Praise for *New York Times* bestselling author Heather Graham

"This thriller [is] a steamy one.... Will keep you turning the pages."
—*Florida Times-Union* on *Danger in Numbers*

"*Danger in Numbers* is a captivating cop fiction with an extra serving of gruesome crime and grit, layered onto a unique setting described in such detail that it transports you right to the middle of it all.... Loaded with gripping detail... A well-developed and twisted read!" —*Mystery and Suspense Magazine*

"Fast-paced...twists and turns...steamy... This book doesn't disappoint."
—*MysterySequels.com* on *The Final Deception*

"Heather Graham delivers a harrowing journey as she always does: perfectly.... Intelligent, fast-paced and frightening at all times, and the team of characters still keep[s] the reader's attention to the very end."
—*Suspense Magazine* on *The Final Deception*

"Taut, complex, and leavened with humor...[a] riveting thriller." —*Library Journal* on *A Dangerous Game*

"Immediately entertaining and engrossing."
—*Publishers Weekly* on *A Dangerous Game*

"Intricate, fast-paced, and intense, this riveting thriller blends romance and suspense in perfect combination and keeps readers guessing and the tension taut until the very end." —*Library Journal* on *Flawless*

Dear Reader,

Wow, 75 years!

I was a lucky kid. My mom had come from Dublin and my dad's family from Stirling, Scotland. Between them, they had books! So many books. For my dad, it was history and mysteries, and for my mom, archaeology, gothics and romance. One of the first books they bought me as a child was a *Reader's Digest Treasury for Young Readers*. I loved it!

I read more and more. And through my mom, I discovered incredible gothic stories that combined history, romance and some creepy scares. The Brontë sisters, then Mary Stewart, Phyllis Whitney and finally...

Harlequin! As I came of age, these contemporary stories were changing, too. Reflecting first a human dream, our greatest emotion, love. Then our roles within that world shifted as we began to aspire toward careers—or not—choosing the road that was going to be best for us!

Reading, of course, fed my desire to create my own stories. And to this day, I'm thrilled to be with Harlequin—reading and writing!

Thank you for being a reader, too!

Heather Graham

A MURDERER AMONG US

NEW YORK TIMES BESTSELLING AUTHOR
HEATHER GRAHAM

FREE STORY BY
JUNO RUSHDAN

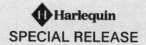

SPECIAL RELEASE

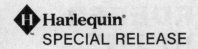 **Harlequin®**
SPECIAL RELEASE

Recycling programs
for this product may
not exist in your area.

ISBN-13: 978-1-335-01682-9

A Murderer Among Us
First published in 2024. This edition published in 2024.
Copyright © 2024 by Heather Graham Pozzessere

Wyoming Mountain Investigation
First published in 2024. This edition published in 2024.
Copyright © 2024 by Juno Rushdan

 Harlequin Enterprises ULC
22 Adelaide St. West, 41st Floor
Toronto, Ontario M5H 4E3, Canada
www.Harlequin.com

Printed in U.S.A.

CONTENTS

New York Times and *USA TODAY* bestselling author **Heather Graham** has written more than two hundred novels. She is pleased to have been published in over twenty-five languages, with sixty million books in print. Heather is a proud recipient of the Silver Bullet from Thriller Writers and was awarded the prestigious Thriller Master Award in 2016. She is also a recipient of Lifetime Achievement Awards from RWA and *The Strand* and is the founder of The Slush Pile Players, an author band and theatrical group. An avid scuba diver, ballroom dancer and mother of five, she still enjoys her South Florida home but also loves to travel. Heather is grateful every day for a career she loves so very much.

For more information, check out her website, theoriginalheathergraham.com, or find Heather on Facebook.

Also by Heather Graham

Harlequin Intrigue

Visit the Author Profile page at Harlequin.com.

A MURDERER AMONG US

Heather Graham

In loving memory of my mom.
Born in Ireland, she embraced her new country,
became a copy editor for an ad company and
was my first before-I-dared-send-it-out editor.
Strong, fierce and kind—but mostly fierce,
when it came to the English language!

Prologue

1949

"Oh! He kicks and punches and—" Cindy Ferguson broke off with a gasp and a shriek "—he's either a football player or a soccer star!" she finished. She shrugged through the pain and said softly, "Or a rock star, like his dad! You know, you're supposed to be doing studio work right now—"

"Hardly a rock star—just a studio musician. There are other studio musicians," Aidan Ferguson assured her. "This kid has one mom—and one dad. I'm a so-so musician. I intend to be a great dad!"

"You're already a great husband," Cindy assured him. "And don't kid yourself, a great musician. You could play with so many groups, but you stay with me!"

"Pain meds are making me look good," Aidan teased.

"If only I had some pain meds!"

Her water had broken; they'd rushed into the ER and were assured her doctor would be right there.

Aidan watched his wife in distress, trying to return her smile. He reminded himself that childbirth was a natural event.

The pain that came with it was natural, too. Cindy would be fine.

But he was worried. They had come to the hospital too late. Cindy was already in heavy labor, fighting the pain.

The nurse had been in, but along with his worrying, he was growing nervous and angry—where the hell was the doctor?

As if on cue, Dr. Jamison walked in, wasting no time on small talk. He gave Cindy a lightning-quick examination and shouted, "Delivery room. Now!"

Cindy was whisked out.

Aidan was left to pace the room until a nurse showed him out and into the waiting room where it seemed he joined a cavalcade of marchers: fathers, others, just pacing in circles as they awaited news of the births of their children. He thought about how his phone was probably ringing: his world was a good one, and even though he was just a studio musician he knew that big names would be calling to congratulate him. That made him smile, and, of course, thinking about them helped make the time go by. And he'd been warned that even now, it could be a while.

He was stunned when the doctor who had so recently left with his wife appeared again almost immediately.

"Mr. Ferguson?"

"Yes, yes!" Aidan wasn't sure why the mere mention of his name frightened him so much. He didn't mean to be a pessimist. But…

"Something happened, something is wrong!" he said anxiously, reaching the doctor.

"Uh, no, Mr. Ferguson. They're seeing to your wife and child now. A little boy, sir. Or, should I say, a big boy. He's ten pounds one ounce. Mother and son are doing fine. You'll be able to see them soon."

Aidan thought he muttered a thanks—he wasn't even sure. He sank into one of the chairs, his head falling into his hands.

Ten pounds. Kind of giant for a newborn? A boy. Every dad's dream, ten pounds, big and strong, maybe he was going to be a star football player!

In thirty minutes, he was allowed to see Cindy and his newborn son.

And the baby was beautiful. He looked as if he was a few weeks old already, as if he could walk out of his bassinet. He had a full head of dark hair.

He kissed his wife, shaking his head as he sat next to her, stroking her hair, leaning over to give her a gentle kiss. "Thank you, thank you," he told her. The emotion welling in him was almost unbearable.

"Thank you, Dad," she teased. "I couldn't have done it alone."

He grinned. "Well, you had the hard part."

"No, actually, you had the *hard* part!" she teased.

A nurse cleared her throat from the doorway and they both looked up, reddening.

"Um, sorry. I have papers here. Have you thought about a name yet?" she asked.

Aidan looked at his wife. She smiled. "Jake. For your dad," she said.

"Jake. For my dad," he agreed. And nurse or no nurse, he leaned over to kiss her again.

"Thank you. That boy is like…my life!"

"He is *our* lives," she corrected. "Our beautiful boy."

Jake Mallory Ferguson *did* become their lives. Cindy Ferguson was diagnosed with cervical cancer a year later; her life was saved, but their son was to be their only child.

And for years, he was their beautiful, beautiful boy. He had a thick thatch of dark hair, amazing, riveting blue eyes and a smile that could charm the coldest heart.

Through grade and middle schools, he was a wonderful student, popular *and* smart.

He did play football, even through his senior year, when he found two things: that he loved the guitar, which was great, and drugs—not so great.

In fact, the alcohol and drugs had gotten so bad that

when he graduated, he knew his father was going to let him be drafted.

Aidan and Cindy were deeply distressed. A neighborhood boy had already been killed in Vietnam.

But a neighborhood girl had already died of an overdose as well.

And all their efforts, punishments, encouragements to get help...all had done nothing.

Aidan had served in World War II himself. Jake had been born as part of the baby boom that had come when the war had finally ended. Aidan had seen bad action: he knew the price of war. And he knew, too, he was still glad he had fought, that he had been privileged to help liberate one of the concentration camps.

And so, when Jake came to his father, begging for the money so he could opt out of college, Aidan hesitated just briefly in agony before giving his answer.

"Son, if you're going to kill yourself, you might as well do so for your country."

Of course, Jake hated him. But he went off and enlisted in the navy before he could be ordered into a different branch of the service.

And in the service, he found help rather than death. He found others who had suffered from his same addictions and an organization that helped in a way no lecture or punishment could.

He still loved his guitar. And when he emerged from the service, he decided to make it his focus.

A truly beautiful boy. And in time, well, in time he became something Aidan had never imagined for his son. Something wonderful, and scary, of course.

He followed his dad into music.

But he didn't become a studio musician.

He somehow became a rock star.

Amazing. Terrifying.

But the lifestyle didn't alter the joy he had learned with his group in the navy, it just put him in a great position to write songs, to handle the band's business, to live…wonderfully.

He bought his parents a great new house in Palm Beach with a heated pool and a Jacuzzi. He lived down the street.

But Aidan continued to worry as the years passed.

Not because Jake fell back—miraculously, he never did. But neither did he fall in love. Oh, well, of course there were women in his life. Some stayed a while. But it seemed he was never really going to fall in love.

He'd never know what Aidan and Cindy had now been sharing all these years, through World War II, Korea, the sixties—being kind of flower children—the seventies, tragedy in the country, days of peace, days of faith…

The eighties, when Jake's band became about the biggest thing in history—well, after the Beatles, the Rolling Stones, and a few others—maybe.

The nineties, the Gulf Wars…

And then, a bit before the millennium…

It was only then, when Jake Ferguson was about to turn fifty, that he found the love of his life. He and his group had been playing at Madison Square Garden and she had been with the backup singers for their opening group. They'd gone for coffee together, and in the days to come, they went to the Met, to the Museum of Natural History, for long walks in the park, to the zoo, to the theater…

He brought her home to Florida and announced to his parents he was going to be married at last. Her name was Mandy Mannix, and she wasn't as old as Jake, but she was a respectable thirty-eight. They teased Aidan and Cindy about heading to Vegas to be married by an Elvis impersonator, but they were married at the church the family had gone to forever, even if it was a quiet affair for their families and closest friends. Jake hadn't wanted a media frenzy.

He went on to write, play and perform with his band—with Mandy singing backup for his group, Skyhawk.

Then something that seemed miraculous happened. Jake and Mandy had their own baby.

A little girl, a beautiful little girl with dark hair and stunning blue eyes. Because of those eyes, and partially because of the name of Jake's band as well, the baby was named Skylar and called Sky. Sometimes, Sky Blue.

She became everyone's life, and Aidan was beyond grateful both he and Cindy were still alive and well—old as dirt, but alive and well—to see the birth of that baby. They both got to see her first toddling steps, hear her first words, hear themselves called Nana and Papa.

They both made it until their loving little granddaughter arrived at her fifth birthday.

Then, in Aidan's arms, Cindy passed away, whispering her last words.

"I love you."

He knew that he would follow her soon enough. In return Aidan whispered, "I will find you in clouds of peace and beauty."

It was another six years before Aidan was to join her.

And while it broke Skylar's heart to see her beloved grandfather die, she was almost grateful after another six years had passed because he didn't have to witness what happened.

Because then, she lost her beloved father...

His father would have been devastated by the way it all happened.

When she received the strange call seven years after his death, she was reminded. And she was as angry as she had been devastated and determined that she would find out what had really happened, and she would clear his name for the ages.

Jake Ferguson had been an incredible man. A legend,

a rock legend, and yet a wise man who had turned his life around and become an amazing human being as well. And he deserved to be remembered in all the best ways.

So...

Yes.

She would join Skyhawk for a special anniversary performance.

She would take her father's place.

And maybe, just maybe, she could figure out what the hell had really happened.

Chapter One

"Hey, our guys are young in comparison to a few of them out there!"

Sky smiled as she listened to Brandon Wiley, five years her senior and the son of Chris Wiley, bass guitarist for Sky-hawk—not quite as late of a bloomer as her father. "Come on, now. My dad wasn't even twenty when they put the band together," Brandon continued. "He's a mere sixty-nine!"

"And I take nothing away from your dad, for sure!" Sky promised. "He's an incredible performer. And I'm betting that my dad still would have been incredible, even at seventy-five!"

"Agreed. Hey, Mick Jagger is over eighty and I saw one of his performances last year—the dude still rules the stage," Brandon said. He paused, looking down. "Sky, I'm so sorry about your dad—"

"Thank you. I know." Her smile was a constricted one. "And my mother would have insisted on an autopsy, even if the supposedly accidental death hadn't called for one. There were no drugs in my father's system. What happened was—"

"Truly a tragic accident," Brandon said quickly. "We all know that. And, of course, we went over and over it all when it happened, and I didn't say that to dredge up the past."

They stood in the studio in the New Orleans Central Business District where Skyhawk had recorded their first album. Sky turned, wincing, because on the wall, there was a picture of the original band members of Skyhawk: her father, Jake Ferguson, vocalist and lead guitar; Brandon's dad, Chris Wiley, bassist; Joe Garcia, keyboards; Mark Reynolds, rhythm guitar; and Hank McCoy, drummer.

Her dad—at the ripe old age of twenty-five when he'd started the band—had been the oldest in the group. And it was true—compared to some of the rockers still dancing their hearts out on stage, the remaining members of Skyhawk were just in their sixties. Back from the service and freshly graduated, her dad had been asked for help from Hank McCoy, a neighbor, and in helping out someone he saw as a little brother, Jake had wound up creating Skyhawk.

And the remaining members of the group could still rock the house—now sometimes with the help of children and grandchildren.

Sky had been asked to join with the group before. The band was still getting gigs—good ones. But not the instantly sold-out gigs they'd gotten when her father was alive.

For years, she'd politely refused any interaction with the group. Her mother had remained close friends with many of them and their assorted wives, ex-wives and children. But the publicity surrounding her father's death still plagued her.

He'd been electrocuted by a faulty amp. The accident had been deemed *user error.*

She had never believed it. Her father had known how to set a stage, but, of course, once Skyhawk had gotten big— and then huge—they had roadies to handle all of that for them. But something had been wrong that night, and Jake Ferguson had gone to check the amp and…boom. Electricity had crackled, and the explosion of the equipment and the ensuing fire that might have engulfed the entire place had taken his life.

Drugs had immediately been suspected, and headlines had read different versions of *Did Ferguson Crack after Nearly 50 Years of Clean Living?*

She'd been furious, of course. And the autopsy had served them well: no, he had been clean as a whistle.

Accident. It had been a tragic accident.

Somehow, though, Sky couldn't accept it. The part of her who had adored the man who had received such adulation and still been the best husband and dad in the world argued that there had to have been something amiss. Her logical self argued that even if there had been something off, there would be no way she could discover what it was this long after the fact. Because while the facts of his death had gotten out, she knew there were many among his fans and his doubters who were convinced it had all been a cover-up.

"Sky."

She was startled to hear her name spoken softly in a deep, rich and quiet voice. Swinging around, she saw that Chase McCoy, the grandson of the drummer, had arrived.

She winced. She'd been eighteen, Chase twenty-one, when they'd fallen into a wild crush. Life had been fun then. She had just entered college, following in her parents' footsteps, majoring in music. Chase, three years her senior, had been sitting in for Hank, playing drums for several of the gigs, making his own name. Her dad had brought her on stage for a ballad he had written, a song that still commanded the airwaves, as well as several music platforms.

And Chase...

Well, she'd been eighteen, and a pretty typical eighteen. Bursting into adulthood with tremendous excitement. She had the most loving and supportive parents in the world, wise beyond their years, parents who had seriously taught her the dangers of excess and more.

Somehow, they hadn't prepared her for Chase.

First, of course, at that age, she had gone for the physical. Chase was simply striking. A solid six three of lean muscle with dark auburn hair and hazel eyes that could burn like crystals. He could play, and he had a voice that lent incredibly to Skyhawk songs and backup vocals. Jake Ferguson had loved him and his talent and had been writing a song especially for him when...

When the accident had occurred.

And at that point, she'd backed away from the band and, to the best of her ability, anyone associated with it.

She'd heard that Chase was now doing much more than music. While many thought that garage-band talent was instinctive and natural, both Hank and her dad had believed in higher education, and while Chase had also continued his music studies, she understood that after her father's death, he had opted for a major in criminology, had graduated and was working in that field somewhere. She wasn't sure who he worked for or what he was doing.

Except now, of course, he was filling in on drums for Hank, who had recently had heart surgery. Hank was going to be around, supervising and commenting, Sky was certain. But Chase would be the drummer for most of the numbers they were doing.

"Chase. Hey. How are you doing?" she asked, relieved her voice sounded completely casual. She still felt anything but casual regarding Chase.

But everything that had happened had been her fault.

That had been years ago now. They had both gone on. But there had been a time when they had lamented being the daughter of one rock star and the grandson of another.

Not as bad for him as it had been for her, Chase had always told her. The lead vocalist was always the front man, the name and face people knew. Those who just listened on the radio or bought the music knew the name of a group if they loved it, and after that, the name of the lead singer, and not so much the other members of the band.

She wondered now if that was still true. There had been so much publicity when her father had died. The media had hopped on it, interviewing band members, fans, producers...

She had managed to hide away. Mostly. Once upon a time, she'd recorded with her father. And that recording had hit the airwaves big-time.

Chase was studying her. She wondered if he was reading her mind.

"So, cool," she murmured. "I'm going to be my dad, and you're going to be your grandfather."

"And you are going to have to rehearse like hell," Brandon said dryly, grinning. "I've only been asked to sit in on a few numbers and some backup vocals. You two... What is Skyhawk without the lead vocalist and a kick-ass drummer?"

"Well, here you go, Brandon. We grew up with these guys, with this music," Sky told him.

"She's right. I think I knew a lot of the Skyhawk lineup before I knew my ABCs," Chase told him. "So today is—" He broke off, looking around the studio. It was meant for recording, but today, they would be putting together the fivesome playing the main frame of the performance, Joe Garcia still on keyboards, Mark Reynolds still on rhythm guitar and Chris Wiley on bass—except on a few numbers where he wanted Brandon to sit in. "Today, we're just seeing how we do," Chase finished.

"Yeah. My dad and Mark and Joe should be here any minute," Brandon said. He looked at Sky. "Are you going to do your dad's ballad?" he asked quietly. "My dad said that you've turned them down every time they've asked you on stage, even to do the ballad."

Sky forced a smile and shrugged. "I don't know. You mean 'Grace,' I take it. My dad wrote several ballads."

"Yeah," Brandon said. "That one. Come on, kid, that video of you and your dad years ago is *still* viral. It could make this whole thing for everyone!"

"Maybe," she murmured.

"Hey," Chase said. "If it hurts you to do it—don't. But think about it. Maybe doing it in his memory will be good for...well, for you remembering the good times and...learning to go on despite what happened."

"I am going on!" she protested. Though, in truth, telling her that to do or not do the song was her decision was Chase standing up for her. "My dad has been dead years now, and I am a normal, functioning human being," she assured them both.

"Oh, yeah, of course!" Brandon said. "It's just that music is something you always loved so much—"

"And then again, define *normal*!" Chase teased.

Sky found she was laughing—*normally*. Chase had a way of saying things that made uneasy moments easy. Teasing, gently. And yet, when she looked at him, she thought she remembered enough about him to see that behind his banter, he was worried about her.

She forced another sweet smile.

"Let's face it, we're the family members of rock stars. No one expects us to be normal," she assured Chase. "And you! More than anyone. As amazing on the drums as your grandfather—and you stopped music to major in criminology. What? Have you decided to be a cop? May have to change your name for that, and unless you have major plastic surgery, you'll never be able to go undercover."

Chase shrugged. "I found out that I liked it, that it's fascinating."

"What? Ugh. Studying blood and guts?" Brandon asked.

"All kinds of cool stuff—not so much blood and guts," Chase countered. He shrugged. "I already had my arts and music degree, but I realized I find fingerprints, shoeprints, fibers and especially the psychology of crime to be fascinating. It is really amazing what profilers can come up with."

"And screw up with, too, right?"

"It's an inexact science, but right more often than not. It's not a be-all and end-all. It's a tool like dozens of the machines out there that can pinpoint where certain soil particles might have come from and where fabrics were made... Trust me, it's cool. Fun, intriguing," Chase said. "Anyway..."

The door to their rehearsal area opened and closed. Joe Garcia and Mark Reynolds had arrived.

"Sky!" Mark exclaimed, stepping forward to encompass her in a great hug.

She'd communicated with him—and Joe, Hank and Chris—through the years, politely refusing every time they'd asked her to join them.

She'd even seen them a few times: her mother had remained friends with everyone, grateful for their support, she had told Sky.

She'd never understood Sky's aversion to her father's people. And Sky couldn't explain to her mother that she just didn't trust any of them.

A therapist would tell her that she just couldn't accept the truth.

But that wouldn't cut it. They would never understand. She couldn't accept what she didn't believe to be truth. Her mother had tried so hard to help her, and for her mother's sake, she had pretended she was accepting her dad's death and moving on.

And as far as her father's band, well, it had been simpler just to go her own way.

But now…

"All right, then!" Joe Garcia announced, grinning. "Let's start with some of our hard rockin' tunes and go on from there. Everything is here: drums, keyboards, guitars and, most importantly, us! Let's get to it. Sky of Skyhawk!"

She smiled. She had always loved Joe. He was a good guy. The youngest in the group at a mere sixty-seven, he could pass for a man twenty years his junior. He had a rich headful of snow-white hair, worked out daily, she was sure, and looked more like a rugged action star than a musician. He had a keen sense of humor and, more importantly, a solid grip on life, reality and the simple fact that fame meant nothing if you didn't have your health and people to love. His wife, Josie, was one of Sky's mom's best friends. Joe and Josie had never had children of their own; instead, they had spent their time helping out at children's hospitals and seeing that those in areas devastated by wars, famine, fires and storms found the care they needed.

She reminded herself she believed someone here was guilty of being involved in her father's death.

But not Joe.

"I'm sitting in for my dad until he gets here," Brandon told them. "But I've done it before. Chase, you've actually sat in a few times, too. So… Sky. You ready for this?"

She smiled sweetly. "As ready as I'll ever be," she assured them.

Mark Reynolds, slim, wiry and with his own full head of snow-white hair, touched her gently on the shoulders.

"Your dad will be smiling from heaven," he said softly.

"Thanks for that. So…"

"Hey, Chase has been the drummer before, and you've played and sung for your dad before, and Brandon sits in, too, so it's just darned cool we're together and doing this. Think about it! Your dad would be seventy-five, and he created the band in the seventies, several decades of music. We're pretty darned…"

"Old?" Brandon suggested dryly.

"Hey!" Chris protested, glaring at his son when he arrived.

"Sorry, Dad!"

"Jagger is still older. Sir Paul McCartney is older! We're classic rock," Chris said.

"*Classic*, okay!" Brandon teased. "Come on, my fellow generationers," he begged. "Help me out here."

"Oh, hell no, you're on your own!" Chase teased.

"Right. Age is all in the mind, and you've got a young mind, right, Dad?"

"Yeah. The mind is still young. The knees—not so much. But when the music is going… I'm young at heart."

"Right. And whatever! Let's go. I've got a list. We'll start with 'Rock the World.' And go, go, go!" Mark said.

Chase slid onto the stool behind the drum set, Joe moved over to the keyboards, and the others picked up their instruments.

Sky knew the songs. She feared, though, that she'd be awkward, that her timing would be off…that something wouldn't be right.

But she moved her fingers over the opening chords and slid easily into one of Skyhawk's most popular songs.

"Rocking the world, in the best way, come on,

I say, let's make her the very best today.

There was a time my soul was sad, out there everything was bad,

in a world so bad, let's change the fad, it's time, it's time, it's time, today,

because *we* are the way.

In a world of troubles, we can hit a few doubles,

being the good

the way that we should.

Now my heart sings as I rock the world, rock the world, rock the rockin' world!"

FAST, WITH GREAT riffs and a drum solo, it was one of the songs that could just about wake the dead and cause the staidest human being to dance or, at the very least, wriggle in a chair to the music.

Chase killed the drum solo.

She picked up with the second verse, thinking of the person her father must have been back in 1974. He'd fallen into a horrible place but come back from it, even through war and the horror of seeing friends blown to bits. But he was determined, as he had once told her, that the more good done in the world, the less the bad could conquer.

She sang the second verse, and they held a long note before the drums slammed in for the crescendo.

And while Chris Wiley was playing his guitar, Brandon was at a mic for backup on the chorus refrains, and to Sky's surprise, the signature song went off without a hitch.

They were all silent.

"The rest of this can't possibly go so well," Joe Garcia said, shaking his head. "Wow."

"Onward," Mark said.

"Yeah, yeah, of course," Joe agreed.

"No, I meant 'Onward' is the next song on the list," Mark said dryly.

"Onward and onward," Sky said, surprised that, once again, her fingers moved over her father's guitar strings, and the words came swiftly to her lips.

There were a few snags, a few suggestions from one band member to another, and a little reworking, but for the most part, they sailed through the rehearsal.

And they were shockingly good, in sync.

Sky found she was enjoying herself. Skyhawk songs,

mostly written by her dad, perhaps didn't comprise the most brilliant lyrics known to man, but with the music that was catchy and almost magical, the pieces stood the rigors of time.

"Sky, ready?" Joe Garcia asked her.

She was startled. The ballad. They wanted her to do her father's ballad.

"Intro is the keyboard," she said. No way to put it off. And it was ridiculous. But it was the one song she had done at home with her father, sitting in the living room, talking about life. He wanted her to live her dreams, never his or her mother's, but *her* dreams. They didn't have to be musical dreams.

And she had assured him she didn't know what she wanted out of life—except to have a family as beautiful as the one he and her mom had created for her.

He'd hugged her. She'd asked him about his favorite song.

The ballad. "Dreams."

Keyboards, a gentle guitar entry, then the lyrics…

"Like the falcon soars to the skies
My heart is lifted with a magic like their wings,
For in the depth and beauty of your eyes
All that is me, deep in my soul, rises high
And sings.
There is magic, magic, in this thing I feel,
Magic, magic, my heart on fire
And I know that it is real."

Chase joined in on the chorus, his voice deep and rich. She was pleased at how wonderful he sounded and that it was oddly good while it hurt at the same time. She turned to glance at him as she sang. He was looking at her.

And she wasn't sure of what she saw in his eyes. Empathy? Strangely…worry.

"There is magic, oh so real, beauty in this thing I feel, my heart rises to skies,

For the magic in your eyes. Magic...magic..."

She almost missed the first beat of the second verse, but in the end, she finished the song—again with the chorus.

Again, with Chase McCoy.

She was stunned when the rest of the group applauded energetically. She turned to see Joe heading over to her, taking her into his arms in a warm hug.

"Oh, Sky, your dad would be so proud!" he exclaimed.

Mark said softly, "Tears in heaven, that was so...beautiful. You did him proud, kid."

Brandon and Chris Wiley echoed their congratulations.

"Skyhawk is going to soar!" Brandon added excitedly.

She thanked them all.

Only Chase hadn't spoken. He was still at his drum set. Watching her, that strange mix of empathy and concern in his eyes.

"Okay. So much for flattering ourselves!" Mark said. "Tomorrow afternoon at the arena, and the night after—showtime."

"And remember, we've been in a studio rehearsal space—next will be at the arena, and we all know that we have to adjust to the size of a location," Mark said.

"We'll have the crew there, too," Joe reminded him. "Setting up the amps for sound—"

He broke off awkwardly. There was silence.

"Guys, it's okay," Sky said. "The world will always be filled with amps. I can hear the word."

"Right, just sorry, sorry!" Joe said.

"We're all sorry," Chris Wiley said. "We'll miss your dad 'til the day we die ourselves, Sky. He wasn't just a bandmate and a friend, he was one of the finest men I've ever known."

"Thank you. And it's okay. Seriously," Sky said. She looked around.

And she thought of the years and years her dad had played with Skyhawk. Like Chris had said, these guys weren't just workmates, they had been Jake's friends, dear friends, more family than anything else.

How could she possibly believe one of them may have wanted him dead?

"Okay, I have date night with the old ball and chain," Mark said. "Ouch! Did I say that? I meant my beloved wife. Hmm. No wonder your dad wrote the best ballads, Sky. I'm a jerk. I love Susie, been with her thirty years, so..."

Sky laughed. "It's okay. You can joke around me, too."

"Yeah, just offensive, but cool," Joe assured him. "Anyway..."

Mark waved and headed toward the door. He paused, looking back. "Chris, Joe, Hank and I have been doing these songs forever, and you three—Brandon, Chase, Sky—have sat in at various times through the years. But I never expected today to go this well. Okay, so...for some of us, after all these years, it would be pathetic if we weren't in sync, but you kids were. Well, thanks, and great!"

"Thank you, Mark," Chase said. Sky smiled and nodded, ready to head out herself. This rehearsal had been her return intro.

Now she needed to think. Maybe make a few notes.

A few notes about what? Did she think if one of them was guilty, they would just fall apart in front of her today?

"I'm heading out for a beer after that," Brandon said. "Anyone want to join me?"

"I'll go with you, kid," his father said. "Joe?"

"Yeah, sure. I'm in," Joe said.

"Sky, come on!" Brandon said.

"Maybe tomorrow night. I didn't sleep well. A little nervous, maybe," she lied.

"We'll hold you to it!" Chris said.

"Chase?" Brandon asked. "You're not going to make me go out alone with the old guys, are you?"

"Rain check for tomorrow night, too," Chase said. "I have some work—"

"Work! Why do you work when you could hit the road with us forever?" Mark asked him. "Your granddad would love it!"

"I love sitting in. Not sure I'm ready to be a forever drummer," Chase said. "Anyway, good night, all!"

He headed out as well with everyone trailing him. They waved again, breaking apart to head to their various parking places.

Sky was in a garage off Canal, and she walked down the street, deep in thought at first.

Then something seemed to disturb her; she *felt* as if she was being followed.

When she stopped and turned to search the area, no one was there. Well, people were there, but no one who seemed to be paying the least bit of attention to her.

No one from Skyhawk.

She shook her head, wondering again if she wasn't crazy and if she wasn't letting her suspicion turn to paranoia.

With a shake of her head, she hurried on to the garage.

It wasn't until she reached her car on the third level that she stopped dead, staring.

Chase was there. Leaning against the front of her little SUV, arms crossed casually over his chest as he watched her approach.

"What are you doing here?" she demanded.

But he shook his head, staring at her curiously. "The question is this. What the hell do you think you're doing?"

She angled her head and narrowed her eyes. "I'm taking my dad's place. Just like you're sitting in for Hank—"

"I've sat in before. You've avoided the band like the plague."

"I've changed my mind."

He walked over to her, not touching her, just standing a few inches from her. "I know you," he said softly. "And I know how you felt about your father. I don't know what you're up to, but I do know this. You've got to be careful, Sky."

"I'm not up to anything. Why should I be careful? My dad died because of a tragic accident, right?"

"Please, be careful."

He turned and left her. She saw that he had parked in the same area of the garage.

Had he followed her?

He was already in his car.

"Chase!" she called, walking toward him. His engine was running.

She stepped in front of his car. He wasn't going to hit her; she was sure of that.

Of course, he didn't. He looked to the side.

She walked around to the driver's seat. He lowered his window.

"Why do I need to be careful? What do you know? Who do you think—"

"I don't know anything, Sky. But if there was anything to know, you slinking about trying to make someone guilty of something could put you in extreme danger."

"You do know something," she said.

He let out a soft sigh, staring straight ahead. "Again, I don't *know* anything. But I do know if there's anything to know, you snooping around could put you in danger. Sky, just—"

"You're just repeating yourself. I don't need you to worry about me," she said.

He turned and studied her. "Yeah. You made that perfectly clear a few years back," he said softly. "But you know, sorry, in memory of your father, I worry about you anyway."

She was suddenly afraid she might burst into tears. And it was all so ridiculous. She had walked away. Her father's death had been devastating to her, and she'd probably hurt herself—and her mother—with the way she'd retreated inward.

But that was long ago now. And she'd heard that Chase had moved on. He had kept studying, but he'd sat in with other groups in the past years. He'd been seen with a few of the hottest, newest female acts out there.

She lowered her head. She wasn't about to cry.

"My father didn't make a mistake with an amp," she said simply. "Sorry. Something happened the night he died. And since you're so determined that I'm up to something, you might as well know I will never accept that it was his fault in any way. Good night."

She turned to head back to her own car.

And she wasn't sure if she was relieved or disappointed that he didn't follow her.

If she closed her eyes, she could remember the past too clearly.

Along with all she had so foolishly thrown away.

Chapter Two

"Well?"

"Well?" Chase replied.

He'd come home to find his supervising director, Andy Wellington, was on his couch, stretched back comfortably, watching a sitcom and waiting for him.

Of course, Wellington had necessarily approved his undercover investigation into the death of Jake Ferguson. That he had done so had surprised Chase—Jake's death had been accepted as an accident and had occurred years earlier. Even if it had been deemed suspicious in any way, a homicide case would have been tossed in with the rest of the cold cases by now.

Wellington didn't have a personal interest in the case; he'd admired Jake Ferguson and liked the fact his undercover agent was part of the music world.

But his interest wasn't personal, and customarily, Chase's personal interest would have kept him on the sidelines.

But it was hard to find his kind of an in.

Chase had meant to take part in the show, one way or the other. But he'd expected he'd be taking personal days to do it, and Wellington might have even tried to stop him for being too close to any possible suspects if there was a case. Then, of course, he would have had to try to convince Wellington that no, he was just sitting in for his grandfather and if he didn't, it could injure any good Chase did in undercover work since it was known—by hardened fans, at least—that he was the grandson of legendary rock drummer Hank McCoy.

Wellington sat up, folding his hands idly on his knees as he waited for Chase to talk.

The man was a good boss. Chase had read up on him and knew he was fifty-one, married, with two kids in college. He'd started in the field just like the agents he supervised now and worked his way up to his position, one he'd held for almost ten years. He could have a stern demeanor or a casual one. Six one, with a clean-cut head of silver hair and dark brown eyes, he was an impressive figure who could also look like a friendly dad.

"So? Anything?"

"Yeah, a good session," Chase told him. He shook his head. "I have known these guys my whole life—Joe Garcia, Mark Reynolds, Chris Wiley and, of course, my grandfather, Brandon, Chris's son and Skylar Ferguson. We rented the space—no roadies were with us."

"And you want to believe it was a roadie and not a friend you've known all your life," Wellington said flatly. He lifted his hands in the air. "That's all well and good, except this person has to be someone who had worked with the group time and again. The particular—and deadly—brand of stuff they discovered has shown up in every area where the band played."

"Yes, I want to believe a roadie is involved. And that it's not Joe, Mark or Chris. Honestly, I think I'd know if it was my grandfather, and you know that—"

"Yes, he's rehabbing from heart surgery," Wellington said.

"And," Chase told him, "a roadie would have had greater access to the stage and the stage equipment—including the amps."

"There is logic in that. Just don't wear blinders."

"I never wear blinders."

"But what you think is that Jake Ferguson was killed because he suspected what was going on, that someone involved was selling drugs, and he had to be shut up before he turned them in?"

Chase hesitated and shrugged. "Yeah," he said at last. "And, yes, it shouldn't be, but it is personal in a way. Jake was clean as a whistle. He had been since he'd returned from fighting in Vietnam. He wasn't a monster who lit on anyone who ordered a beer, and if his friends wanted to light up a joint here or there, he could shrug it off. But he would have never tolerated someone selling drugs—especially when so many customers might be kids or young adults. And especially since the drugs had been showing up now and then where their shows had been playing. Yes, Jake was killed, I'm convinced, and for a reason. The same reason that has you agreeing with me, when protocol suggests that it's not."

Wellington actually grinned. "Yeah. I can't bring back your rock-star friend. If my sanctioning your investigation while 'just playing with your gramps's band' can manage that, then I can blink easily enough. But you will keep me posted every step of the way."

Chase nodded. For a minute, he wondered if he should tell Wellington he was worried. Skylar Ferguson didn't know a thing about the suspicions the FBI was harboring regarding drug sales revolving around the band, but she didn't believe her father's death had been an accident.

It worried him. It might worry Wellington enough to pull the plug.

Then he'd be more worried than ever about Sky, Chase knew.

And, really, what could he say about Skylar?

"So, is it going to be a hell of a show? Shake the arena?" Wellington asked.

"You bet."

"And you have tickets for me, right?"

"Backstage passes included, Uncle Andy," Chase assured him.

Wellington frowned at that.

"It's cool," Chase assured him. "We all called friends Aunt this or Uncle that back when I was growing up. They'll just think you're a family friend they've never met."

"But your folks—"

"Aren't coming. They've been in Ireland for the last six months. My dad flew in and out to make sure I was taking good care of *his* father. This has been a great opportunity for my mom, working at the museum in Dublin, so Gramps and I both insisted that Dad get back over there."

Wellington nodded. "I trust you. Obviously, you wouldn't be working for me if I didn't. All right, so I'm out of here for tonight."

Chase stood to walk him out.

"Great place you have here," Wellington told him, standing on the porch and looking toward the path that led around to the side courtyard. "You're right in the French Quarter, away from the fury of Bourbon Street, just two blocks off Esplanade and about that distance in from Rampart. Very oddly neighborhood-y."

Chase grinned. "Yeah. My grandfather, Hank, bought this place when the city was a disaster, right after Katrina. He paid too much for it, but he's a good guy, too. The family he bought it from was in trouble, no jobs, kids in college... And, yeah, I have to admit, being the grandson of a rock icon has its perks. He gave me the house as a gift when I graduated from college."

"You grew up here."

"Yeah, in New Orleans. In a house my folks still own in the Irish Channel area."

"And you're working for me," Wellington said, shaking his head.

"They still call it home, but they travel all the time."

Wellington looked around, nodding. "Well, keep your head down. See you rockin' out."

Chase nodded and watched Wellington walk away, headed down the street. He paused for a minute. No way out of it, his grandfather's success—or the success of Skyhawk—had given him amazing privileges. But he had always known that, and he had known it was because his grandfather, like Jake Ferguson, was just a good guy. From the time he'd been a child he'd been taught they were blessed and lucky and that meant they had to help others. Hank McCoy had practiced what he preached, and he was one of the few people who knew what Chase really did and who he worked for. Hank had been surprised at first about Chase's deepening interest in criminology. But when Chase had been about to graduate with his second degree, he'd told Hank a little impatiently, "You told me to help people, that we'd led a charmed life and that meant giving back. Gramps, I think I can be good at delving into things, discovering the truth. I think I can really help people this way!"

Hank had grown silent, and then he'd smiled.

"All right. Maybe you're right. But don't forget the drums, huh?"

"I love the drums. And the guitar, though I'm better at drums."

"Genetics," Hank told him. "Go out and save the world. Do me proud. But remember this. Music. Seriously. Like love, it makes the world go around."

Chase headed back in, locked the door, grimacing when he remembered it had been his idea to give Wellington a key for the times now when he might be waiting to see him privately, wanting a personal update.

His office was on the right side of the house, just behind the music room. He headed there, determined to go over everything he knew about the major players in the case.

Of course, that started with the band.

And his memories of the last concert Jake had played, and the last words Jake had said to him.

There had been about seventy thousand people in the audience, just as there had been for U2 and the Rolling Stones.

Seventy thousand suspects?

No. Because Jake wouldn't have known or had contact with the majority of the audience, though of course, New Orleans had been his hometown, so he'd have had friends there. And the other band members would have had friends. And family.

But Jake wouldn't have been talking with many people right before the show: he'd have been with the band, with the roadies and perhaps the venue supervisor. But he was angry about something he'd seen just as they had been setting up. Something he had seen someone do.

And because of the emotion involved, it suggested someone close to him.

Back to the band and the roadies.

Sometimes, roadies were attached to a venue, sometimes to a performer or group, and sometimes, a combination of the two were working.

That night…

Chase closed his eyes and leaned back. Though he'd already been intrigued by other courses in college, his focus in life that night had been music. And he'd been standing stage left, ready to sit in for Hank, something that still thrilled his grandfather since his father had chosen to follow another path, the restoration of ancient art pieces. Chase's father's work was impressive since he'd worked on pieces in major museums across the world—it just didn't compare to the fame of being a rock star. Though Chase had failed miserably at drawing so much as a stick figure, his dad had never minded that he didn't follow him into the art world, but rather he was glad that Chase made Hank so happy.

Jake hadn't just been the lead singer. He'd been the true front man. He knew how to work a crowd. He also knew how to share, kicking over to other band members, never doing a show that didn't feature each player, each instrument.

After his death…

The gigs hadn't been enormous. Joe Garcia had taken over most of the vocals, Hank had taken on a few, and Chris and Mark the rest. During his life, Jake Ferguson had recorded sessions with his daughter, wildly popular on social media through the years.

Everyone had been beyond thrilled that she had agreed to be part of this concert. It was taking place in her hometown, and the guys had assumed that she had finally agreed in a moment of weakness. She'd never shown any of them hostility; she had always been not just cordial but friendly because she didn't ever want to ruin the fact that her mom was still friends with the group and their families and when she'd been at the same place at the same time, she'd hung out with them.

But Chase knew her better. Even if it had been years now since…

They'd been together.

He winced. They'd been darlings on stage together, beloved by the group and by the crowds. So young and sweet in their puppy love, and how perfect that the grandson of the drummer and the daughter of the vocalist and lead guitarist should fall in love.

It wasn't their time together on stage that he remembered.

It was her laughter, her smile, her eyes when she looked at him. Her way of making sure that she tipped any musician they ever saw playing on the street—and there were plenty. It was the spring break when they'd escaped their families and everyone to head to St. Augustine Beach. Days in the sun, nights spent on history and ghost tours and just being together.

And then Jake had died. And she'd never said another word to him; she'd stepped away. And when he'd tried to reach her after the funeral, she had told him that she couldn't, just couldn't, see him again. Ever.

After today, he thought, leaning back and stretching in his desk chair, he knew why.

To the best of his knowledge, she'd never taken any courses in criminology. And she hadn't been near the stage when her father had died.

She couldn't have heard her father's last words—spoken just to Chase as he'd taken over for Hank on a number—so she couldn't have his reasons for suspecting that something more than an accident had been involved.

But she thought that someone in the band had killed her father. And she had surely had him on that list along with Hank.

He was convinced himself that whoever Jake had been talking about had realized that Jake was going to blow the whistle on them.

Who it was and what they had done, Chase didn't know for sure. But he suspected that it was selling drugs, that they were responsible for the contaminated drugs that had killed several people, young people among them, in the areas where the band had played.

Jake's last words had echoed in his head through the years.

"I know what's going on, and I saw... I'm going to put an end to it as soon as this gig is over!"

Then his showman's smile had taken over his face, and he'd stepped into the spotlight.

He'd seen something. Someone. And he'd meant to call the cops when the lights were down and the music and applause and screams in the crowds had ended. Whoever had been selling drugs would have known that if Jake had seen them, it was all over. He'd cleaned up the hard way himself; he'd seen too many people die who had lost their grip.

And he had known whatever he knew before the show started...

Chris Wiley, Joe Garcia, Mark Reynolds, and, of course, Chase's own grandfather, Hank McCoy.

He knew his grandfather didn't do drugs. No one could hide drug use that well, especially on the rock trail. In his time getting to meet or know about some of the most famous musicians out there, he'd seen too many who had been lost to addictions. He'd also seen those who had started out with some hard partying—something easy to fall into when you were young and suddenly rich and famous—but totally cleaned up their acts and were still performing at the ages when many people were ready to hang up their hats.

But Skyhawk...

He shook his head. Joe Garcia had never done drugs, but he still enjoyed a few beers. Mark Reynolds was known to chill with a little marijuana.

To his knowledge, none of them did cocaine, heroin or any of the hard stuff. Then again, the best dealers probably never touched the stuff themselves.

They were the four surviving original members of Skyhawk. He sat in sometimes, Sky had come with her dad, and Brandon Wiley sat in for Chris.

Sometimes, Sky's mom had come up as well.

Joe Garcia was married. Mark's one son was the CEO of a major tech company, one he had created himself. His name was David. He always seemed to be a great guy, proud of his dad who was, in turn, proud of him. Mark had shrugged when people had asked him if he hadn't wanted his only child following in his footsteps. "Just glad I could pay for the education that helped him get where he is today!" Mark said.

Then, of course, there were the roadies. The band had three that were on their payroll. Justin West, Charlie Bentley and Nathan Harrison. They were in their forties, men who had started with Skywalk at least twenty years ago when they'd been in their twenties themselves, young and eager to be with such a prestigious band.

So...

That was his suspect pool. Four surviving band members—their family members at the stage that night—himself, Sky and Brandon—and the roadies.

He was forgetting one person. Kenneth Malcolm.

Malcolm. Malcolm worked the venue. But...

The effects of the strange drug sales that seemed to follow Skyhawk had been found in various places, not just New Orleans. So that should eliminate Malcolm, but...

Sky.

He bit his lower lip, shaking his head.

She had been so loyal to her father, and he understood why. Jake had been amazing; he'd been amazing to Chase as well, all of his life. A man who truly believed in the human family and in his responsibility to give when giving was needed. The band had begun in a garage in New Orleans, but Jake had been there not just for the aftermath of Katrina, but for any other disaster hitting the country as well. He encouraged the young. He was dedicated to education for everyone. He could joke and laugh and somehow be a kind human being with the strength of steel.

That show...

He could close his eyes and still see the massive concert. The seats and floor filled, people watching and waiting, the light show beginning, the display of the colors over the crowd, over the stage, blues, pinks, reds, more.

The venue host welcoming "the amazing Skyhawk" to the stage, the band members heading out and Jake at the mic, welcoming and thanking the crowd, the beat of the drums, the chords of the guitar as Jake strummed the first notes, and the bass and rhythm and the keyboards coming in...

The crowd screaming as they began, the vibrancy, the excitement in the arena...

The first hour had gone brilliantly. Jake had called out for Hank's drum solo, he had highlighted Chris on bass, Joe on the keyboards, and Mark on the rhythm guitar. All the solos had ended with the group coming in together again, setting off into a medley of several songs. Then Jake had announced that a family member was stepping in, and Chase would be drumming. He'd walked off to escort Chase to the drums as Hank had bowed and taken off to the side. Chase had heard Jake muttering those last words, then Mark had warned there was something wrong with the amp and then...

Jake had exclaimed to the audience, "Give me a sec here, my friends... Don't want anything missed for my hometown crowd!"

They had applauded and screeched out their appreciation, and Jake had walked over to the amp and there had been a spark, a small spark, and then a sizzle that had seemed to burst through the entire massive arena before the explosion at the amp, the burst of flames...

Smoke and screams. Security trying to initiate evacuation, roadies trying to reach the band, and Jake...

Jake lying there, eyes wide open, even in death, his look stunned as the fire burned around him, charred his body...

He'd tried to run to Jake. Someone had caught him, screaming he'd been burned alive, and dragged him back to the wings and offstage and out into the night air while he'd screamed and screamed himself, knowing that Sky was there, that she would run right into the blaze.

He understood Sky's feelings, but still...

He stood suddenly. He had to talk to her. She really didn't understand what she could be setting herself up for.

He headed to the front door.

The years had been so strange. They'd avoided each other in an area that was close. Then again, he'd been studying and then working, and his strange job had taken him around the country just as it had now taken him home.

His hometown. Yes, it was where Skyhawk had begun, where Jake had lived next door to Chris Wiley, and the others had been nearby. Jake had been writing lyrics for years, strumming notes to them, and with the others, the music had been created to go with the words, and bit by bit, they had formed their first album, scraped together the money for the studio to get it recorded...

And history had been made.

It was where Jake had been born, and where he had died.

And where Chase was suddenly extremely worried that Sky Ferguson, named for the band itself, might well die.

He couldn't let it happen.

She was so determined. But she didn't know what she was doing.

She didn't know the suspected why of his death, why a killer would seek a way to end his life before Jake's sense of life and justice might bring down that quiet and subtle killer...

Yes. Time to pay her a visit.

SKY WAS STARING blankly at her schedule for the coming week. She had determined that she was going to keep moving when she wasn't with the band, but despite her resolve and opening the computer, she was simply staring at the screen, moments of the past seizing what was supposed to be her focus on the present.

She hadn't scheduled work for the next few weeks, determined that she would do the show and work with whatever aftermath there might be. She had never left music behind but rather turned it into something that gave her real pleasure. She took music lessons to troubled kids, kids of any age. Sometimes, it was working with four-and five-year-olds with behavioral issues as they entered prekindergarten. Sometimes, it was working with teens who were acting out. She'd become a certified therapist with her specialty, but she'd also discovered that the theater classes she'd taken worked well with it all, especially those in improv. Other times, she worked one-on-one with children or sat in on classes. She used her mother's maiden name as her business name, and while students often knew who she was, they thought it fun to keep the secret. The little kids had no clue what *Skyhawk* was anyway, but for the teens, it was a nice thrill that made them respect her with a bit more awe.

She traveled wherever she was needed. She had discovered that doing what she did was great for the mind. Keeping at what she did, of course, she'd never get rich. But she didn't need to get rich. Her dad had seen to it that she and her mom were taken care of for life.

She closed her eyes for a minute, wincing. She was glad to be home. She had a wonderful old house in the Garden District, secluded behind a tall stonework wall and gate. The home was one of the oldest in the district, and when they'd bought the place, they'd had to redo all the plumbing and electric, the kitchen and the bathrooms. But she had worked on the house with her dad who had never minded getting his hands dirty. He never expected others to accomplish every piece of what he saw as his manual labor. And, she remembered, smiling, he had also told her that they never knew when the tide might change, when his music might become something that was seldom played and of the past. The world could be a fickle place.

She started when she heard the buzzer that meant someone was at her gate. She hadn't been expecting any friends that night: they all knew that she was going to perform with Skyhawk.

But there was a telecom on her desk, and she pushed the button. "Hello?"

"It's me, Skylar. Let me in, please."

Her heart seemed to skip a beat. Seeing Chase again...

She had been so head over heels in love with him. And then she had just walked away. He'd tried to reach her.

But...

It had seemed the only way to get through her father's death had been to turn away from Skyhawk and anything and everything that had to do with it. That included the people.

And so—as she had found herself prone to do several times during her life—she had cut off her nose to spite her face.

Now, seeing him again... Nothing had changed about him that would alter her concept of what she had seen in him years ago. He was still a striking individual. No matter the passage of time, she still felt as if she...as if she could just touch him. Crawl into his arms, maybe now, at last, feel something in his warmth that was comforting to the soul...

And probably so much more! she told herself dryly.

"Skylar? I need to speak with you," he said impatiently.

Of course, he was impatient. She had been the one to build the wall. And whatever it was that he wanted...

Well, maybe his empathy had come to an end.

"Sorry. I'm here." She still hesitated, wincing. Then she pushed the button that would open the gate and then the front door.

She pushed away from her desk and hurried out to greet him at the entry.

He opened the door and stepped in. "Hey, um, sorry," she murmured.

He arched a brow to her. "For answering the door slowly? Or being incredibly rude for year upon year?"

She made a face at him.

"Sorry," he said with a shrug. "That's not why I'm here."

"Why are you here?"

"You. I'm worried about you," he told her.

She frowned. "Why?"

"Because, whether you like to admit it or not, I know you. You loved Skyhawk when your dad was alive. Now you hate it and everyone and everything around it."

"*Hate* is a strong word."

"So what are you doing?"

She shrugged, trying to avoid his eyes. He had always seen too much. He did now with her. More than physical attraction, it was part of what had made them such an incredible couple: they knew one another. They understood their different family dynamics. They'd respected one another's thoughts, shared explanations...

"Kind of late, but would you like some coffee? Soda, water? I may have something stronger, a beer maybe?" she suggested.

"Let's have coffee," he suggested.

"Uh...okay."

He led the way to the kitchen. Apparently, she hadn't changed much of anything through the years. She had a new coffee maker with all the bells and whistles for just about any kind of coffee someone might like, but it sat right where the old one had with the pods in a little drawer attached to the machine.

"Regular with a hint of cream?" he asked her.

"Yeah. Black?" she asked in turn.

"Yeah. I guess coffee tastes don't change through the years."

"Oh, but they do!" she protested. "I sometimes enjoy an espresso, straight and strong, and on occasion a vanilla latte."

He didn't respond.

"And you?"

"Espresso, black."

"Well, it's something," she murmured.

She headed to the refrigerator, getting cream for her coffee. He'd made hers first, so she added cream to her cup while he put through a second.

"Got any food?" he asked her.

"I'm not sure I invited you to dinner…"

"Dinner was hours ago. It's going on breakfast. I'll settle for—"

"You always were hungry. You must have the metabolism of a hummingbird."

"That doesn't answer the question."

She sighed. "What do you want? Yes, I keep food here. I know… I have cheese grits and shrimp in the fridge from yesterday, should still be good."

"Perfect."

"I'll just microwave a dish—"

"No, I'll heat them up on the stove," he said casually. "Hey, Hank always hated the microwave—said it was giving us weird brain waves. I'm not antimicrowave, just learned that a lot of things heat up better on a stove."

"Knock yourself out," Sky said. She opened the refrigerator again, digging out the container with her leftovers. She handed it to him. "There's quite a lot there. I placed an order and didn't realize I'd ordered the family size until I got home. They didn't have that kind of ordering before the pandemic years, but during that time, I guess they learned that people decided they liked picking things up to take home."

He knew to look in the lower cabinet next to the stove for the frying pan.

Sky thought that she really needed to change up her life a bit.

"Where's your mom, by the way?" Chase asked her. "Is she coming to the concert?"

"She wasn't planning to. She's in Ireland with her sister. They're doing a whole heritage kind of a thing. But..."

"Now that she knows you're going to be taking on your dad's role, she wants to come?"

Sky sighed. "Yep. I told her she's heard me all her life. That she knew Skyhawk all her life. She doesn't need to come."

"Did you argue her out of it?"

Sky shrugged. "I hope!"

"Ah, which leads to a further question."

"I didn't think you came just for shrimp and grits."

"Cheaper than a restaurant," he said.

"Right. Like you need to worry about that. Just what are you doing now? Working in some kind of lab somewhere? Never seemed like you."

"Call me a perpetual student," he said lightly, using a spatula to move the grits around in the pan as they heated. "Anyway, if it was just to see you sing your dad's songs, why wouldn't you want your mom here?"

"It's not a matter of not wanting her," Sky said. "I just don't want her feeling that she has to leave a trip she's wanted to do to come back for what she's already done."

"You're lying, aren't you?" he asked her.

"Why would I be lying?"

"Because you don't want me to know the truth," he said quietly.

Again, she felt as if her heart skipped a beat, froze in her chest.

He did know her too well.

"I don't know what you're talking about," Sky lied.

He turned off the stove and lifted the frying pan, setting it on a cold burner. He turned to her, his hands on his hips, and she knew why he had come.

Of course.

"Sky," he said flatly, "you think that someone deliberately killed your father. And you think that somehow, doing this show, you're going to figure out how and why. But that's crazy. Don't you see that it's crazy? It's been years now. Even if we were all forensic scientists, it would be too late. No clues would have survived this amount of time, this amount of people in and out—"

She didn't realize that she'd walked over to him until she set her hand on his arm, shaking her head in protest and interrupting. "You've taken too many classes! It's just New Orleans. Hometown. I said that I'd do my dad's songs, that I'd be him for this."

He looked at her a long moment. She realized she had come too close. She still remembered far too much about him, the scent of him, the feel of him, and in that moment, she wanted to forget all her misery, to lay her head against his shoulder and let him hold her and tell her that everything would be all right and then...

And then touch her and let the touch become something deeper and more intimate and then, in his very special way, make her forget for a while that anything in the universe could be wrong, that there was light and beauty and incredible wonder in the place that he could take her to...a place that they never really left because they remained curled together, legs draped over legs, flesh still damp and hot and touching...

"Sorry!" she murmured. "I just—"

"You never need to be sorry with me," he said softly.

She had to step farther back, make a much lighter situation out of it.

"Oh, thought you came here tonight so that I could give you a massive apology!" she teased.

He smiled. "Oh, trust me, I haven't expected that for years." His expression grew serious again. "I meant that you never needed to apologize for touching me."

"Your grits!"

He turned to look at the pan. "Yeah. They're still there."

"Getting cold. I'll get you a dish," she said.

"Get yourself one, too."

"I'm not hungry—"

"You're never hungry until I'm eating and then you're hungry. Get two dishes."

She hadn't realized it, but he'd made her smile again.

She got two plates.

He spooned the shrimp and cheese grits onto both of them, and they sat at the kitchen table.

"I wasn't expecting dinner—"

"I already tried to tell you," Sky said. "Dinner was hours ago."

"I wasn't planning on a meal—"

"You asked for one."

"You might have refused. So this is nice. And still…"

"You came to warn me that I shouldn't mess with the past, that doing so would be worthless," Sky said. "I'm just singing."

"Stop lying."

"Just singing and playing the guitar."

"Sky." He looked at her while chewing and swallowing. He set his fork down and took a sip of his coffee.

She realized she had frozen, watching him.

He reached over and took her hand.

"You know, I love you. From the minute I first saw you,

I think even as kids, I was in awe of you and in love with you. But that's really neither here nor there as far as this all goes. Sky. Listen to me. Leave it alone. Sing, play, have a good time, honor your father. He wrote great songs. He reigned with the hottest band over several decades. But don't do anything else. Don't question people. Don't interrogate the roadies. Leave it."

"Why? If everything was so innocent—"

She was startled when he winced and slammed a fist on the table.

"Sky! Listen to me, damn it! Don't you understand? If any of this was real, anything you suspect at all, then you'd be putting yourself in danger. Honor your father, Sky! How the hell do you think Jake would feel if you died because of him?"

Chapter Three

Chase had tried. He had tried everything in hell and in his legal power.

He couldn't just knock her out, kidnap her and keep her away until after the show.

Well, he could. But it wouldn't be legal. And that would definitely be something that she wouldn't forgive.

"Chase," Sky said, looking steadily at him, "trust me. I have no intention of getting myself killed. And the fact that you're here tells me something."

"That I'm a glutton for punishment?" he said dryly.

She let out a sound of exasperation. "No! You think that something is off-kilter, too. You know that what happened to my father was not an accident. You don't know what happened, but you know that something was wrong. Very wrong."

"Sky—"

"What? It's okay for you to be there and suspicious as all hell but not me?"

"Sky, first—"

"There is no *first*."

"Well, yeah, there is," he told her. "You know what I've been doing. I got my major in criminology and I've kept at it—"

"Professional student, yeah, I got it."

"No, you don't. Yes, I've taken a lot of classes about poisons, blood spatter, DNA and fingerprints. But I've also spent hours upon hours at a shooting range. I know how to use a gun. I know how to aim. I've taken classes in self-defense—"

"And would a gun have protected my father from an amp that had been purposely set up with a frayed wire, something timed to go off after the show started? Was he going to shoot at the electricity?" Sky demanded.

"Okay, no," Chase agreed. She had a point.

"I'll be on stage, you'll be on stage," she reminded him passionately.

He sighed, looking down, shaking his head.

"Look at me, Chase, please!" Sky begged. "I know you, too, remember? I know that you suspect that someone on the stage that night—or near it, someone with easy access to the instruments and the amps—meant for my father to die. I can't begin to understand why anyone would want to kill him. Everyone loved him—seriously. He—"

"Sky, stop. Yeah, he was one of the nicest human beings I have ever encountered. One of the best. But he was no doormat. He held his own when he had an opinion. And he was always a staunch defender of anyone he saw as downtrodden."

"So," she said slowly, studying him, "you do know that he was killed."

"Sky, I don't *know*—"

"You suspect. And you've figured out what I hadn't—that he was probably killed because he was going to do something for someone and someone else didn't want him doing it, or—"

"Sky, don't you understand? That's why it's dangerous."

She nodded. "I repeat. I'll be on stage. You'll be on stage."

"I'm not going to talk you out of this," Chase said.

She shook her head.

"All right. Then, do me a favor," he said.

"Of course."

"You let me know anything that you think, feel or suspect," he told her.

"On one condition."

"What's that?"

"You let me know anything that *you* think, feel or suspect," she said sweetly.

He let out a sound of aggravation.

"That's the deal," she told him.

"All right, then, I have another idea," he said.

"Let's hear it."

"Okay, we're in this together, that's what you want?"

"*Demand* is more like it," she said casually.

"Then, we pretend that we're a thing again. That way, I can be at your side. That way, I can at least attempt to protect you."

She looked startled for a minute, and then as if she was about to protest.

But she didn't. Instead, she smiled. "At least that way, maybe *I* can protect *you*."

"Sure, cute, of course," he said. "The point is we stick together and we have one another's backs. How does that work for you?"

She nodded slowly. "There's not a lot of time. I've made lists of everyone there—"

"I did, too."

"But," Sky continued, frustrated then, "we only have two more rehearsals and then the show."

"Lunch."

Sky's face knotted in confusion. "Lunch? It's past midnight, and you've just finished a nice big plate of cheese grits and shrimp and—"

"No. Let's invite the guys to lunch."

"Oh! Smart. Think they'll come?"

"To the best of my knowledge, they have nothing else

to do until the show. Brandon Wiley is the only other family member, and he's here with Chris, so they'd be having lunch together somewhere anyway. Of course, every one of the guys—"

"We need the roadies, too," she reminded him.

"They'll come. It will be a free meal."

"Okay, so…"

"Why don't we send out an email invitation," Chase said. *"We?"*

He smiled. "Of course. We're a thing, right?"

"I'll write it or you'll write it?" Sky asked.

"Doesn't matter, we just need to get it out."

Sky nodded, rose and walked from the kitchen to the dining room and back across to her office. She sat at her computer and started filling in addresses. "Okay, I have Chris, Mark, Hank, Joe and Brandon. Not sure I have all the roadies in my address book."

"I'll fill them in," Chase said. "May I?"

She shrugged and started out of her chair. He was already sliding in before she could slide out. She moved quickly.

Chase entered the extra addresses and then a message.

Hey, guys! Rare opportunity! Lunch in the French Quarter—seriously! We'll meet at Chase's noonish, unless that's too early for old rock stars.

"Your place?" Sky asked. "I thought you meant here."

"My place is more convenient for those not living here—French Quarter."

"Okay, whatever. But as for lunch…"

"Delivery. It will be great."

Sky looked at him, nodding. A little blip caused them both to look at the computer screen. "An answer already," Chase noted.

Sky stood to look over his shoulder. "Joe Garcia! He says he's in. Excellent. And he gave us an LOL, telling us that old people have a tendency to be early risers!"

"We'll have them all here, trust me," Chase said. "And—"

He broke off. A dog was barking loudly enough to raise the dead. The sound was coming from somewhere nearby.

From right next door.

Chase leaped to his feet and hurried out of Skylar's office to the front, throwing open the door.

He could swear he saw the gate at the front rattling. And the dog continued to bark. He hurried outside, looking just beyond the gate.

There was nothing. And the barking stopped abruptly.

"Chase!" Sky called, hurrying outside to join him. "Hey, people walk on the street. And that's King from next door, a big old shepherd, but sweet as a baby. He's—"

"He's what you need," Chase told her.

"Chase—"

"Let's get back in. You need a big old dog like King."

"I love dogs. But I travel too much. And, please, come on, Chase, this is getting ridiculous! No one is going to come after me here. I mean, why would they? As far as anyone knows, I'm filling in for my dad. It's just a show, a show—"

"Unlike any other," he said. "Damn, Sky, if I know what you're up to, someone else may suspect that you're looking for them, too. Move."

"Right. And not you?"

"Jake wasn't my dad," he said quietly. "I loved him, but others loved him, too. Come on. Let's get back in the house."

"But seriously, I have the gate, you have to buzz to get in—"

"Or jump the wall."

"King is out there," Sky reminded him.

"All night?" he demanded. She wasn't going to lie. She shook her head.

"But still—"

"I'm not leaving."

"What?"

"I'm not leaving."

"I'm not inviting you to stay!"

"You don't even have your own dog."

"I'll get one tomorrow," Sky promised.

King suddenly started barking again. Chase couldn't leave her. Whether she liked it or not, he couldn't leave her. And it would be hell all night, knowing that she was upstairs, that they were close, that years had dripped away as if they'd never been apart, and he couldn't leave her.

"You have a lovely sofa," he said.

"That's not... I mean, the house has four bedrooms upstairs. Chase, you know that's not the point."

"Hey, we'll put on a good show."

What the hell did he have to do? Tell her the truth about what he now did for a living, the truth about who he worked for...

"Sky, I am worried for your life. Because someone besides me suspects that you're not just singing with the band for old times' sake, for your dad."

King barked and stopped again.

"I would appreciate a pillow and a blanket," he told her, prodding her through the entry to the parlor.

"Really? If you're insisting, there are guest rooms—"

"No, I'll be down here. Where I'll know if someone is fooling around with the house."

"Super hearing? After being a drummer?"

"Cushioning earplugs. Hank told me too many of his friends have gone deaf. You need someone else here. Sky, what the hell. This is real. Someone could break in. With a gun. You need protection. Tonight, I'm it."

"And what are you going to do if someone breaks in with a gun?" she asked.

"Shoot him," he said flatly.

CHASE WAS DOWNSTAIRS. Sky had provided him with two pillows and a blanket. The furniture in the large living area that consumed the center of the house was old—dating back to the 1800s—and she doubted that there was any way anyone could sleep comfortably on the one sofa that sat with a group of upholstered chairs in front of the fireplace.

But he was there.

Of course, she couldn't quite figure how she hadn't realized that he was armed. But she didn't know anything about guns. She'd never wanted to know anything about them, even when crime rates had gotten higher in many of the country's major cities.

And yet now...

She'd asked him, of course. With a shrug he'd explained it was all part of the classes he'd been taking in criminology, right along with blood spatter and fingerprints.

She'd provided him with the little he had asked for and he'd escaped.

But she knew he was there. And it was hell.

And then again, it wasn't.

While she was in a turmoil of hell where the past had come to life, she also felt...safe. She believed him. He knew how to use a firearm, and she figured he probably knew a lot more. He'd always been—perfect. Tall, broad-shouldered, lean-muscled, agile...a diver, a guy who could ski, skateboard, swim, kill it on a football field.

It had never occurred to her before to be afraid; she had simply been determined. In fact, even being her father's daughter, she'd never been afraid. The house was in a great quiet residential neighborhood, not too far from Lafayette

Cemetery, Commander's Palace and a place she loved, Garden District Book Shop. Still close to a few iconic places, but private and off the beaten path. When she had turned eighteen, her parents had put the house in her name. When her dad had died, her mother had started traveling and when she was home, she liked to be in a little condo she'd purchased down in the French Quarter near Café du Monde.

Both of her parents had always been low-key, friends with their neighbors, quiet in their lifestyles when they weren't performing. They had loved being together. And yes, while he was recognizable, as he'd often explained with amusement, it just wasn't like being a movie star. The good majority of people in the world would have no idea of who he was when he walked down the street.

And she wasn't well known at all, so there had been no reason...

Of course, she could have done a few simple things. Like having alarms installed for the gate and the house. That might have meant that Chase McCoy wouldn't have insisted on spending a miserable night on her sofa.

And she wouldn't have spent the night knowing that he was there.

So much distance between them. Years! But...

When she was near him, all that they had shared might have been yesterday. She could remember the subtle way his scent, clean and masculine, could wrap around her: it was as if she could breathe him in. She loved the sound of his laughter, the look in his eyes...

And it was ridiculously tempting to walk down the stairs, just squeeze next to him, look up at him and pretend that time had not created a wall between them, a wall that she had somehow pushed into being.

But it was there. He was here because he was afraid for her. And because he had loved her father. And for no other reason.

She winced and tossed, plumping her pillow. She had to grow up. She couldn't erase the past, but it was behind her. She had to behave like a normal human being with him, except...

They were playing a game. A dangerous game. Pretending they were a couple who had simply fallen back together so that others might not suspect anything amiss if they whispered to one another, slipped together as a couple if they saw or heard something...

She had to grow up. Play the game. And for a minute, she was a little amused. Chase and all his criminology classes and work—doing whatever it was he did with most of his time.

Undercover!

Undercover in plain sight. And if it got her the answers she wanted, total justice for her father, well then, it was worth whatever she had to do.

Decided. Simple. Done.

And it was still the wee hours of the morning before exhaustion claimed her. Because he was there, downstairs, so close, and she didn't understand herself why she had thrown away such an incredible man, such a beautiful relationship.

SKY HAD STILL been sleeping when Chase called; he could hear it in her voice. He wondered if just maybe she'd had as much trouble falling asleep as he'd had. No matter. It was late. Time to move.

"Hello?" she murmured, curiosity in the very sleepiness of her voice.

"Time to rise and shine up in the... Sky!"

She groaned. "Oh, that was bad."

"Yeah, I know. But you need to wake up."

"Wait a minute. You're calling me—from downstairs?"

"Seemed the best way to wake you up," he told her.

"Okaaay."

"We need to get to my house."

"Um, the lunch thing, right. But it's still early."

"I know you want to shower. And then at my house, we'll have to check our RSVPs and order the food in, I'll need to shower, and I'm hoping there's time for us to go through a few things."

"A few things?"

"Our suspect list, what we know about each of the players, the band, the roadies, anyone who might have been close. If what happened was more than an accident, there had to have been a reason."

She was quiet over the line for a minute. Then she told him, "You forgot something," she told him.

"What?"

"A dog? If I get a nice big dog, you get to go home at night."

He shook his head. "A nice big dog would be good, but I won't be leaving you."

She let out a sound of aggravation. "What? You're going to guard me the rest of my life?"

"I believe that between us, we'll glean the truth. We'll find out if there was more than the many law enforcement and fire personnel saw that day."

"They were looking for cause, not a reason," Sky murmured. "Should we make coffee first, grab something—"

"Believe it or not, I have coffee. And food. We need to go."

"I'm going to shower and come down," she said, ending the call.

CHASE LOOKED AT his phone for a minute, grimaced to himself and rose to wander the living room. The house was a beautiful one, but he knew that it had been falling apart when Jake had purchased it. He'd always loved period things.

There was a picture on the mantel, and he walked over to it. The photo had been taken when he and Sky had first started dating. But Hank was in it as well, along with Jake. It had been taken on stage one night, maybe at the casino stage in Florida, a smaller venue, maybe about seven thousand people, and it was one of the nights they had each come in for just a song or two. But the pride that both Jake and Hank wore on their faces was wide and touching, just like the way they all stood together, he and Sky in the middle, Hank and Jake flanking them.

He turned away from the picture, reminding himself that he was working. Someone in or connected to the band was selling drugs. Bad drugs. Not that they couldn't kill on their own, but these had been contaminated with fentanyl.

Jake had known it, and Jake had died.

And if there was anything he could do for Sky's father, it was going to be to keep his daughter safe. And between them, they would find the truth.

Sky HEADED FOR the shower. She realized she was arguing with him just to argue. She should be glad. Chase was on her side. Since she'd get nowhere by looking at the players and roadies and demanding to know if one of them had killed her father, it was great to have someone on her side.

Then again…

Hank McCoy was Chase's grandfather. And he was on the suspect list. Was Chase open to believing his own grandfather might have killed Jake?

She doubted it; if someone had told her that her father was a murderer, she wouldn't have believed it.

She turned the water on, not sure if she wanted it to be hot and soothing or cold enough to really wake her up and straighten her out.

Sky tried both, and both were good. But she hurried and

dressed quickly and casually in jeans and a tunic and hurried down the stairs.

"Let's go."

"Don't we both have cars here?" she asked.

"Leave yours."

"Why don't we leave yours?"

"Are you being argumentative for the sake of it? We're going to my house."

She winced. She was doing it again. Arguing just to argue.

"Fine. We'll take your car."

The distance between the Garden District and French Quarter wasn't great, but Jake was an expert of winding his way around the tourists who seemed to think it was fine to suddenly step out into the street at any given minute.

"The problem with the French Quarter," she murmured.

"Wandering tourists?" he asked. "No big deal. There's not so many this close to Esplanade and Rampart. Anyway...we made it."

He hit a button on a remote, and the gate that led to his courtyard swung open. He pulled his car into the garage, leaving room for those who were due to join them.

"They'll take rideshares or walk, depending on where they're staying," Sky commented.

"Probably, but just in case...we've some room here. And it's even possible to find spaces on this street this far from the river. Anyway, I've got to shower. I've ordered food, so if it gets here before I'm out—"

"I think it will be safe for me if I see that a food delivery is arriving."

He didn't reply but led the way through the kitchen entrance.

She remembered his home. And like her own, she thought, it was a great one. Having survived a number of serious fires, it was one of the oldest in the area, stemming from the late 1700s. But it had been treated with care through the years. It was a smaller house than hers with a narrower stairway, with touches of the period in the archways and architectural details. Her home was decidedly Victorian while his was more French Gothic, but both were part of what they loved about New Orleans: the history, the color and the music. Especially the music. She smiled, thinking about the wonderful performers she so often saw when she just took a walk down Royal Street.

"What?" Chase asked.

"What?"

"You're thinking something and smiling," Chase said.

"Just that I wonder… I mean, the guys started as kids, basically. My father being the grand old man in his twenties. And I wonder if they hadn't all grown up surrounded by so much great music if they would have become the group that they were. It wasn't one song—it wasn't a vocalist or a guitarist or any one instrument. These guys loved and grew up with and studied music, all of them," she said.

"As did we."

"And I still love it and use it, just in a different way," she assured him.

"Okay, so…the kitchen is smaller, but it has an island. So just in case—"

"I can safely handle food," she assured him.

"Okay, I'm headed upstairs."

"Go!"

He did, hurrying up the narrow flight that led to the second floor. He had a great balcony up there; they'd watched a few parades go by from that vantage point, though they took different routes now.

When he was gone, Sky slowly turned around, taking in the house. He'd either remained a fairly neat person or he had someone come in to clean. And while not the size of her place, he had a table in the dining area that stretched straight into the parlor that would seat eight, and there were plenty of sitting spaces in the parlor.

She walked to the left side of the house and found that one room was all but filled with a drum set. But Chase also played guitar, and he had a collection of tambourines and maracas. She smiled when she actually found a cowbell on the shelf along with the other smaller instruments.

What was he really doing with his life? she wondered.

When she'd hear about him through one of the band members or their families, he was just taking another class, sitting in with a group somewhere, working on something in a lab. He seemed to travel a lot, too.

She hadn't been there long before she heard a buzz and remembered that he had a gate bell, similar to the one she'd installed. She quickly headed for the front, freezing in the parlor when she looked up the stairs.

Chase was there, bottom half wrapped in a towel. His shoulders were bronzed and glistening, and his abs and pecs had remained smoothly muscled.

"I've got it!" she cried to him. "For God's sake, get dressed!"

"I don't know if you should answer the door—"

She ignored him, hurrying on to the front. She pushed the button at the door that opened the gate and stepped out to the porch. It was the food arriving, two burly men bearing boxes and bags. She greeted them pleasantly and directed them to the island in the kitchen and the long table in the dining room. They'd barely gotten things on the table when Chase came hurrying down, now in jeans, a T-shirt and a casual jacket.

She realized the latter probably concealed a weapon.

But he thanked the delivery men as well and saw them out.

"See?" she said. "Food, delivered, safely, and I managed it just fine on my own."

He didn't reply to that but said, "Let's start getting this stuff open and out. Oh, paper plates. There's a tray of plastic forks and all on the counter… We'll be ready, and if there's time…"

"If there's time, what?"

"We'll quickly run up to my office."

"Shouldn't we do that first? Food gets cold. I see you have crawfish étouffée, gumbo…all the right stuff, huh?"

"One hopes. You're right. Leave it all covered. That's a salad—doesn't matter. Come on upstairs," he said.

He hurried ahead of her, turning to the right.

His office was impressively neat and well equipped with his computer, a good-sized monitor, printer/copier complete with a scanner and a tray with neatly folded papers. His desk was large with an ergonomic chair, and there was a love seat in the rear of the room and another chair that could be brought up to the desk.

She wondered who he might work with here at times.

And she couldn't help but feel a bit of jealousy. Did he write music sometimes? Maybe with someone…with whom he could make beautiful music?

"All right, the remaining group. Four guys—one of them my grandfather. Hank always admitted he did some pot in his day, doesn't care for it now, says he can take a nap at the drop of a hat without it. Drinking—a bit to excess in his younger days, wild, crazy and a success—but he says he respected Jake so much, even when he didn't realize it, and he learned to temper himself. Yes, he's my grandfather, and yes, I want him to be innocent."

"Did any of them go crazy on drugs at any time?" Sky murmured.

"Not really, and certainly not in comparison to a lot of groups out there who suddenly had tons of money and adulation. I looked up a bunch of public-domain stuff. They never went crazy peeing on stage à la Jim Morrison or anything, but Joe Garcia once drank himself into a stupor and ripped up a hotel room and cooled his heels in jail overnight."

"Brandon?" Sky asked.

"He's been rowdy a few times, but whatever he has or hasn't done, it was never bad enough for an arrest. I've been with him during Mardi Gras when I was worried that he'd get himself in trouble and I wanted to make sure he'd get home okay. Brandon...he was there that night."

Sky nodded. "I've never seen Mark or Chris have anything more than a beer or two. And if he does drugs of any kind, Brandon certainly has never asked me to join in. Then again, other than being polite when my mom has had anyone around, I haven't really hung out with these people for years."

"Your dad never frowned on anyone having a drink. Even sober, he'd buy a beer for a friend. He'd be out of there if people were drinking to excess, they... Well, they just didn't. They respected him, and they followed his lead. They might all owe him their careers—and their lives."

"Roadies?" Skylar said.

"Okay, let's just remember we can't label them as guilty of anything just because we were never as close to any of them as we were the band members," Chase said.

Sky smiled. "Gotcha. So...?"

"So. Justin West, Charlie Bentley and Nathan Harrison," Chase said. "Justin has been with the group longest, he's turning fifty in the fall, and has no arrest record that I can find, and records like that are accessible. I have seen Justin kick back after a show with a lot of tequila, but he's also a family man, two sons in college, still married to Julia, his wife of twenty-seven years. Charlie Bentley, forty-three, divorced, handsome man, glad to sweep up the ladies after a performance. He had a DUI back in 2008. He was young, and in the biz... Driving under any kind of influence is a sin in my book—plenty of rideshare companies out there—but that's a personal thing."

"Not personal at all. Too many people have been injured or killed by impaired drivers," Sky said.

He nodded. "Still, doesn't turn him into a murderer or…"

"Drug pusher?"

"Right. Then we have Nathan Harrison. Also in his early forties, also divorced—a couple of times—still a good dad to his kids, so I hear. Coaches his son's Little League team and is on decent terms with both his ex-wives, no arrest record, but again, likes to party after a show and considers himself quite the hunk for those young women who like to hang around rock stars."

A buzzing sounded.

"First of our lunch guests," Chase said, rising. "Let's see who it is."

"Everyone responded. Hanging around until sound checks and all tonight," Sky murmured. "Well, except for Hank, of course—"

"Because Gramps is in the hospital," Chase reminded her.

"He's doing okay?"

"He'll be in there another week or so and then… He'll be out of any kind of heavy lifting until he finishes with his cardio rehab."

"Puts you in a bad position, doesn't it?" Sky asked him.

"What do you mean?"

"Skyhawk with no drummer."

"You don't hang around a lot. They have no lead singer and they've managed."

Sky laughed. "All those guys sing, and they've divided the songs well. But being a drummer…hmm, harder call."

"And the rock world is filled with them."

"But not drummers who belong with Skyhawk."

"Hey, let's focus. Be charming and fun and see what we can learn about people."

Sky nodded gravely. "Someone fixed that amp. And they knew how to do it. Fray it just enough that the band would be in the middle of something and that would mean my dad would be impatient enough to fix it himself without stopping the show."

"They're all fairly tech-savvy when it comes to the shows."

"No, seriously, think about it. There's so much going on. The light show, the mic stands, the amplifiers, all usually run by a good DJ until the band's front man takes over. I think—"

"I think we're talking about a single wire—one mic."

She stopped, almost tripping down the stairs. She grabbed his arm to steady herself. Naturally, he was there, catching her. But she looked into his eyes.

"You knew—you knew long before all this came along. You have known that what happened to my dad wasn't an accident and—"

"I haven't known anything. I've suspected some things, yes. But don't you understand? We don't know who to suspect, and even if we did, damn it, Sky, the legal system works on proof. I don't like that you're here, because yes, I think something was done on purpose to your dad. And if whoever did it thinks you're on his trail, there's going to be another so-called accident!"

She was still holding his arm. His hands were still on her shoulders.

The buzzing sounded again.

He released her and turned and headed on down the stairs, hitting keys on his system that opened the gate and the front door.

He stepped out to the porch.

Their lunch guests were arriving.

Chapter Four

"Skylar of Skyhawk! Wow, kid, it is great to see you!"

Nathan Harrison was the first to arrive. He greeted Skylar with a massive hug, pulling her tightly into an embrace, then setting her at arm's length to study her. "Honey," he added, "you are beautiful like your mama, but man…do you have a lot of your dad in you! That dark hair and those blue, blue eyes! I'm thrilled, and I swear," he added, suddenly serious, "your daddy is going to be smiling up in heaven, knowing his girl is doing his stuff with a voice to challenge the angels!"

Nathan was a solid, strong and good-looking man with red-blond hair, a beard and a mustache that made him look like a Viking roadie. He'd always been nice to her, but she knew he could be wild.

She liked Nathan. His hug was warm. His welcome seemed real.

But then, who? She had always cared about these people, her "uncles" when Skyhawk had performed with all this crew for years and years.

"Hey!" Chase said lightly. "Watch the merchandise."

"Aw, come on! Jealous of an old man?" Nathan returned. He cast his head at an angle, arching a brow. "Hmm. You young-uns are hosting this luncheon together, I surmise?"

"Well, it's lunch, and we're both here," Sky said lightly. "Nathan, great to see you. How have you been?"

"Up to no good, like usual!"

Stepping from behind Nathan, Joe Garcia was doing the talking. He wasn't a short man, being about six feet even, but Chase and Nathan were about six three or so, making him appear small in their presence. But Joe was a showman, too. He'd kept in shape and could move like a man thirty years his junior.

He must have also been a mind reader because he quickly said, "Come on, now! The best things come in small packages!"

"There's nothing small about you," Sky assured him dryly, giving him a hug, too.

The buzz sounded again.

"That's going to be Justin and Charlie," Nathan told them. "You know, both moved out of New Orleans. Justin's living down in Orlando and Charlie headed up to Baton Rouge. The pandemic years were hard, Skyhawk wasn't performing and…"

"Hey!" Joe protested. "We kept you guys on payroll all the way through it." He looked at Sky and gave her an encouraging smile. "That was something your dad insisted on—none of the usual bonuses and perks, but a paycheck at the very least."

"And were we grateful! But in Orlando, Justin could have his family near the theme parks, and there wound up being some work down there. But you know Justin—he'd never let anything interfere with Skyhawk." He laughed suddenly. "He liked being a three-to four-hour drive to the Fort Lauderdale and Miami areas, too. 'Cause, you know, Skyhawk isn't the only group heading out there! He took the kids down to see Cheap Trick last year, and he worked some old-timers, too. Anyway, he's super excited. Says that age doesn't dull a rocker—like Cheap Trick commanded that state. But this show has you, Sky! The Sky of Skyhawk.

Sold out, you know, and resales… People are asking like crazy—in the thousands—to get in. This is going to…"

"Rock?" Chase suggested.

"We will rock it," Joe promised. "Hey, it's Itch and Scratch, Mr. Mom Justin and Wild Man, Crazy Charlie. Now, there's a pairing for you!"

Justin and Charlie came in, making faces at Joe. "Hey, Mr. Mom?" Justin demanded.

"Said with love and all good things," Joe promised him. "You managed this all being a great husband and dad."

"Hmm. Wild Man? Crazy Charlie?" Charlie asked.

Skylar had a smile plastered on her face as she accepted hugs from the two of them, too. There was nothing wrong with Justin's looks; he was a young, strong sixty-plus, but he tended to have a more serious demeanor, and she'd noted through many occasions that he was happiest when his wife was able to attend whatever gig they were working and that he worried about the right gift for her on any occasion. On the other hand, Charlie had dark brown eyes, almost platinum hair and a smile that made him alluring—except to Sky, it also made him appear a little…smarmy. If that was a word.

"You are a wild man," Joe said simply. "But hey—"

"Hey, yeah, the invitation came from Sky's email—to come to Chase's house. So, hmm, should we assume some old fires have rekindled and we have a hunk, a hunk of burning love going on here?" Charlie asked.

"Charlie," Joe murmured. "The kids…"

"Kids? Joe, they grew up!" Justin protested.

"My question is purely selfish. If the studly drummer is occupied with the luscious young singer, that leaves more adoring fans ready to pounce on a roadie just because he's close to the band!" Charlie said.

Sky smiled and said, "Thank you. I think. Yeah, um, I

mean, who knows? But…yes…we're having this luncheon together."

"You two are together?" Joe said, looking at them. He seemed surprised at first and then pleased. "Jake would be pleased," Joe said softly. "Chase is a good boy—"

"Joe! These *kids* are both over twenty-one now and, from what I hear, leading full and responsible lives," Nathan said, stepping back into the conversation. "Then again," he added with a shrug, "you guys will be kids to Joe and the other oldsters as long as we all live."

"True," Chase said, setting his arm around Sky's shoulders. "Guess what, Nathan. Hank calls you guys *kids*, too. He told me he used to call anyone under forty a kid, but now it's anyone under fifty."

"We're going to miss Hank," Joe said. "But! We want him better. The world is revolving again, and we've gotten so many offers."

"And," Charlie said, "let's hope you're going to take them. Have to stay relevant. I mean, we may all know you, Chris and Mark are older than dirt, but between us all, we caught some great acts last year! I saw the Stones, still amazing. I saw the Eagles, Def Leppard, U2 and more, but I believe putting the *Sky* into Skyhawk is going to be something amazing!"

"Hey," Chris protested, "I may be older than dirt, but I have a full head of hair, dark bedroom eyes—if I do say so myself—and I can pass for…well, at least five years younger. Neither here nor there. Back to it. So… Sky?"

"I can't promise a tour," Sky told him.

"But she's not *not* promising a tour, either," Chase said.

"Well, cool, young McCoy. We believe Hank will be back," Joe said, "but we all know you're welcome for half the gig anytime."

"Hey—and there, at the gate. Mark, Chris and Brandon!" Sky said.

Sky wanted this lunch; they needed the gathering. Or did they? Was it going to help any? They knew the players… Nathan, reserved, glad to be behind the curtain. Charlie, always out there, the guy to overdo things.

But did that make him…homicidal?

But something *had* happened. Chase had always known it; he had been working it, and maybe what had happened had turned him onto the path he'd taken as what now seemed to be the life of a perpetual student.

And she felt uncomfortable, standing there as they were.

"Hail, hail! The gang's all here!"

"You're here," Mark said, looking from Nathan to Charlie to Justin. "You're here. But tonight, we have our chance at the venue—"

"Are you kidding, man?" Justin asked. "We started last night, and we finished up this morning. All we need is Skyhawk up on the stage."

"Sky and Skyhawk!" Charlie said, turning to look at her. His expression was serious, and his words were spoken with what seemed like real warmth. "Seriously, Sky. Your dad was always so proud of you. On stage and off. Someone asked him once what he wanted you to be when you grew up—a rock star, or maybe president of the United States. He said he just wanted you to grow up to be a good and decent person doing what you loved for a living, whatever that proved to be. He would be so proud."

"Charlie," she said softly, "thank you. That's very sweet of you." She turned to the others. "Come on, we've provided all kinds of our city's finest choices. I mean we are a music city, and we are a food city! Let's eat! We have jambalaya, crawfish étouffée and so much more! Let's do this!"

"Fine!" Chris said. "Boy, and it's as if he heard the dinner bell—here comes Brandon now!"

Chase moved ahead and did a presentation of all the

dishes he had ordered, with Chris Wiley laughing and telling him it was a feast for kings—on paper plates.

"I have important work tonight. No time for dishes," Chase explained. "Eight chairs at the table, but we can drag in the stools from the kitchen, or anyone can sit wherever they want to sit. Just dig in. It's great to be together."

"Let's do a video chat with Hank, too, huh? Could we?" Mark asked.

"Sure, he has his phone," Chase said. "I'll try to reach him."

He stepped into the kitchen area to make the call while the others grabbed plates and piled them high.

Sky waited for the others and realized she was standing back. To her surprise, Charlie turned to her and spoke softly. "Sky…"

"Yes?"

He looked pained. "I… I know how to work a stage. I know we weren't blamed, and the fire marshal said there was a faulty wire, no one could have done anything. I just… I always felt guilty. As if there should have been something…that I should have seen something, that…"

"Charlie, stop, please!" she said, setting an arm on his shoulder. He was the wild one. The one who might have gone off the deep end at one time or another.

But she believed he was sincere. His eyes were filled with pain.

"Charlie, I know that you know wires, and I know you'd never have allowed anything bad up there. I know you loved my dad. Please, the pain of loss is bad enough. We never blamed you, my mom never blamed you."

"Thank you," he said quietly. "I appreciate your words. They help."

"Got him!" Chase said, walking back in from the kitchen. He lifted his phone. Hank was there in his hospital bed, but Sky was relieved to see that despite his recent health scare,

he looked good. Full head of snow-white hair, handsome
face betraying his years and a smile that was still great. She
imagined after many years had passed Chase by, he might
look much the same.

"Hey!" Hank greeted the others. "Get out there tonight
and knock 'em—"

He broke off. Of course he'd been about to say *knock
'em dead*.

But no one in Skyhawk was going to use that expression.

"Knock 'em off their feet! Rock the house down. I can't
be there," Hank said, "but in my mind, your substitute may
be the better choice."

"Never, Gramps," Chase told him. "But I'll do my best."

"Sky, you look stunning! Then again, always," Hank
told her.

"Thanks, Hank. And you feel better soon. You are still
one handsome devil!" she assured him.

"I wish I was there for the food."

"Soon enough, Gramps," Chase said sternly. "You're
going to follow the doctors'—"

"Orders, yes, Chase, I promise. Because if Skyhawk is
hitting the tour circuit along with a lot of our fellows from
the seventies and eighties, I'm going to be well and hitting
it with everyone again. Nathan, Justin, Charlie—great that
you're on it. Where's whatshisname?" Hank asked suddenly.

"Gramps, who is whatshisname?" Chase asked.

"You are talking about Malcolm—Kenneth Malcolm?"
Nathan asked.

"Yeah. He's still working the place, right?" Hank asked.

"Oh, yeah," Mark said. "Sorry, I thought I'd mentioned
that when I visited to tell you we'd been to the place."

"His name was on the paperwork when we made the
plans," Hank said. "Months ago. Didn't know, though, with
the way things go these days—"

"Oh, yeah, he's still there. And guess what? He's been really decent," Charlie told him. "I think he had tickets and the thing is sold out and he's raking it in on resale."

"Whatever, as long as it all goes well. Sky, I swear, I dreamed about being on a cloud with your dad watching, and he was beaming," Hank said.

"Thanks, Hank," Sky told him.

"And get the video chick or whoever is on doing the Jumbotrons to make sure she's got me on the wire while it's going on!" Hank said.

"Will do, Gramps," Chase promised.

"Go eat!" Hank commanded. "Oh, wait. I can see Mark and Joe chewing. But the rest of you—have lunch! I can almost smell it from here. They have me on a cruel diet— yeah, yeah, yeah, I promise I'm going to stick to it! But go—quit torturing me, showing it all to me."

"Bye, Hank, just get well," Charlie said, and his words were echoed around the room.

Chase ended the video call.

"We never answered him," Joe said. "Did you guys invite Kenneth Malcolm?"

Chase made a face. "I didn't think of him."

"Neither did I," Sky admitted.

"He's a jerk anyway," Justin said with a shrug. "He's being nice because he's making money. Doesn't matter— I'm still glad to be away from him for this. Tonight, during tech, he'll be all over us, I promise you. So… Gumbo! I love it!"

Food and good humor went all around, different band members and stage techs sitting next to each other, switching around for dessert—bread pudding and pecan pie—and exchanging seats again.

Then Justin glanced at his watch. "Let's get over there. We've a host of other people working under us on this. The

MC, the light crew, the computer geek…and because of Mr. Kenneth Malcolm, I'd love to see it all go right."

"We're out of here!" Nathan agreed. "Charlie, come on. We're aiming for perfect!"

"Nothing is ever perfect," Joe warned.

"But we gotta aim high, right?" Mark asked, studying Sky. "Aim high, like our founder, but now we've got his daughter, and…"

Chase slipped his arms around Sky, pulling her back against him as he spoke over her shoulders. "Jake's beautiful Sky, as perfect as we can get, right?"

"No, no, no, no, no—not putting it all on me!" Sky said lightly. "Anyway, thank you, guys, all of you. This was great."

"No, thank you and Chase, our legacy, eh?" Chris offered.

"Aw, chopped liver over here?" Brandon asked, causing them all to laugh.

"Prime sirloin," Mark assured him. "And Chris is bringing you in a lot for this one, right?"

"Oh, yeah. Hey, when time starts going by, well… It's nice to see you've passed on something of value—and whether you kids decide to keep at it or not, you made us feel good, so…prime sirloin!"

"Personally, I was thinking of filet," Sky said, smiling at Brandon. He grinned in return.

"So we'll meet up again in a few hours," Mark said. "After last night, I have nothing but faith. Oh, for the performance, we'll have the ballad as the encore. And maybe—the encore should have at least two numbers—we'll also do 'Real Paradise.'"

"Gotcha," Chase assured him.

One by one, their guests filed out. When they were gone, Chase was silent.

"Well, did you get anything?" she asked him.

"Charlie would have been first on my list," Chase said. "And no more."

"Really?" Sky pressed. "I mean…he's…he was super and kind, but he is the one most likely to fall to excess."

Chase let out a long sigh. "Okay. We both think it was more than an accident. That means that your dad was going to do something after the show that involved someone— who or what, we don't know. He didn't care if other people had their minor vices, but…"

"He'd care if someone was selling drugs," Sky said.

"And those who use recreationally—sometimes a little too recreationally—aren't usually the ones with the control to make money on the scam."

"So…why?" Sky asked, perplexed. "Skyhawk started off in a garage, and they all struggled. But then they got hot, and everyone involved made money. Why—"

Chase frowned. "I don't know. I've deep-dived into the financials—"

"What?" Sky interrupted explosively.

"Hey, years of criminology courses can pay off," he said lightly. "We have a few hours—"

"Dog," Skylar said.

"What did you say?" he demanded.

She smiled. "You said I needed a dog. Let's head to the pound."

He was quiet for a minute and then looked at her, a half grin on his lips. "We can get a dog. You should have one. A dog is always good. But you won't get rid of me. Not until—"

"Until we get through this? Because," she added, frustrated, "we never got any answers."

"But we will," he assured her. "Still, a dog. A big one with a bark that shakes the very trees."

"No Teacup Yorkies or the like, eh?" she said lightly. "What if a big dog is mean—"

"Wait!" he said. "I have the perfect dog. Let me get this all cleaned up, and then I have a friend you should meet. Great guy, with great, perfect dogs."

"I thought I was going to adopt a dog that needed a home."

"You'll be adopting. Wait and see. I've got the ticket on this one."

He turned away from her, taking out trash bags. She hopped in to help him, separating trash from recycling. They were quickly done, and he swore he'd be right down as he ran quickly up the stairs.

"Let's go," he said, descending almost as rapidly as he had left.

"Okay. Where are we heading?"

"Tremé," he told her. "A great piece of property there… well, you'll see!"

They headed out, leaving the French Quarter to cross Rampart. In a few minutes, they came to a solid block that seemed to be mainly pasture and stables.

"Someone who owns a carriage company?" Sky asked.

"No, Trey owns horses, but not carriage horses. He's just a friend who…lectured one day. He's retired now and came into some family money."

Chase spoke as he pulled into a parking space outside a wooden fence. They had barely gotten out of the car when a gate opened and an older man appeared, a welcoming smile on his face.

"Chase!" he said with pleasure.

"Trey!" Chase called in return, and leading Sky forward, he introduced her and then said, "Sky, this is Trey Montgomery, and I think we might just call him an animal whisperer since he has enormous talents with all kinds of creatures!"

"Come in, come in, and welcome!" Trey said. He was

almost Chase's height and, though lean, seemed to be made of sinewy muscles.

"Retired—teacher?" she asked him.

"Something like that," he told her. "I sure love what I do now, though." He pointed out a pasture where five horses were wandering about, snatching bits of grass here and there from the earth. "The paint there—that's Sally. She just came in last week." He paused, shrugging. "Most workhorses are tended to carefully, fed, seen by the vet… then you hit an idiot who should never be around any kind of animal—including humankind—and he abuses a creature to no end. We've finally taken care of the sores in her mouth from having a bridle ripped around like a hockey puck, and she lets me approach her. I don't think we'll ever see her coat grow back over some of the scars she got from a whip, but…hey, at least they got the bastard on animal-abuse charges!"

"And you got the horse," Chase said, smiling.

"Sally already comes to me," Trey said happily. "But you don't want a horse. You want a dog. I think I have the perfect new friend. Come on to the house!"

His house was a simple ranch-style dwelling; when Trey opened the door, he was greeted by a bevy of dogs, most of them German shepherds or shepherd mixes. He made a point of petting them all, as did Chase and then Skylar.

"So…" Chase said.

"Larry," Trey said. "Right there. He's a shepherd/Lab mix, a big boy, trained in all kinds of disciplines, and doing great since he has been with me. He was injured on the job and retired."

"Injured—" Sky began.

"He was a police dog, worked with the canine squad," Chase explained.

"And he's already taken to you!" Trey said happily.

He had, Sky realized. The dog they called Larry was by

her side, wagging his tail as he looked up at her. He looked mostly like a shepherd, but his coloring was golden Lab. He was a handsome creature, and his tail kept wagging away as he stood by her side.

"Think Larry chose you!" Trey said.

"Sky?" Chase asked.

"I—uh—I think Larry is great. I just worry—as Chase knows—because I travel on business—"

"Larry is welcome back here whenever you need to go. As you can see, I have ample room. So can I get you kids some coffee or anything? Have you had lunch?"

"Enough lunch to last forever," Chase said. "Thanks, Trey. We have to get to the tech rehearsal, too, so—"

"And you did get me tickets?" Trey said.

"Oh, you bet," Chase affirmed.

"His collar is on him. I'll get his papers," Trey said. "Happy dog, happy owner!"

Sky blinked, looking at Chase. She realized her hand was still on Larry's soft head. She had always loved dogs—it had just seemed too cruel to own one and board it every other minute.

But this...

He was an amazing dog, and one that came with boarding when necessary?

"What are you, a magician, or friends with half the city?" Sky asked Chase.

He shrugged. "I've met a few people along the way. We'll get Larry to my place and—"

"Hey! My dog, my place," Sky said.

"Okay, but—"

"Right. You're not leaving me. You'll spend another night crinkled up on the couch."

"You got it," he told her.

She let out a frustrated sigh. "Knock yourself out, then."

"It's getting late. Onward to your house. And you don't

have to worry about him being housebroken—all of Trey's pups are."

"Naturally. What other magic tricks do you have up your sleeve?"

Trey returned, bringing her Larry's vet papers and license information...and a bag of dog food.

"Thought I'd get you started out right," he told Sky. "And I'm glad you like him. Looks like Larry has truly chosen you."

Sky thanked him, still a little amazed she'd been the one to remind Chase he'd suggested she get a dog.

And he'd found her Larry—housebroken, trained, loving—so quickly.

Chase thanked Trey who told him he was thrilled Larry was going to such a good home. In a few minutes, they were on their way.

He shrugged, ushering Larry into the back seat of his car. She slid into the passenger's seat. Larry took a seat without protest. Naturally, he was well behaved in the car as well.

They drove in silence to Sky's house. "Give him some water and a bowl of food, and he'll be fine until we're back," Chase said.

"Okay."

"I'll wait in the car. We want to be on time."

He stayed in the car on the street. Sky keyed in the gate and the front door and led Larry in. "Larry," she told the dog, "I didn't know I needed a dog, but you're pretty darned cool, and I hope you like this place and... I don't really care if you get on the couch." She laughed suddenly, rubbing the dog's head. "Get lots of hair on it for that guy out in the car. I want to see the two of you sleep on that thing!"

Larry barked and wagged his tail.

She quickly found bowls for water and food and assured

the dog she'd be back. He curled up on the kitchen floor, and she could almost swear that he nodded.

Then she left the house, reassuring herself that the door and the gate were securely locked.

"Ready?" he asked as she slid back into her seat.

"Well, I'm here. And Larry is sleeping on the kitchen floor. Hey, who names a dog Larry?" she mused.

"You don't like it? I guess you could rename him."

"Larry is fine," she said, looking out the window as they drove through the city she'd known all her life, a city she loved.

The city her dad had loved so much.

"You okay?" he asked her.

"Yep. Except…"

"You're frustrated. And it's okay. We're here. Just…act normal."

"Right. *Normal*."

Parking by the doors had been arranged for the band, and it was easy to reach the backstage doors. As they stepped around in the wings, Sky saw the crew was already rehearsing with the lights. Hundreds of lights were spread about the stage and the massive audience. They turned to various shades of blue, pink, orange, yellow and purple.

"It's fantastic, and wait until you see the spotlights going and everything up on the Jumbotrons!" said Justin, who was adjusting the levels on the giant soundboard.

"Can't finish that setup until I have the band all here," he said. "And if there's a problem, I'll be right there in the wings, ready to run on out. I'm going to be switching out the mics and the instruments when needed, too."

"Thanks, Justin. We're the first?" Chase asked.

"No!" Mark Reynolds said, hurrying in from the opposite wing. "I was just talking to Kenneth Malcolm, assuring him we'll be perfect with two techs, more than we've had a dozen times in the last decades. But…this is his place, so…"

"Sky!"

She heard her name called and turned to see Kenneth Malcolm was coming out. He was smiling broadly, ready to greet her.

She forced a smile to her lips.

He drew her into a hug instantly, and she tried not to stiffen, tried to return his touch. He drew back, a man like the roadies, somewhere between forty and fifty, lean and sharp with a full head of neatly combed dark hair and light gray eyes. And, always—always—the businessman, wearing a perfectly tailored suit.

"I can't tell you how delighted we are that you're here. I know you've avoided the spotlight, but people see it as extra special that you're doing your dad's numbers. He was such a showman, writer, guitarist, vocalist…talker! You're going to talk to the audience, too, I hope."

Sky glanced at Chase.

"Oh, she can talk!" Chase said.

"Oh, Chase, cool, welcome, and I can't tell you how glad we are that you're here, subbing for Hank. How's he doing?"

"Great. He'll be back to it all very soon," Chase said.

"When you can't have all of Skyhawk, it's amazing to have a Skyhawk legacy!" Malcolm said. "Seriously—"

"Ah, there's Joe!" Chase said. "We can get this started, and thanks, the venue looks terrific—"

"We have a great staff here, and they've worked great with Skyhawk's guys," Malcolm said. "I'm out of here— or out into the audience. I want to see all that's going on tonight, make sure… Well, you know, tomorrow night, I'll be dealing with all kinds of stuff, so…"

"Great to see you, and thank you," Sky murmured, noting that Chris and Brandon had come in and Justin was talking to them.

"Ready to get some sound checks going!" Mark called.

Brandon walked up to her with a guitar. "One of your dad's," he told her.

She thanked him. He headed to the side, saying that everyone had everything.

Before he walked to the drums, Chase paused by her.

"You okay for this part?" he asked her.

She nodded. "I… Yeah. Probably not so much talking tonight—"

"Tonight is sound and light check. Channel Jake tomorrow night," he said, lightly touching her hair.

"Ready to go. List is up on the screen right now!" Mark called.

Sky held her father's guitar. She closed her eyes tightly for a moment, and a sad smile came to her lips. Jake would be glad to see her there.

If only the cloud wasn't there, gray and creating something over it all…

But minutes later, after the first numbers, she let her fears, her anger, her loss and her pain all go. She thought of the amazing artists she had seen just walking down the streets of New Orleans, artists who would have given just about anything for the chance Jake had given her, the chance to do what she loved on such a stage.

No matter what, music and family had been Jake Ferguson's life.

And she would give his music everything that she had within her.

The spotlight fell on her, and there seemed to be a hush despite the music as she sang—and channeled Jake.

She did talk. She introduced the drum solo, spotlighted each member of the band, drew Brandon out from the sidelines and had him play and sing with her.

She heard the others come in on the harmonies, Chase pick up on the duets. And always, the lights glimmered around her.

She realized she could compartmentalize what they were doing…

They would get to the truth.

But she would do the show, too, with all of her heart, in memory of the man she had loved. And in doing so, she took a minute between the songs to just talk about her father, about the amazing man he had been…

And it was good.

There was a silence following her words as she prepared to say goodbye so they could walk off—and then, of course, return for the encore they believed the audience would demand.

Then there was applause, real and spontaneous, from the band members, the crew, everyone out adjusting lights and screens and everything else that would go with the show.

"Thank you!" she cried. "And Skyhawk thanks you! Good night!"

She and the others headed off.

Charlie, Justin and Nathan were there, nodding to her, beaming, each congratulating her and Chase and Brandon.

"Now, let it go a few beats and then…everyone back out!" Mark said.

They headed out and did the last two numbers.

"If only the real show goes so remarkably!" Joe Garcia said, grinning. "Sky, thanks, that was… Man, your dad is grinning from ear to ear up in heaven!"

Sky thanked him.

"Hey, you are joining us for a quick drink tonight, right?" Brandon asked. "You said you would!"

"Um, well, I was going to, but today I got a dog—"

"Cool. Dogs are cool," Brandon said. "But come on, another thirty minutes. There's a great quiet place in the Irish Channel, and we can slip away for just a few minutes!"

"Sure," Chase said, sliding up behind her and slipping an arm around her. "Sky, come on, let's hang for just a bit."

She looked at him, a question in her eyes. He didn't have to nod. She almost smiled. There had been times in the past when...

She was feeling that now. That sense of both security and sensuality when he touched her.

Compartmentalize! she reminded herself.

But that night, it seemed they were joining the crowd.

"Sure," she said.

"Hey, guys! Barbie and Ken are coming with us!" Brandon called. "Drinks on us after that great lunch."

"Snacks, too—no dinner tonight," Chase said. He frowned suddenly, and she realized his phone was vibrating as he reached into a pocket to retrieve it.

"A sec, guys. I'm right with you."

He stepped away for a minute. Sky smiled at Brandon as he called out to the others, finding out who was driving with who.

Chase stepped back up by her and put his arm around her shoulders again.

Something about him had changed. Others wouldn't notice.

But she had once known him oh so well.

"We're going to take my car—probably a quick drink and then out of there. New dog, remember? Anyway, see you there," he said to the others.

There was a lot of tension in his touch. He led her out through the back. Quickly.

"What's wrong?" she asked him as they reached the car.

He shook his head. He wasn't speaking; maybe there were ears somewhere near them.

Skylar crawled into the car and waited.

Once he had gunned the engine and they were moving, she turned to him. "Chase! What the hell is going on?"

Chapter Five

Chase kept his eyes on the road and sighed inwardly. He hated lying, and yet he'd spent a whole two days with Skylar. Intense days that, when he touched her, seemed to wash away the years.

But she had turned away from him. And he wasn't in a position now to bare his heart—and his life—to her.

"Call from a friend," he said.

"And?"

"They had a death down by the river," he said. "A kid... it was just marijuana. College kid, with friends, took a few puffs...seized and was dead. The only good thing is that watching him freaked out his friends and none of them touched the stuff after that... It's headed to a lab. But sounds like the weed had been contaminated with fentanyl. Apparently, it's a huge problem now, pills, uppers, downers, weed, cocaine...tons of drugs contaminated."

"Wow. That's horrible. And your friend called you?"

"It's all over the news."

"Right. But the friend called you," she pressed.

He turned to look at her briefly and then quickly returned his attention to the road. He didn't have to look at Sky to see her face in his mind's eye. Eyes bluer than the bluest sky, hair like her dad's, dark as ink, flowing around her shoulders. He'd fallen in love with her when he was young. And in all the years that had gone by...

He'd been practical. She was gone. He'd met people. But he hadn't had a real relationship since they'd been together. Young Chase had believed they'd eventually marry, that some people were lucky in life and they met someone who was there for them for the rest of their lives.

"Chase?"

"Yeah?"

She let out a loud sigh of exasperation. "Chase! Friends call you to report the news? Why? What is going on?"

He shrugged. "Hey. We're with a rock band. Everyone knows rock and roll may lead us all to some kind of excess," he said sarcastically.

"Chase—"

"Oh, come on! You know what? I'm scared to death for you, and I need to trust you right now. And I'm not really sure how to deal with either."

"Why wouldn't you trust me?"

"Oh, I don't know. Never returning a call, email or text. Pretending as if I'd fallen off the face of the earth—"

"Chase, I couldn't deal! I just couldn't deal, and I... Look, I'm sorry! But you're the one scared to death for me, so please, let me in on whatever the hell it is that's going on," she pleaded.

"You know what's going on," he said quietly. "This whole thing has to do with drugs. And I think someone involved—close, at the very least—has been involved with some very bad drugs that have been going around. Yeah, I have friends. You do, too. The old couple next to you with the dog—Tim Hanson and his wife, Liz. I know you are friends with them. Oh, I also know you like to sing sometimes at Jazz Mass."

"What? Wait! Have you been—"

"Did I try to follow you a bit and make sure you were moving on all right with your life? Yeah, I did. I cared. Sue me. But now..."

"Now, yeah, I got it. Bad drugs are out there. My father might have known something. And so he died, because he wouldn't let innocent people be harmed by others. And despite being clean, he didn't care if someone had a joint or a beer, but he would have been furious if—"

"If," Chase finished, "someone was out there purposely trying to addict the youth of America or, worse, to kill innocents, your dad would have acted. Because the big players out there up the profits in drugs by cutting them big-time. As in with fentanyl."

"So," she said slowly, "someone out there knows you believe someone in or around Skyhawk is doing this? You have some interesting friends."

"Well, of course I do!" he said. "You know I've worked in labs, and I've taken all kinds of classes in criminology."

"Are you sure they are all friends?" she asked.

He groaned. "I got a call from a friend, yes. A trusted friend."

"How do you know them?" she asked.

He was going to have to tell her at least something of the truth. But first, they had reached the bar where they were supposed to meet the others. He found street parking, turned off the car and sat for a minute.

"Because my friend is someone I met at a lecture. And he's with the FBI."

"Oh," she said simply. "Well, that's good, right? Is this friend going to be coming to the concert?"

"Yes," he admitted.

"That's cool," she murmured, looking down at her hands. Then she turned to him. "Though, neither of us is going to be electrocuted. The guys made a point of saying anything to do with electric or sound or even lights, they'd be handling it."

He nodded and turned and said fiercely, "And that's for real. You don't touch anything. Anything at all. Promise!"

"Of course. But you have to promise me the same."

"I do, of course. But the drummer isn't the front man—or woman. You are."

"I promise. Should we go in?" Sky asked.

He nodded. "Yeah. But…"

"But?"

"You don't drink anything that I don't give you, okay?"

"Now you want me to worry about drinks? In a bar that's been here forever?"

Chase didn't get a chance to answer. He saw Joe Garcia was on the sidewalk, hurrying toward them and tapping at Sky's window.

He indicated that they were getting out, and he and Sky exited from their respective sides of the car.

"Chase, Sky," Joe said excitedly, "this is a cool happenstance. A reporter from *the* major music magazine is in the bar—recognized me and Mark—and is dying to interview Sky!"

"Oh, well, I'm not—"

"Honey, please. No, it's not like we're hurting, like we won't survive, but anytime something like that goes around, songs are played and played on the radio and… Please, it will only take a few minutes, I promise!"

Sky glanced over at Chase and he nodded. "I'll be right there," he promised.

"Okay, um, sure, if it helps everyone, then…sure."

They headed back in together. It was a neighborhood kind of place—not like a bar on Bourbon Street, blasting music and catering to tourists. It was somewhat surprising that a reporter had made his way here, but when Joe introduced him and Sky to the man, it turned out his name was Jimmy Broussard. He had been born in New Orleans but headed out to California for work. Naturally, he latched on anytime he could when a known band was playing in the vicinity.

Broussard was maybe in his late thirties, and despite the fact he'd probably interviewed dozens of music celebrities, he seemed in awe of Sky. He shook her hand, telling her she looked like her father and added quickly, "A beautiful, feminine version of your dad, of course."

She thanked him and glanced a little nervously at Chase.

"The two of them are a thing," Joe said. "If you want Sky—"

"Please, Chase, join us!" Broussard said. He pointed to a table at the back of the bar. It was quiet there; music was playing, but it wasn't a live band. It was controlled from behind the bar and was kept at a volume that allowed for conversation.

"Sky, Chase, what would you like—" Joe began.

"No, not to worry. I know what she likes," Chase said. "Mr. Broussard?"

"I'm good, got a beer," Broussard said.

Chase hurried to the bar himself and asked for two beers—in bottles. He brought them back to the table where Broussard was smiling at Sky as they waited.

"Thanks," Sky murmured.

"Broussard, you're sure—"

"Got my beer right here, never go for more than one. Anyway…" he turned to Sky as Chase took a seat at the table "…I just loved your dad's work," he told her. "You know, some songs are catchy just because you've got a beat that people can't resist. Words don't even matter—it's the tune. A tune that makes you move, that is just peppy. But so many of the groups from decades past had some real songwriters in them, too," he told her.

She smiled at him in turn. She seemed okay with the reporter, which was good on many fronts.

"Yeah," she said. "My dad loved what he called the storytellers. He was a big fan of Roger Waters and Pink Floyd. The Who and Pete Townshend with *Tommy*, the rock opera…there were a lot of great writers out there, really. And there still are! Music keeps growing. Oh, that was something else my dad taught me. Every genre has good music, just as every genre has music that will fade. He told me one time that rap really wasn't his favorite form of music but that there was good rap and that you could combine all kinds of music. He and my mom got to see *Hamilton*, and he fell in love with it and Lin-Manuel Miranda. He was one of those guys who truly appreciated the talents of others."

"So I heard," Broussard said. "He's also known for helping young musicians—and anyone who needed help, really."

"He had a lot of pet charities. I try to keep up with them, as does my mom."

"That's great. I mean, growing up with that kind of a rock legend…"

"He was a great father. He taught me good lessons for life. I didn't get away with anything—"

Broussard laughed. "Can't imagine Jake Ferguson spanking his kid. Did you spend a lot of time in time-out?"

She shook her head. "I was a good kid. There was something about him and my mom. I wasn't afraid of horrible things happening if I misbehaved, I just didn't want to disappoint anyone."

"Wow. Great. And what about you?"

"What about me?"

"Sorry. I'm usually a great interviewer, right on with questions. I'm in awe. Anyway, what about you? Favorite group, singer—"

"I couldn't pick a favorite. If I'm looking to some of the artists from past decades… Freddie Mercury, amazing vocals. Roy Orbison! Hmm, oh, wow, Nancy Wilson from Heart. My God, what a voice! There are others, of course, so many…and…"

Broussard laughed. "It's an amazing world. Glad to be

on the sidelines, though…" He paused, grinning. "My dad was an attorney. Loved boats, and we took a lot of holidays down in the Caribbean. He ran into a fellow at a local place where people just sat all together. Started talking to the fellow next to him who said he was a guitarist. My dad told him that he could help him get a real job. Turned out the fellow was Eric Clapton, possibly the best guitarist out there!" He turned to Chase suddenly. "Wow. I'm sorry, didn't mean to be ignoring you. You are… Hank McCoy's grandson, right?"

"I am," Chase said. "And don't worry about ignoring me at all. No problem."

"Hey, drums are a big deal. And I've heard you. This is off the record—better vocals from you than your grand-dad, but…hey, who am I to judge?"

Sky was gazing at Chase, and he caught her eyes, and they both laughed. "A guy who has listened to more rock bands than anyone can possibly imagine?" Chase said lightly. "Anyway, I take any and all compliments. Back to Sky."

"You still play. You still sing."

"I like life low-key," she told him.

"So—kids and Jazz Mass."

"You do your homework," Chase told him.

"It's my life!" Broussard said lightly. "Anyway, Sky, thank you. I was in love with your father's talent. I think this is going to be an amazing gig."

"You'll be there?" Sky asked him.

"Oh, you bet. Hey, can I get a shot of the two of you together?"

Chase noticed Sky seemed to miss a beat, but she was quickly back with the plan.

"Of course!" Chase said quickly.

"Of course," she echoed.

They'd been sitting in chairs at a square table. Chase

stood and walked around behind Sky, ducking down with an arm around her and his head by hers.

Broussard said, "Well, should have had my photographer here, but this was truly happenstance, so... Well, they say phones take incredible pictures these days."

"Any device can only take what it sees," Sky murmured.

"It sees pure beauty!" Broussard said, snapping his pic. "And handsomeness, of course," he told Chase.

Chase laughed aloud at that one. "Hey, how about 'the group at play at home'— This is where Skyhawk began years ago in a little garage," he reminded Broussard.

"Yeah, cool!" Broussard said.

The others—including roadies Nathan, Justin and Charlie—were at one of the long plank tables. Chase motioned to them and they scrambled, half the table heading to stand behind the other half, allowing room at one end for Chase and Sky.

The picture was taken.

When several backup shots had been made, Broussard thanked them all, as they did him and he was gone and the bartender-owner, Danny Murphy, came over to express his appreciation.

"The real deal. You guys are the real deal!" he told them. "And Sky...wow. Thanks. I mean, thanks. What that will do for this place... Major league!"

"Yeah, but keep it real, okay, huh?" Joe Garcia begged. "That's why we love to come here, it's just...real. Not a gig, just a beer!"

"Oh, always," Murphy promised.

"Anyway, we're going to get home—" Chase began.

"No! Hey, we're all just finally together!" Brandon protested. He went silent, though, suddenly. There was a TV screen behind the bar. A twenty-four hour news show was on and the headlines were running.

"Oh, my God!" Joe said.

"Another one," Mark added, shaking his head. "Man, am I glad I'm not young anymore."

"You'd think, too, that kids would cool it right now! I mean that poor kid, from what I'm seeing, he was just going to have few tokes!" Chris Wiley said. He looked at Brandon. "Don't even think about buying any weed right now!"

"I'm here, with you, drinking a near beer, Pops!" Brandon protested. "Not to worry. What the hell kind of a dealer does that?" he added. "Kills their customers?"

"Some ass who doesn't know that overcutting stuff to make bigger bucks doesn't do the trick. Man, that's right… poor kid," Mark said. "We haven't had trouble like this in a while now. What a…well, what a mess and a tragedy."

"Absolute tragedy," Charlie agreed, standing. He shook his head. "What is the matter with people? I'm almost glad Jake isn't here. He'd be so upset over…"

His voice trailed, and he looked at Sky. "I'm so sorry."

"It's okay. My dad would be furious, you're right," Sky said. She looked around at them all. "Everyone should be furious. This is random murder for profit. But the cops get on to people eventually. And I hope whoever did this is charged with murder."

"They'll get them. They always do," Joe said, nodding his head sagely.

"But they don't, do they?" Brandon asked, looking at Chase. "Hey, you're the guy who has taken all the classes. They don't get them all the time, do they? I mean, look at the serial killers who were out there for years and years—and those who were never caught."

"Most of the time, from the lectures I've heard, criminals eventually make mistakes," Chase said. "Any of us who might want to take a puff now and then…wouldn't be doing it right now! Hey, one more round of bottled beers. We'll play everything safe!"

He headed to the bar, keeping his eye on the table. They

all seemed perplexed, horrified by what they had seen on the news.

And yet one of them...

He snatched a tray off the bar to carry the beers back, placing them in front of everyone.

"Hey, cool," Chris Wiley said, smiling at Chase. "When all else fails, you can be a bartender!"

"Aw, he's aiming higher than that!" Mark said. "What are you going to do with all these classes? You know, I just never saw you working in a basement lab, kid!"

Chase shrugged. "Thanks to you guys, I get to be whatever I want." He laughed. "Never worked in a basement. Most labs would be underwater soon in this area!"

They all laughed. Mark, Joe and Chris, the remaining original members of Skyhawk, all seemed to be at ease. Older men, those who might have retired in another life, but all still strong and vibrant. Chase was grateful his grandfather, Hank, would soon regain his strength, and he would still be part of what he had loved all his life again. And still...

Brandon? Wild child? Sometimes what was in plain sight was the simple answer.

But for some reason, Chase just didn't think it could be that easy. Gut reaction. A man's gut could be wrong.

But it could also be right.

Then...the roadies. Charlie, like Brandon, the wild child in the group. Justin, a man who by all appearances loved his wife of years and years and his sons, both in college, one headed for a career in medicine, the other in banking.

Nathan...divorced. A few times. But a man who coached his one son's team, a guy who seemed to love his children...

"I think it's time, children, that we do get back. Last tech tomorrow, and then show goes up at eight!" Mark said. He looked around the table, grimacing. "I am the oldest dude in this fizzy party now, so children, all of you—off to bed for a good night tomorrow!"

They all stood and headed out. Chase paused on the sidewalk.

"Chase?" Sky asked softly.

"Such a beautiful night!" he said.

"Yes, it is," she agreed. "For…for most of us."

"Let's get to the car. Get some sleep."

He nodded. The street here, off the tourist path and in a neighborhood section of the city, was quiet. His car was just down a block or so, and they started for it in silence.

Maybe it was the quiet, maybe it was his training, but he heard someone slip almost silently down the street toward them just as he opened the driver's door to his car.

He spun around, almost reaching for the small sidearm in its holster at his waistband which was hidden by the jacket he was wearing.

But again, gut sense had kicked in.

It was Brandon Wiley, looking at him anxiously.

"Brandon?"

"Sorry, sorry, I didn't mean to sneak up on you. I mean, I wanted to get to you without anyone else seeing… I, man, I don't know. Well, I mean, you do know. I swear, no hard drugs, but I do some weed now and then, and now…"

"Do you have something on you?" Chase asked. "Brandon—"

"Yes, yes, I do. And I don't know, Chase, I mean no one really understands what you're up to all the time, but I thought that—"

"Brandon, yeah, I know some people, and I can—"

"Please, please, please, I'm going to be sitting in for many of the numbers tomorrow night, and it all means a lot to me. I don't want to get in any trouble—"

"Brandon," Chase promised, "I'm not going to get you into any trouble. I'm going to be grateful as all hell you came to me if the stuff you have turns out to be tainted. Thing is, if there is something… Brandon, we have to know where you got it."

Brandon nodded. "I didn't buy it. There's a guy who works the spotlights over the audience at the arena. I gave him a few joints a few years ago, he caught up with me after today's rehearsal and gave me these."

He produced two joints, handing them to Chase.

"I'm going to need to know this guy's name," Chase told him.

"But if there's nothing wrong with these—"

"Look, laws about pot have changed. Possessing a couple of joints is nothing. Let me find out what the story is with this. First off, you no longer possess it, I do. And as for anyone else…at tops, small amounts are a fine and a few days in jail. But I'm not after you or anyone else just smoking a joint—we need the source."

Brandon nodded seriously. "Don't worry. Nothing for me in the next days except for a beer—in a bottle that's sealed when I get it!"

"Good thinking. Okay, I'll get this somewhere. I promise. And I'll let you know what's up in the morning. And if there is something in this…"

"I know, I know, I know. I got it from a guy named Bobby Sacks. He works lights."

"Thanks. Let's keep Bobby alive, okay?" Chase said.

"Thanks," Brandon told him. "Okay, uh, see you love-birds tomorrow, huh?"

"Yep, good night."

Brandon walked away. Knowing Sky was watching him, Chase still knew he had no choice.

"Just a sec," he told her, dialing Wellington's number. "Hey, um, a friend of mine got panicked when he saw the news. I have a couple of joints…um, yeah. I'll give you an address. You can pick them up from me there? I mean, I know you're a lecturer, but with what's going on… Great. I thought you might know what to do."

He hung up. "A friend who knows everyone in every lab from here to the ocean."

"Chase, my God, do you think—"

"I don't think anything right now. Let's let my friend get these to a lab, huh?"

She nodded and crawled into the car. They were silent on the way to the house. When they arrived, Larry was overjoyed to see them.

Sky might have said she didn't want a dog. But Larry evidently loved her.

And she loved Larry, it seemed.

"He's been sleeping on the couch, you know. And there are guest bedrooms here—"

"I guarantee you, when you go to bed, Larry will park himself in front of your door," Chase told her dryly. "I have to wait for my friend."

"I'll wait with you."

Before long, there was a buzz at the door. Chase looked out— Wellington had come straight to Sky's house when he had called him.

"That's him?" Sky asked.

He nodded, hitting the release for the gate and the door. A minute later, he opened it to meet Wellington on the porch.

"Don't be rude—invite him in," Skylar said.

Larry woofed; she set a hand on his head, telling him that it was all right.

Chase had no choice. He stepped aside as he greeted Andy Wellington and introduced him to Sky as one of his lecturers.

"Sky Ferguson, what a pleasure!" Andy told her.

"And so nice to meet you, too. Brandon is a dear friend of ours, and we're so grateful he came to Chase and that

Chase…knows people. Can we get you anything?" Sky said pleasantly.

"No, it's late, I'm just going to get these joints to friends I've met along the way," Wellington said politely. "But… Chase scored me some tickets for tomorrow night. I can't wait—you mostly disappeared, Miss Ferguson, and like me, tons of people out there are anxious to see you step into your father's shoes."

She shook her head. "I can't step into his shoes. I can only hope to honor him."

"I'm sure you will. He had an excellent reputation, and Chase tells me that all the amazing things written about him being an incredible human being are true."

Sky smiled and nodded. Wellington asked if he could pet the dog, and Sky assured him it was fine because he'd been identified as a friend.

Andy's eyes locked with Chase's for just a moment, and then he was gone.

"We'd really best get some sleep," Chase said.

"What did you think about Brandon? And…do you know this guy he was talking about? Bobby, who works lights?"

"I don't know Bobby. But—"

"Chase, if this stuff is laced, more people could die!"

"Wellington will get back to us as soon as possible and…" he shrugged "…I already told him Brandon got the stuff from Bobby Sacks."

She arched a brow at him.

"A little note I passed to him along with the joints."

She stared at him suspiciously. "Hey, let it get to the right people! If it was no big deal, it was no big deal. Well, hopefully, some lives will be saved."

"Shower," she said.

"Pardon?"

"There are three guest rooms upstairs and two more bathrooms. I'm for a shower and bed. Sleep wherever you like. I mean, we do have a dog now—one that your *friend* very specifically picked out for me. I'm going to assume he's an exceptional guard dog. Good night."

She turned and disappeared up the stairs. He watched her go and winced. There were moments when...

Time. Time could have gone away. He'd be holding her, just as he had those many years ago, he'd almost feel the softness of her flesh, the look in her eyes when...

First things first.

Keep them all alive.

Hell, they did have a big dog. He'd take a shower. And his firearm would be on the sink, right next to the shower. No chances could be taken now.

A SHOWER FELT GOOD. Delicious. Hot water, and then, as it sluiced over her and she felt the steam and replayed the day in her mind, the day, and Chase...

Cold water.

Didn't help a lot.

He was there. There in her house. Close. She was standing in the shower, naked. He was probably in a shower, too...

Maybe. Maybe not. He seemed...

Well, he was paranoid about her, but with all his so-called friends, she couldn't tell what was really going on with him.

What the hell was he really doing for a living? He did love his grandfather, he'd always seemed to care about everyone involved with Skyhawk...

Impatiently, she turned off the water, stepped out and dried off, wrapping the towel securely around her. She stepped from her bathroom into the bedroom area, opened the door to the hallway cautiously and looked out.

Larry had indeed taken up a position right outside her door.

One room down, the door was closed.

She smiled. With Larry in the house, it seemed Chase

had chosen to make use of an actual bed. As she stood there, she heard the faint sound of water going off.

Chase had opted for a shower and a bed.

She petted Larry's head, closed the door and headed for her dresser, seeking one of the oversize soft cotton T-shirts she liked to sleep in.

And then she had no idea of what really happened next. The show was coming up tomorrow—or later today, since it was after midnight.

Life…

Life was so fragile.

And at this moment her mind was, too.

And people in one's life were unique and rare, and she knew that and she'd never understood herself why she'd had to learn to live with loss on her own, why she hadn't clung to others who had cared.

She didn't know what she was thinking. No, she *wasn't* thinking. But she found herself stepping back out into the hall, heading to the door to the guest room that was closed, and opening it.

Chase was there, wrapped in a towel as she was, sorting through the clothing he had discarded but stopping dead as he saw her there.

"Sky?"

She shook her head. "Shut up. Please, just shut up."

She walked over to him, putting her arms around him, and drawing him into a deep, long kiss. And as she had hoped, prayed and maybe imagined, he pulled her closer to him, his arms wrapping around her, both towels slipping and falling away, and then their flesh, flesh touching, flesh, melding…

Time. Gone. An amazing burst of diamond and crystal light, the world exploding around them as they fell together onto the bed.

Touch came so easily, sweet, soaring sensuality as kisses

roamed intimately between them, as the need and urgency grew, and they were together again…

Soaring, sweet ecstasy, excitement and the comfort of… Love and security that had always been there, waiting. As if they'd never been apart.

Chapter Six

"Why? Why did you push me away? Right when I might have helped you the most?" Chase whispered.

Sky looked at him, eyes a little desperate and, he thought, gave him the only answer she had.

"I don't know. I don't know! I was just…"

"Please tell me you know that I'd never have hurt your father," he said, his eyes on hers, searching, seeking.

"Maybe you'll never really be ready to forgive me!" she whispered.

He moved his fingers gently through her hair and then cupped her chin as he told her, "The past is gone, it is history, and we can't change history. But I loved you then, Skylar. I never stopped loving you, and I love you now."

She let out a soft cry, clinging closer to him, parting her lips as his mouth met hers in a passionate kiss that seemed a true promise of the words he'd spoken.

And later, they lay together, and he told her again that he'd always loved her and always would.

She smiled.

"Hey, that was an amazing declaration of my feelings, heart on my sleeve," he told her. "A response would be great."

She rolled over on an elbow to look down at him.

"Well, you know, you said it would be best if we pretended… I use all kinds of acting and improv techniques when I work with my students. When I'm doing something, well, you know, I try to do it right!"

He laughed, and she fell next to him again, whispering that she'd never understood, that maybe her pain had needed a different pain to twist her from her feelings. "I'll never understand myself, much less be able to explain myself!" she whispered.

"And it doesn't matter. What does matter is that we get some sleep," he said, wincing at the thought of the day to come.

She nodded, curling closer against him.

He closed his eyes, smiling. Amazing. If they could get past tomorrow...

He couldn't believe that they were together, that this... had happened. And for the moment, he was just going to hold her close.

SKY SLEPT AMAZINGLY WELL. She woke because light was coming through the windows, and she actually felt a chill.

She shouldn't have been cold with him next to her. But he wasn't there.

She must have slept incredibly deeply; he had gotten up and dressed and she hadn't heard a thing.

"Chase?" She said his name softly and sitting up, she was startled to see that there was a note taped to the inside of the door.

Frowning as she rose, she collected the note. She knew his handwriting.

Please don't freak out. I had to leave for a few minutes. Couldn't leave you alone. Andy Wellington is downstairs with Larry. I asked him to watch over you.

Her frown deepened, but she quickly hit the lock on the bedroom door. Andy Wellington might be a friend and some kind of a law-enforcement lecturer, but she didn't know him. And this was her house! Chase shouldn't have...

Whatever!

She quickly gathered clothing and headed into the shower, anxious to bathe and dress as quickly as possible, reminding herself she was going to have to come back upstairs to choose an outfit for the show. She had a little rhinestone-studded tunic, and she thought she'd wear that over black jeans…kind of feminine, but pants to go with the guys.

Neither here nor there at the moment.

There was a stranger in her house!

She hurried on downstairs and found that Andy Wellington was indeed in the living room, seated on the couch with Larry curled at his feet. He had either a small tablet or a large phone, and he was engrossed in studying something that was on it.

He quickly looked up and rose as she entered the room.

"I'm so sorry. I don't mean to be intrusive, but we really didn't want you to be alone—even with Larry here."

She frowned, looking at him. "I really don't understand. I mean, you're a friend of Chase's, and that makes you welcome in my home, but…"

He looked down and when he looked up, his expression was acutely uncomfortable.

"I know that Chase is concerned, and other than that…"

She wasn't going to pick a fight with a stranger. She lifted a hand and said, "Not to worry, I'll speak with Chase. Would you like coffee or anything?"

He shrugged. "I took the liberty. There's a pot made in the kitchen."

"Great. Thank you." She headed into the kitchen, followed by Larry, who was wagging his tail wildly.

Whatever else came of all this, she did love the dog. She checked his water and food bowls and realized that Chase had already seen to them.

"Well, Larry," she mused, "did you get to go out yet? Want to run around the yard?"

She walked back out. Andy Wellington was studying his device again with a frown on his face. She opened the door to let Larry run out joyfully into the yard. Then she approached Wellington.

"Is everything all right? Oh! By the way—the stuff that Brandon had last night, was it…tainted?"

He hesitated and then nodded. "Not to the point of instant death, but yes, it was contaminated."

"Oh, what about the guy that he got it from? Is he…?"

"Dead? No. I'm not sure what's going on exactly. We reported it to the right people immediately."

She nodded. "More friends of Chase's?"

"Friends of mine," he said. He shrugged. "I held a position in law enforcement for years. I know the right people."

"Ah. Well, I'm hoping he gets back soon."

"Me, too!"

"Don't let me interrupt your work," Sky told him. "I'm going to head to my office and go over the set list for tonight."

"Great. I'm here if you need me," he said. "Hey, can I get your phone number, please? I should have gotten it from Chase. I mean, well, seriously, there is bad stuff going on, and we should have each other's numbers."

She handed him her phone. "Grab my number and call me, and I'll have yours."

"Perfect, thanks."

She waited for him to get his number and call her. Then she took her phone back.

She smiled. "Just let Larry back in when he scratches at the door—which I believe he will in a few minutes."

"You got it."

She headed to her office thinking that she was going to have a hell of a lot to say to Chase when she saw him. She wasn't going to take it out on Wellington. The man was doing a friend a favor. It wasn't his fault that Chase had neglected to talk it all over with her.

Last night had been so good. So amazing...

And now? Now she realized that time had passed, and that there was so much she really didn't know about the man at all.

And yet...

There were still things she knew in her heart. He might annoy her—even anger her—but he was a good man. Trying his best, worried about her.

Still...

He had some answering to do!

THERE WAS ONE chance with the kind of overdose Bobby Sacks seemed to have suffered; luckily, it was something Chase had been trained to deal with and was prepared to administer: naloxone. He shot the dose into Bobby and began CPR.

He waited anxiously as Bobby's wife, tears in her eyes, looked on.

Then...

A gasp. Bobby inhaled. And by then the paramedics had arrived, and Chase could tell them what had happened and what he had done.

"That is one lucky man! I don't know if we'd have made it in time," one of the medics told him as Bobby was lifted onto a gurney and rolled out to the ambulance.

Chase shrugged. "I had a great mentor," he said. "Have you been called out on more of these?"

"So far, from what I've heard, anyone else afflicted has made it into the hospital," the medic told him. "Thankfully, people saw the news, and they're smart enough to get in—or throw away whatever the hell they bought. Carefully, I hope."

"Me, too," Chase murmured. "You'll be met at the hospital. When I called in, I was assured that this was something the FBI was on, so…"

"Got it. They'll be waiting until he can talk."

"I'll check on him later," Chase said.

The medic nodded; there would be police officers at the house, too, but he was grateful that Nancy Sacks, Bobby's wife, had called him. Apparently, she hadn't wanted Bobby arrested, but she'd been afraid of his behavior.

"Cops are coming?" she asked Chase when the paramedics were gone. "Bobby is going to live, right?"

"I believe so—we got him past the first hurdle in time. But I'm not a doctor—"

"But you did know what to do."

Nancy Sacks was an attractive woman with long brown hair and enormous hazel eyes. Chase had planned on paying Bobby Sacks a visit; he just hadn't expected to find him as he had.

Bobby had given the stuff to Brandon. But if he had been the one dealing it, he'd have known better than to indulge in his own product.

"All right, Nancy, from what I've heard, this has happened before—and it's the federal government that's following the trail. Someone will be here, yes. I take it you didn't join him for his little bit of recreation?"

"I hate pot—just makes me fall asleep," Nancy said. "But I never cared if Bobby had a puff here and there. I've known some drunks, and they're feisty and get into fist brawls. I've never seen a few puffers get dangerous toward anything other than a pile of food."

"Nancy, this is so important. Where did he get the stuff?"

She shook her head. "I don't know. From someone last night, I imagine, but I have no idea who. I mean, you know, he works those lights all the time for whatever is going on,

and yeah, most of the time, things are available from someone. They kind of work on a trust arrangement, I guess. I
don't know! Oh, Chase, I wish I knew. I mean… I knew
how close you were to Jake Ferguson and I figured you
learned a lot from him, but… Yeah, I guess we've all heard
you're in some kind of a forensic school, so… I didn't know
how bad it was going to get, I just called you—forgive me—
because I didn't know I was going to need an ambulance…
But, oh, my God, thank you! Bobby isn't a bad guy, he's
good, he just…"

"Nancy, it's okay. But someone will be here and they'll
want a statement. Or if you like, I can bring you to the hospital, and you can be there with Bobby and people will talk
to you both while you're there."

"Please," she said.

He nodded and put a call through to Andy Wellington, telling him that he'd be back as soon as he'd dropped
Nancy off.

"Well, that will be good," Wellington murmured.

Chase winced inwardly. He hadn't been sure how he
was going to explain this one. And he didn't know why.

Gut fear, maybe because of everything going on.

But even with Larry in the house, he hadn't wanted Sky
to be alone.

A dog could be shot. Then again, so could a man. But
it was unlikely that a man like Wellington, who had spent
his life in the service of the government after a stint in the
military, was going to be taken by surprise.

Unlike Larry, he could shoot back.

"Let's get to the hospital," he told Nancy.

He hoped that Bobby might be conscious, but he doubted
it. He believed that the man might make it.

But it would be a while before he could talk.

Chase just hoped it would be before the show that night.

SKY LIKED ANDY WELLINGTON well enough. There seemed to be little to dislike about him. He was polite and courteous, pleasant in every way.

She just didn't know what he was doing in her house. So, Chase had taken all kinds of classes. He knew all about so many things.

And they were both convinced her father had been murdered.

But what was he really doing?

She had left her office to make sure that Wellington was doing all right, still just seated on her sofa, when she heard the buzz that warned her someone was at the gate.

Larry woofed excitedly, wagging his tail.

That meant that Chase was back.

She hit the button that allowed the gate and door to open, and then she waited for him to come in. Naturally, he saw her staring at him the minute he walked in. And he knew she was going to want answers.

"Hey! Sorry, I had to run out. But under the current circumstances, I wanted someone to be with you and thankfully, you'd met Andy and you know—"

"Yeah. He carries a gun," Sky said, arms crossed over her chest.

Chase shrugged. "Yeah, I know you're safe with him."

Andy sat there silently, shaking his head, looking at Chase.

"I thought I was safe once I had a big dog," Sky said.

Andy spoke at last. "I didn't mean to be intrusive—" he repeated.

"You weren't," Sky quickly informed. "You're a perfect gentleman, welcome anytime. That's not the point."

They both just stared at her.

And then at one another.

"Just what the hell is going on here?" she demanded.

"I suggest you just tell her," Andy said quietly.

"Please! I suggest you just tell me, too," Sky said, staring hard at Chase. He couldn't mean her harm; even angry as she was, she couldn't doubt the feelings that enveloped them, as real as anything had ever been in her life.

But...

"Andy isn't just my friend. He's my SAC," Chase said.

"Sack?" Sky asked, confused.

"No, *SAC*, Special Agent in Charge," Chase explained.

"Um...in charge of what?" she asked.

Andy walked toward them both. "It's imperative that you keep this quiet. Special Agent Chase McCoy has been with the bureau for over two years, and he's an invaluable player in his undercover operations."

Sky shook her head, completely confused. "Undercover? Everyone knows who you are—well, anyone who is into rock bands and that kind of thing."

"Exactly," Andy Wellington explained.

Chase looked at Sky. "I'm sorry," he whispered.

"Well, yeah, you pretend well," she said. "But I still— you mean, none of this is because of my father, you're really working for...the government?"

"Yes and no. I really work for the government, but no one knows except my folks and Hank. And as to your dad? I work for the government because of him," Chase said flatly.

Sky stared at him, frowning. Chase explained, "I never believed it. I never believed that Jake Ferguson would inadvertently rip up an amp when a wire had come loose. I—I believed he saw something that night, and whatever he saw caused someone to make sure he never got a chance to tell anyone else."

She shook her head. "I don't understand—"

"No one knows, Sky. I told you. No one knows but Wellington, some fellow agents, my parents, and Hank. And now you. Because it's imperative for the kind of work I do that everyone thinks I am what I am in the other half of my life, the grandson of Hank McCoy, drummer and vocalist for the rock band Skyhawk."

She was silent, not sure what to think or feel.

"Why didn't you tell me?" she asked.

He didn't reply.

"Be fair, Sky," Wellington said quietly. "He hadn't seen you in years."

"But…"

She just shook her head and turned away.

"Sky," Chase said.

"Let me deal!" she snapped.

And apparently, her state of mind wasn't the most important thing at the moment, because Wellington was quickly speaking with Chase.

"Bobby. You got to him in time."

Chase nodded. "I don't know what's out there, if it's the same source… The stuff Brandon had was contaminated, but not badly enough to kill. This stuff that Bobby had… was bad. And the thing is, Bobby can't be the dealer—small stuff, giving to friends or whatever. He has a great wife, good work—I don't really know him, but from what I've seen when I have been around the venue, he's a solid worker and loves his wife and family and has no desire to die."

"You know him enough—his wife called you," Wellington said.

"And I think it was the right call for me to get there," Chase said quietly.

"Yeah. You've done this—had the equipment and the knowledge to do what was needed. Let's hope he makes it. And that he comes around…in time."

"We have no idea how much is out there," Chase said.

Sky was watching and listening in astonishment. She thought she knew Chase. Even after years away. She'd asked about him casually. She'd looked him up online. It always seemed that he'd been playing or taking classes or…

Maybe she actually knew Chase better than she'd imagined. This was, on the one hand, all a shock. On the other hand…

It wasn't surprising Chase would be an agent, that a young man who had listened to and admired her father had learned to save lives…

And to fight the bad guys.

"All right. We know Brandon had stuff—and Bobby had it. We need to find the main snake and cut its damned head off," Wellington said. "This has gone on too long."

"My grandfather and Bobby are at the same hospital. I thought I'd take a minute to visit Hank, and then I can check on Bobby as well. NOPD is on it—guards are in the hall," Chase said. "Sir, if you could be with Sky a bit longer—"

"No, no, no, no, no," Sky said flatly.

They both stared at her.

"Now that I know what the hell is going on, Chase, I'm sticking with you. I haven't seen Hank, and I'd very much like to. You just said NOPD is at the hospital, too. I'm going with you." She turned to Wellington. "Thank you, Mr. SAC, sir. I appreciate everyone worrying about how I get to keep on living. But I will be fine now with Chase, and I'd very much like to see Hank."

Chase and Wellington stared at one another for a moment.

She had a feeling Wellington was silently assuring Chase it was his call.

"All right. So Larry guards the house, and we all head out," Chase said.

"And you'll be at the venue by four?" Wellington asked Chase.

Chase nodded. "Last tech."

"I'll be there, an old lecturer, in awe of a classic-rock band," Wellington said.

Chase nodded. "And we may find nothing, despite all our determination."

"Something is going on. And we will find the truth," Wellington said. "Well, I'll leave you for now. Give Hank my regards. I'll just say goodbye to Larry and be out of here."

"Thank you, sir," Sky told him.

He smiled at her. She did like the man. And if Chase was working directly beneath him, it was good to know him.

When he was gone, Chase watched her in silence.

"So nothing about you is real."

He shook his head. "Sky, everything about me is real. And that's why…it's why what I do works."

"Hey, you were honest at first. You said we needed to pretend."

"Sky, nothing with you is pretend!" he vowed.

She nodded. "Well, we'll see. Busy afternoon—let's get to the hospital."

"I'll see to Larry—"

"I have food and water set out for him already," Sky said. The dog was next to her, her constant companion—and guard.

Well, if all else went astray, she'd gotten a great dog out of it all.

She petted Larry's head and told him to guard the house and started out, leaving Chase to follow her and check on the locks to the house and the gate as they left.

His car was there, ready, on the street right in front of her house.

She was silent as they drove. So was he.

But when they reached the hospital, he turned to her at last. "Sky, please. I swear this is true—what happened with your dad set me on this path. But it's incredibly important that no one else knows."

"Did you think I was going to announce it on stage tonight?" she asked him. She knew her tone was sharp and sarcastic, but she had trusted him. And she had thought that he trusted her.

Even if they'd been apart.

He didn't respond. They exited the car and headed up into the hospital, pausing for their visitor credentials at the desk.

Sky followed him as they walked straight to Hank's room.

Hank was in a chair by the bed, watching the news. Sky was glad to see he looked good: his color was healthy, and he smiled broadly as he saw her coming in behind Chase.

"Sky!" he said with pleasure.

She smiled and hurried to him, bending to give him a hug and a kiss on the cheek.

"Sweetie, it's wonderful to see you," he told her.

"You, too, Hank. And you look—"

"Thanks! I get out of here in a few days. I think they're being overly cautious, but, hey…my grandson is a dictator. And I will do everything they tell me. I'm anxious to come back to the drums myself. Oh, and if you're going to start playing with those guys often, I have a great gift for you. Seriously, half the drummers I know are deaf now! But I found these great earplugs—they let you hear, but they keep out the deafening volume. These are just about perfect!"

"Thanks, Hank. I'm sure Chase appreciates them," Sky said sweetly.

"There are tons of perks to what we do," Hank said. "And a few drawbacks, but there's a set of the earplugs in my drawer. I'd love you to have them." He grinned. "There's no way I get to play this gig, so please take them?"

"Take them or he'll make me crazy," Chase said.

"Hey! You have hearing thanks to me!" Hank said.

Chase grinned at him. "And I can play the drums, too, thanks to you. No lack of appreciation meant, just—"

"He's a dictator!" Hank assured Sky, grimacing, and shaking his head. "But other than that, a good enough kid. So how are you? Ran into a friend of yours before I found myself in here, Sky. Virginia Hough. She said you were a miracle worker with troubled kids, that they spent time with you, got deep into music and showmanship and stopped being so much trouble."

"Virginia is a lovely woman," Sky said, shrugging. "I like kids. I like working with them. One of the students I had the first year I was working went on to become great at improv—he's working at an improv comedy club in South Florida. It's great, Hank. Really rewarding."

"Like the boy here," Hank murmured. He looked quickly at Chase. "Always trying to learn something new!" he added.

"It's all right, Hank. She knows," Chase said. As he spoke, he frowned suddenly. She saw he was looking out the small window of the door to Hank's room. "Excuse me," he said. "I'll be right back."

He left the room. Sky watched him go, lowering her head and smiling slightly.

The place was crawling with police. That would be the only reason he'd be away from her, she knew.

"Kid he saved is down the hall," Hank said quietly.

"I heard…something," Sky said.

"I am proud of him. Chase was in a place where he could have gone on to be the top of top—but he went on to do something he saw as being more important."

"And he knew what to do for…for what happened," Sky said.

"He still takes classes all the time. He's like a sponge, wants to know everything and it all makes him invaluable. And…" Hank looked down, a frown tearing into his forehead.

Hank, as a grandfather, was still an impressive man.

Even in a hospital chair, he had a strong face, solid jaw, bright eyes and his headful of handsome white hair.

She imagined that one day, Chase would look like him. Or maybe Chase did look like a young Hank, as he must have looked all those years ago when Skyhawk had first hit the scene.

"He never believed what happened to my father was an accident," Sky said.

Hank looked up at her. "Neither did I," he told her. He shook his head. "Your dad and I... You know, I was the one with the garage. My folks let me have a drum set out there. And your dad started coming over, and the two of us were the beginning of it all. He just...he just had it! I'd heard the story that his dad wanted him drafted, that he wouldn't do anything about getting him into college to get out of Vietnam. I thought it was the cruelest thing I'd ever heard. But Jake told me, no, that it was the best thing in the world for him. His dad had told him that if he was going to kill himself, at least he could do it for his country."

"I heard," Sky said softly.

"He said war was brutal. And it hurt him—he lost friends he made in the service. But for him, it turned out to be a lifesaver. He'd been given back a chance in a double way, and he was going to be smart and grateful for all his years to come. I loved him, Sky."

"I know you did, Hank. He loved you, too."

"He made us all better musicians—and better human beings."

Sky smiled, hunkered down by his side and took his hands. "Thank you, Hank. I know that after what happened... I was horrible for a while. Now..."

"Now you want the truth. And I understand. So does Chase. And I believe in him, Sky. I believe in my grandson. If something can be done, Chase will be the one to see that it is."

"Where do you think he's gotten off to?" Sky asked.

Hank shrugged. "Well, he knows the place is swimming with cops, and you're safe in here with me. That kid he saved—I say *kid* loosely at my age—anyway, like I said earlier, he's just down the hall. Maybe he's conscious."

"And Chase is trying to find out what he can from him?"

"I would think. So tell me about tonight. Are you at all excited? Did you really want to perform? Are you doing it just to try to discover what happened in the past?"

"Both. If I can honor my dad, I'm glad to do so. If I can find the truth, so much the better. I should have said if *we* can find the truth. I didn't realize until we got into this in the last couple of days just how ill-equipped I was to find out anything."

Hank smiled. "You're in good hands, I promise. Even if…"

"If?"

Hank shrugged. "I read people."

"Oh?"

"Well, hmm. You care about Chase. You two were like a pair of lovebirds back then, and I got the feeling…well, the feeling is there. But you're not sure you trust him."

"Okay, truthfully? I just found out he was working for the government."

"He's not at liberty to share that, you know."

"*You* know," she said softly.

He nodded. "I know. Being him… Okay, he is my grandson. But he's also an amazing human being, Sky. Then again, so are you. You're both the family of rock royalty, and yet you see the world in a bigger way. And that's great. But don't forget one thing."

"What's that?"

"Your dad invented and loved Skyhawk. The rest of us… Well, he was the one who found out how we could make and record our music, he was our main songwriter. He loved the band, and he loved telling stories with his songs. Remember that. You're truly honoring him when you get up there on that stage and channel him and all that he loved."

"Thanks, Hank."

He nodded. "And trust Chase. It's not his fault he can't tell anyone."

"I'm not just *anyone*. He knew what I was doing right away, and right away he wanted to help me. But he didn't trust me."

"Forgive him. He has his reasons for keeping his life a total secret."

"Right, but...it was *me*."

"And I'm sure he was in torture over not being able to say anything. In fact—"

He broke off. His door suddenly burst open. A man entered, leaned against the door to shut it, and looked out through the window. While carefully studying the hall, he pulled out a gun.

Chapter Seven

Bobby Sacks was awake and aware, but just barely.

Chase should have felt relief, grateful when he spoke with the man's doctor and was told that his arrival and quick action had saved Bobby's life.

The doctor himself had been the one to summon Chase; there was an officer from NOPD just outside his door. Another officer had just gone downstairs with Bobby's wife so she could take a break and get something to eat in the cafeteria.

"Also figured you might want a minute—just a minute, he's not very strong—to speak with him alone," the doctor had said.

Chase had appreciated his help: naturally, it was imperative to save a life first. And sometimes, law enforcement really had to wait to question a suspect or a witness.

This man had seen to it that he'd get a few minutes immediately.

Bobby opened his eyes as the doctor left and Chase stood by his bed. He winced and tried to smile. "You're supposed to be a drummer. My wife said you're known for taking forensics classes and that…you saved my life when she didn't know what to do. Thank you."

"I'm glad you're alive," Chase assured him. "But, Bobby—"

"Yeah, I know. I saw a guy briefly when I wasn't really…

well, aware enough to say much. I know. I don't want others to die."

"But you gave Brandon some weed."

"Different lots."

"Where did you get your drops of the drugs? Different drops?"

"I… I don't know."

"How can you not know?"

"I leave the money wherever I'm told to leave it. Then I get a message back. I…well, I meant to be generous with friends. I made a buy twice."

"How do you make the buy?" Chase asked.

"The web." He hesitated. "The dark web."

"So you make arrangements online—on the dark web—and someone tells you where to leave money and then where to pick up the stash?"

Bobby Sacks winced as he nodded. "I never thought… I mean, I'd heard about drugs that were laced, but I never thought… It's been a long time… When Skyhawk is playing…" He shrugged weakly. "Maybe some other times. I don't… I don't know. I guess that sometimes when other groups or acts are performing…"

"I'm glad you're going to be okay, Bobby, really. Thing is, what happened to you could happen to someone else. I mean, I'm not up on the dark web, but I'll let the cops or whoever know, and they'll get someone to you with a computer, and you can help them find the source of whatever is going on here. I've got to do that."

"I know!" he said, wincing. "Chase, believe me, I don't want anyone dying! I don't want anyone hurt or dying because of me!"

"Right. I'll—"

A male nurse was coming into the room, carrying a tray with a shot of medicine to be added to Bobby's IV.

"Hey," he said, greeting them both. "Doc just ordered this

for you. It will take me two seconds. Oh, I've been asked to tell your visitor he's been here long enough. You need to get some rest."

Chase glanced at the needle. There seemed to be something off. It should have been an ordinary procedure; he'd seen the staff add medications to his grandfather's IV often enough.

But something looked different. The man was dressed in the same scrubs as the other nurses, but something didn't seem right.

"What is that?" Chase asked him.

"Oh, uh, just a little more saline, get him better hydrated," the nurse said.

He looked to be a man in his late thirties or early forties. And if he was a nurse, he shouldn't have suggested that a shot so small was but saline.

"You're not putting that in his arm," Chase said.

"What? I just told you—"

"No. Step away from him," Chase said.

He saw the man reach behind his back and knew that he was reaching for a weapon. He could have pulled his own. Instead, he made a flying leap, bringing the man down to the floor before he could draw his gun.

The weapon went flying across the floor.

The ostensible nurse went for it, stretching to retrieve it.

Chase caught him by the ankle, shouting for one of the cops.

In two seconds, NOPD's finest were in the room with him. He explained quickly that the man had tried to put something in Bobby's IV then gone to draw his weapon. He needed to give this one to the cops; he didn't want to have to show the credentials he kept but never used.

The officers quickly had the guy cuffed and up. He stared at Chase with loathing and then started to laugh. "Hotshot drummer. Think you're tough 'cause you got the money for hours at the gym, huh? You'll get yours—trust me. You'll get yours!"

"We've got him, Mr. McCoy. We've got him," one of the cops assured him.

"Thanks!" Chase said.

They dragged the suspect out of the room, aggravated that they hadn't seen that something was wrong when he'd gone in.

Chase made a mental note to tell Wellington they needed someone in the hospital who knew something about medicine—either that or make sure nothing went into Bobby's IV unless the doctor himself administered it.

"Man, wow, you are…well, one hell of a drummer," Bobby said, looked at him in despair and shaking his head. "You did it again—you saved my life again. How the hell…"

"I knew that wasn't saline. I've had my share of family in the hospital," Chase said, shrugging. "And what the hell, I haven't even done any drumming here. Listen, I'm going to see to it that the people who matter know what happened and make sure you're safe. I'll take care of that right now. Your wife will be back up in a minute, and they'll let her stay—but I'm going to see to it that someone who knows what's up is here, too. At all times."

"Man, thank you. Thank you, thank you!" he said softly.

Chase nodded, heading for Bobby's door. As he set his hand on it, he heard a sound that could only be that of a shot, explosive, painfully loud in the peace and quiet of the hospital floor.

SKY DIDN'T MEAN to scream; the sound of the shot was so startling, so loud, she let out a gasp that was part squeak and part scream.

"It's all right, it's all right!" the man in Hank's room quickly informed them. "I'm Luke Watson, NOPD. There's—

I don't know what—but you're safe, my job is to stand right here and shoot anyone who tries to come near either of you," he assured them.

Sky swallowed hard and said the only thing that came to mind.

"Thank you, thank you. But Chase—"

"Chase will be fine. There are cops all over this place. Whatever is going on, we all have our assignments, and you are mine," Watson said.

Sky nodded, hoping against hope he was for real, because he wasn't wearing a uniform.

As if he could sense her thoughts, the man turned, still keeping his peripheral vision on the door but reaching into his pocket.

Not for a gun, she prayed.

His credentials.

"Thank you," she whispered again, gripping Hank's hand tightly.

She had wanted to find the truth. Now, she was sure she knew it. Her father *had* seen something, known something, and he had died for it.

Just as someone was apparently trying to kill others now.

Fear seemed to grip her like chilled and bony fingers around the heart.

She needed to know. She needed to know so badly. And yet…she had never imagined this kind of danger, a killer slipping into a hospital, shots fired *in a hospital*!

She thought about being on stage that night but remembered there would be security stations and security guards. Bags would be checked and arrivals would go through metal detectors.

What had happened with Jake had been far more subtle.

Whoever was doing this didn't want to get caught. But then…

The man drew the door open, letting Chase enter. He

was anxious and tense, asking quickly, "You're all right? Everything is all right?"

"We're good. Officer Watson here is great," Hank assured him quickly.

Chase stared at Watson and gave him a nod of thanks.

Then Chase was gone again.

"Where... He needs to be here!" Sky whispered.

"Trust him!" Hank whispered.

"Trust is a two-way street!" she whispered in return. But she realized she was afraid.

Afraid for herself. And worse.

She was afraid for Chase.

"STAIRWELL!" ONE OF the uniformed cops in the hall shouted. "Headed down the stairwell!"

He was moving quickly, racing to the stairs.

Chase hurried behind him, drawing his weapon and assuring him, "I have a permit! I can help, I swear, I've worked with lots of cops, and I am not at all trigger-happy."

The cop nodded as they headed in the direction of the gunfire.

They almost tripped over one of the police officers who had just been in Bobby Sacks's room, one who had cuffed the fake nurse.

He groaned; the man was shot but still alive.

"LeBlanc!" the officer with Chase cried, hunkering down by the fallen man.

"Stay with him—get help!" Chase ordered, knowing he needed to move fast.

"He got Harvey's gun...he's got Harvey!" the man on the floor moaned.

"I'll get him!" Chase promised, hurrying down the stairs. He didn't hear the explosion of another shot. He did hear scuffling and then a whisper that was oddly echoed in the stairwell.

"Move, move, move…and you may live!"

Despite his speed, Chase forced himself to move as quietly as possible, finally seeing the nurse and the cop as he rounded one turn. He took aim at the nurse's head, shouting out, "Stop now! Lower the gun!"

Instead, the nurse laughed and took aim, pointing his weapon directly at him. But Chase was ready, sliding back to avoid the bullet that plowed into the wall while carefully returning fire.

The nurse didn't let out a peep.

Chase had caught him squarely in the forehead. He fell, rolling down the last few stairs to the first-floor landing.

Chase cursed himself as he hurried down to reach the officer—Harvey as the other man had called him. He was staring at Chase with gratitude.

"He was going to kill me. He shot my partner—he was just using me to get out of the hospital. He would have killed me. How…"

"I've worked with law enforcement and have the proper credentials to carry, and he was after people in this hospital. My grandfather is here," Chase said.

The cop looked at him. "You're one hell of an interesting drummer, Mr. McCoy."

"Um, yeah, I've heard that."

"Thank you. I need to see to my partner—"

"He was talking, and being in a hospital, he'll get immediate help."

"And…well, we'll need your weapon, and you'll have to make a statement. I mean, you saved my life, but the world runs on paperwork. Real paper, sometimes."

Chase nodded, looking at the dead suspect.

Was he the pusher? He'd never seen the man before.

"Well, I guess you have to call someone, but I'd like to get back to my grandfather," Chase said. "If that's okay. I'll be here… I am due at our tech rehearsal at four, but—"

To his relief, Chase saw that Wellington had arrived with the captain of the local PD.

"Mr. McCoy, the police need your weapon, and they'll be asking you to sign a statement. We need to do this quickly. Captain Hughes and I both have tickets for tonight's event—we can't have you missing anything and we don't want to miss anything, either!"

"I need to see my grandfather and Sky," Chase said.

"Of course. You are something, Mr. McCoy. Johnny-on-the-spot, and a big show tonight! Grateful you were here," Wellington said. "Come on, son, we'll head on back up, I'll get you onto the paperwork, and then we'll get you to the show!"

OF COURSE, Sky figured, Wellington had all kinds of strings he could pull. He left Hank's room again with Chase, but the two returned within a few minutes—paperwork all done.

Even for Wellington, that must have been quite a feat. But then, from what she began to understand, Chase had now saved the life of a cop as well, and that had to sit well with whoever pulled all the strings.

They finally bade Hank goodbye with Chase warning him to do everything the doctors told him to do—and Hank warning Chase to be careful.

"Always careful," Chase told him.

"I didn't see today as—"

"That's because you weren't looking. I am always careful," Chase assured him.

Hank's face—half smile and half frown—showed his pride in his grandson. Sky, of course, was grateful. Chase did seem to have a knack for getting the bad guys.

Her father had given him that determination.

Of course, she was proud, too. And still a little bit scared. She'd been angry that he hadn't trusted her. But inwardly, she could admit she now understood. He was undercover. Undercover…as himself. And all his classes had been real—apparently, he'd learned a great deal about drugs, drug overdoses and how to reverse them.

He also seemed to have instinct, something one probably couldn't get in any class, more likely something that was basic to certain people.

She was quiet as they headed to the last rehearsal before the concert.

She was surprised when Chase spoke, his voice pained. "I'm thinking we should cancel the show. Wellington even mentioned it to me."

"What?" she demanded.

He shook his head. "It's one thing for me to step into something that could turn very bad—I made that choice. But after the events at the hospital, I don't know what we're looking at."

"I put me in it—I'm choosing to do so."

"It's a concert. No one should die over a concert."

"People are dying without the concert. The concert is your way of finding out what is really going on, just how deep it all runs. Chase, I want to do it. Not just for…not just for one reason. I want to do it for my father. Hank reminded me of something today. My dad loved the band—he created it. He truly believed in that saying, that music could soothe the savage beast. And I've got it—someone is using Skyhawk events for something so bad it's pure evil. But this is the chance to stop it. To save lives. You got to do that today. Chase, I want my chance to be a part of something bigger, too."

He was silent.

"Wellington would understand. Oh, and Wellington will make sure the metal detectors are working overtime, and the audience is half cops and agents, probably, Louisiana State Police, you name it."

Again, he was silent.

"I'm right, aren't I?"

"You'll be center stage," he said quietly.

"You betcha!" she said determinedly. "Chase, people have seen on the news that drugs have been laced and contaminated, that people are dying. I don't think so many will be wanting to buy stuff. But I do think that whoever was doing what—the person my father knew was involved—is going to be there. And under these circumstances..."

"Yeah, he could slip up," Chase admitted. "Still—"

"I'm going to be all right. Chase, Charlie made a point—none of us touches equipment. If something is going to happen, it will be to one of them. Not that I want anything to happen, I don't mean it that way, but—"

"I don't think whoever from our group is involved is the kingpin—but if we can get someone who can talk—"

"Bobby didn't help any?"

"I think he will help. Wellington is getting a computer whiz in there with him." He hesitated and shrugged. "Bobby knows he almost died. And he has a great wife, a good job."

"So what did he tell you?"

"The dark web."

"It is real," she murmured.

"Very real."

"I mean, I knew that, I just..."

"We'll see," he said. They'd reached parking for the performers, and he turned to her again. "Sky, if anything was to happen to you—"

"And if anything was to happen to you," she interrupted.

He nodded slowly. She set her hands on his. "Okay, seriously, I know you think you're stronger, that some machismo is kicking in—"

"No. Honestly. Training. Sky, you know I've been to a million classes—"

"That won't stop a bullet."

"No. But I know how to watch and hit a fly at a hundred yards when I need to. But I don't think there are going to be firearms at the concert—"

"Then, you don't need to be worried that I'll be a target."

He was silent. She knew he really didn't think firearms were something they needed to concerned about.

But he was still worried.

"I'm not going to touch any equipment, Chase," she told him. "I'm just going to be there—drawing out whoever might be doing something, or not even drawing them out. I'll just be making sure the show goes on so they can do whatever it is they do."

He nodded. "Yep, right. Okay then, shall we?"

The exited the car and headed in. Chris Wiley and Brandon were there, checking mics and instruments with Justin, Nathan and Charlie.

Charlie, naturally, looked at them anxiously. Chase clapped him on the back, and Sky knew he was hoping Charlie would act normally.

She assumed, however, that Chase had gotten with him. He knew about Bobby Sacks. He would have made sure, too, that Charlie was all right.

And that he should keep quiet.

"Hey!" Chris called, greeting them. He hurried over and gave Chase a pat on the back and hugged Sky.

"This is going to be amazing! Sky, so cool," he said softly.

"Thanks. Of course."

"Mark has the set list. Sound checks…"

"Wait, wait!" Mark came hurrying in from the stage-right wing. "Sky, we've another reporter who wants to speak with you before we get started. Obviously, we want the best tech we can get, but I also know that you knew your dad, you'll play it by ear and audience cue once we get going—"

"Mark, yes, I'll be fine." She smiled and added sincerely, "I'm happy to be here. And I will be my dad to the very best of my ability."

Mark Reynolds smiled at her. "No, Sky. Honor your dad, but be you. This band, the group of us, we're his legacy in a way. But you're his real legacy. Be you!"

Joe Garcia had followed Mark in. "Be you, Sky," he echoed. But then he grimaced and added, "But you might tell the reporter you think we're ultracool."

Sky laughed. "Joe, I've got it. No worries," she assured him.

"Hey!"

She turned around. Charlie was attaching a wire to an amp.

"Hey, Charlie."

"You're all here. No one, and I mean no one but Nathan, Justin or me, is to touch anything electric or electronic, got it?" he demanded.

"You got it!" Mark assured him, glancing worriedly at Sky.

She set a hand on his arm. "It's okay." She turned, smiling. "Not to worry, Charlie. I won't even fool with my own fuse box!"

He looked at her and nodded. She smiled. He was definitely looking worried. She decided it was a good thing Chase was the one working undercover and not Charlie.

"I've got the reporter just back there. Her name is Marci Simmons. Seems nice and already told me she loves her job because she loves rock bands," Mark said.

"Great. I'll go talk to her." She turned and almost tripped over one of the workers she didn't know.

"Sorry, sorry!" he said. "I'm, uh, Noah. Noah Lawson.

I'm kind of new. But I'm super happy to be here, and I didn't mean to be in your way!"

"No, no, it's fine!" she reassured him.

Smiling, she headed into the stage-right wing. A woman was waiting for her by the dressing rooms.

"Hi, I'm Marci!" she said, offering Sky a hand. "I realize you guys want to get to it, but I'd love to ask you a few questions. This is a really special occasion. Chase McCoy sitting in for Hank—and you, which is truly rare, taking your dad's place."

"I'm happy to be here," she said.

"Even though…"

"My father loved the band. He loved music. All forms of music. And he was from New Orleans, fell in love with street musicians, Frenchmen Street and all the venues. Dad loved his songs. I'm happy to do his songs."

"He was all about the music, right?"

"And people," Sky said. "He truly enjoyed other musicians. Oh, and musical theater! He told me he'd been crazy about *Godspell* and *Jesus Christ Superstar* when he'd been young. He loved *Tommy*, and then, coming up to closer decades, *Hamilton* and *Next to Normal*. He appreciated so many of his fellow performers."

"They say he admired others. Some rock stars want it to be all about them and don't really care to watch other—"

Sky interrupted her with an honest laugh. "Trust me! My dad wanted to go to just about any concert—he loved his old friends and acquaintances and new talent. And then again, any musical theater anywhere near him."

"His songs—"

"Tended to reflect his life."

"Well, here's an important question for you. We understand you use music to teach, often with those who are having difficulty with behavioral problems or fitting in—kids maybe even at risk. Will you keep doing that, or will you be with Skyhawk full-time now?"

"I love what I do. But I'm not saying I won't be with Sky-hawk again. On the one hand, I was my father's baby. On the other hand, the band was equally his creation. I'd like to honor music in the way that he loved it and the band."

"That's great, and thank you so much!" the young woman said. "I am truly anxious to see the show and equally grate-ful for this chance to chat briefly with you."

"My pleasure," Sky assured her.

She left Marci, aware that activity was already hap-pening on the stage, with sound and mic checks. They'd be ready for her.

She paused. Brandon was next to Chris, listening to all last-minute instructions from his father. Nathan was working on something with the keyboard. Joe and Mark were both strumming guitars, talking about chords. Char-lie and Justin were working on something with an ampli-fier and the drums.

But she wasn't the only one who hadn't been on stage.

Chase wasn't there.

Frowning, she looked around and saw he was in the audience. He was engaged in conversation with an audi-ence member.

Andy Wellington. She knew Chase: while it might ap-pear the two men were having a casual conversation, she could tell he had just learned something. Something that brought a furrow to his brow. But Brandon approached the two of them, and Chase quickly smiled and introduced the two men.

"Sky?"

She spun around. Nathan was there. "Mic check?" he asked her.

"Um, yeah, sure, of course!" she replied.

She went through the motions. And she hoped she'd

get a private minute with Chase again before they plowed straight into tech…

And the performance.

One that might be far more than anyone involved had begun to imagine.

"Bobby has been great, amazing, really," Wellington told Chase. "Of course, we have some great people working for us who can crack almost anything ever done on or with a computer."

"They found the source?" Chase said.

Wellington nodded, smiling, as if they were speaking about songs or the weather. "The signal bounced all over, from here to Asia, Europe, Africa… South America, and back here. But in the end, the origin was right here, in Orleans Parish. Finding the actual physical place where the initial site was created is proving a bit difficult—personal computers move all over the place, and registrations can be as false as anything else. But someone here is being played by someone bigger. What I'm trying to figure is why? We've checked the financials on the band. You know yourself every member does well enough. No one is in this for the money, so…"

"But you think it is someone with the band."

"Someone close. The band or the roadies."

Chase had nodded, then lowered and shook his head.

Who? Why? None of them needed money.

"So," he said, "no one with a gambling problem, no one who lost big in cryptocurrency or anything of the sort?"

"We have truly had people all over this. I'm convinced they are working through one of the cartels. But again, *why* is a mystery. These guys don't need money."

Chase knew they didn't have much time for a private conversation. As others moved near them or passed by, he introduced Wellington, who behaved like the perfect—if slightly reserved—fan.

He glanced on stage, wishing that his heart didn't skip a beat as he watched Sky at the mic.

She wasn't touching it, she was standing back, singing a few bars, doing a sound check. They were testing just her mic, she was singing a cappella, and he was touched by the song she had chosen, her dad's ode to the beauty of life once one learned how to live it.

"The sun so bright, such a promise, beauty and light,
Yet those same lights can turn to night,
Darkness deep, with just a blaze, one that burns,
While it promises to amaze,
But the pain sets in, and there seems no hope,
Tangled there in a million ropes,
Just broken bits and pieces of me
Pieces longing again to see…
Find the freedom in true light,
Seek the stars in the darkness of night,
And finding the light is hard, so hard,
But it can be captured if you fight the fight,
And once again, you'll find true light,
Hold it loose and hold it dear,
and you'll discover that the light is near…"

There were choruses that came in, harmonies, and it was an amazing song, both beautiful and with a rock beat that had made it an instant success. But that day, listening to Sky, knowing what it had meant to her because of what it had meant to Jake, was beautiful.

Jake had found the true light. He'd battled hard, he'd tortured his parents and others who had loved him, but he'd proved himself in the end.

And then he'd died, determined that he would do what was right for others.

They were doing a sound check, just a sound check,

and yet when Sky finished, there was silence in the room. Then applause.

Applause…

Except Chase noticed Justin. He wasn't applauding. He was staring at Sky. Staring at her…as if something inside of him was broken and burning as well.

He felt his phone buzz.

He glanced down.

Dark web encrypted but the source—here.

He closed his phone and looked at Justin again. He had to get the man alone.

Chapter Eight

Sky found herself chatting with Joe about the songs, and then Mark about their set lists. Chris joined them as well, telling her that the full rehearsal with her the night before had been like speeding back through the years to a beautiful time.

"You, Brandon, Chase...having you guys here is incredible," he told her, smiling. He grimaced. "You kind of, hmm...what are the words I'm looking for? Make everything perfect. We were good from the beginning—your dad made us good musicians, and he kept us all together as friends. I mean, a lot of the old groups are still playing, but most have new members in them somewhere. Folks like us, from the seventies and eighties...we lost a lot of amazing artists. Janis Joplin, Elvis, Michael Jackson, Prince, so very many...and then, hey, you get where we are and there are deaths from natural causes, too. But think of the groups and performers still out there—Bruce Springsteen, Elton John, Billy Joel—your dad loved all of them, said they were real songsters! 'Piano Man,' Billy Joel, one of his favorites. The Eagles! So many more. But with us...your dad is gone and Hank is recovering, but we have family members! True legacy."

"Thanks, Chris," she told him. "It's great fun to be with Brandon, too."

"Yep, the boy is coming along nicely. But..." He shrugged.

"What?" Sky asked him.

"Thing is, being us has been great. We made money, and your dad was the guy who led us. We were so young, but we never went crazy. He got us the right management and the right financial advisers. Thing is, as much as I've loved being Skyhawk, what I want to leave behind is hard to explain."

Brandon walked up, joining them. "You're not going anywhere for a long time!" he told his father sternly.

"Not planning to," Chris assured him, "but none of us ever really knows. I don't know how to express it, but I'm so glad, so damned glad, you three younger people are with us—but what I hope we leave behind is something that isn't performing in front of a crowd or getting a good paycheck. It can't really be touched. It's just the love of music, what music can do when you're down, how it can help bring you back up, how... Wow. I just sound weird—"

"Nothing new there!" Brandon teased.

"Hey! Careful, I'll ground you!" Chris teased in return. He ran his fingers through his hair and then paused. "Like this stuff on my head. It's white—"

"Ah, but still there! You still look like a great rocker!" Sky assured him.

He laughed softly. "Like I said, it's just darned great that there are a bunch of us still out there—some of them even make me feel young! Anyway, Sky, hope you'll join us now and then. Thing is—well, I know you love what you do. You take music someplace special and do special things with it when you work with kids, so... I hope you can keep doing what you love, and still throw some gigs in with us old-timers now and then, too."

She gave him a quick hug. "Chris, thank you, and I hope so, too."

Nathan called Chris, asking him to come check something on the keyboard. Chris hurried off, and Brandon grimaced at Sky.

"And here we all are."

"And you, sir, are great on the keyboards and backup. And you play lead guitar, too!"

Brandon laughed. "I try. Anyway, I'm happy to be here. We'll have fun."

She smiled. "Sure. Lots of fun!"

"The special friend group is arriving," Brandon said using air quotes and almost whispering as if someone might have heard them from the audience. "There's that guy Chase knows—some kind of a forensic expert, does all kinds of lecturing."

"Yeah, I met him. Andy Wellington. Nice guy," Sky assured him.

"Yeah, he seems okay. And there's Justin's wife, Julia," Brandon pointed out. "Wonder who that guy she's with is. She usually shows up with the kids. Well, adult kids—both of them just finished college." He laughed suddenly. "And there—Nathan brings two of the kids from Little League— they get to win tickets. Not by playing. I guess he channeled your dad. They get two backstage tickets for helping others to improve most. Kind of cool, huh?"

"Yep, very," Sky agreed. She smiled. The kids were in their midteens. Half grown-up—half not. They were watching everything that was going on wide-eyed and seemed thrilled when Charlie approached them, asking them to stand in different spots to make sure the revolving, colored lights looked good over the audience.

She glanced at the man with Julia. She'd never met him, but she assumed he had to be a relative or a family friend. Justin's marriage had always been solid as a rock, and she'd met Julia several times through the years. She was a woman who seemed to love what her husband did—and loved getting to see all the various performances he might work.

"Sky, did you want to take lead guitar on the ballad or just the vocals? I mean, you can do both, and I know that you might prefer both, but—"

"Brandon, can you take lead on that?" Sky asked. "I think I do want to concentrate on the vocals."

"Honored, Sky," Brandon assured her.

"Pulling in a wire!" Justin called, heading backstage right.

Sky couldn't help but notice that Chase idly followed him, stopping to talk briefly to Mark, check something on the drum set—and then head on back.

She wanted to follow, too.

But…

How did she do so without being obvious? Take a casual wander. Charlie was working with Joe, checking on the keyboard.

But as she moved, Mark was suddenly in front of her, grinning.

"You know, your dad really loved everyone. Different people for different reasons. Loved Roy Orbison's voice, the way Clapton could play… Who is your hero? Besides your dad, of course."

"And Skyhawk?" She smiled, looking back. She couldn't see Chase or Justin.

"Who else?"

"Um, hmm. Nancy Wilson, Heart! Killer voice. Oh— and I'm always a kid at heart. It wasn't live performance, but I loved, loved both Idina Menzel and Kristin Bell in *Frozen.* Wow. Hmm, oh, well—loved Idina Menzel from the get-go—saw *Wicked* on Broadway as a kid, and she was killing it then. And who wouldn't love Joan Jett? And I'll never forget Delores O'Riordan, beautiful voice! Seventies, hmm. Wow—how could anyone leave out Aerosmith? Journey?"

She kept smiling, talking.

How the hell could she casually get by him?

But...

Why would Chase be suspicious of Justin, of all people? Justin, great worker, solid as a rock, no overindulgences, great husband, great father...

But there was Julia, chatting now with the boys. Her friend, the stranger who had come with her, was just standing back, watching all the proceedings.

"Mark, Julia is here—Justin's wife. I'm going to go and talk to her, tell her that...that it's great to see her," she said.

"Oh, yeah, Julia! I'll come with you."

Great.

They both hopped off the stage, Mark turning to give Sky a hand. They walked over to Julia and the teen boys.

Sky barely got a chance to say hello before one of the kids said, "Wow, man, you're her! You're Skylar Ferguson."

She smiled. "Yes, I am. And thanks for being here. Oh! And I know how you got tickets to the show, so thanks for being such great young men."

They flushed, one speaking after the other, talking about Skyhawk numbers.

Julia looked uncomfortable. The strange man who was with her was watching.

He looked ready to move, almost ready to spring at any minute.

"Well, welcome, and we'll be seeing you!" Sky told the boys. "Julia, it's so great that you're here. Anyway, I just remembered I have to check to see if I brought clothes in for a change—"

"What you're wearing is cool. Love those jeans and that...shirt thing," one of the kids said.

"Tunic. It's a tunic," the other told him.

"Well, thank you, because at this point, if I did forget everything, it is what I'll be wearing!" she said.

Then she turned quickly, heading back to the stage, determined she was going to find out what Chase was doing.

And why Justin was…so strange.

"YOU NEED TO…UNDERSTAND," Justin told Chase. The man was crying; tears were streaming down his face.

And he was terrified.

"I understand you're the one who managed to fray that wire. You were best friends with Jake, and you knew he'd be ready to do things himself to keep a show flowing smoothly. You knew he'd go to fix the amp."

"I…loved Jake!" he whispered.

And that was true; Chase believed him.

But something had clicked when they'd discovered that the places to drop off the money and to pick up the goods were right here.

And when he'd seen Justin…

He'd known. And he'd accused him in a straightforward manner when he'd gotten him alone, repeating the last words he'd heard Jake Ferguson say before he had died.

"I know what's going on and I saw… I'm going to put an end to it as soon as this gig is over!"

Justin caught his breath, trying to contain the violence of his sobs.

"He saw, he knew, and he was going to report you to the police. Because despite his own sobriety, Jake didn't mind others who could have a recreational drink or even a joint—what he minded was drugs being sold to children—and people dying!"

"I know, I know… I didn't care. I thought it would be over. They could arrest me—I didn't care about me. I had no choice. Then…or now…"

"Then, what the hell?" Chase exploded.

Justin looked toward the stage anxiously, trying to dry his face with his shirt sleeve, terrified as he looked toward the stage. "I never knew about the…fentanyl. That they are using it to cut hard drugs and handling it so recklessly. I didn't. I swear. But they got to me, they let me know, and even now——"

"Even now, what?" Chase demanded.

Justin looked at him. "If I don't—if *we* don't—walk back out there looking calm as can be, he's going to kill Julia. And as soon as word gets out, he's going to see that my boys are killed, too."

Chase stared at him. He had never believed that Justin was the head of their snake.

But just how deep did it run?

Back to the cartels theory. So who was the man with Julia today?

"All right, we'll talk quickly. Who is the man with your wife right now?"

"His name is Drew Carter. He's…been ordered to kill Julia if I don't make things happen the way that they're supposed to," Justin said.

"That's easy enough. I'll get out by him and——"

"No, no, he's just a…a pawn like me. His wife is in the hospital with a new baby. And there's a man there…ready to take her out along with the infant and…you don't know, you don't understand how bad all this is. And it's not just my wife. He's going to go after Sammy and Jeff—my sons. He's got them covered, too. Don't you see? There's no way out of this. He can kill anyone at any time with a snap of his fingers. His enforcers are everywhere."

"And so are the good guys and law enforcement," Chase told him.

"But if I don't——"

"You do what you're supposed to do. We're going to go through the show with you having done what you've been ordered to do. And by then…"

He broke off. He could see that Sky was coming into the wing.

"Hey!" she called cheerfully. But he knew Sky. She wanted to know what the hell was going on.

Did he dare tell her this was the man who had killed her beloved father?

"Can you get Wellington back here?" he asked her.

"Um, sure. But—"

"Now. Please."

"Sure. Okay."

She hurried back toward the stage. "Hey, Andy! Can you come here for a minute? Chase wants to see what shirt you like best!"

Andy came on back quickly, excusing himself to the others. As he arrived, Chase told Sky, "Please, get back out there. Try to talk to Julia again and keep her with you."

"Why—"

"Please, please, just act normally, in a friendly manner." He looked at his watch. The doors would start opening in less than hour.

Whatever Justin was supposed to be doing, he was supposed to be doing it now.

The man still looked like hell. With Wellington there, he explained what he knew quickly, adding that Justin needed to get it together, to act as expected.

"My wife...the boys and...the others—"

"I'll get to the guy out there watching over Julia," Wellington promised. "Justin, do as Chase says—do what you're supposed to do. And don't be afraid. We'll get to your children before anyone else can."

"You don't understand how powerful—"

"Actually, I do. But you need to understand how powerful we can be when given the chance," Wellington told him. "I'll go have a discussion about lights with Drew Carter right now."

Wellington disappeared. Justin still looked like hell.

"Pull yourself together, man!" Chase ordered him. "This show has to go on as planned. All right, where does everything go?"

Justin shook his head. "There's not everything. I just put the money I got from the last haul—" He broke off, looking worse than he had. "Blood money," he said. "Right before we open the doors, I slip it beneath a particular seat, changes every time."

"Do you have your orders yet?"

"Yeah."

"And putting the money out was what Jake saw?"

"Yeah."

"And no one else ever saw you?" Chase asked.

He shrugged. "I just walk around the seat, look at the lights. Sometimes sit a few places. Everyone thinks I'm just checking it out."

"Do it. And quit crying. Justin, this truly has to be the performance of a lifetime for you."

"I'm not on stage. I head back to the wings. Then I get a message about where to find the stuff I'm supposed to distribute along with what I get to keep."

"Right now, come on. You can help salvage all the harm you've done. And you are performing now. All right. Go do your walkabout. Where exactly will you be putting it?"

"First balcony, front, center, dead center."

"And don't worry. In fact…"

He looked out. Wellington was standing with Julia, a laughing Sky and the man he'd been told was Drew Carter.

And he knew Wellington had seen to it that Carter knew it was over—and had given him everything he could possibly give him.

Agents would already be in the field.

They'd have the families safe. And they'd be watching. And waiting. Because when it was known that whatever lackey was the pickup man had been scooped, the so-called snake would probably see to it himself that his death threats against the families of those who had failed him had been carried out.

It was all a long shot.

And a real takedown might not happen. But Wellington would see to it that no innocents were harmed. Even if it meant giving up his own life.

But Wellington would be here tonight.

Watching. Waiting. And they all had to play it out.

"Justin? This all depends on you!" Chase said.

Justin straightened. "Yeah. I've got it. And I don't care what happens to me—"

"I know. Your family. I promise you, the people out there will see that they are safe. Justin, it's all in motion already. Just one more question before you start out. Who is the head of this thing?"

He shook his head miserably. "They call him El Rey."

El Rey.

Chase had heard the name before. And Wellington had been right. El Rey was really Miguel Esposito, head of one of the largest cartels, suspected to have slipped into the country illegally to take out a witness in a trial scheduled for just months ago.

No one had even imagined just how far this all reached.

"Showtime," he said.

SKY DIDN'T GET much of a chance to talk to Wellington, but she did know that he and Chase were working furiously at whatever it was that was going on.

And that Justin was involved somehow, and he'd been scared. No... Terrified.

But she had to have faith in the men. Her part in this was important, and her part was to get on stage, perform as she had never performed before, and make it all appear as if nothing was wrong at all, as if the world of rock 'n' roll was everything.

She saw the crew working quickly, leaving the audience, heading to the wings. Mark called out to her that they needed to get back, that the MC would be taking over the booth.

Wellington had Julia and Drew Carter somewhere—she didn't know where. But she had a feeling a few of the extra crew members were his men.

That Wellington was a man with the power to make things happen quickly.

"Heads up!" It was Kenneth Malcolm calling out. "House lights up! Doors are open!"

He was in the wings, impeccable as usual in a casual beige suit. Sky couldn't help but wonder about him.

After all, other than the three who worked specifically for Skyhawk and those who worked for other bands, Kenneth Malcolm was the man who did the hiring.

He had hired Bobby Sacks.

But Bobby Sacks had been a victim.

She wondered bitterly how anyone, including a drug kingpin, could expect anyone to keep payments coming in, taking the big deliveries from him to disperse for the megamoney to be gained on the streets, when the customers were dying from the product.

But she doubted that whoever was behind it all cared. Could a man like Kenneth Malcolm have been involved? How could he and still keep his job?

Then again, who knew the venue the way he did?

Mark and Joe were laughing together as they headed stage right; Chris was behind them, reminding Brandon which numbers he wanted him sitting in for. Sky naturally reminded him where she wanted him to take lead guitar and, of course, he should stay on backup vocals through the whole show, if he wanted, although he probably knew them all as well as she did, if not better.

She didn't see Justin; Nathan was heading stage right with them while Charlie was heading stage left.

Curtains were opened as people continued coming in.

Lights on the stage blazed as they did so, people in twos and threes and larger groups, loud and excited as they came in, some with drinks and snacks, others just anxious to find their seats.

The MC spoke over backup music as the crowd came in, talking about the show, the weather, the city, welcoming everyone.

Every seat was filled when he announced, "And now, ladies and gentlemen, boys and girls, and whoever! Let's welcome to the stage, Skyhawk!"

It was time to make their entry.

Skyhawk. Her father's creation, the music, his love. And tonight, Skyhawk was the three older rockers, Chris Wiley, Mark Reynolds and Joe Garcia, still looking the part, agile, vibrant for their ages, long hippie hair, and all that they needed to be.

And then her, Brandon and Chase. Second and third generations.

Skyhawk, changing, growing—and yet the embodiment of love that her dad had created.

Her part in all that was just to play with all her heart.

They ran out, waving to everyone and going for their instruments, Chase bowing broadly as his name was shouted, grinning and then maintaining a fantastic drumroll.

They burst straight into one of Skyhawk's most popular numbers, "The Path I Took," and from there, they moved straight into one of her dad's older ballads.

Act normal, behave normally, give the show all your heart and...

Trust in Chase, in Wellington, and that everything is

being handled. Her part was to keep this moving, give them the opportunity to do what was needed…

"Welcome! We are Skyhawk, and we're thrilled to be here, thrilled to have you here with us! I'm Sky Ferguson, and you have known Chris Wiley, Mark Reynolds and Joe Garcia for—"

"Decades!" Joe put in dryly, bringing a bout of laughter to the crowd.

"We have Chase McCoy on drums tonight—though Hank has told him he wants his place back as soon as possible! But we'll make do, right?"

Her words were greeted with laughter and another round of phenomenal drumming.

Chase, too, was playing his part.

"We also have Brandon Wiley with us tonight, and this guy does just about everything!"

Brandon created a combo of melodies quickly, then they moved into a fast, heavy rock piece that had once ruled the airwaves.

She moved about the stage, forgetting she'd told Chase she wouldn't carry the mic. But her father had moved; it was natural, swirling and dancing while doing the songs, the numbers she had known since she was a small child…

Songs she had done with her dad. And she gave it her heart as she went along, because as serious as the night had become, it was also her ode to him.

Mark stepped in when it was time to take a break, announcing with her that they were giving everyone a chance to head out for drinks, snacks and merchandise. Hey, the place was in it for the money, right?

They could bring the crowd to laughter and applause, and it felt good.

Even if…

Running to the stage-right wing, she found herself crashing into Chase's arms.

"Our guys have the families!" he whispered to her, pretending to nuzzle her ear. "Kids, wives, good... They went in the back. They'll be waiting."

She smiled at him, pretending to whisper in his ear as well.

"Ah, lovebirds!" Mark said. "It's adorable to see you two together again."

"I'm adorable?" Chase asked, grinning.

It was going the best that it could. But she didn't see Justin anywhere. She knew he had to be playing whatever part it was that he needed to, but...

She managed to slide back into his arms and ask softly, "Justin?"

"He's good. Agent at his side."

She nodded. They weren't playing, but the canned music and the noise of the crowd was almost deafening, still. They waited, talking about where they were going next. Mark and Joe reminded her of the songs they would do for the encore; it was apparent that this crowd would demand it.

Then the MC announced the return of Skyhawk to the stage. It was time to run back out there.

Next...

Drum solos, songs that featured each instrument and each player. A wonderful crowd in the audience, cheering them on, moments when she needed to chat, to laugh, to draw the others in, moving across the stage, covering the stage...

And all the while wondering what was going on, how Chase, too, was managing to bang away, come in with drumrolls when she was about to speak, to bring them back to their performance, to follow her as she crossed the stage, paused to make comments to those off the apron by the stage...

Then she thanked everyone for coming. For supporting Skyhawk.

She thanked them for having loved her dad and all the music he had created.

Then they were running off stage, listening, waiting, hearing the crowd roar, screaming that they come back, and then the MC announcing they'd return for the last few songs...

Her father's songs. Songs about life, learning about the dark side and how to find the light, about love, about the strength to be found in the eyes of a loved one...

Then it was done.

"Thank you! Skyhawk thanks you, I thank you, and among the angels—trust me!—my dad thanks you!"

She ran back offstage. Show over. Encore over. And...

She stood with the others in the wings, just breathing, as the MC announced safe paths out, as crowds of people began to leave from the floor, from the balconies.

Chase was right next to her; she had a feeling he wouldn't be leaving her.

Justin was nowhere to be seen.

Neither was his wife, nor the man who had been with her.

She looked at Chase, but he evidently didn't intend to say anything at that moment, other than to join in the happy banter that was going around, everyone congratulating each other on the success of the show.

Andy Wellington was not backstage.

The teenage boys were, and a few other special guests. A few reporters, a few photographers, but all of them gleaning and snapping what they could.

And finally, Chase whispered to her, "Let's escape to a dressing room!"

She nodded, feeling his arm around her, leading her.

But a man with a recorder stopped them.

"Ferguson and McCoy, together again!" he said.

Chase smiled and looked at Sky. "Were we ever really apart?" he asked.

"Aw, man, but now…will you two be continuing with the band?" the reporter asked.

"Oh, well, the band…the main members of Skyhawk were friends before they were the band—our families have been friends. We've been friends. I'm sure we will be playing together again. When, where and how often, well, that will remain to be seen."

"Skylar, you work with kids—"

"Kids and music," she said, glancing up at Chase.

She wanted to talk to him alone!

"Okay, Chase, so, we understand that you've been working in a number of labs, that you've gotten into forensic sciences. Will that continue into your future?"

Chase laughed easily. "Right now, our future is getting home—we have a new dog! So, hey, thank you, thanks so much for your interest, but…"

"We're just dead tired!" Sky said.

She winced inwardly, wishing she hadn't used the word *dead*.

Chase was already leading her away. "Thank you! Thank you so much for your interest in Skyhawk!"

He managed to get her to one of the dressing rooms, pushing the door open and then leaning against it, shaking his head.

"Chase, what's going on?" she asked.

"Wellington is a good man and good at what he does. He had agents with Justin's family—and with Drew Carter's—before we were halfway through the first set. Now…he's got people trying to get the place cleared out while following whoever goes for the money. We need to just sit tight for a minute and wait—"

His phone buzzed, and he looked at it quickly. "They've

got something. Stay here, don't move. Keep the door locked. Don't answer it to anyone—*anyone*—but me."

"Chase, I—"

"Please, Sky, I'm begging you, just listen to me right now."

She nodded.

He slipped out. She locked the door.

And she knew that every second would seem like an hour until he returned.

Chapter Nine

The houses were covered; agents were waiting. Justin was safe, Julia was safe...

But something had happened. What should have been an easy and clear operation had changed when the lackey picking up the funds Justin had left managed to sense the agents about to nab him. The place had been almost clear, but a woman with a teenage girl had been just exiting when the man doing the pickup had grabbed her and the kid. He threatened to throw them off the balcony, and law enforcement had backed off, giving him time for an agile leap down to the sound booth, onto the floor and up again onto the stage and into the wings.

He was back there now, joining the friends, reporters and others who grouped backstage after a performance.

Chase sped through the wings, seeking anyone who matched the poor description that they had so far. White, medium height, medium build, brown hair.

And, it seemed, they were hiring their lackeys from the ranks of acrobats—he should have broken a leg attempting his escape route.

But he had made it. And in the arena where there were still a few people milling about, the agents had refrained from firing so they wouldn't hit an innocent or worse, create a panic that would allow the perpetrator even greater leeway.

Chase stepped from the dressing room just in time to see the door to the performers' parking lot begin to swing closed.

He took off, slamming it back open, racing into the back.

He saw a man. Medium height and build. Brown hair.

He tore after him; he was in decent shape himself, but contrary to what he saw on TV most of the time, he hadn't been in that many situations where a perp had run.

But he was after him in a flash.

This guy could run.

"Stop!" Chase shouted.

The man turned to look back—and in doing so, he tripped, thankfully. Chase didn't think that he could have outrun him.

But he was on the ground, moaning. Chase reached him, dug plastic cuffs from his wallet and dragged him to his feet.

He frowned as he did so. The man didn't seem to have packets or...anything.

And, as Chase looked at him, he started to laugh.

"You'll never beat a king, you know."

"You handed it off!" Chase said.

"Me? I didn't do a thing. In fact...hey, you're the damned drummer. Cool. I can sue the venue, the promoters—and Skyhawk!"

"Oh, I don't think so!"

Chase pushed the man along before him, wishing he'd gotten set up with earbuds and a mic, but that hadn't been feasible when he'd been playing the drums, and he had to keep one hand on the guy while he used the other to call Wellington.

"I've got him, but he's passed it off!"

"Get him in here."

"He's suing us all," Chase said dryly.

"I don't think so. Too many witnesses, and I'm willing

to bet he's got a rap sheet a mile long. Who did he pass it off to?"

"I don't know—"

"Back on lockdown. Now!" Wellington said. "Agents ready to get him—"

"I have to get back in—Sky—"

"Agents at the door. Hand him over—get to Sky."

"On it."

He ended his call, dragging the man back toward the stage doors.

"He's going to shoot your ass, you know."

"Who is?"

"The king."

"Well, he can try. What's the king's name?"

"It's *King*, obviously," the man said.

"What's your name?"

"Myron."

"Myron what?"

"Myron Mouse. What the hell. Hey, I want an attorney."

"That will all be arranged for you."

"You should stick to the drums. Now I'm just suing you personally!"

"Yeah, go for it!"

Chase was finally getting him back toward the rear-stage doors. As Wellington had promised, the door opened, and two agents appeared. He knew the one man—he'd worked with him before in Baton Rouge in a small sting at a bar. He was Gene Shepherd, another agent who worked a lot of undercover cases and was excellent at sliding into just about any group anywhere.

He and his companion, an attractive female agent, were casually dressed. He was wearing a Skyhawk T-shirt while she was dressed in jeans and a soft, light sweater—but one bulky enough that he knew she was armed beneath it.

They'd naturally been filtered into the audience and looked the part of any couple heading to a rock concert.

"Got him," Shepherd assured them. "Hey, cool, thanks, we weren't expecting this kind of help from a drummer."

"Hey, he's trying to ruin what was a good concert. And he might be an accessory to murder," Chase said.

"Murder! I didn't murder anyone!" the man protested. "Hey, I wasn't here when Jake Ferguson was killed!"

"Who knows what laws we can make stick?" Shepherd asked. "Good prosecutor, a jury tired of drugs killing people—"

"I didn't kill anyone!" he protested again. "No one is dead—"

"Yeah, people are dead and dying from that stuff you sold," Chase told him.

"I didn't sell it! The king sold it. I mean, maybe someone got carried away. Look, I don't make the stuff. I don't package the stuff. I'm a messenger, that's all. I'm told to get drop-offs, nothing else. I didn't kill anyone, I didn't. Wait! Not only did I not kill anyone—I didn't do a damned thing. There's no money on me, nothing—you need to let me go this instant. Brutality! Oh, hell, yeah, I am going to have a field day with you in court!"

"We'll see," Shepherd said. "Chase, you can—"

"You idiots! I'll be out on bail in an hour. And when I'm out, you're going to be so sorry! You're going to wish for death before you get to that sweet peace—"

"He's threatening us now," Shepherd said. "I'm pretty sure that death threats are illegal in themselves. Man, we've got him on so much!"

"You have nothing!"

"Enough to see that a jury puts you away forever and ever. Then again, this is Louisiana, and if it weren't, we're federal, and sometimes—" Shepherd said.

"You're threatening me! Wait until I talk to my lawyer!"

"You'll get a lawyer," Shepherd promised.

"Yeah, you will," Chase said, but he took the man by the shoulders, spinning him around to stare at him and demand, "Who did you pass it off to?"

A shot suddenly rang out. It missed the man by about half an inch.

Chase threw himself on the suspect, bringing them both down flat. Shepherd and his companion were already down, weapons drawn, and Shepherd was speaking into his body mic.

"Shots fired! Sniper in the rear-stage parking!"

Chase dragged the culprit behind a dumpster along with Shepherd and his partner.

"Your king will be happy to kill you! If it was me, I'd be throwing myself on the mercy—and safety—of law enforcement!" Chase told him.

"No, no, they were aiming at you!"

"Were they?" Chase asked. "You know that isn't true. You failed. You're a liability now. Better off dead to those who pay you. Who the hell did you give the packet to?" he demanded again. "Hey, we'll fight for your life, but..."

The lackey must have known that his so-called king killed anyone who failed him, because he suddenly started shaking.

"You don't understand—"

"Oh," Shepherd said, "with your crowd, failure is death. So maybe you want to join a new crowd. We can keep you safe."

"He has a long reach. Even in prison."

"Solitary confinement. You can live. Maybe one day, the king and his royalty will be gone, and you can have a life again," Shepherd's partner said quietly.

"All right, all right!"

He told them who he had given the packet to.

And Chase was stunned. He might have known. He might have suspected.

But still…

"I've got to get back in!" he said.

"We'll cover you," Shepherd assured him.

Chase leaped to his feet, diving for the door. It was still wedged open, and he ripped it the rest of the way, sliding behind its protection as quickly as he could.

A shot rang out.

But as Shepherd and his partner returned fire, the door closed behind Chase.

He was in.

He had to get back to Skylar.

"SKYLAR!"

She heard her name being anxiously called just seconds after Chase left.

"Skylar, Skylar Ferguson! It's Special Agent Brent Masters. Wellington sent me to get you out of here. I can show you my credentials."

"Chase said to wait for him!"

"No, it's all gone to hell. There's been a pass-off, and we have to get you the hell out of here. Now. Look…look through the little hole. You can see my credentials."

There was a peephole in the dressing-room door. She looked through it. The credentials looked real enough. But…

"I have been ordered to get you to safety!" the man said.

There had been a pass-off?

"Aw, hell, Miss Ferguson…"

She heard a key rattling.

This guy had the keys to the dressing rooms. She prayed that made him real.

The door opened. He looked enough like an agent. But maybe he looked like a drug smuggler, too.

"Come on, please, Wellington is across the stage, and he knows Chase is out and wants you with him. I'm the real deal, I swear it—"

He never finished his sentence. She never saw the person who slammed his head with a guitar, sending him crashing down to the floor.

Out like a light.

But then she did see who had wielded the weapon. And to her astonishment, it was someone who hadn't dressed to blend in with a bunch of rockers.

It was Kenneth Malcom, and as usual, he was dressed impeccably in one of his suits.

"Skylar, that guy was a phony. He thought he'd knocked me out over there, and he stole my master key... Let me get you to Wellington before another of these perps gets over here!"

Wellington had filled the place with undercover agents.

But it seemed that head of the drug cartel or whoever was pulling the strings had filled it with his own people as well.

"Come on!" he told her anxiously. "Skylar, hurry, I owe it to your dad to make sure that you're safe!"

She looked at the man on the floor; he was out.

If nothing else, Kenneth Malcom knew how to play the guitar as weapon.

"Skylar!"

She followed him out. The dressing rooms were stage left while most of the workings of any show there took place stage right.

"We'll head around the back. You don't see anyone, right?"

She shook her head, hurrying by him, ready to run across the back of the stage until she met the one man that she knew Chase trusted entirely.

But she had barely gotten around the back before she saw Chris Wiley coming her way, looking anxious.

"Skylar! Thank God. Brandon is going around the other way for you. Seems Chase headed on out, getting himself involved in all this—"

"Chris," Kenneth Malcolm exploded from behind her. "You! You're the one. You saw to it that Justin was played because you knew that he loved his wife and kids more than his own life. Get the hell away from her now, Chris."

"What?" Chris demanded.

"You heard me, move aside. I'm getting her out of here!"

Brandon appeared then, coming from the other direction. "Thank God! You found her. Skylar—"

"Both of you! Back off, you bastard pushers, get away from her."

"Kenneth, what in God's name is wrong with you?" Chris demanded. "Leave her alone. Let Skylar come with us right away, and go and do whatever the hell you need to be doing—getting out of here yourself, getting to safety—"

"Move. Now. I don't trust you—either of you," Malcolm said.

"Malcolm!" Brandon exploded.

Sky stood there, torn, incredulous.

And not at all sure who to trust.

"Let me just go back to the dressing room!" she said. "All of you, leave me alone. I'll be with Chase soon enough, and you guys can argue this out with the agents—"

"Where's the agent? The guy who was going to get Skylar?" Chris demanded.

"There was no agent—just another pusher who was better disguised," Malcolm said. "Now, I mean it, you two, get the hell out of the way."

Chris Wiley shook his head. "Jake Ferguson was my best friend and, however it played out, you had something to do with him dying. You get the hell out of my way, and you get the hell away from Skylar!"

Chris and Brandon stood together, staring at Sky and Malcolm, hands on their hips, determined.

She couldn't believe it.

Chris had been one of her father's best friends. And Brandon was far from a perfect human being, but they were all far from perfect.

And Kenneth Malcolm...

She turned. And she turned just in time to see him smile and reach behind his back, under his always-perfect jacket, and produce a gun.

"Sorry, Skylar, I was going to try to make this a little easier for you... I really do like your father's songs and the way that you do them, but..."

"Let her go!" Chris demanded. "What, are you going to shoot me, with FBI agents running all over the place?"

"Uh, yeah, no problem."

Kenneth Malcolm fired, and Chris went down and before she could run to him, Malcolm had his hands on her, fingers through her hair, dragging her with him and away from the fallen man and his stricken son.

She let out a scream that could have wakened the dead, but Kenneth Malcolm shouted almost as loudly.

"One more sound out of you and I shoot Brandon, too!"

He aimed at Brandon.

She gritted her teeth, stared at him and said, "Don't you dare—lead the damned way!"

And he did, lifting a ring in the floor and forcing her down a ladder ahead of him.

CHASE HEARD SKYLAR'S scream just as the door slammed shut behind him. He hurried toward the sound and was just in time to see that Chris Wiley was on the ground, bleeding, with Brandon hovering over him, screaming for help.

He paused by Chris, hitting a speed dial that instantly brought Wellington's voice to his ear.

"Man down, we need an ambulance, now," Chase said.

"It's a flesh wound," Chris groaned. "Go, go, go—he's got Skylar."

"Malcolm?"

"He threatened to shoot me, too, if Sky didn't move. She basically told him to go to hell, but...she moved. She wouldn't let him shoot me," Brandon said.

"Please..."

There was no pretense going on anymore; Chase could hear sirens blazing through the night.

"Chris, they're on the way—"

"I'm fine. My shoulder...well, hell, it's good I'm not the drummer!" Chris said.

"Where?"

"Into the floor."

"The floor—a trapdoor, there!" Brandon said, pointing it out. Chase had to admit he hadn't even thought about a stage basement. They didn't use it for their rock shows; when theatrical performances were put on, characters and set pieces could be moved up and down.

He nodded, feeling like an idiot, hurrying to the spot where there was a small metal ring that brought up a three-by-three piece of the flooring, revealing a ladder.

He moved down it cautiously, quickly speaking with Wellington, advising him as to his position and letting him know that the man had Sky.

Only dim light filtered through from above. No one had thought about the area—it wasn't being used.

But then, maybe they'd figured this would just be too simple. Wait and see who was picking up the goods and nab them after making sure that threatened families were safe.

He should have known better. Nothing in life was ever easy. He shouldn't have left Skylar, but if he hadn't...

They would never know that there had been a pass-off, that there were more people involved here than they had imagined.

Malcolm. Chase had thought of him. But he'd also set his name aside because he hadn't been at the other venues. Apparently, this whole thing was bigger than even Wellington had imagined.

He reached the ground. The area was empty, other than a few large storage containers. He drew a penlight from his pocket, desperately searching.

If they had come down here, where the hell—

He saw a panel to his left and determined that it had to slide, lead somewhere.

It did.

Across the area to the rear of the stage, beyond, and to another ladder that led up to...the door backstage. The one he had come through. The one in lockdown now...

But Kenneth Malcolm was the one who managed the venue. The one who had probably studied the blueprints a zillion times over.

He was the one person who would know how to silence alarms and bypass a lockdown.

Swearing, he ripped open the door, heedless of the sound that instantly keened through the venue. The cops were there.

Agents were there. All good men and women, steady people who knew their jobs...

But hadn't known Kenneth Malcolm.

SKYLAR HAD NEVER been below the stage, and she didn't know what to expect once they went down the ladder.

But once they were away from others, she didn't intend to be so obliging.

"Move!" Malcolm told her.

"I'm moving. What? Do you want me to break a leg

and slow you down even more, you idiot? And you are an idiot. Now everyone is going to know who you are and what you did—"

"And no one will give a damn when I'm on a beach in Mexico!" he promised her.

"Oh, am I going to Mexico?"

He started to laugh. "Skylar Ferguson, child of Jake, beloved by all, little nightingale, and now… Well, you guys were good tonight. You know, there are probably a thousand men out there who would love to take you to Mexico! But I'm no fool. You'd kill me the first chance you got."

"Because you're the one who ordered Justin to fix the amp that killed my father," she said flatly.

"No, it was my suggestion, and I was the one on the dark web that gave the order—promising to see that Julia and the kids were killed if he failed—but I'm not the be-all and end-all," he said. "But you look like such a beautiful, sweet thing. I know, however, that you're a raving bitch."

"So what's the deal? You're going to kill me, too?" she asked.

"Not quite yet, not if you try to be a good girl."

"If you're going to kill me anyway, why would I be a good girl?"

"Because there's always hope, right? You can live on the hope that your boy toy will make it to you somehow, or one of his lecturing friends." He laughed. "Hope that you move and that your idiot drummer boy doesn't pop up in front of me, threatening me."

"If not insurance against such a thing, what am I?"

"Okay, you are insurance. But seriously, try to be nice, Skylar. I know you can do it. I've seen you with other people. So behave…"

"I see. You're taking me so you can get to Mexico. I hate to tell you, but it's not going to work."

"And why would that be?"

"They'll shoot down your plane."

"No, they'd kill an innocent pilot. They don't want to do that, right?"

She started to laugh suddenly. "And you think you have a plan that will get you to a plane and off the ground and no one is going to know? You're an idiot—"

"That's not being nice," he warned, thrusting the nose of the gun against her skull.

"Well, you are. If you hadn't come for me, you could have walked out on your own, and no one would have noticed."

"No, that fool knew. He knew when he saw me with the packet."

"The fool? You mean the real FBI agent who came to the dressing-room door."

"He would have told Wellington. I had to take him down, and I'm not sure I killed him, and there you were, so…now you're insurance. And again—"

"Okay, so I'm going with you to a car. Whose car? How—"

"You don't need to worry about whose car."

"Oh, I see. The idiot who picked up the package passed it on to you when he realized that he was seen and being chased. And the FBI agent saw the exchange. And with all the metal detectors, no one other than law-enforcement officials should have had firearms, but you didn't need to bring a firearm in because you'd already stashed one here for emergencies."

"So smart. Wow. A real Einstein."

They were still on the ground. It was dark, but she could see the hatred in his eyes as he shoved her.

"Move, Einstein."

"Where?"

"The panel, you dolt."

"Hey, I've never had an occasion to be down here before!"

"That's right. You horrible, elitist, wretched, conceited performers! You think that you walk on stage and the world adores you. You don't give a damn about anyone working— you just want your music, your drinks and your drugs, and your good old rock 'n' roll."

"That's bull. My father cared about everyone. He cared about kids being given drugs, and he's turning over in his grave right now because you're killing people everywhere with drugs that aren't just addictive, they're lethal—"

"Oh, no, no. I'm just this venue. The king has many subjects. Now, get the hell through the panel."

Sky moved toward it. He reached past her to shove it open.

If she pushed him, if she went for his arm…

"Don't even think about it," he told her.

She pushed the panel, went through the door. They started to move up to the main level again, reaching the door to the backstage parking.

"An alarm will raise all hell. If you just go and leave me—"

"Not on your life!"

"But—"

"You forget. I run this place," he reminded her, smiling grimly.

Of course.

He hit a code in a box by the door and pushed it open. The door silently moved, and they stepped outside.

There were agents everywhere!

Except out here.

Because, of course, they'd had the place locked down. The agents were approaching, questioning and perhaps even searching everyone.

Somewhere busy talking to Chris and Brandon and others...

No. They would know. Brandon would have told them about the entry to the lower-stage area and they would be coming after her...

"Hey!" someone shouted.

But Kenneth Malcolm didn't hesitate. He turned, taking a wild shot, not really caring if it hit its target or not.

They heard the sound of a thud. Someone had hit the ground.

And there was no fire in return.

"So you just killed another innocent?"

"Maybe I just wounded a bastard cop. No time to figure it out."

"After all this, you think your king is going to get you to Mexico? I hear he kills people who don't carry out all his plans."

"I'm not just a flunky."

"Hmm. That could be all the worse!"

"Shut the hell up and move. Over there. That nice little SUV that looks like every other SUV and has the dirtied plates. I am not an idiot, Miss Ferguson. I'm a smart man—the one who will kill you if he has to."

She moved ahead as he prodded her with the gun, praying that whoever had called out to him wasn't dead.

Chase would come after her. She knew it.

But she knew, as well, that she needed to keep herself alive. He'd pointed out that she had no training.

But she had instinct, and she desperately wanted this man brought to justice, to pay for what he had done to her father and others.

She had to watch and wait because...

He would make a mistake. She didn't know when or where, but he would make a mistake.

And when he did, she swore silently to herself, she would be ready.

She had wanted the truth. She had wanted it so badly because there should be no disbelief, no skepticism ever, that her father had found his focus in life, that he had never fallen again, that he had lived for his music—and for others.

She closed her eyes, remembering him. He'd had such strength and such courage. Seeing him, in her mind's eye, in her memories, she knew that he had served his country and more, and he had lived every day of his life with courage, the courage to be his own man, the best husband and the best father.

He had given her music. And so much more.

And this...

Whatever happened, she would face it, manage it, do what she could...

This man had caused her father's death. She wouldn't falter. And with faith in his memory, and men like Chase, she just might make it. And who knew? Others knew that Malcolm had taken her.

Chase knew.

Malcolm had told her about hope. Hope was good to cling to. Hope, courage...and faith.

She had been lucky in life because the men in her life had all three. She would have all three, too.

Chapter Ten

Chase burst out the rear-stage door.

At first, he saw nothing, no one. Then he heard a groan, and he hurried over to the dumpster.

He found another man down and recognized him as Victor Suarez, again, a man he knew to be a good agent.

His eyes were closed; he didn't appear to be moving. But he'd made a sound, and that meant that he had to be alive. Chase called Wellington as he hunkered down, telling him they needed med techs outside as soon as possible. He checked for the man's pulse; his heart was still beating.

His eyes fluttered.

"Black...black SUV," he muttered. "Plates..."

"Hey, help is coming," Chase told him, searching for the injury that had caused the large stain on his lower right gut. He ripped a piece of his shirt, pressing the wound, knowing that the blood flow had to be stopped. "Can you hold this?" he asked. "Victor, the bleeding..."

Suarez nodded and placed his hand on the pressure dressing Chase had created. He pressed down himself.

"Got...it."

"Can you tell me... You said 'plates.' What about the plates?" Chase asked.

"O-obscured," the man said. "Muddied. On purpose, I'd bet. He has her...she's..."

"Hurt? Is she hurt?"

The man on the ground moved his mouth. No sound came, but he formed the word *no*.

Then he winced and managed to open his eyes, looking up at Chase. "Go! You've—you've got help coming. I think... I was a damned idiot, warning him...should have shot him flat out. No, right, we are the law, we don't just commit murder, but..."

Black SUV, plates obscured.

The man's eyes opened again. "Mic and buds...take my mic. Easier..."

"Thanks, thank you!"

Brilliant idea. He reached gently for the little button on the man's collar and even more lightly for the buds in his ears.

"Wellington, have you—"

"Got you loud and clear. And help is there. EMTs are headed out the door right now."

"Thanks. I see them, and I'm heading out after Sky. She may have her phone in her pocket, and he may not have thought of it if she didn't pull it out. Can you—"

"You bet. I'll get a trace on the location."

"Thanks. I'm heading out."

"Listen, I can get a trace on her phone going, but it will take me a few minutes. You can hold position—"

"No. I've got something else I have to do quickly," Chase said suddenly. "Get back to me, please, as soon as possible."

The med techs had arrived, and Chase stood, nodded to them and took off. His car was just a few feet away.

There was only one exit from the passenger lot, but he needed to think.

Where the hell would the man be going?

But first things first: he was going to take a lightning-quick side trip. Sky's place was close.

If it came to a point where he might need help...

There might be no better help than some he had quickly available to him.

He was out and moving in seconds. At Sky's house, he was grateful he knew the code as well as he knew his own.

He was in and out in seconds with Larry at his heels.

"Now, boy, where did he take her? He should be calling, asking for money, demanding clearance to get away... something. Unless..."

The *unless* was just grim. She might be a human shield for him, insurance, a hostage for bargaining.

Where? Esposito was still somewhere—he hadn't gone to the homes where he had sent his assassins to take care of the families of the men who had failed him.

Would he welcome Kenneth Malcolm, anyway?

As he anxiously asked himself questions, he heard Wellington's voice. "You're right, Chase, she's got her phone on her. He's heading west, out of the city. There's a small airport there... He's no good to his cartel king anymore, but he's got a major payoff on him, and there's a small airport—"

"I know it," Chase told him quickly. "I know exactly where it is."

"Sending backup."

"Fast as you can."

"We've got the control tower. They'll stall on the plane."

"Gotcha. Thanks."

He turned toward the highway, glad he knew the city and the route to take.

Grateful, too, when Wellington's voice came to him again.

"He had one hell of a lead, but you're closing in. The airport is right ahead—"

"Yeah. I know."

"Backup—"

"May be too late. Still no sign of Miguel—"

"No. As I told you, the families are safe. Agents got his assassins, and I think one of them is a major player. That part of the takedown went as planned—even though we were hoping these were hits the man might have wanted to take himself." He was silent just a moment and added, "We should have been on Malcolm," Wellington said.

"*I* should have been on him," Chase said, furious with himself that he had missed the man. But they hadn't known the scope of what was happening.

Now they did.

"Half a mile. I think they're turning into the airport."

"Yeah."

Chase was on them. They *were* turning into the small airport. But he knew that if Malcolm saw him, he'd probably shoot Sky on the spot just to kill her, because he wouldn't go down alone.

He drove the car to the side of the road, drew his weapon and warned Larry, "Stay close to me! Duty, Larry. We're on duty."

Larry gave a little sound of agreement. He'd been trained in many disciplines and was still a police dog to the core.

Chase leaped over the small fence, followed by Larry, and they headed along the outer shell of the place, watching as the black SUV came to a halt.

"Stealth mode, Larry," he said.

He hadn't had much of a chance to work with the dog, but he had faith that Sky had been given one of the best, an animal deserving a good life after taking a few shots in the line of duty.

Creeping along the buildings, they came within earshot as Malcolm got out of the car.

Sky apparently had no intention of helping him. He walked around to the passenger's seat, searching the area as he did so, grabbing her arm and dragging her out of the car.

"Now!" he told her harshly.

Larry was tense, letting out a low growl.

"Steady, boy, steady. On my command," Chase told him.

He could hear Sky. She wasn't rolling over—or shaking in fear.

"Why? You said you didn't want to take me to Mexico!" she said harshly.

Malcolm was looking at the plane, frowning. "Where the hell's the damned pilot?" He drew his gun, looking around.

As he asked the question, a man appeared at the top of the short flight of stairs leading to the body of the jet.

It wasn't the pilot.

Chase had never seen him in person before, but he'd seen pictures on the screens at the New Orleans offices.

It was Miguel Esposito, head of the major crime ring behind it all.

"So, here you are!" Esposito said to Malcolm. "And with a hostage. You have the money?"

"Right here," Malcolm told him. "Yeah, I've got a hostage."

"So…who do we have here?"

"Just a disposable, as soon as we get the bird in the air free and clear."

"Ah, but maybe not so quickly!" Esposito said, eyeing Sky with amusement.

"Disposable, trust me. She's trouble," Malcolm said.

"But so are you. You screwed the pooch, Malcolm. We lost major players."

"That wasn't me!" Malcolm told him. "Idiots—"

"Idiots you dragged into the ring, *mi amigo.*"

"I've got the money. The operation wasn't going to run forever. I did my part."

Malcolm was dragging Sky to the plane, looking back to see if anyone was coming.

"Well, we have a long flight in which to discuss the future," Esposito said. "For now…send up the *chica*!"

Chase quickly weighed his options—and his chances. Sky was with two men who were hardened killers, both armed. While it would be one hell of a thing to bring down Esposito, Sky was his priority. If he shot, he had to do so damned fast: kill one, the other might instantly aim at her and…

Esposito turned back into the plane. Malcolm was forcing Sky up the small set of stairs.

But Sky was apparently going for broke. Even though Malcolm held his weapon loosely in his hand.

Maybe she knew that Malcolm would eventually have his way. That Esposito might have fun with her for a bit, but eventually…

She wasn't suicidal, Chase knew.

But she was no one's patsy.

She spun suddenly, quicker than lightning, slamming a knee into Malcolm so hard that he teetered on the first step behind her and started to fall. And Sky was ready to pounce, ready to fly for the gun he was holding.

But she might not make it.

Chase wasn't alone: he had Larry.

He fired.

His aim was true. He caught Malcolm dead center in the back of the head, and the man went down.

Esposito reappeared, gun out. He didn't know what had happened, but he was ready to take on the woman who had already leaped down the last steps and ducked behind the ladder in hopes of reaching for Malcolm's weapon which had now flown just steps away…

But Esposito didn't see her right away. Of course, he would have known from the sound of the shot that it had been fired from a distance.

"Now, boy, now!"

Larry went running out for his new mistress, barking and growling furiously.

Esposito was distracted, trying to take aim at a dog that seemed to have the speed of a greyhound.

Chase stepped out where he could be seen.

Esposito whirled around, taking aim at him then.

Not fast enough.

Chase had known exactly where he was aiming, and with Esposito determined to fire, he had no choice.

He fired himself. The king went down. Sky emerged from her ducking stance beneath the steps.

Larry threw himself at her, and she almost fell backward again, taking the giant pup into her arms. She soothed the dog, assuring him she was all right, and stared at Chase incredulously.

He ran toward her, just as an explosion of sirens burst into the air, and the backup he'd been promised came barreling through the gates to the private airfield.

SKY COULDN'T SPEAK as she held Larry, and Chase came to take them both into his arms. She'd been thinking that she was an idiot—when she'd been thinking at all. Fear had all but paralyzed her when she'd seen that she wasn't up against just one man with a gun but two.

And still…

She wasn't going to be taken. She wasn't going to be tortured before she was killed. There had been no choice. Her plan had been to throw Kenneth Malcolm off so badly that she'd seriously injure him and grab the gun and then duck under the plane until she got a chance to either *try* to shoot the other man or somehow escape.

She'd thought she had a chance.

Because while she might have been *disposable*, she was certain that, to the man on the plane, Kenneth Malcolm was equally disposable. And whoever the other man had been, Malcolm had caused him some considerable trouble.

Considering the consequences, if Kenneth Malcolm was down, he might have shrugged it off and left without her.

No. Probably not. But there was always hope, even if it hadn't done too much for Malcolm.

She'd prayed that help might be coming...

How, she wasn't sure. But Chris and Brandon had known that Malcolm had her and...

"Oh, my God!" She found speech at last, pulling away from Chase and asking him desperately, "You got Larry. You and Larry—but, oh! Chase! Chris! Chris Wiley. He was shot, and a man in the parking lot—"

"They are being taken care of. I truly believe they're both going to make it," Chase assured her. "Skylar...oh, God, Skylar!"

"You came in time!" she told him. "How...?"

She loved the smile that touched his lips. "Well, Larry and I were pretty good. But you, Skylar Ferguson, gave us what we needed when you fought for yourself!" he whispered. "I don't know if you were entirely foolish or amazingly brave."

Looking into his eyes, she shook her head.

"I couldn't get into that plane. I just knew I couldn't!"

"Well, we can talk more later!" he murmured.

He didn't let her go, but he turned to the first man who came rushing from one of the cars that had burst onto the field, briefing him quickly on what had happened.

The man nodded, wanting to know if there was anyone else anywhere, and Chase told him that they hadn't seen a pilot and didn't know if anyone else was in the plane, but if so, they hadn't appeared.

Other agents were out of their cars, communicating in a way that Sky didn't understand. But two headed up the steps to the plane, one right behind the other, weapons drawn, ready for what they would encounter within.

Another car drove in.

It was Wellington himself who jumped out, rushing over to them. He looked anxiously from Sky to Chase, frowning.

"You got Malcolm—and *Miguel Esposito*?" he exclaimed.

"I had some help," Chase said, managing a grin. "A really great dog—and then a true heroine not about to go anywhere quietly."

Wellington frowned, once again looking from Chase to Sky.

"And Larry. Hmm. They may want that dog back," Wellington said.

"They're not getting him!" Sky said, smiling. Her eyes fell on Malcolm and then Esposito, and she shivered and looked away.

She was so grateful to be alive.

And still...she wanted to be away from the blood and the horror and the fear.

"It will all be in my report," Chase said, "but there's something I never knew about Sky. She's got one hell of a kick and a tremendous sense of balance. It helped that Esposito ducked back into the plane at the right moment and Sky had made a dive to safety. But—"

"Sir!"

One of the agents who had gone into the plane reappeared.

"Yes, Cooper. Empty?"

"No, sir. Just a terrified woman who doesn't speak English. My Spanish isn't great, but I think that she was kidnapped and forced to act as a server on the plane and—and I'm not sure what else. She was hiding on the floor in the galley."

Wellington nodded. "We'll get her some help and figure out her situation. Can you talk her down so we can bring her in?"

The agent nodded. The woman emerged, looking at them terrified. Then she saw Esposito's body, fallen to the tarmac.

She let out a cry, but it wasn't a cry of loss or pain.

It was one of relief. Shaking, she turned into the arms of the agent who had to catch her before she, too, became a casualty of the short flight of steps.

"It's okay, you're okay, you're going to be okay!" the agent reassured her.

He helped her down, and as he escorted her to one of the vehicles, she looked over at Chase and Sky and suddenly broke away, running to hug Sky, speaking so quickly.

Sky, knocked a foot away from Chase, thought that the poor woman had been a victim—like so many others. Kidnapped? Maybe members of her family had been threatened, too.

Larry was amazing; he didn't growl. He knew the woman was no threat. The shepherd/Lab mix sensed her fear and trauma and leaned his furry body next to both her and Sky.

Sky wasn't sure what to do, but she hugged the woman back, smoothing her hair and telling her that it was going to be okay.

The woman broke away at last, hugged Chase and then hurried to join the agent.

"We'll find out more about her," Wellington said, looking at Sky and smiling. "Maybe you should be on our payroll."

She smiled and shook her head. "Um… I think I'll stick to teaching kids."

"Far more dangerous!" Wellington said lightly. He hesitated. "We're going to need a debriefing on all this, of course. And Sky, I'm sorry, I hope you're feeling up to—"

"I'm here. I'm alive. And I'm up to anything needed," she said. "But, please, do you know anything more about Chris and the other man?"

"In surgery as we speak, but the prognosis on both is

good," Wellington told her. "So I'm afraid that there are a few things that still need attention…"

Chase was smiling at her. "She is the bravest individual I know," he said. "And we'll be fine. Paperwork. It comes with everything."

Medical techs had arrived; gurneys were coming out. Forensic crews were heading onto the plane.

"You are something!" Chase told her very softly. He hesitated. "You are your father's daughter."

"And that," she told him, "is the greatest compliment I could receive. Thank you. And thank you—and Larry. You saved my life."

"You saved your own life. And Larry played his part, distracting Esposito after Malcolm was down."

She hugged the dog again. "And to think I didn't even know I needed a dog! But Larry, I promise you the best treats forever and ever."

She saw Chase smiling slightly and turned to him. "Do I get the best treats forever, too?" he asked.

"Yeah. This time, forever—and ever!" she promised.

Chapter Eleven

The night was long.

"Worst part of the job," Chase teased as they sat at headquarters. He had to speak lightly. He was afraid that if he didn't, if he thought of the way it might have all ended, he'd cease being rational.

He thought about Sky, about meeting as kids...friends. Friends who came together again when they were of age, friends who fell in love then, and...

Maybe there were such things as soulmates. He hadn't lived like a monk, but in the years between he'd just never fallen in love. He'd had relationships, but...

Nothing right.

Then, when it seemed that pretend might turn to reality—or might have been real all along whether that had been admitted or not—he might have lost her.

Forever.

"Hey!"

Sky touched his arm. It was morning; there really hadn't been a night. But despite her worry that they bring Larry back home and give him the assurances he needed, she'd insisted that they get to the hospital.

Miraculously, while several agents had been injured, none had been killed.

And Chris Wiley was going to be fine.

When they arrived at the hospital, Chase told Sky,

"We're going to have to see Hank quickly before anyone else. He won't believe that *you* are okay if he doesn't see you himself. We'll be brief because I know—"

"I'm happy to see Hank and then Chris," she replied.

"And we'll check in on Bobby Sacks, too. Bobby was a hell of a help in this."

"Oh, did they find out anything about the woman—"

"Alina Gomez. She's fine. Wellington is going to help get her asylum status. Esposito's goons killed her father for refusing to distribute his goods at a school. Then, he just swept up Alina as his personal property. She's going to be fine," he reiterated.

She smiled. "Okay, onward to Hank and then Chris!"

Chase's grandfather was awake when they entered the room.

"About time!" he boomed. "Thankfully, I didn't know about most of this until it was over. You two…you know, you did good. You did really good. But don't do it again! You scared the bejesus out of me!"

Chase and Sky both gave him hugs, and Hank told them that he'd be transferring into rehab the next day, and that by the end of the month…

"I'll be drumming my heart out again! And you!" he said, wagging a finger at Chase.

"Gramps, I—"

"I'm not suggesting that you quit anything. You don't have to worry. The news is filled with the whole event, but a lot is focused on you—not as an agent, Chase, but just as the drummer who went after his beloved. The word is out there that supposedly law enforcement brought down a major drug ring and just that you…you're a hot drummer and lover. And you, Miss Ferguson! Like a new age Disney princess, kicking ass!"

"Um, thanks," Sky murmured.

"Your dad…well, you know what I believe? I believe he

was looking out for you from the clouds, and that… My God, girl, he would be so proud. No, I believe we'll meet again. He is proud. And your mother—"

Sky let out a squeak. "Oh, my God! I haven't called my mother, and she'll see the news!"

"Maybe you should do that," Hank said.

The look Sky gave Chase was a little panicked. He smiled and told her, "Step out, give her a ring. Make sure she knows that you didn't get so much as a bruise from the whole thing."

Sky nodded and went out into the hall.

Hank watched her leave and turned to Chase.

"Don't let her get away this time," he said.

"Well, I didn't mean to let her get away *last* time."

"Make it permanent, then," Hank said.

"Gramps, I can't force her into something. These have been the most intense days of my life, but we've just gotten together again—"

"I don't think that either of you were ever really apart. You know, I remember when Jake fell in love with Mandy. There had never been anyone he loved like her before in his life, and he knew that there never would be again."

"I know that Sky is all that to me," Chase told him. "But I can't make her—"

"Marry you?"

He turned. Sky was back in the room, grinning and looking relieved as she walked in.

He ignored the question first, asking her anxiously, "Your mom?"

"Oh, she's mad at me, but she says that she's way more relieved than angry. And she's coming home from Ireland. I told her the events were over…but she's coming home."

"That's great! I look forward to seeing her," Hank said. "Now, as to the other. This big, brave undercover agent is afraid to ask you to marry him."

"Gramps!" Chase protested.

But Skylar turned to him, grinning. "Yes, of course."

"Pardon?"

"Oh, come on. Don't make your grandfather do everything! Yes, I think we should definitely get married. I don't want a crazy wedding. I want our families. And Skyhawk. Oh, wait. Skyhawk is kind of my father's other kid, so that's family, too."

He looked at her. He'd loved her forever. And maybe that was why time had slipped away, and why time, now, was everything.

They weren't going to waste any more of it.

But two could play the game.

"Sure," he said. "I'll marry you."

They both laughed. And it was, in truth, nice that right there, in his grandfather's hospital room, he drew her into his arms for a kiss that was a promise for a lifetime.

"Okay, okay, get a room!" Hank said, shaking his head. "Oh, yeah, you have rooms. Nope, you have houses. So..."

"We still need to see Chris, and I want to check on Bobby Sacks," Chase told him.

"Then, go do it. You can stop by tomorrow afternoon and see me here. Rehab place after that, and I'll be working hard, I promise. I'm not handing over my drum set entirely yet!"

"You better not do that," Chase warned him. "I'm not ready. All this is..."

"It's a lot," Hank agreed. "All this tonight...and I was here. Well, thankfully, they're going to let me see Chris soon. Maybe now! Hey, ring the nurse. See if you can walk me into his room."

"They'll want you in a wheelchair," Chase said.

"They can put me in a rocket ship if they want. I'd just really like to see my old friend."

"I'm on it," Sky said, hurrying out.

In a minute she was back with a wheelchair—and a nurse. The nurse saw to it that her charge was safely seated.

"Now, please, this isn't at all regular... You shouldn't even be visiting at this hour, but keep the noise level down. It's just five a.m., and the patients need their rest!"

"Yes, ma'am!" Chris promised.

"Well, good to see you all. Mr. Wiley needs to sleep, but he's too worried about events and Miss Ferguson and... please. Go in."

They entered, and Sky hurried to Chris's side, taking his hand.

As she did so, Chase noticed that Brandon was asleep in a chair by the window.

And Mark Reynolds was there, too, standing now, though he'd been seated in a chair by the bed. Chase realized that Joe Garcia was also in Chris's room and he smiled, surprised that the hospital had turned a blind eye to so many visitors.

Especially at this hour, as the nurse had pointed out. But they were there.

Skyhawk was there. The old group, friends before they'd been a band. All—thankfully—innocent of the machinations and terror going on around them.

Chris looked up at Sky, smiled and squeezed her hand.

"I was so worried!" Sky told him.

"We all were," Mark Reynolds said quietly. "Worried about you, too—crazy worried about you."

"I'm fine, I'm fine. It was Chris who was shot!" Sky said.

"Chris, what did they tell you? I mean, you were in surgery—" Chase began.

"Funny thing is, the guy played so many people—but he was a lousy shot," Chris said. "Caught me below the bone, didn't even shatter anything. They got the bullet out, they sewed me up, and I'm just about as good as can be."

"Hey, Chris is tough!" Joe said.

Brandon had woken up, and he blinked and stood, coming over to the bed. "Dad! You are not good as new. You're going to behave. You were warned that the big fear is going to be infection, and you'll have to be careful—"

"I will!" Chris argued. "You're the wild child."

"Not so much anymore, trust me," Brandon said, looking around at all of them. His eyes fell on Sky. "And you!" he said softly, turning to Chase. "She walked out with Malcolm, you know, because he threatened to kill me."

"But it all worked out!" Sky said.

"How the hell?" Brandon asked.

"Teamwork!" Chase said. "Sky kicked ass, Larry distracted the one guy, and…"

"You brought 'em down," Brandon finished. "It's been all over the news. Right now, a lot of confusion. Apparently, reporters know that Esposito was running a major drug-distribution ring through several venues. Working with people like Malcolm—threatening families, little children—to get what they wanted done. Right now, they're just saying that members of Skyhawk were injured, but that—hmm, how did they put it, Dad?"

"They said that members of Skyhawk held their own and helped bring down a crew of major criminals. People knew you were kidnapped, Sky, and they knew that Chase came after you—I think they even knew a dog was involved, but the reporters have been shockingly careful about what they're reporting. Still…"

"Still, there's going to be enough publicity to make us all crazy…and rise to the top of the charts!" Mark said. He shook his head. "But that's not what matters. I'm just grateful, so incredibly grateful, that we're all here. That Chris is going to be okay, that Hank is on the mend. That Sky and Chase—"

"And Larry!"

"And Larry? Okay, the thing is, we made it. And we

know the truth behind what happened to Jake, all those years ago, Jake meant to get it all torn down. And… Chase, Sky, you knew. The rest of us were devastated but never saw it as anything other than an accident. We always knew that Jake was best, and thanks to him, we all know how to be our best, and thanks to you, Sky, and you, Chase, we've all survived—and lots of people will live. All is good. Hey, I could pass out some Jell-O and we could all toast one another?" Mark finished.

They all laughed softly.

"Think I'll pass on the hospital Jell-O," Chase told them. "And I want to go and check on Bobby quickly. If they'll let me, of course."

"I think they'll let you do just about anything tonight— or this morning," Hank asserted.

Chase nodded. He glanced at Sky and smiled and slipped out into the quiet hall. He spoke briefly to the police officer on duty, who assured him that he was welcome to look in on Bobby Sacks, though the patient might be sleeping.

But when Chase stepped silently into the room, Bobby's eyes were open.

"I'd hoped you'd stop by to see me!" Bobby said. "I…oh, man, I've got to admit, after I talked to you, I was pretty terrified. Because there were layers to what was going on, people who did know who the players were, people who didn't…and everyone worried about their loved ones if they didn't follow through. But…is the news real? They say the FBI brought down the kingpin, but they say that they followed you, that you were involved."

"I think it's safe, Bobby. And I just wanted to say I know that you were scared to say anything. You did. You talked, even terrified. So you were a help, just as much as anyone."

Bobby smiled. "That's great news. I have other great news."

"That's great. Really great!"

Bobby's smile deepened. "I'm going to live! No permanent damage to my major organs. Somehow... Well, you really saved my life. I owe it to you."

"No. You owe a good life to yourself," Chase told him. He patted Bobby's shoulder. "Just stick with it, keep getting better and better. And right now, I'm going to leave you before they throw me out."

Bobby nodded. "Thank you!"

Chase nodded and waved, leaving Bobby's room and heading back to Chris's.

The nurse met him in the hall.

"There are sick people in this hospital, Mr. McCoy. Now, I am aware it was a difficult night for you all, but you've seen your friends and your grandfather, and now it's time for you to leave," she informed him.

He smiled. "Yes, ma'am. We'll be getting right out of here," he promised.

Stepping back into Chris's room, he saw that everyone in the room seemed comfortable and relaxed. His grandfather sat in his wheelchair, Chris was in his bed, Joe was on the chair in the corner with Brandon perched on the edge of it, Mark was still standing by the bed, and Skylar was seated at the foot of it.

They all looked up when he came in.

"Bobby Sacks?" Mark asked.

"Pulling through fine, too," Chase informed them. "But we've just been thrown out. Hank, we need to wheel you back, and the rest of us—"

"Need to go. Right. But we'll see you in the morning," Brandon promised his father.

"It is morning!" Chris reminded him. "Go home, all of you. Adrenaline has run out. You had a great show—and then all hell broke loose. Go!"

"Wait!" Hank said. "Someone has an announcement for us."

Hank stared at him hard.

"Oh! Yes, we do—"

"But we don't have a date, we want to see my mom—" Sky began.

"Oh, my God, took you two long enough!" Brandon exclaimed. "Wow, and yay!"

"Legacy," Mark said, looking around the room. "Chase, Sky, beautiful. We couldn't be happier for you. We'll have to hire a band for the wedding because—"

"Because we hope you'll all be celebrating with us!" Sky said.

"Because the lead singer will be a bit busy," Joe said, laughing. "Seriously, guys, we couldn't be happier. And I know that...somewhere..."

"My dad is happy and proud," Sky finished.

"So before the demon nurse gets back," Chris said jokingly, "we should probably clear out. You have to roll me back to my own room, and then—"

Apparently, the group did still think alike. It was almost as if they'd planned it, rehearsed.

Chris, Mark, Joe, Hank and Brandon all shouted, "Get a room!"

Larry. Larry was the best dog ever, Sky was convinced.

When they reached her house, her first move was to drop down by the dog and embrace him, scratching and petting him, telling him just how much she loved him.

Larry, of course, lapped it up.

Chase hunkered down by her, stroking the dog as well.

She looked at him. "Hmm. Trey Montgomery was a lecturer turned dog rescuer and trainer?"

Chase shrugged. "Trey spent thirtysomething years of his life working with the police canine division. He worked with all manner of disciplines—drug dogs, cadaver dogs, missing-persons dogs—and he had several of his own that could do just about anything." He hesitated. "I told him that—that I needed a dog for a very good and loving person who seldom thought about her own danger. Larry had taken a few bullets, and like any good cop, he was rewarded with retirement. But…"

"In the middle of all that happened, you thought to come back for him," Sky said.

"I was afraid I might have followed you into the bayou or a forest or… I didn't know. But I knew that if it was necessary, Larry could follow your trail. As it happened, we didn't need to find you. But everything was on split-second timing, and Larry bought us what we needed." He hesitated. "I was so afraid that if…"

"That if you hadn't gotten there when you did, Malcolm or Esposito would have shot me?" she asked, smiling. "Well, my plan was to knock him down and get his gun and hope that I could fire it," she informed him. "I mean, I did have a plan. I knew I wasn't just getting on that plane. But…"

"But?"

She smiled. "You did come."

He leaned over, delicately kissing her lips. "How did we let the years go by?" he whispered.

She shook her head. "It was my fault."

"No. There is no fault. Sky, I couldn't put the past to rest, either. And Wellington is an amazing man, brilliant at what he does. He believed in me—which was important. Of course, there were also a number of bad things happening around the state. They'll still be trying to clean it all up, but that's going to be for other agents. Hey, no one does this job alone, trust me."

"And yet you've managed to keep it secret—undercover you!"

He shrugged. "No one expects a guy born with a silver spoon in his mouth to run around really working."

Sky smiled and nodded. "Are we really getting married?"

He adjusted to be on his knees, dodging one of Larry's paws as the dog rolled over, expecting a belly rub.

"Larry, wait your turn!" Chase said. Then he turned to Sky. "Skylar Ferguson, it would be the greatest honor of my life if you would marry me. Um... I'm supposed to have a diamond. I'll take care of that—"

"I don't really care about the jewelry," she assured him. "You gave me a few amazing gifts already."

"Oh?"

"Well, Larry for one."

"Larry is cool. I grant you that."

"And in truth, you gave me my life."

"No, kid. You are your father's daughter. You had everything to do with saving your own life."

"Okay, then...you're giving me something I value as much."

"What's that?"

"You're putting *your* life in my hands!"

He leaned over the dog, taking Sky into his arms, kissing her long and deeply with all the emotion from the depths of his heart.

Larry let out a little disgruntled moan of protest, and they broke apart, laughing.

"I'll see to Larry's bowls and all," Chase said.

"I'll start the shower."

"Yeah, shower, that will be good."

"All touch of monsters gone!" she told him.

And that was it. They scrambled up, Chase heading for the kitchen, Sky streaking up the stairs. She realized how much had happened, and all in the last sixteen hours or so.

And now...

She wanted a good, hot spray. Lots of heat and tons of mist. She stepped in ahead of Chase, glad to have the heat, to feel renewed from all that had gone on.

She'd been so close to...

Death.

But now life loomed ahead of her. She had been right: she and Chase—with the help of agents, police and friends—had proven the truth of the man her father had been, never careless, always clean, always caring about others.

And even before that...

She had realized what she had thrown away. But Chase had never forgotten. Never really left her. And now they had a chance.

He slipped in behind her. She felt the heat of his body, deeper, more encompassing than any other. She turned into his arms, and with the water sluicing over them they kissed and touched and scrubbed. They managed to laugh as the soap slipped to the tub bottom, as they both reached for it, crashing into one another, nearly falling, catching each other...touching and kissing again.

Then they were out, so they wouldn't fall, drying, laughing...

Making their way back to the bedroom.

Making love.

She had no clue how many hours passed, but at one point, she rolled over, half-asleep, and noticed that there was a gun on the bedside table, not the one he'd had earlier—

He noticed her curiosity.

"A service weapon is always taken when it's been fired under such circumstances," he told her. "They'll return my regular one."

"And that—"

"Is a personal backup. I think... I think it's over. But like it or not, fame follows what we've done and..."

"You went into what you do because you knew that something had happened and happened very wrong," Sky said seriously, looking into his eyes. "I don't know everything you've done through the years, but I know it's been important to you."

"I—I can stop."

She shook her head. "No, Chase. You're the man I love. And you're the man I love because of all your determination, because you do want... Well, none of us can fix the world, but you want to do what you can to stop very bad things. I don't want you to change."

He ran his fingers gently through her hair, shaking his head. "You are amazing. And you—"

"I love what I do. I'm not always sure I'm changing the world, but I love kids. I love working with them, and I always hope that I've given them something that they can love, that they can do, that can keep them from...other things."

He nodded. "I love kids, too. We are having a few, right?"

"Five or six."

"What?"

She laughed. "One at a time, and we'll see how it goes."

"Legacy!" he teased.

"Legacy. So..."

"We don't have to be anywhere at all today. We can just..."

"All right!"

She rolled back into his arms.

A while later, they finally slept. And it was night when they woke up, ran down to take Larry out and dig around in the kitchen.

And then, of course, they realized that they had dozens of missed phone calls, and that while the night of both amazement and horror was over, other things might be just beginning.

But that was okay.

Because now they both knew they had a lifetime together.

Epilogue

The events at the arena had naturally created a media sensation. While Sky would rather have been kept out of everything, there were too many people who had been involved, and the coverage went on for weeks.

And, in due time, Mandy Ferguson returned from Ireland, a pile of mixed emotions. She had been terrified for her only child, and then, of course, grateful.

She didn't seem the least surprised that Sky and Chase were together again.

"Honey, honey, you are the best daughter, loving your dad so much!" she told Sky as she hugged her repeatedly. "I mean...who knew we were waiting for this, but..."

Unsurprisingly, Sky was wanted for interviews. At first, she'd wanted nothing to do with them. And then she realized that she didn't want to be seen as a pathetic victim, but when he'd talked to the press, Chase had let them all know that she'd been instrumental in saving her own life.

And she was grateful—grateful, too, that was Chase just being... Chase.

More than anything else, she wanted the world to know that they were all lucky, that all law enforcement involved had been exemplary, and that it had been a far-reaching thing.

And even now, years after his death, they could be grateful to her father: he'd been the one to first realize what had been going on, and it had been the knowledge that he would never have let it go on that had gotten him killed.

Amazingly, Chase being undercover was never revealed. He had just so happened to be the drummer that night.

And in interviews, he would just smile and remind the world that he'd acted like any man in love—he'd gone to find his fiancée.

In the midst of it all, Hank McCoy was let out of the hospital. The rehab he was going to be at for the next several weeks was in Arizona and, as much as she loved her home state, Sky was ready to leave it for a while.

Mandy suggested that they all head to Arizona for a while, find a quiet place and let things settle down.

Sky wasn't so sure; she made her own schedule. Chase didn't.

But Wellington came through. At Sky's house, visiting the happy couple, getting to know Mandy, he assured Chase that a vacation was going to be something that he both needed and deserved.

And so they headed out to Arizona to spend some time simply getting away.

They planned a small wedding because Sky really wanted it to be special with just the guests they knew and loved in attendance. They would head to her favorite church in New Orleans, and the service itself would be part of Jazz Mass.

Their reception would be small as well. They would have it at home.

Something else happened while they were in Arizona.

A second romance bloomed.

Chris's wife had been gone many years.

And at first...

It just seemed like two old friends spending time together, making the days go by. Mandy was in good health—

always grateful for it, she often assured Sky—and she was very happy to be there and help Chris through his rehab.

Wonderful.

They were often together working while Sky and Chase headed off to the OK Corral, a museum, Sedona, or...

Just off alone!

But when Chris had finished his rehab and they were all seated in the little house they had rented for the stay, Mandy said seriously that she had something to tell them.

They gathered around the kitchen table.

Mandy lowered her head. "We're going to be m—"

Sky glanced at Chase, frowning, and Chase glanced back at her.

"What's happened? Has something happened, suggested that anything bad is going to happen? M—murdered?"

Mandy looked up at them. "Married! We're going to be married. I'm sorry. I mean, we never want to upset you kids and, Sky, I know how you felt—"

Sky couldn't help it. She broke out into relieved laughter.

"Mom! The one thing I know for sure about Dad is how much he loved you—and he loved Chris, too. If I know anything at all about my father, he'd want you both to be happy!"

Her mom jumped up and ran around to hug her.

They all wound up standing. Hugging. Laughing and happy.

"But," Sky said, "no double wedding!"

Mandy laughed. "We're running off to Vegas."

"That'll work," Chase assured them.

"Well, we mean today!"

"Go for it!" Sky said.

And so, Mandy and Chris went on to Vegas, and Sky and Chase returned home. And in another month, they had the small but beautiful wedding she had wanted, and even though she loved every minute of it, the wedding it-self hadn't mattered.

Making something wonderfully real on paper that already lived in her heart and soul did. And, of course, at the house for the reception...

They didn't hire another band. They wound up jamming...

And when Mark Reynolds asked her what the future would bring, she assured him, "Chase and I have to live our own lives, but we will be around!"

She lifted her glass and said, "Skyhawk forever!"

Her words were echoed by the group.

Chase slipped around behind her, pulling her tight.

"*Sky-lar and Chase forever*!"

She smiled, leaning against him.

"Sky-lar and Chase. Forever and ever and ever!"

And she knew that it would be so.

* * * * *

A Q&A with Heather Graham

What or who inspired you to write?
I think many factors in my life inspired me—my mom
came from Ireland with all kinds of wonderful books to
read and my dad's family were Scots with all manner of
great books as well. From an early age, I was devouring
everything that they had. But I also had a truly eccentric
great-grandmother who told endless stories about fantasy
creatures. She once caught a leprechaun but let him go
without getting his gold because he cried so hard. She also
managed to tell my sister and I, "Don't be misbehavin'! The
banshees be gettin' ye in the outhouse!" We were teenagers
when we realized we never had an outhouse!

What is your daily writing routine?
I think it's just like a Dr. Seuss book. I started writing with
five small children and I wrote when I could. Turned out to
be a great way to learn self-discipline and keep going. The
kids are grown up but we all know that life can intrude on
any schedule. Therefore, I can still write on a plane, on a
train, in a car, going far!

Who are your favorite authors?
I have way too many to say! But a favorite book of all time?
A Tale of Two Cities!

Where do your story ideas come from?
Life! Places, people, the news. I do love to travel anywhere and having five kids paid off—their friends grew up to become detectives, US Marshals, and one of my sons' friends became my favorite: a "fabricator." She creates the charming characters we see on ads and in movies, costumes for "superheroes" and more. I toured the studios where she worked seeing an adorable, smiling pig next to the creepiest zombie ever. The experience gave me a great character!

Do you have a favorite travel destination?
I have several. New Orleans is considered to be my home away from home. I love my mom's home, Ireland, and, of course, Scotland. I also love Italy—and New Zealand! New York, Chicago, tons of places in California…oh, Dubai! I am so grateful that I have been able to see so many wonderful places.

What is your most treasured possession?
I'm not a "thing" person. My favorite things in this world are all people, family, friends—and those friends I've not yet met!

How did you meet your current love?
I met Dennis at a Halloween party when I was a teenager. We were married when I was eighteen after graduation and went off to college together. The kids like to say that "It's been trick or treat ever since!"

How did you celebrate or treat yourself when you got your first book deal?
Mainly, just being grateful and amazed. But way back, I was honored to earn RWA's Lifetime Achievement Award and when I received the call, my granddaughter Chynna was the only one there and she was about six at the time.

She stared at me very concerned and said worriedly, "But you're not dead yet!" Celebrated with dinner out—as we did when I gratefully learned that I was to receive the Thriller Master Award as well. And again, thankfully while I'm still here!

Will you share your favorite reader response?
Hmm. Well, I can tell you my strangest. I was at an American Booksellers Association event signing books when a young man asked me to sign his arm. I thought it strange, but I smiled and signed his arm. He came back the next day to show me he'd had the signature tattooed on!

Other than author, what job would you like to have?
I started out life working in the theater, children's theater, and then dinner theater and commercial work. But when our third child was born, I couldn't spend the time away anymore. I bought *Writer's Digest* and *Writer's Market* and started looking at where to send things, what kind of work, and to who. My first sale was a short horror story to *The Twilight Zone Magazine*. And then, thankfully, a book sold! To this day, I love theater, and my kids say that I became a writer so that I could write my own dinner theater scripts for certain conferences and, of course, cast myself in them!

Juno Rushdan is a veteran US Air Force intelligence officer and award-winning author. Her books are action-packed and fast-paced. Critics from *Kirkus Reviews* and *Library Journal* have called her work "heart-pounding James Bond-ian adventure" that "will captivate lovers of romantic thrillers." For a free book, visit her website: www.junorushdan.com.

Visit the Author Profile page at Harlequin.com.

WYOMING MOUNTAIN INVESTIGATION

Juno Rushdan

For all the survivors of tragedy
who never lost faith or hope.

Prologue

Wild Horse Ranch
Located between Laramie and Bison Ridge, Wyoming
July 3
Fifteen years earlier

Sprinting as fast as possible, lungs burning, he ran full-out from the clearing into the dark forest to be sure no one saw him. Once well in the woods, he stopped and leaned against a tree. Heart pounding, he caught his breath.

Beneath black clothes, he sweated from exertion. From the sweltering July night despite the strong breeze. From anticipation pumping in his veins. From fear that his plan might not work.

Come on. It should be an inferno by now. What was taking so long?

Another full minute ticked by. The big house should've gone up like dry kindling.

What had he done wrong? Did he need more accelerant? Should he go back to check?

Patience. Just wait.

Looking past the horse stable and two cabins of sleeping teens, he stared at the main house on the hill where Dave and Mabel Durbin lived. He'd made sure no one could help the unsuspecting Durbins. First, he'd locked the doors of the summer camp cabins and then the bunkhouse that was located far behind the stable. The barracks-like building was full of men who worked on the ranch.

Sweat dripped down his face and body, collecting everywhere on his skin. He clenched his jaw, his breath still coming hard from his chest, his nerves strung tight.

A gust of wind whipped through the dry leaves, rattling the brittle branches of the trees overhead. On the hill, smoke rose in the air, the smell filling his nose. Finally, the fire was taking hold. Flames burst to life on the house with a crackle that swelled to a roar. Like a supernatural monster, crimson and gold, it clawed and crawled its way up the sides of the house.

More perspiration rolled down his face, stinging his eyes. He lifted his mask and wiped his face with a gloved hand, but caution had him pull it back down *just in case*.

The fire blazed bright now, pulsing with hunger, growing bigger and hotter, spreading across the roof. He stared with grim satisfaction.

So beautiful. Powerful. Hypnotic against the pitch-black sky.

His creation. He'd been the one to give it life and set it loose.

A sudden gust of dry wind, bearing hard from the north, swept over the house, fanning the flames. Carrying sparks on the breeze to nearby trees. Glowing embers rained from the branches, falling on the two cabins. It wasn't long until the timbers of both roofs caught fire. The flames swirled and swelled, slithering down the walls, burning faster than he imagined possible. Much faster than the main house.

This wasn't part of his plan. A few of those sleeping teens trapped inside were innocent. The rest he blamed even more than the Durbins. He'd intended to make them suffer, too, once they were older and had more to lose than just their lives.

Fate was intervening, making it happen sooner rather

than later. In a way they were all to blame. Guilt by association. The fire would make them pay. Without remorse. Without mercy. It would punish those responsible. This was sweet vengeance.

After tonight, the summer camp on the ranch would close forever.

He smiled, excitement bubbling in his chest. Watching the flames do what was necessary, he was enthralled. No. He was in love. This was the best high of his life. Better than playing football and scoring touchdowns. Better than sex.

If only he'd known what a thrill this would be, he would've done it sooner. For Timothy…and for Birdie.

There weren't any screams yet. The cabins weren't up to code and didn't have smoke detectors. No alarms to wake them. Maybe the smoke would kill them in their sleep before the flames. Not quite the punishment or death he'd wanted for them. They deserved much worse.

Twigs snapped, hurried footsteps trampling the earth. He spun in the direction of movement—to his left in the woods. Two figures raced toward the clearing.

No!

A teenage girl darted from the tree line first, her long hair flowing in waves under the moonlight. Lean, pale limbs pumped hard in panic.

Liz. She worked at the camp and was on his little hit list. Why wasn't she locked in the girls' cabin with the others?

The answer burst from the woods, not far behind her. Sawyer Powell. Her stinking boyfriend. He wasn't a camper or a worker and had no business being there.

Sawyer was like his self-righteous brother, Holden. The former was the star of the basketball team, the latter was the quarterback. Golden boys who thought they walked on water at high school. Did whatever they wanted. Of course, he'd break the rules by being here.

"I'm calling 911." Liz was dialing as she ran.

No, no. Liz and Sawyer, a pair of meddlers, getting in the way. The dude ranch was smack-dab between both towns. One of the fire departments might get there in time.

Liz bolted to the double doors at the front of the girls' cabin and yanked on them. "I can't get it open! They've been tied shut!"

Although he'd made knots that would be hard to undo, in hindsight, chains and padlocks would've been smarter than using ropes.

"Break a window!" Sawyer grabbed a rock and shattered a windowpane, smashing around the frame. The lanky guy hopped up, disappearing inside the boys' cabin.

Liz did the same, scrambling into the other cabin. Those two were ruining everything.

Fists clenched, every sense alive, he gritted his teeth. This was not how it was supposed to end, with Liz Kelley and Sawyer Powell being heroes.

Teens dressed in pajamas funneled out through the broken windows, jumping onto the grass. Coughing and gagging, they backed away from the cabins. Some of them hurried up the hill toward the main house, shouting for the Durbins and yelling for help.

Liz and Sawyer might have stopped his plan, but they wouldn't stop him.

Everyone involved with what happened to Timothy would either burn or wished they had after he was finished with them. All the people who'd remained silent. Those who had looked the other way. Those dirty souls who benefited.

He saw their faces. Knew their names. Not only the ones on the ranch tonight. There were others and there would be justice. He would light their world on fire and burn it to the ground. One day. No matter how long he had to wait.

Liz emerged from the fiery cabin with the last girl. They backed away from the flames as Sawyer climbed out the boys' cabin window. Dropping to the ground, he gulped in air. Liz turned away from the cabins. Her jaw dropped and she took off.

He pivoted to see where she was going. The horse stable was burning, too! The wind was spreading the fire with blistering speed, feeding it fast, making the thinner structure of the barn go up like tinder. Horror whooshed through him. Helpless animals weren't supposed to get hurt.

Liz threw open the doors and rushed into the stable. A moment later, horses darted from the barn, one at a time. Could she get the stalls open and save them all in time?

For a painful second, his heart squeezing in his chest, he contemplated helping the horses. But he'd be seen for certain. He would be caught.

Hacking on the ground, Sawyer glanced around. He stumbled to his feet. "Liz!"

"She's inside the stable!" a girl screamed, pointing at the building engulfed in flames, and Sawyer made a beeline for it.

Men busted through the door of the bunkhouse, storming outside and sprinting into action. Some ran toward the main house while the rest headed for the stable.

Horses were still being set free. Sawyer was almost there. Another horse charged out of the burning barn, but no sign of Liz. Fire shot out through the roof. Sawyer hesitated. Afraid.

With a thunderous crunch, the roof of the stable collapsed, sending sparks shooting into the air like a million mini flares.

Two men wrapped themselves in blankets. Others threw buckets of water on them. Then the men rushed into the stable.

Why bother? Could she have survived?

Doubtful. Even if she had, the chances were slim they'd get her out alive. The only thing that could save Liz now was luck.

Chapter One

Fifteen years later
Present day

Special Agent Liz Kelley made her way through the Denver International Airport, eager to get back to work at Quantico.

Her cell phone buzzed. She fished it out of her oversize laptop bag. Glancing at the caller ID, she groaned. "Hi, Mom," she said, forcing herself to sound upbeat.

"How was the law enforcement symposium, sweetheart?"

"Fine, I suppose, all things considered."

"I'm sure it was better than fine," her mom said, ever the optimist. "I bet you did fantastic."

Only if *fantastic* meant "regrettably stilted and anxious." Since she survived a tragic fire as a teenager, she preferred to stay in the shadows. She still carried scars from that night on the inside and out. Being in the spotlight, the sole focus of more than a hundred people for an hour, had been brutal. She'd choose taking down a serial bomber any day instead.

Reaching her gate, Liz took a seat far from the desk and most of the other passengers, sitting with her back to a wall. Scanning the area, always assessing whether any potential threats lurked, she parked her rolling carry-on beside her.

"Not really, Mom." She adjusted her scarf that covered

the puckers on her neck. In her profession, it was easy to hide the telltale signs of the numerous skin grafts and most of the remaining scars that ointments didn't smooth out with long sleeves, her shoulder-length hair and trademark neckerchiefs. "The only reason my boss chose me is because the book has gotten so much attention. Public speaking and teaching really aren't my forte."

"You have to stop downplaying your achievements, Liz. You wrote an insightful book, and you're one the FBI's top profilers working for a special task force."

"It's called the BAU," Liz said, referring to the Behavioral Analysis Unit, where she'd worked at Quantico for the past eighteen months. A series of tough cases and a track record of impressing her supervisors had earned her a coveted spot. "It's a specialist department, not a task force." They coordinated investigative and operational support functions, as well as criminological research to assist federal, state, local and foreign law enforcement agencies investigating unusual or repetitive violent crime.

"Anyway, my point is that you're exceptional, and the FBI recognizes it."

Shaking her head, Liz smiled at how her mother looked at her through rose-colored glasses. "It does take a certain type of person who thrives at getting into the minds of the sickest, darkest criminals out there. An achievement that I'm sure is hard for you to brag about during your quilt guild meetings or bridge club."

"They're not the right audience, but it's their loss. Your dad's hunting buddies think it's cool." Her mom's voice brightened with enthusiasm. "Sweetheart, I hope you appreciate how lucky you are."

Lucky Liz. That's what everyone in her hometown had called her after she had survived the fire on the dude ranch. The one that had killed Dave and Mabel Durbin. Yet they'd always said it with a wince or such unbearable pity in their eyes that her parents decided to move from Bison Ridge, Wyoming, to Missoula, Montana, to give her a fresh start, where she could heal. Homeschooled for the remainder of high school. Gone were the days of wearing shorts and tank tops and running on the cross-country team. An end to nosy townsfolk and concerned friends dropping in un-invited, forcing a smile at the sight of her, with stares that lingered too long. No more whispers when they thought she couldn't hear them. *At least her face wasn't ruined. That's still pretty.*

Her parents had sold most of the land on their prop-erty to the Shooting Star Ranch next to them, owned by the Powells, but had kept the house, which had been in the family for generations. They hoped she, their only child, would want it someday.

As far as Liz was concerned, she never again wanted to set foot within a hundred miles of where she'd suffered and had lost so much. Too many painful reminders.

Even being in Denver was cutting it a bit close for her liking.

"Yeah, Mom, I know I'm fortunate." And she was. To be alive. To have a successful career where she got to make a difference and save people.

But the blazing inferno that summer had robbed her of beauty and the chance for a normal life at only seventeen years old. In its place, she had been given a need—an ob-session—to understand the mind of someone like the ar-sonist responsible for changing her world forever.

None of it felt like the kind of luck that was good.

Her phone beeped. She glanced at the screen. It was Ross Cho, the special agent in charge of her subsection, BAU 1. "Mom, I've got to go. It's work on the other line. My boss probably wants to hear all about the symposium as well."

"Okay. Love you."

"Love you, too. Give Dad a hug from me." Liz disconnected and answered the other call. "Kelley."

"Where are you?" SAC Cho asked, his tone curt.

Liz stiffened. "At the airport, sir. I managed to get a standby seat on an earlier flight back to Virginia." There was no need to stay for the entire symposium once she'd done her part.

"Glad I caught you before you boarded. There's a change of plan. We received an urgent request for assistance from a fire investigation office that find themselves under an accelerated timeline. There appears to be an arsonist who is rapidly escalating. He's struck four times in the past twelve days. Five dead so far, another hospitalized in critical condition and not likely to make it. The most recent fire was earlier today, around eight this morning. Based on how things have been spiraling, we extrapolated that it's likely there could be another incident within the next day or two."

This was perfect for her instead of being a show pony at a conference. She lived for this kind of case.

Standing, she hoisted the strap of her laptop bag on her shoulder and pulled up the handle of her rolling carry-on. She had everything she needed, including her field jacket—windbreaker with FBI identifier—and agency-issued Glock. "I'll change my flight. Where am I headed and who is my point of contact?"

"We've booked a rental car for you. Check your email for the reservation. Looks as though driving is faster. Should take you roughly two and a half hours to reach Laramie."

A chill ran through her veins as the breath stalled in her lungs.

Laramie.

Time froze, as if her brain had shut down.

"The deputy state fire marshal there made the request and will be your POC," SAC Cho said. "He'll meet you at the site of the latest incident. I forwarded the address to you along with his information. The name is Powell. Sawyer Powell."

Sawyer, her ex-boyfriend? He's a fire marshal?

She hadn't seen or spoken to him since she'd moved away. Not that he hadn't tried to stay in contact after she left, but it had been too hard for her. The sight of him over video chat, the sound of his voice on the phone, even his bittersweet emails—all cruel reminders of another thing that she had lost.

Her first love.

Quickly, she banished the resurrected demons from her mind and gathered her thoughts. "Why me, sir? Surely there's someone in the Denver field office who could take this."

"You're the best I have on arson and bombings. There's no one in the Denver office more qualified to handle this than you. Besides, you're from Laramie. Don't you want an all-expense-paid trip back home?"

It was the last thing she wanted, considering the emotional havoc it might wreak for her.

"I'm from the neighboring town, Bison Ridge," she said, needing to make the distinction for some odd reason.

"Regardless, you know the lay of the land and you're in the area, more or less. What are the odds, huh? I guess the stars have aligned in your favor, as luck would have it."

Yeah, just her brand of luck. *Bad.*

Her voice, when she spoke again, was a rasp. "I guess so."

"I thought you'd sound more enthusiastic about being assigned this case," SAC Cho said. "It's the type you'd beg me to give you, but I'm sensing otherwise right now. What am I missing here? Is this going to be a problem?"

Squeezing her eyes closed, she reminded herself of what was most important, why she did this job. Her tragedy had led her to the FBI, to become a criminal profiler with this specialization. What most civilians didn't understand, the part that wasn't shown on TV or covered in the newspaper was the long-term impact of arson. What it did not only to property but also to people, to families, to neighborhoods, to businesses. How it could destroy a small town.

If she could prevent another fire and the loss of more lives, then she had to do everything in her power to try. No matter the personal cost.

Liz opened her eyes and headed toward the rental cars. "No, sir," she said, stripping any weakness or doubt from her voice. "This won't be a problem. Thank you for the opportunity."

"That's more like it." Papers shuffled across the line. "There's one more thing before you go," Cho said, no doubt saving the best part for last. "This is about to get national coverage. Powell can't dissuade the mayor any longer from talking about it live on a major network."

Her stomach cramped. "Does the mayor have any idea how dangerous it is to give that kind of media attention to the UNSUB?" she asked, referring to the unidentified suspect. It would most likely make matters worse, only encouraging further incidents.

"Powell also thinks it's unwise, but the mayor isn't listening to him. It's an election year, citizens are dying, and businesses are being burned to the ground. Doesn't look good. The politician wants to control the narrative." He sighed as though there were more. "Listen, you've closed every case you've been assigned. Your record is flawless. I need you at your best on this one. Do you understand what I'm saying?"

Failure wasn't an option and she wouldn't have it any other way. Even though she was going back home, where the worst thing in her life had happened, all she had to do was keep the past in the past. There was never any room for feelings on an assignment. This time, it was especially true.

"Yes, sir. I understand." Absolutely nothing would get in the way of doing her job.

ARSON. AGAIN.

In his gut, Sawyer Powell was certain of it. Soon enough he'd have the evidence to support his hunch. Wearing his full PPE—personal protection equipment—kit, he followed protocol, starting with the least burned areas and moved toward the most damaged ones. Firefighters worked around him, making the scene more chaotic than he would've preferred. The fire had been extinguished, but now they were conducting overhaul. The process of searching for and putting out any pockets of fire that remained hidden under the floor, the ceiling or in the walls was laborious, but a single cluster of embers could cause a rekindling.

Ideally, he'd examine the area before overhaul began to ensure important evidence wasn't lost or destroyed. The station didn't enjoy having him underfoot, either. Yet they were working in tandem since time was something neither he nor the fire department had.

Sawyer was under mounting pressure from the mayor while the station was operating with only a small crew. They barely had enough for their three shifts that worked forty-eight hours on duty and ninety-six hours off duty. In their small town, where most of the action came from wildfires, that wasn't a problem. Until now.

He slowly walked the perimeter of the charity thrift store, jotting down notes for his report and taking photographs like an archaeologist mapping out a ruin. The air smelled of burned rubber and melted wires. Damp ash covered the floor, sticking to his boots.

Fire was a predictable beast. It breathed. It consumed. More importantly, it also spoke, telling a story. Sawyer only had to interpret. One thing he loved about his job was that fire didn't lie. Whatever it showed him would be the truth.

He picked up a large piece of glass from one of the broken windows. On it was a revealing spiderweb-like design. *Crazed glass.* A key indicator that a fire had burned fast and hot, fueled by a liquid accelerant, causing the glass to fracture.

He pushed deeper into the two-thousand-square-foot building. Ducking under insulation and wiring that hung down from the exposed ceiling, he came to the front of the office, where the victim who was now in the ICU fighting for her life had been discovered. Two firefighters inside had already opened up the walls and were getting ready to pull the lathe in the ceiling.

"Hey, guys, stop!" Sawyer called out, and the two looked over at him. They weren't from the station, but he recognized them from the volunteer crew that were sometimes called in. Many of them he knew by name. Not these two. "What are you doing? I need to examine this area before you destroy any potential evidence."

"Oh, okay," one said. "The chief told us to clean out the whole room. Nobody wants the dreaded and embarrassing call back to the scene because of a rekindle."

Sawyer tamped down his rising anger. "Slow everything down and think about what you're doing. In fact, why don't you take a break until I'm done?"

"But we were called in to give some of the station guys a break," the other one said. "We're fresh and ready to help. What do you want us to work on?"

Sawyer didn't care as long as they got out of his way. "Go ask the chief."

The pair shrugged and vacated the area.

Exhaling a perturbed breath, Sawyer looked around. He cleared some of the torn-down gypsum board and noticed deep charring along the base of the walls. Gases became buoyant when heated. Flames naturally burned upward. But this fire had burned extremely low down.

Near the door inside the office, he moved the remnants of a chair out of the way. Peculiar char patterns shaped like puddles were on the floor underneath. The type produced by a flammable or combustible liquid that caused a fire to concentrate in those kinds of pockets, creating *pour patterns*. What made the char strange was the intensity of the fire.

The same markings had been at the other two crime scenes along with something else. He removed more debris, sifting through ashes until he found it. Remnants of a mechanical device. He collected it, along with some of the surrounding rubble.

He snapped pictures and took samples to send to the crime lab. The bad news was it'd take several weeks to get the results. He glanced up at the ceiling and smiled. The good news was the clues the substance left behind pointed to gasoline as the accelerant. It burned downward, producing a hole exactly like the one at the center of the pour pattern on the floor. Then there was the highly volatile air and vapor mixture that always formed above burning gasoline, rising to the ceiling where it would ignite. He took photos of the severe ceiling damage over the spot.

Searching for any other similar burn patterns throughout the building, Sawyer identified a total of three points of origin. A fire had been set not only in the office but also by the rear and front doors. No doubt the fire had been intentionally set, creating a barrier to prevent the victim from escaping and from help easily reaching her.

The sadistic perpetrator had set a death trap. Disgust welled in Sawyer.

Stepping outside the building with the samples and his camera in the toolbox, he winced at the size of the crowd that had gathered nearby, a combination of civilians and reporters. It had doubled since he'd arrived.

Sawyer spotted Fire Chief Ted Rapke speaking to the two volunteers who had almost messed up the scene. He braced himself in expectation of the conversation that was to come.

They never got along when they worked side by side as firefighters, and after Ted was promoted to chief while Sawyer became the new fire marshal, instead of Ted's close friend, Gareth, things only got worse.

Ted raised a hand in Sawyer's direction and headed over to him. "There must have been some miscommunication, but there was no need for you to snap at those guys. Unlike us, they don't get paid to be out here. They freely volunteer their efforts as a way of serving and giving back to the community. I can't afford to lose them while some firebug is torching the city, killing people."

Sawyer pulled off his helmet and tucked it under his arm, aching to remove the rest of his gear in the sweltering ninety-degree August heat. "And I can't afford to have them tearing up valuable evidence if we're going to have any chance of catching whoever is doing this. Look, I get that your people are getting hammered."

"Try completely overwhelmed. I won't have you scaring off essential volunteers."

"That wasn't my intent." Sawyer took a breath, not wanting to utter the words on the tip of his tongue, but it couldn't be avoided any longer. "Overhaul is strenuous. The firefighters involved in suppression may be so fatigued afterward that they overlook hazards, along with evidence. As for the volunteers, they're not focused on preserving the scene so I can do my job. Their only concern is to help put out a fire and prevent a rekindling. Perhaps you should consider sticking to thermal imaging until after I've investigated and you can get a fresh crew for overhaul."

Ted folded his arms across his chest and narrowed his eyes. "Did you have the audacity to try and tell me how to do my job?"

"It was only a suggestion." One given to help them both be more effective.

"That takes some nerve, buddy," Ted said, "after Mayor Schroeder just got on national television and basically called you incompetent."

Clenching his jaw, Sawyer didn't even want to get started about the *mayor*.

Someone cleared a throat behind him. "Excuse me, gentlemen," a woman said, the voice familiar.

Sawyer pivoted, facing Liz Kelley, and the world dropped out from under him. Special Agent Cho had told him she was coming. Part of him refused to believe it until he saw her himself. The mention of her name alone had sent his pulse racing with anticipation.

Now, here she was standing in front of him. Her pale green eyes met his and he took in the sight of her. Same long wavy light brown hair. Same rose-colored lips. Trim figure albeit less gangly and curvier. A decade and a half older, and she still took his breath away.

"Oh yeah," Ted said. "Forgot to mention an FBI agent is out here waiting to do *your job* since you're having so much trouble on your own." The chief stalked off.

Ignoring Ted and their typical friction, Sawyer didn't take his gaze off her. "Liz." He stepped in to hug her as she extended a hand to shake his instead. In the awkwardness, they both backed away, not touching each other at all. "Have you been here long?"

"Only a few minutes. The chief told me you were inside."

"It's good to see you. I only wish it was under better circumstances." Unease—the same he'd carried since Liz ended any contact—churned through him. All he wanted was to close the distance between them and be free of it.

They'd once been inseparable, sharing everything, including a vision of the future. He missed that. Missed her.

She adjusted the scarf around her neck, pulling it up a bit over her scars. "Me too."

"FBI. How do you like working for the bureau?"

"It's fine. Good to have a purpose." She walked around him and faced the ruined building. "Are you sure this one is also arson?" she asked, cutting straight to business.

He removed his gloves. "With the classic V, multiple points of origin, crazed glass and puddle configurations caused by an ignitable liquid hydrocarbon accelerant that has a high boiling point, my guess is gasoline. I'm one hundred percent positive," he said, confident she understood all the jargon after having read her impressive book on behavioral analysis of serial arsonists and bombers.

She studied him a moment. Did she doubt him?

"I can get you some gear and we can take a look inside together," he offered, and it occurred to him she might not be comfortable going into a building that had been on fire only hours ago. How foolish to even suggest it. Then again, he wasn't sure how to manage this situation. Walking through the aftermath of a fire was probably regular protocol for her, but still he said, "Sorry if you'd rather not go inside."

Taking another step back, she shook her head. "It won't be necessary. You're the expert in determining the cause. I'm here to help you figure out who's behind this."

It was the reason she was finally back in Laramie. To see justice served. To stop a sadistic killer.

He understood the drive and respected her for it. If only he knew how to handle working this case with her and the total gut punch he felt every time he thought about her.

"Do you mind?" he asked, opening his coat, not wanting to endure the heat any longer.

"Go right ahead." She took his toolbox and helmet, giving him a hand.

He stripped off the heavy turnout gear, leaving his pants and boots and his navy blue T-shirt that read Wyoming State Fire Marshal on the back.

"What can you tell me about the latest victim?" she asked.

"Ermenegilda Martinez. Thirty-one years old. Married. No kids. She runs the Compassionate Hearts charity and is currently in the ICU. It doesn't look good."

"This place doesn't open until nine. Any idea why she was here so early in the morning?"

He shook his head. "I'm hoping her husband will be able to shed some light on that."

"Have you been able to find a link between the victims?"

"Nothing so far." A failure that ate away at him, keeping him up at night.

"I haven't had a chance to review the case file since I drove straight here. I'd like to walk through all the details with you."

The back of his neck tingled, and he got the sense someone was watching him. He scanned the crowd of gawking spectators.

Of course, he was being watched. Right along with everyone else working. Many of the people in town were friends and associates. Most he knew by sight if not by name. Only one high school served both Laramie and Bison Ridge. He'd gone to school with almost everyone around his age, who'd grown up here, and had played sports with at least half of those working in the department. Scanning the faces of those who'd gathered, no one stuck out as a stranger.

Still, he couldn't shake the prickle of warning, which was worrisome. "Let's go to my office," he suggested, "away from prying eyes. And we can go over everything there."

"All right."

"Where's your car?"

"About three blocks away," she said. "There was no place to park around here."

"My truck is closer. I'm over there." He gestured in a direction less than a block away. "I'll take you to your car and you can follow me."

They walked past the fire station ambulance parked off to the side and around the crowd-control barricade, avoiding the mass of spectators. Serial fires and murders were unusual in the small, quiet town, where neighbors looked out for one another, and were bound to draw a ton of macabre interest.

A woman darted from the cluster of onlookers, rushing straight for them. He gritted his teeth at the sight of her, wishing they had been able to sneak by.

"Excuse me, Fire Marshal Powell!" She held out a recorder as she caught up to them. "I'm Erica Egan from the *Laramie Gazette*."

"I know who you are." *A menace.* Sawyer picked up his step and Liz kept pace with him.

Egan drew closer, her arm brushing his. "I've been trying to pin you down about the fires."

"I'm aware." He'd been warned about her. She had a reputation for pinning down and cozying up to guys for an exclusive. Didn't even matter if they were married. Sawyer wasn't one to buy into distasteful gossip that could ruin someone's career, but he didn't care for Egan's brand of reporting. Pure sensationalism.

"Would you care to comment on the things Mayor Schroeder had to say about you and the fires on the *Morning Buzz*? Is it the reason the FBI is here?"

He glanced over at Liz's jacket, which conspicuously announced the presence of a special agent. "I didn't watch or read about the mayor's appearance because I've been too busy working." It made him wonder how Ted had so many colorful details.

His truck wasn't much farther ahead. In a minute, he could hop inside and dodge answering any more questions.

"I'll recap for you." Egan shoved the recorder closer to his face. "The mayor said, and I quote, 'Arson Investigator Sawyer Powell'—"

"Hang on. Can you be quiet a moment," Liz said, putting a hand on his forearm, forcing him to slow down. "Do you hear that?"

He was about to ask, *What?* but in the quiet, it became obvious. There was a faint clicking sound. Was it coming from his vehicle?

"Bomb!" Liz yelled.

In the next heartbeat, his silver truck exploded in a fiery burst of heat and searing light, the violent boom rattling him to his core.

Chapter Two

Liz threw up an arm to shield her face. The ear-shattering blast rocked the ground, propelling the rear of the truck into the air and slamming it back down. The punch of the explosion knocked them off their feet as Sawyer wrapped his arms around her and the reporter.

Breath left Liz in a whoosh, pain shooting through her back when they landed hard on the pavement. Sawyer's sharp exhale rushed across her cheek. Her heart jumped into her throat.

A firestorm of blazing metal rained onto the street and over other vehicles. Liz was stunned, shaken but needed to get her bearings. Needed to move.

Get up. Get up!

She rolled Sawyer off her and started to sit up. A second explosion sent one of the truck doors whizzing through the air, flames erupting out the windows. Sawyer was back on top of her, protecting her with his body as fragments of glass and shrapnel sliced into the storefront sign beside them.

The smell of melting rubber and burning gasoline filled her nose. Her ears rang. Her eyes stung.

Liz pulled in deep breaths, trying to shake off her daze. Sawyer rolled onto his back with a groan.

She glanced to the right. "Are you okay?" she asked the reporter, who was lying face down with her hands covering her head. "Are you burned?"

"No. I don't think so." The woman whimpered. "Is it safe to move?"

"Yeah. I think so." Liz turned, checking on Sawyer.

Sitting up, he hissed in pain. She looked him over for injuries. There was a gash on his thigh and along the side of his torso where pieces of hot metal had scorched across his skin. His arm was pink, slightly singed.

"You're hurt." If only he had left his gear on or hadn't tried to shield her and the reporter from the eruption of fire and killing debris. She caressed his cheek, thankful it hadn't been worse.

"Oh my God." The reporter sat upright. "I—I can't believe what just happened."

Neither could Liz. Someone had tried to kill Sawyer and had nearly succeeded.

He fingered the rip in his trousers. "It's a clean cut." His gaze drifted to the pile of burning metal that used to be his truck.

"Can't say the same for your abdomen," Liz said, taking a closer look. A shard of metal was embedded in his flesh. "I'll get an EMT."

"No, I'll go." The reporter brushed off her clothes and slowly climbed to her feet. "It's the least I can do." A slight tremor rang in her voice. "You two saved my life."

Sawyer remained riveted on the wreckage. A bit of color had drained from his handsome face. Flames danced in his eyes. "A few feet closer, seconds really, and we would've been toast." He shook his head at the inferno that had been his truck.

Liz gingerly peeled up his shirt and looked at the wound. "It's bleeding pretty bad." But she didn't dare put any pressure on it with the piece of metal lodged in his side.

"I'll hurry." The reporter took off.

"Any chance you've upset someone that you know of?" Liz hiked her chin at the fireball.

"Enough to kill me?" He shook his head.

"Then whoever our suspect is did this."

"But why?" His voice dropped into a graveled tone.

Possibilities ran through her head. "They don't like the investigation. Maybe you're closer than you think to figuring this out. But the more important question is, why aren't we dead?"

Sawyer pulled his gaze from the flames and looked at her. "Come again."

"That bomb was planted with the intent to kill you."

"Maybe it was an aggressive tactic to scare me off."

She gave Sawyer a slow, noncommittal gesture with her head as she considered it. "Maybe." Although she doubted that was the case. "The bomb was big enough to set off a secondary blast," she said, thinking aloud. "That kind of explosion was meant to kill, not scare."

"Then why didn't he wait until we were in the vehicle to let it explode."

More possibilities rushed through her mind. "I can't say for sure, but I do know that it's one thing to kill a fire marshal and quite another if it's a federal agent," she said, and he grimaced. "No offense, but it's the difference between a state level and federal crime. Not to mention drawing the ire of the entire bureau by blowing up one of their own. The BAU would descend upon Laramie like the four horsemen of the apocalypse determined to bring the end of days to the perpetrator. Anyone smart would avoid that."

Smart enough not to let their agenda override common sense. She hoped her presence was the reason they hadn't been in the truck when it exploded. If it was something else, then this was bigger than she feared.

The ambulance pulled up. Sawyer tried to take the toolbox full of evidence with him, but Liz took it from his hands. She'd ensure it stayed in her possession or locked safely in her trunk.

Once the paramedics got him on a gurney and loaded into the back, she ran to her rental car and raced over to the emergency room at Laramie Hospital. After she flashed her badge, a nurse didn't hesitate to show her to the bay where they had put him.

Sawyer was lying on a bed propped up with pillows. She'd kept pictures of him, but all the photos were of him as a teen. Today was the first time she'd seen him as a man, and seeing his face after all this time was just short of ecstasy. His intense baby blue eyes met hers, a grin tugging the corner of his mouth, and her stomach fluttered. She drank in the sight of him. His sunny blond hair was too long in the front, still curly at the top in a way that had always made her want to run her fingers through it, and messier than before the explosion, but the rough-and-tumble look on him was appealing. His jaw squarer than she remembered and covered in stubble.

Pulling her gaze from him, she stepped inside the bay.

"A doctor will be in to see him shortly," the nurse said.

Liz gave her an appreciative smile. "Thank you."

The nurse left, drawing the curtain behind her, giving them some privacy.

"My personal hero returns," he said.

Liz shook her head. "I'm no such thing."

"All evidence to the contrary. You've been here less than an hour and already saved my life."

"I can't take credit for being a default deterrent." Possible deterrent anyway. The culprit deliberately triggered the bomb early, which had caused the clicking sound—something they wouldn't have heard until they were inside the truck if the intent had been to kill them. Clearly the person didn't mind taking lives, enjoyed it even, but was fear of committing a federal offense really the reason they were alive right now? Maybe if they were able to figure out the answer, it would help them find the killer. "How are you holding up?" Liz asked, going to his side.

"I'm alive, so I can't complain."

Well, he could, and she wouldn't blame him if he did. But the old Sawyer she knew never was one to complain or criticize and always the first to give a compliment. The best type of friend, who'd never let anyone down, especially not someone in trouble. Kind. Confident. Strong. In high school, he loved basketball, her, and numbers. He had talked about having a double major in college, business and finance. The perfect combination to become a quantitative analyst. A far cry from what he did today.

"How did you end up a fire marshal?" she wondered. "I thought you wanted to be a *quant*."

"I guess the same way you ended up an FBI agent." The humor bled from his tone as the light in his eyes dimmed.

Her dream of wanting to be a museum curator felt like something from a past life. In fact, it was distant enough to have been someone else's desire.

The tragedy that summer had altered the courses of their lives forever.

"I was a firefighter for a long time," he said, "until I realized I was better suited for going into the building after, piecing it together and figuring out the why."

Sawyer had always been a handsome hunk with picture-perfect looks, but she'd found his analytical mind even more attractive. It was good he was using it to help stop criminals instead of finding ways to make companies more profitable.

"Is there anyone I can call for you to let them know you're in the ER? Your wife? Girlfriend?"

Part of her hoped he had found happiness with another woman. A larger part wished he was unattached, which didn't add up in her head since she had been the one to cut him off. What he did with his life, the job he chose, who he loved, shouldn't matter, but in her heart, she'd clung to him. Out on a run, making dinner for one, in bed alone, in the stillness of the dark, he'd emerge like a phantom, haunting her.

"Nope. Not even a lover to complain when I work overtime," he said, and relief trickled through her. "I never got into anything serious, and anything fun tends to fade fast. More often than not, being with the wrong person is lonelier than being without them."

Something in his voice saddened her, too, making her regret her selfishness. He deserved to have the full life that she never would. "I'm surprised. You wanted to be married by twenty-five and have a couple of kids by now."

"After all this time, you still don't get it." His gaze narrowed on her as he cocked his head to the side. "That was *our* plan. The life I wanted with you."

His words sliced at her heart with the precision of a scalpel, but she didn't dare allow long-buried feelings to bleed through.

The bay curtain opened with a whoosh, thankfully diverting their attention.

"Hello," said a woman, entering as she stared at a medical tablet. "I'm Dr. Moreno." Her head popped up and she flashed a smile. "I hear you're not having a good day."

"You have no idea," Sawyer said.

Dr. Moreno set the tablet down and pulled on latex gloves. "Let's take a look."

"I'll step out," Liz said.

Sawyer put a hand on her forearm. "I'd prefer it if you stayed."

Dr. Moreno grabbed a pair of scissors and set it down on a tray. "He'll need a distraction in a moment."

"Then there's no one better than you, Liz," he said.

The doctor treated his leg first, cleaning the wound and applying a bandage. She slathered ointment on the pink area of his arm. Then she moved on to his abdomen and cut his T-shirt off, revealing his bare torso.

Warmth shot up Liz's neck, heating her face. He'd aged but hadn't changed for the worse in the past fifteen years. Somehow, he'd only gotten better looking. A few small lines etched the outer corners of his stunning eyes. He had quite a bit more bulk. The body of a teenage basketball player had been replaced with ridges and valleys of lean, sculpted muscle on a firefighter turned investigator.

He'd developed this body not only in the gym but the hard way. Hauling eighty pounds of gear and equipment up flights of stairs and into dangerous situations.

At least he no longer battled fires, but unless they found whoever planted a bomb in his truck, he'd be in danger.

"Okay, this next part is going to hurt." The doctor traded the scissors for forceps. She pressed down lightly around the wound and then gripped hold of the piece of shrapnel. As Dr. Moreno began extracting it, Sawyer grimaced. "Talk to him."

Liz took his hand in hers and squeezed. Thinking of something to say, anything to take his mind off the pain, she blurted the first thing to pop in her mind. "Hey, do you remember that time we went swimming, and afterward you surprised me with a picnic?" The lunch he'd packed had contained all her favorites.

He laughed. "Yep. I was the genius who laid out the blanket right under a hive of angry, territorial hornets. How could I forget?" He hissed when the doctor started the sutures.

Liz pressed her palm to his cheek, caressing his flawless skin with a thumb and drawing his full attention. "Right up until we got stung, the day had been perfect. Eighty degrees. Sunny. Warm breeze. Blue skies. Cool water. We swam and played around in the lake for goodness knows how long." He'd even brought an MP3 player. They'd danced and made out, and it had seemed like they'd have forever together. Kissing. Hugging. Dancing. Laughing. Holding each other close. "Another surprise—the tickets to the ballet in Cheyenne. *Swan Lake*." He'd been an A-student and star athlete who also knew classical music and appreciated art—interests they'd shared. Everything she'd wanted in a life partner. "Nothing could've made the day better. Other than not getting stung."

There were no more perfect days. She hadn't even put on a bathing suit since...

"None of that is what made the day special." He tightened his fingers around hers. "It was perfect simply because we were together." The sincerity in his voice caused a pang in her chest.

"All done." The doctor removed her gloves with a snap of latex.

Liz slipped her hand from his. In her effort to distract him, she'd only sabotaged herself, rehashing beautiful memories she couldn't afford to dwell on. Every time she thought about Sawyer, what it was like to be with him, she softened.

It made her weak.

"The wound should heal in two to four weeks," Dr. Moreno said. "No arteries were cut, but I'm glad you didn't take the chance of removing the piece of metal. The stitches will dissolve on their own over time. I'll prescribe an antibiotic to prevent an infection and get you discharged. Take an over-the-counter analgesic for pain. Do you have any questions?"

"You have anything I could put on?" He gestured at his bare chest. "Other than a hospital gown."

"Sure. Plenty of scrubs around. I think we can rustle up a top for you."

"Thanks."

With a nod, she whipped back the curtain and disappeared.

"Liz." Sawyer reached for her.

But she stepped away from the bed. They needed to focus on finding a killer, not ancient history. "While we're here at the hospital, we should go up to the ICU. See Mrs. Martinez. Speak with her husband. We can go over everything else pertinent to the case afterward."

"Of course. Back to business. But we should also make time to talk. Clear the air. About us."

"There is no *us*," she said, almost as a reflex.

"You made sure of that by not returning any of my emails or phone calls. I get why you left Wyoming, but I never imagined you'd leave me, too."

They had been connected. The strongest bond she'd ever had, other than the one with her parents, but she'd acted in both their best interests.

"I went to Montana to see you once," he said, and her heart sank, not wanting old wounds to reopen. "Drove all night without sleeping. I need to know. Were you home that day when I knocked on the door?"

Of course she was there. After the move, it took her a year to leave the house. Her father had gotten rid of him without even asking her, which had been just as well since she'd hidden in the closet.

Like a coward.

"I would've sworn you were there," he said, "so I stood outside, calling for you."

The sound of him—screaming her name at the top of his lungs, pain racking his voice—had gutted her. The memory had tears stinging the back of her eyes.

"I was out there trying to remind you what you meant to me until I was hoarse and your dad called the cops."

No reminder was necessary. They'd practically grown up together, with their properties adjacent. Hers on the side of the Bison Ridge town line and his in Laramie. Since they were thirteen and first kissed, they'd been making plans.

Listening to him outside, she hid in the closet, grief-stricken over the end of her world as she'd known it, over the loss of the life they'd never have together. She forced herself to accept the reality that nothing would ever be the same again.

He'd needed to move on without guilt or any obligation to stay with her, the scarred girl who survived. And she had needed something he couldn't give her. To heal on her own. To build a new life. To do what felt impossible—reimagine her future without him.

It was the toughest decision she'd ever made, but she'd thought a clean break was best.

"Were you home?" he asked. "Just answer that much."

She had never lied to Sawyer. Not once. And she wouldn't start now.

Liz swallowed around the tight knot of guilt rising in her throat. "I'm not back in Wyoming for personal reasons," she said, telling him the one truth they needed to discuss at the moment. Emotions blurred lines, leading to mistakes, which endangered lives. After the bomb in his truck, one thing was certain. Failure could get them killed. She stiffened her spine along with her resolve. "I'm only here because of the case. It's all that matters right now."

SAWYER RODE IN the hospital elevator beside Liz, his chest aching. How could she think he'd be engaged, much less married with kids when he was stuck? His heart was trapped in limbo.

Not that she would know. She'd washed her hands of him without looking back and considering the impact of her choices on him.

He'd wished for a chance to talk to her face-to-face so many times, memorized the questions he'd ask, how she'd respond, wondering whether he'd finally get a sense of closure. None of his hopes included the two of them working a case together or her using it as an excuse to avoid having a long overdue conversation. Still, he clung to two little words: *Right now.*

He took that to mean eventually she would be willing to discuss what happened between them. Just not right now.

The pain he'd kept bottled up for a decade and a half—holding him prisoner to the past, unable to move on—would have to fester a while longer.

The doors opened to the ICU floor. He stepped off the elevator with his sole focus on the job.

They headed to the reception desk. "Hello. I'm Fire Marshal Powell," he said, pulling his badge from his pocket and flashing it at the nurse when she eyed his medical scrub top, "and this is Agent Kelley. We'd like to get an update on Mrs. Martinez."

"Her condition hasn't changed." The nurse's face tightened into a grave look. "She's on life support, but the extent of her injuries makes survival highly unlikely. The doctor thinks she has seventy-two hours at the most."

"Can you notify us if there's any change?" Liz asked, handing her a business card, and the nurse nodded. "What room is she in?"

"Three." She pointed to it. "Her husband is there with her. Only one person at a time is allowed inside."

"Thank you." This was the part of the job that sucked the most. Fire marshals had to pay these kinds of visits, too. Tell someone a loved one had died in a fire so severe their body was unrecognizable. Or ask them questions, probing into their life when they needed space to deal with their emotions. It was always hard on him.

They crossed the open space and stopped at the large window that provided the nurses with a view of the patient. Mr. Martinez sat in a chair beside the bed, his head bent, his hand resting near his wife's, wrapped in bandages, like her face, arms, and most of her body.

Her injuries were severe and extensive. Far worse than the condition Liz had been in. Sawyer had been by her side, too, giving her parents breaks, staying during the wee hours so they could go home, rest, shower and eat.

As close as he had been with Liz, their love strong and real, even for teenagers, he didn't presume to understand the magnitude of what Mr. Martinez must have been experiencing.

A thread of anger wove through Sawyer. They had to stop whoever was responsible before more lives were destroyed.

He glanced at Liz and saw the dark shadows swimming in her eyes. A slight shudder ran through her but only lasted a second. Anyone not carefully watching would've missed it. The sight of the latest victim fighting for her life in the ICU had to be hard on Liz, bringing awful memories to the forefront.

Once, when Sawyer was little, he was playing with one of his brothers, racing through the kitchen, and collided with his mom, who had been holding a pot of boiling water. The burn on his arm that formed had blistered and stung for a week. But his pain had been nothing in comparison to the agony Liz had endured.

Running into a burning building to save kids and horses took a singular kind of selflessness and courage. Her reward had been getting trapped under a burning beam that had fallen in the stables, flames melting her flesh and months of slow healing.

After suffering the unimaginable, she chose a career focused on arson and bombings. Faced what she must fear on a regular basis. She was remarkable.

Always had been.

"Are you all right?" he asked.

Her face was calm but her spine rigid. "I'm fine." The tight, clipped tone of her voice confirmed what he suspected despite her words.

She wasn't okay, but she was too strong to say otherwise.

Mr. Martinez looked up, catching sight of them. A burly

man, he wiped tears from his eyes, stood in a weary way as though he might fall back into his chair and approached them.

They met him at the threshold.

"I'm Special Agent Kelley and this is Fire Marshal Powell. Can we speak with you for a moment regarding your wife?"

He nodded and she gestured for them to move over to a corner.

"Do you know who did this?" the husband asked.

"That's what we're trying to find out," Sawyer said.

Liz pulled a small notepad from her pocket. "What time does the Compassionate Hearts store open?"

"At ten. Every day."

"Any idea why she was there two hours early?" Liz asked.

Mr. Martinez sniffled. "To catch up on paperwork. She used to do it late at night, but I used to worry about her. Bad things can happen late. I thought earlier in the day was safer." A tear leaked from his eye.

"Generally speaking, it is," Liz said, taking notes. "Did anyone know she made a habit of coming in early?"

The husband shrugged. "Maybe some of the staff."

Sawyer thought back on how the fire had three points of origin and a theory he had. "When your wife went in early before the store opened, did she lock the door behind her or leave it open?"

"I can't say for sure, but I believe she locked it. Doris Neff worked mornings. She'd know."

"Do you have any idea why someone would have a reason to burn down the charity or harm your wife?" Liz asked. "Please try to think carefully about the smallest thing."

Mr. Martinez shook his head. "The thrift store gives all its revenue to help disabled veterans and impoverished children. Most of the people who work there are volunteers. As for my wife, she's the sweetest soul. No one would have any reason to hurt Aleida."

Sawyer exchanged a look with Liz before turning back to Mr. Martinez. "We thought her name was Ermenegilda."

"It is, an old family name but a mouthful. No one ever calls her that. Her grandmother went by Gilda. So, my wife uses her middle name. Aleida."

Liz tensed. "Neither are very common names. Thirty-one would put her at the right age. By any chance, is your wife Aleida Flores?"

"Yes, that's her maiden name. Do you know her?"

A strange look crossed Liz's face for a moment, and then it was gone, replaced by a stony expression. "I'm from around here. Bison Ridge, actually. I know a lot of people from there as well as Laramie. Thank you for your time. If you think of anything else, give me," she said, handing him a business card from her pocket, "or Fire Marshal Powell a call."

"The fire station can reach me if you dial their main office. We'll let you get back to your wife." They left the ICU. In the elevator, Sawyer waited until others got off and they were alone. "How do you know Aleida Flores?"

It was probably nothing, like she'd said. She knew lots of people, as did he, but something about her expression worried him.

"From the camp on the dude ranch," she said, her voice a whisper. "Aleida was there that night."

Everything inside him stilled. Silence fell like a curtain, the space around him becoming deafeningly quiet.

"One of the girls you rescued?" he finally clarified.

Staring straight ahead, her body stiff, Liz gave one slow nod. The strange expression came over her face again. She was probably thinking the same unsettling thing running through his head. Aleida had been saved from a deliberately set fire fifteen years ago only to be in critical condition with an unlikely chance of survival because of another one.

Coincidences happened every day, but this one he didn't like.

Chapter Three

Emotions seesawed through Liz. Seeing Mrs. Martinez had been harder than she had expected. While staring at the poor woman, for a heartbeat, Liz was trapped back in the burning stable, panic flooding her veins, frenzied horses, the crackling terror of the fire, the beam falling—pinning her, flames lashing her body, smoke clogging her lungs, searing pain.

Liz flinched. She often had terrible nightmares about that night, but this was the first time in over a decade that she had experienced a fresh wave of sheer fear while awake.

She couldn't help thinking back to her own time in the ICU, the mind-vibrating cacophony of the machines, the tubes, being in and out of consciousness while others whispered, thinking she couldn't hear. The shuddery breaths of her mother crying to her father. *Oh, honey, our little girl was perfect. Now I can barely look at her.*

Liz clenched her hands at her sides. Her internal wounds remained raw despite the time that had passed.

The elevator chimed and the doors opened. She shoved the horror of her personal tragedy into a far corner of her mind as they stepped out onto the first floor.

Another shiver ran through Liz. The shock from learning Aleida, the last girl she'd gotten out of a burning cabin and to safety, was Mrs. Martinez hadn't dissipated.

How could the universe be so twisted and cruel?

Or was there something else at play?

There was a saying that if you saved a life, you became responsible for it. Whether or not it was true, Liz didn't know, but she was more committed than ever to finding the monster who was setting the fires.

They had almost reached the doors to the parking lot when Erica Egan hopped up from a chair and made a bee-line for them. The woman did not give up.

Liz hated the journalist's persistence as much as she admired it.

"You again?" Sawyer asked with a disgusted shake of his head.

The double doors opened with a whoosh.

Egan followed them outside. "I have a job to do, the same as you."

"Not quite the same," Sawyer said. "The more you stalk me, the more time you take away from me investigating."

The determined reporter hurried around to the front of them and raised her recorder. "Give me a quote. On the record," she said, but when Sawyer glared at her, she continued. "I just need something to work with. Anything. Come on."

"I've got a quote for you." Liz stepped close to the recorder. "Fire Marshal Sawyer Powell is doing an incredible job, getting closer to the truth each day. That's why he or she—but I'll stick with *he* since ninety percent of arsonists are white males from midteens to midthirties—targeted Powell today by planting a bomb in his truck that nearly took his life, as well as yours and mine."

Sawyer glanced at her with a quirked brow but didn't say a word.

"If that's true and he's doing such a good job, why is the FBI taking over the case?" Egan asked.

Liz folded her arms. "I'm not here to take over. I'm only here to assist. For a complex case such as this, usually an entire Behavioral Analysis Unit is required. Not one fire marshal working alone. Rather than being criticized, Sawyer Powell should be commended for having the foresight to reach out to the FBI."

The journalist cracked a smile.

"That's all for now," Sawyer said. "Egan, if you want to be part of the solution and not the problem, stop glorifying this pyromaniac who's murdering people. Less sensationalized prose about the fires in your articles that will only embolden him. Focus more on the innocent victims and the destruction of property, like a charity. This guy is a monster. Brand him as one and you'll get more quotes."

"Call me Erica." Shutting off the recorder, the pert reporter stepped closer to him, tilting her head as her features softened. Egan's face was classically beautiful. Platinum blond hair. Deep blue eyes. A svelte figure only a dead man wouldn't find attractive. "My writing style has boosted readership, which is what I was hired to do. I'm willing to consider what you've said, but not simply for more quotes. I want an exclusive. From you. We could discuss further over drinks. I'm buying."

Liz suddenly felt like she was intruding on something by simply standing there. Who was she to stand in the way of him having fun if that's what he wanted? "Sawyer, I'll wait for you over—"

"No need, Liz. Ms. Egan is the one leaving." He glanced back at the other woman. "I have no interest in having a drink with you, but if you reconsider your angle in future articles like I've asked, *we'll* give you an interview together when it's all over."

Egan's eyes went sly. "That could take weeks. How about a chat over coffee every morning?"

Liz swallowed a sigh, listening to this negotiation.

Sawyer glanced at her from the corner of his eyes, probably picking up on her irritation. "Once a week?" he countered.

"You don't expect to catch this guy soon, then." Egan flashed a slithery smile. "Every other day, locations to be determined by me."

A muscle ticked in Sawyer's jaw. "Fine," he said, wearily.

Triumph gleamed in the woman's eyes. "By the way," she said, turning to Liz, "what's your name? For my article."

"Special Agent Liz Kelley."

"The one who wrote the book?" Egan asked.

Liz was taken aback. "I'm surprised you've heard of it."

"You're famous around here. Sorry I didn't recognize you."

Was this town and Bison Ridge still talking about that tragic summer? About the *lucky* girl who survived?

Sawyer clasped her shoulder and squeezed. "It's not what you think," he said, his voice soothing. Their eyes met and recognition was written on his face about what was going through her head. "The Sage Bookshop had it in stock. Signed copies. Your mom even had a huge poster made with your picture on it. They hung it in the front window for months."

She remembered her mom had asked her to sign a bunch of copies, so she'd always have an autographed one on hand. Liz hadn't believed the far-fetched story, but she hadn't pushed for the truth, either. When it came to her mom, sometimes it was better not to ask.

The reporter's gaze landed on the spot where Sawyer touched Liz. "What's the history between you two?" Egan switched the recorder back on and held it up.

Sawyer dropped his hand as Liz backed away from him.

If only they could stop touching. "We're old friends. We used to be neighbors. Our properties are adjacent, but there are plenty of acres between us," Liz said, completely caught off guard, hearing herself babble. Not her style. Ever. She simply didn't want the past dredged up and rehashed on the pages of the *Gazette*.

She bit the inside of her lip to stop the verbal diarrhea.

"We're done here. Now, if you'll excuse us, we have work to do." Sawyer took Liz by the arm, cupping her elbow, and walked off.

Liz glanced over her shoulder. Egan watched them for a moment before she strutted off across the parking lot.

"At least you're going in the right direction," Liz said. "I don't recognize Egan. Is she from around here?"

"Moved here a couple of years ago."

Relieved the reporter was gone and hopeful Egan hadn't caught the whiff of a scoop, Liz took a deep breath. "There's my rental." She pointed out the sedan.

"Thanks for the quote." He let go of her arm. "You didn't have to say all that stuff about me."

"Yes, I did. Because it's true." Although she should've given her words deeper consideration rather than spouting off a knee-jerk quote. On the bright side, it was only a few lines in a local paper. Not a ten-minute tirade on a major national news network. "I heard what the mayor had to say about you on satellite radio during the drive. I don't know why Bill Schroeder is trying to hang you out to dry, but I won't stand for it."

She was acquainted with Bill well enough and had never cared for him. They were around the same age, with him being two years older, but Bill's entitled attitude rubbed her the wrong way. He was a bully back then and still was. Only this time he was using his position as mayor to pick on a civil servant who was trying to do his job.

"Voters are going to want to blame someone if I don't catch this guy."

"If we don't. You're not in this alone. Not anymore. We're going to nail this person. Together." Thinking back on Aleida in the ICU, Liz intended to see justice served.

"The one thing I miss about being a firefighter is working on a team. Being a fire marshal gets a little lonely." The corner of his mouth hiked up in a grin, his blues twinkling, making her stomach dip like she was seventeen years old again.

Shake it off, Liz.

She hit the key fob, unlocking the doors.

"Want to grab dinner over at Delgado's and go over the case?" he asked.

Eating at Delgado's with him, the way they used to, was an easy *no*. Too familiar. More nostalgia was the last thing she needed.

"I'm starving, but let's get it delivered to your office," she said. "There we can talk privately and openly, combing through the details while we wait for the food." She pulled on the handle, opening the door.

He put his hand on the top of the frame, blocking her from getting inside the car. "Did you mean what you said about us being a team?"

"Of course."

"Good, but it's going to require trust. The kind of trust where my life could be in your hands and vice versa. Until we get this guy, we're going to be joined at the hip. Can you handle all that?"

She wasn't the same petrified seventeen-year-old girl who hid in a closet because she didn't know how to stand on her own two feet after losing so much. "I can handle anything."

"Even if it's with me?" His gaze held hers, a clear challenge gleaming in his eyes.

He had no intention of putting the past behind them. He would keep pushing for answers, for the discussion that didn't take place in Montana all those years ago. The one she owed him.

She'd thought reliving the trauma of the fire would be

the hardest part of coming back. Instead, the most difficult thing was blond, blue-eyed, six-three and two hundred pounds of pure stubbornness.

Time for her to go into damage control mode before he went on the offensive.

She drew closer, bringing them toe to toe. No more backing away from him, averting her gaze or acting like an awkward teenager scared of the slightest touch, giving him reason to doubt she could handle this—being "joined at the hip." Their familiarity could be a strength. They'd once been so in tune that they finished each other's sentences. They only had to find a new rhythm without letting the tempo get out of control.

"Even with you," she said. "I'll make you a deal. After we catch this guy, we'll sit down and talk." As much as she disliked scrapping her plan to hightail it out of town once the job was finished, it might be the only thing to appease him. "Really talk until you're satisfied. Okay?"

Leaning in, Sawyer brought his face dangerously close to hers, eliciting a different kind of shudder from her, but instead of retreating, she steeled her spine.

"Satisfying me won't be easy." A slow, knee-weakening smile curved his lips.

There went those stupid butterflies in her belly again. She knew from delicious experience what a passionate, generous, tireless lover he was as a teenager. She could only imagine how experience and patience had improved him. They'd fit perfectly together, their limbs tangled, melting from pleasure.

Not that she'd had other lovers to compare. She didn't even wear a T-shirt on a run, opting instead for a long sleeve, lightweight UV top. The idea of taking off all her clothes in front of a guy, the sight of her probably making his skin crawl, was unthinkable.

But Sawyer was the only man to ever give her butter-flies. Let alone with just a smile.

With their lips a hairbreadth apart, she couldn't help but wonder if he tasted the same.

She tried to prevent any emotion showing on her face, not letting him see how much his proximity or his words or smile affected her. "Like I said, I can handle anything."

"We'll see." He stepped aside. "Let's go catch a killer."

Chapter Four

Closing the door to his office inside the fire station, Sawyer gestured for Liz to make herself at home.

"Have you been able to find any connection between the victims?" she asked, sitting on the sofa in the back of the room.

"None so far." Something he'd lost sleep over, wondering, why them?

"It would be good to have someone photograph the crowds at any other fires during the remainder of this investigation." Settling in, she removed her jacket but kept on the scarf, which, he now noticed, matched the color of her slacks.

Gunmetal blue. Custom-made.

Did she always wear a neckerchief around others? Or was she ever at ease in her own skin with someone else?

If so, he wanted nothing more than to be that someone. Still. Always.

"Do you think our suspect will be out there, again?" Sawyer sat behind his desk.

"It's highly likely. From the looks of what was left of the Compassionate Hearts building, he loves destructive fire. Roughly one-third of arsonists return to the scene. The primary attraction can be a desire for control and power. Not just watching the firefighters battle the blaze, but it's the thrill of seeing how much damage they've caused."

He hadn't considered someone would risk raising suspicion by hanging out for hours in this small town, but it was probable, considering the bomb in his truck and the aggressive nature of the fire that had been set. "The office where Aleida Martinez was found went up fast and hot with no windows for her to escape. There was no need to start two additional fires unless the goal was to ensure the whole building burned to the ground."

"If you've got a local law enforcement contact who could handle taking the photos, it would be helpful."

"As a matter of fact, I do. My brother Holden is the chief deputy in the sheriff's office." His cell phone buzzed. He pulled it from his pocket. "Speak of the devil. Give me a minute."

Liz nodded.

Sawyer answered. "I was just talking about you."

"And I was just looking at your truck," Holden said. "Or should I say what's left of it. Please tell me you're in one piece. I don't want to be the one to have to give Mom bad news."

"No worries on that front." Sawyer spun around in his chair, facing the wall and lowered his voice. "Guess who's in my office?"

"I hate suspense."

"Liz."

A long beat of silence. "Your Liz?" his brother finally asked.

It had been a long time since he'd heard anyone refer to her as his. Didn't change how he'd never stop thinking of her that way.

"I can hear you," she said in a singsong voice.

Sawyer winced. "Yep. Listen, I need a favor." He explained to Holden about the need to have a deputy take discreet photos of any crowd that gathered at future fires.

"I'll get on it as soon as we're done collecting what little forensic evidence is left out here."

"Once you get it, hang on to it. Liz has a contact at Quantico who will fast-track lab results. We're sending him everything."

"Roger that. I'm relieved you're okay. Truly. I'll see you tonight. Heads up, Grace might want to look you over."

No might about it. With Grace, Holden's wife, it was a guarantee. She was a nurse, drop-dead gorgeous and the sweetest soul, who his brother was madly in love with. There would be no hiding his injuries from her.

"I've got stitches in my side, a minor burn on my arm and a cut on my thigh," Sawyer said, coming clean.

"Smart man to fess up. It'll make her examination faster. Later."

"Thanks." They hung up and he spun back around, facing Liz.

She gave a wry grin. "You a fire marshal *and* Holden a deputy? Unreal," she said with a shake of her head.

"Actually, all of my brothers ended up in law enforcement."

Liz shot him an incredulous look. "All of you? Wow. What about Matt?"

Matt Granger was his first cousin on his mother's side. After Sawyer's aunt bankrupted her family with gambling debts and ran off with another man, Matt, who was only seven at the time, and his father came to live at the Powell ranch. Matt was raised almost like a brother rather than a cousin and his father became head manager, overseeing the cattle.

"As soon as Matt turned eighteen, he joined the army. Did black ops. Then he came back and believe it or not became a cop. He was recently promoted to chief of campus police at the local university."

"Your maternal grandfather was a cop, right?"

"A sheriff. Like his father before him. My mom planned to join the FBI after she finished her degree. Dad was going to leave Wyoming and follow her wherever she went, but my granddad got sick. My dad had to take over the Shooting Star. Then Mom got pregnant with Monty and all their plans changed."

"I didn't know. I guess law enforcement runs in your blood, but I thought for sure you boys would've taken over the family ranch. At least one of you. My money was on Monty," she said, and Sawyer would've made the same bet. "That was always your father's dream. He must be proud of you guys, but I'm sure he's also kind of disappointed."

The words tugged at his heart. His father had four sons who loved the ranch and enjoyed working on it, but they'd all been called to do something else. "Long story. The short version is my dad isn't thrilled about it but he claims to understand. I think he's secretly holding on to hope that one of us will give up the badge and take over the ranch someday."

Sawyer opened his bottom drawer and grabbed a fresh work T-shirt. As he pulled off the scrubs top, Liz's gaze slid over his body, a blush rising on her cheeks, before she looked away.

He had to check his grin, but it was nice to know he could still catch her eye. That would have to be good enough for right now.

"Walk me through the other two fires," she said.

Although Liz had a digital copy of everything on the case, he pulled out the physical file, crossed the room and sat beside her on the sofa. He set the folder on the coffee table in front of her and opened it. "The first was a restaurant. No casualties. The owner is devastated. He recently spent a boatload renovating the place. The loss financially ruined him since insurance won't cover arson. The perpetrator started a leak from a gas line, let it build and left a device to get the fire started. Caused an explosion. There wasn't much left, but when I inspected, I found remnants of a timer."

"A timer?" She looked over the file.

"Found the same at the Compassionate Hearts and the fires before that. A cabin over in Bison Ridge. I cover that town, too. Four guys hunting over the weekend. And then a nail salon. Happened after-hours when the head nail tech was doing inventory in the basement."

"Our guy loves fire but likes to set it at a safe distance. Doesn't want to risk getting burned himself. The timer also shows control. Patience. Same accelerant?"

"I believe so. Gasoline."

"What was used to ignite it?" She looked up at him.

"My guess, based on the intensity of the burn pattern at the point of origin, something really hot. I'm thinking a flare."

"Like the kind used on the road for an emergency?"

"It's possible. Easy enough to get. Certainly burns hot enough at 1,500 degrees Fahrenheit. I believe the timer was rigged to set it off. I won't know for certain about the flare or get confirmation on gasoline as the accelerant until I get the results from the lab. They're backed up as usual. Could take six to eight weeks."

She raised her eyebrows in surprise. "Long time to wait."

"Welcome to my world." He had to rely on the crime laboratory that processed forensics for the entire state. Waiting two months was standard procedure.

"Actually, let me introduce you to mine." She took out her cell and dialed a number. "Hey Ernie, this is Kelley. SAC Cho sent me to Laramie, Wyoming, to cover the—" She paused as she listened to the guy on the other end. "You saw it on the news earlier. That's the case. Yeah, lucky me," she said with a bit of a grimace. "Listen, we need assistance processing the evidence from the fires ASAP. The faster, the better on this one." Her gaze bounced up to Sawyer's.

She nodded and smiled. "Thanks. I owe you one for this." She disconnected. "Once he gets it over at Quantico, he'll do his best to get us answers in less than forty-eight hours."

"Wow." He was impressed. "Must be nice having friends in high places."

"We'll need to drive over to Cheyenne and pick up what you've already submitted to DCI," she said, referring to the Division of Criminal Investigation, where the lab was located.

"No need. I can have Logan send it to your contact. He's a DCI agent. Still lives on the ranch, like me. Only he has a longer commute."

"Holden is chief deputy. Logan is with DCI. What about Monty?"

"State trooper."

"Do you all live on the ranch?" she asked with a teasing smile.

"Afraid so," he said.

Her smile spread wider. "But why? You're all rich."

Sawyer huffed a tired chuckle. "Correction, Holly and Buck Powell are rich," he said, talking about his parents. "My brothers and Matt and I are living off civil servant salaries." It wasn't as bad as it sounded. Their parents had built Monty his own house on the property after everyone thought he was going to get hitched. The engagement fell through, but the place was still there and his. Last year, Holden and his wife moved from the apartment above the garage to their own home a few acres away from Monty once construction was completed. Sawyer took the garage apartment while Logan stayed in a large room in a separate wing of the house from their parents. Matt built his own place, not wanting to stay in the main house or wait to have his aunt and uncle pay for it provided he ever got married. "Besides, Mom and Dad like having us close." It also made it easy for them to pitch in to help on the ranch when needed. "Speaking of living arrangements, where are you planning to stay while you're here?"

"Home. My mom has an old friend who looks after the place. I called her on the drive up. There'll be a key waiting for me under the front mat."

He turned toward her, and his knee brushed against hers, causing an electric spark where they touched. Holding off on a conversation about the past was one thing, but he found it impossible to ignore feelings that welled inside him every time he looked into her eyes. Feelings that reminded him of what they once had. How only physical contact with her would ease the dull ache in his heart.

Their great chemistry hadn't dissipated, but what he wanted from her wasn't sexual, or rather not only sexual. He longed for the intimacy he hadn't known since her, to hold her while she fell asleep. To listen to her breathing. To feel her heart beating against his chest.

If only she needed the same, but at least she didn't pull away this time. A good sign.

"If you get lonely out there all by yourself," he said, reaching over and putting his hand on her knee, "remember, I'm just a few acres away." On horseback, he could reach her in minutes, but that was still too far for his liking. "You could stay on the ranch if you'd prefer. Plenty of guest rooms, and I can guarantee three things—a comfy bed, hot breakfast and strong coffee. In full disclosure, I make no promises that my mom won't cater to your every whim."

A demure smile pulled at her mouth, holding back a laugh.

What he wouldn't give to hear her laugh again.

"I'll be fine," she said. "I'm used to solitude."

"Just because you're used to something doesn't mean you like it. Or have to endure it. Especially not while I'm around. If you were at the ranch, it'd be easier to talk. About work. Only the case," he said, clarifying. He didn't want her to bring the wall back up between them when he'd just gotten her to lower it. "I won't push on the rest." *Only a nudge here and there.*

She hesitated, her expression tightening.

"It'd be safer for you, too," he added. "You're assuming the bomb went off early because you were there and this guy didn't want to kill a federal agent. But what if you're wrong? What if the detonator malfunctioned? What if he didn't want to kill the reporter? Egan has been giving him a lot of coverage that I'm sure he's lapping up. There are a lot of what-ifs." He'd been calculating them. Each one made her theory less likely. "If he planted a bomb in my truck because of my investigation, then you're going to be a target right along with me going forward."

"I can handle myself."

So could he, with an assailant he could see and fight. He hadn't stood a chance against a car bomb.

"You've never been targeted by someone like this," he said.

"Before I was assigned to BAU in Quantico, I worked a case undercover. I had to infiltrate an extremist group. Find their bomb maker. Some people who make explosives bear the marks of their handiwork. The bureau thought I was a perfect fit. They were right. I was able to lure him in. He was attracted to my scars. A sick, twisted guy, but when I caught him, made the bust, it hit the news. My name, my face were out there. The only good thing to come from having my identity exposed was I could publish the book I had been working on. What most people don't know, the part that didn't make it in the news, was I barely got through that alive. In the end, it came down to him and me, but I didn't let him win."

Sawyer wasn't most people. Although he lacked the resources of the FBI, he stayed abreast of what was happening in her life. He was aware of what she'd been through.

"This is different," he said. "You don't have other agents for backup, surveilling your every move."

What if this guy found out where she was staying and lit the house on fire while she was asleep? Or planted a bomb in her rental?

The horrific idea made his blood boil. Made him want to find the culprit and put an end to him before he had another chance to hurt her. He'd taken a piece of shrapnel in his side, but the door that blew off his truck had nearly taken off her head. They were both fortunate to be alive and he intended to keep it that way.

He realized the nature of her job meant sometimes she would face danger, but if it was in his power to protect her, to keep her from suffering, then he would.

"There are no houses near yours." His place was the closest, but it wasn't as if he could stick his head out the window and see her. Bison Ridge was a small mountain-town with a fairly large surrounding landscape, along with a sheriff, a general store and only a few other ranches. "Anything could happen to you out there. My family's ranch is better. Safer." No one was getting in uninvited. If by chance they did, everyone in his family was an excellent shot, thanks to his father making certain of it. Plus, they had twenty armed cowboys in the bunkhouse and a security system.

Liz stared down at his hand on her knee before putting hers atop his and giving it a small squeeze. Her mouth opened. He knew she'd protest because she was a fighter, but he had a sound rebuttal. A knock on the door stopped her from speaking.

They shifted apart.

"Come in," he said.

The door opened. Gareth McCreary poked his head in. He was the assistant chief, managing day-to-day operations, filling in for the chief or one of the battalion commanders as needed. Catching sight of Liz, he hesitated. "I don't mean to interrupt. Do you have a minute?"

Unlike Ted, Gareth was levelheaded. A relatively nice guy. Sawyer never had a problem with him, even when they were going after the same job as fire marshal. "Sure."

"Glad to see you're all right after the bomb tore your truck to pieces." Gareth stepped inside, holding an armful of turnout gear. "We gathered your stuff for you," he said, setting it down in a chair.

"Thanks. I appreciate it." His gear had been the last thing on his mind once the ambulance had arrived and Liz had the foresight to transport the evidence. "Were you on the team today?" The assistants usually worked different shifts from the chief.

"No. When I heard about the fire, I went to check out the scene. Ted is taking off early. Engagement party planning. I'm filling in for him."

"Great." Since Gareth hovered, Sawyer asked, "Anything else I can do for you?"

"It's what I can do for you. I heard things got heated between you and Ted earlier."

Sawyer shook his head. "Not on my end."

Raising his hands in mock surrender, Gareth kept his expression neutral. "With this recent string of fires and murders, we need to remember we're on the same team. Ted agrees. As a gesture of goodwill," he said, tossing him something from his pocket.

Sawyer caught the keys to one of the station's command SUVs. "I was told there wasn't funding in the budget for me to use a department vehicle."

"You need wheels to do your job," Gareth said. "Until you wrap this case, we'll treat any fire like it might be arson. You go in before overhaul. Also—" he beckoned someone else inside "—I think you know this guy."

Joshua Burfield entered and waved hello.

"I do." Stepping over, Sawyer shook the volunteer's hand.

"I asked Josh to brief the others in the VFD," Gareth said, "to ensure we don't have any further miscommunication. The sooner you catch the sick guy doing this, the better for everyone. Including us."

"Please let the volunteers know I appreciate their efforts." Sawyer wanted to make that clear. Their assistance was essential during a crisis such as this. "I hope there are no hard feelings."

Josh shrugged. "If there are, I'm sure it'll blow over. We're here to make things easier. Not harder for anyone in the department."

"One more thing, and we'll let you two get back to it," Gareth said. "Dinner is ready in the kitchen. I volunteered to cook and picked up groceries on my way in. Spaghetti and meatballs. My mother's recipe. You two feel free to help yourself."

"Thank you," Liz said. "Very kind of you."

"Unfortunately, we've already ordered from Delgado's." Sawyer sat back on the sofa.

"If you change your mind, you know where the kitchen is," Gareth said before leaving with Josh and shutting the door behind them.

"That's a first. Make that two," Sawyer said. "I was one of them for more than ten years, I work in the same building, and I haven't been made to feel welcome to join any meals since I started this job. Now I get a dinner invitation and keys to a department vehicle in one day."

Another knock on the door. This time it was their dinner delivery. Sawyer tipped the driver and they dug into the food.

Liz moaned. "I didn't realize how hungry I was," she said around a mouthful of food.

"Ditto." He bit into his burger.

"Or how much I missed Delgado's beef French dip sandwiches with au jus."

He hoped she'd realize there were other things and people she missed, too.

"Hey, what does Ted have against you?" Liz asked before stuffing some fries in her mouth.

How nice to see she had a healthy appetite and didn't only stick to bird food. "He thinks—well, they all think I got the job over Gareth because my last name is Powell." It was a fact and no secret that his parents had friends in high places and enough influence to give him the advantage if he and Gareth were equally qualified. It was also a fact, but a lesser-known truth, that they never would. They came from the school of hard work and had ingrained in their sons the importance of earning their achievements. The only handouts were free room and board, only to keep their kids close, but Sawyer and his brothers even paid for that by working on the ranch. He had the calluses and occasional sleep deprivation to prove it.

"If only they knew you better." Liz patted his leg. "You'd never accept a job you hadn't earned on your own merit," she said with such confidence it filled him with warmth.

She had been more than his girlfriend. More than his lover. She was his best friend. The one person outside his family who knew him, had his back and believed in him without question. Something he hadn't been able to find with anyone else. To be so completely loved. To be the center of another's life.

"Take the invitation and the vehicle as an olive branch." She set down the sandwich, wiped her hands and picked up the file.

"Lizzie, staying at your house alone—"

"If he used a timer and a flare, how did he hide it?" she asked, cutting him off.

"I believe he planted some kind of canister filled with

gasoline, the timer or detonator and flare attached, all concealed in something nondescript. Like a box. At Compassionate Hearts, I found the remnants under a chair in the office and two other spots. He probably planted it the night before around the closing of the restaurant, the nail salon and the thrift store when workers were tired, eager to leave and wouldn't have noticed a small box. It would've been easier to do at the cabin in the woods."

She riffled through the pages. "Where was the device left at the salon?"

"In the basement. Near the stairwell. The fire would've blocked the only way to escape."

"Located in the back of the building?"

Sawyer nodded. "Both of them."

"Then he would've wanted to make sure the nail tech and Aleida were in the right spot when it went off. If this guy was watching, he couldn't have seen them from the street, known for certain they were where he wanted them."

Sawyer connected the dots. "Unless he'd called them. There was a phone line in the basement of the salon and office. They answer, he gets them talking, keeping them on the line until the timer goes off."

"I'll get the phone records. Maybe this guy was stupid enough not to use a burner." She flipped through a couple of pages and stiffened.

"What is it?" he asked.

The color drained from her face. "Can't be," she said, her voice barely a whisper as she stared at the page. "Look." She pointed to the four victims of the cabin fire. "Do you recognize the names? Those three?"

Sawyer glanced at the pictures and the names that went along with them, but nothing rang a bell. He was acquainted with most of the victims. More than a handful of times, he'd been in Compassionate Hearts, had spoken with Martinez in passing. He'd eaten at the restaurant before it had been renovated and burned to the ground. His mother had gotten her nails done at the salon often, and everyone there was pleasant enough. All of them, including the hunters he'd gone to high school with, though he hadn't known them. But that didn't give him the answer as to why they had been attacked.

They didn't go to the same church, belong to the same clubs or even use the same banks. Four lived in Laramie, the other two in Bison Ridge.

"What am I missing?" he asked.

"The hunters, Flynn Hartley, Scott Unger, Randy Tillman, the nail salon technician, Courtney O'Hare, and Aleida Martinez. They were all there at the summer camp the night of the fire."

Sawyer took the file from her and looked it over. He hadn't attended the camp and wasn't familiar with those who had. Though the fire had left indelible scars on the inside for him, he hadn't memorized the list of teens who had escaped. "What about the fourth hunter, Al Goldberg, and the restaurateur, Chuck Parrot? Were they there, too?"

Liz thought for a moment, squeezed her eyes shut and shook her head. "No. They weren't."

He took the file and turned to the incident where the nail tech had been killed. "What about the owner of the salon? Do you recognize the name?"

She glanced at the page. "No."

"What if the murderer had mistaken the tech for the owner and killed O'Hare by accident. This might not be what you're thinking." He hoped like hell that it wasn't.

She sucked in a deep, slow breath, and then her gaze lifted to his. "Five out of the seven people targeted were there that night. You're the math guy. Statistically, is that a coincidence? Or are we dealing with something else? Could the connection be the fire?"

"It's possible Goldberg is an outlier. A result of human

error. The murderer didn't care if Goldberg was in the wrong place at the wrong time and was acceptable collateral damage in order to kill the other men. But why Parrot's restaurant?"

"Maybe our guy torched the restaurant to hide his real motive. Arsonists do it all the time. With Goldberg, perhaps it's like you said, he's an outlier. Wrong place. Wrong time."

They needed to be careful not to skew the data to fit an emotional model. The fire fifteen years ago changed the trajectory of their lives, upended their worlds. The cloud of it, hanging over their heads to this day, could be overshadowing the way she looked at the facts. "We can't jump to conclusions and see threads where there aren't any. There has to be another link we're missing between them."

Liz nodded but with a doubtful expression.

Whatever the connection, they had to find it and be certain. Fast.

Chapter Five

He checked his watch. 10:35 p.m.

Time to shake things up.

He whipped out his burner cell phone and made the call.

On the third ring, the line was answered. "Hello," Neil Steward said.

"You deserve what's about to happen."

Neil didn't respond right away. "Oh yeah, and what's that?"

"Fireworks."

"Bob, is this you messing around?"

"This isn't Bob. The fireworks and much more you deserve. Your son is a different story." The authorities would find his twenty-three-year-old son's body inside the Cowboy Way Tattoo Parlor, where he worked at his father's shop. He'd killed Mike a little earlier. Slit his throat. Then set the devices to start the fire. "But sins of the father..."

"Who is this?"

He triggered the timer and counted down in his head. "My name is Vengeance. You're guilty for what happened to Timothy. You stood by and did nothing to stop it. You stayed silent. Sold your soul. That's why I've taken your boy and your shop." To teach Neil about true loss.

"I—I—I don't know what you're talking about or what you want, but if anything happens to my son, the police are going to get involved. You hear me?"

If only he'd told the police the truth years ago, Mikey would be alive now. But then Neil wouldn't have been paid for silence or had the money to start his own tattoo shop. Neil was a liar and a coward who valued money more than doing the right thing, and when the authorities questioned him tonight, the odds were he'd even lie about this phone call.

"Listen to me, Neil. You're going to burn in hell." *Three.* "No need to call the cops." *Two.* "Your son's body will be found before long." *One.* "They'll be in touch shortly."

The fire had started. Too bad he couldn't be there to see it just yet. Soon. Patience.

Right on cue, Neil yelled colorful expletives over the line, but that wouldn't bring his son back.

He disconnected.

Neil would try to call his son first, then go looking for him at the shop.

Any minute now, a passerby on the street would smell smoke, notice the flames and dial 911. The fire department would be on the scene in less than ten minutes, and a large crowd would gather once more.

Then he could see the Cowboy Way burn.

But how long until you arrive, Liz?

LIZ PULLED UP to her family house and parked the car. *Home.* She'd always think of it as such even if she didn't want to stay.

Sawyer was right behind her in the department vehicle.

She'd declined his offer, again, to stay at the Shooting Star Ranch, but he insisted on making sure she got to her place safely.

Popping the trunk, she hopped out of the car. "See. Nothing to worry about."

"Let's check the place out, sweep for any planted devices before we issue an all clear. Okay?"

Wise words. She wouldn't protest since it had been her plan to search the house.

He reached for her bags, but she grabbed them.

"You're injured." She frowned at him. "And I'm more than capable of carrying my things. I do it all the time."

He took the bags from her hand and closed the trunk. "First, I'm fine. Second, you've been gone so long you've forgotten how a cowboy operates."

Chivalry was not dead in the Mountain West. Another thing she missed.

She led the way up the porch. Under the mat, she found the key and unlocked the door.

Sawyer's phone rang. As they stepped inside, he answered, "Hello." He got quiet as he listened, his features tightening with worry. "You've got to be kidding me." More silence. "We'll be there as soon as we can." He hung up. "There's another fire."

"Already? We extrapolated that there wouldn't be another for a day or two. Not in less than twenty-fours. It's too soon."

"I don't care about FBI projections. I care about the firefighters. The team is exhausted from putting out and overhauling the one at Compassionate Hearts. Not only are innocent civilians being killed, but with this grueling pace of these attacks, the lives of firefighters are being jeopardized."

After they stepped outside, she locked the front door. "Where is it?"

"Back in Laramie. Town center."

Thirty minutes away.

"I'll drive," he said, heading for the SUV.

BITING BACK A SMILE, he watched Liz Kelley climb out of the red LFD SUV and fall into step beside Sawyer, her gaze glued to the fiery beast devouring the Cowboy Way Tattoo Parlor.

Magnificent.

As much as he wanted to stare at the flames and savor the devastation on Neil Steward's face, he kept Liz in sight.

FBI was printed in bright yellow letters on the jacket she wore like armor. The same way she wore the scarf that hid her puckered skin. Relying on her attractive face to appear normal when she was anything but. Covering up her scars when she should've exposed them with pride. The marks of a survivor.

All proof she was still clinging to who she had once been—a pretty, vapid doll, good for nothing besides spreading her legs for Sawyer—instead of embracing what the fire made her, forged into someone new.

A wasted gift. One he'd take back.

It was no coincidence Liz was in town.

Providence brought her to Laramie. Vulcan, the god of fire, summoned her...just for him.

At first, when he spotted her in front of the smoking heap of what was left of Compassionate Hearts, it had been a shock. Then his surprise slowly twisted to anticipation.

Years ago, he thought Liz would be the one to get away. The fire had taken everything from her. Left her scarred and scared. On the run from life itself, which had been sweeter than killing her. But here she was, bigwig FBI agent, risen like a phoenix from the ashes, returned right on time.

Back on his list with the others who would pay.

Earlier, he had salivated at the idea of taking her out along with Sawyer Powell in one fell swoop with the truck bomb, the remote detonator itching in his hand.

But the reporter, covering his handiwork with such flourish, had been with them. Gave him reason to reconsider. So he'd set it off early and got to witness how the air shook with the explosion, glass bursting from the windows, flames lapping at the metal. The second concussive blast was better than the first, with the truck door nearly decapitating Liz and shrapnel wounding Sawyer.

Good thing they hadn't died quickly and painlessly.

The explosion gave him insight. In the aftermath, watching them—how Sawyer tried to shield Liz, the way she caressed his face, the worry in her eyes before she ran to her car, no doubt to race to the hospital—was like old times. Something still burned between them.

Sawyer was a nuisance that he simply wanted out of the way, but with Liz, he could do something special. Toy with her. Break her. Take away someone she loved to show her how it felt before he killed her.

Even if she was FBI.

He wasn't a fool and didn't need the Feds breathing down his neck. So he'd wait until she left Wyoming to end her. After all, he was a patient man. Better to torch her in Virginia anyway. Then her death wouldn't appear related.

Finishing the list and keeping his promise would be worth it in the end. It was the only way to get what he wanted. Needed more than anything else in the world.

Staring at Liz, he knew exactly how to have fun with her while he bided his time to kill her.

He wondered if she could feel the heat of his flame standing so close or sensed what was to come.

Chapter Six

"Is it our guy?" Liz approached Sawyer, who had snagged Gareth's attention as the assistant chief came out of the tattoo shop. "Did he do it again?"

Gareth moved them farther away from the building. "It appears so."

"What happened?" Sawyer asked.

"The owner of the shop next door smelled smoke, went outside to check it out and reported the fire at about 10:40 p.m. Our company and the VFD responded at 10:47 p.m. and 10:55 p.m., respectively. Once we got inside, I immediately saw the similarity to the other fires. That's when I came back out and called you. After I hung up, I heard Neil Steward, the owner, screaming that his kid, Mike, was inside." Gareth gestured to the poor man. "His wife, Evelyn."

Horror and sad resignation welled in Steward's glassy eyes as he held his wife, who was sobbing.

Liz swore under her breath. Her heart ached with pity for the couple.

"Two went in to look for him," Gareth said. "The pair checked the first floor where they do the tattoos, but he wasn't there."

"Did they search the basement or office?" Sawyer asked.

"The office is on the second floor. Can't get close enough yet. Two more devices went off near a pile of flammable materials that were in the shop."

Dread slithered up Liz's spine. "Has that happened before, devices going off while you were inside?"

Gareth shook his head. "No. First time."

"Were the devices exposed or were they hidden inside anything?" Sawyer asked.

"Concealed in cardboard boxes."

Sawyer sighed. "This guy is escalating things. Deliberately endangering firefighters."

"Well," Gareth said, tipping his hat back, "he's definitely slowing us down."

"Strange," Sawyer muttered, staring at the blaze.

She studied his face. "What is it?"

"Our guy wanted the other places to burn to the ground. Hot and fast. Why not this one?" Sawyer mused. "With the other devices going off later, he wanted to take his time for some reason."

Turning, Liz stared at the tormented looks on the faces of Mr. and Mrs. Steward, their gazes fixed on the inferno that had once been their business. "Maybe it's not about the firefighters. I can't imagine anything worse for a parent than this. Having to watch the fire that has taken away their livelihood while waiting to find out if their child is alive or dead."

She scanned the crowd. This guy was out there, taking it all in, relishing the pain and devastation he caused. No way he'd miss it.

Liz spotted someone on the periphery of the crowd discreetly taking pictures. A woman with an athletic build and long hair in a ponytail. "Hey, is that a deputy in plain clothes?" she asked Sawyer.

He followed her gaze. "Deputy Ashley Russo."

"Good." Liz nodded once, briskly. "We'll have a picture of him. He's here. I'm sure of it."

Sawyer leaned in, putting his mouth close to her ear.

"The Stewards, were any of them in the fire at the camp—Neil, Evelyn or Mike?"

"They weren't there." She knew the names of every camper that had been locked in the cabins and all the men from the bunkhouse who had worked to save her life and rescue the Durbins that night.

How were the Stewards connected to the other recent victims?

Two firefighters emerged from the tattoo parlor.

"We want to talk to them," Sawyer said to Gareth.

"Come on. It's Anderson and the probie Johnson. Hey!" Gareth started toward the fire engine where the two were headed. "Anderson, Johnson, over here!"

The two turned and trudged toward them in full turn-out gear with their breathing apparatuses hanging around their necks. One was a woman, which surprised Liz. She wasn't sure why. In her job, she'd met more than a few female firefighters. Maybe she hadn't expected to find one here in Laramie.

Both had looks of weary devastation.

"Anderson, Johnson," Sawyer said, "this is Agent Liz Kelley. Well? Did you find Mike Steward?"

"We thought we had a chance of saving him," Anderson said, her voice rough from the smoke. "The fire didn't reach the second floor. We managed to put it out, but he was already dead."

"Smoke inhalation?" Sawyer asked.

Johnson shook his head. "His throat had been cut. I thought I was going to retch right there. Never seen anything like it."

"Me either. My God." Anderson's voice was heavy, horrified. "Do you think the fire was set to cover it up?" she asked.

"He wanted us to find the body like that." Liz crossed her arms. "Otherwise, he would've set a device upstairs.

Probably would have doused it in gasoline, too, to hide the wound until the ME examined the body."

"Tell me what you saw when you first went in," Sawyer said.

"Not much at first." Anderson opened the top part of her coat. "Smoke was too thick. Black."

"The spray turned to vapor straight away," Johnson added.

"You should know the fire was up high, Sawyer," Anderson said. "In certain areas, the ceiling looked the same as the recent fires."

"He used gasoline again."

"Same accelerant," Anderson said with a nod. "The others got a handle on the secondary fires." She tugged off her gloves. "We kept moving. Checked the basement first since we found the nail tech down there. But nothing. We finally got up to the second floor."

Johnson closed his eyes. "I almost—" he paused and swallowed convulsively "—slipped in the blood. There was so much."

"It's not an easy sight," Liz said, trying to console him. "Even if you've seen it before, you never really get used to it."

Anderson looked at Sawyer. "Got a second?" She hiked her chin to the side, and they took a couple of steps away.

"You all right, Tessa?" He pushed her hat back and put a comforting hand on her shoulder, and unwelcome annoyance prickled Liz.

"I've been better." Even dirty with a soot-smudged face, she was girl-next-door cute. "When my shift from hell ends, I really need to blow off some steam. Decompress. You interested in having some fun tomorrow night?"

One side of Sawyer's mouth hiked up in a wry grin.

The idea of him having fun with the pretty, probably

flawless, firefighter sent a wave of jealousy through Liz so hard and fast it astonished her.

Get a grip. Although she had been living like a nun, there was zero reason for a handsome hottie like Sawyer Powell to be celibate. Girls had been throwing themselves at him since high school. He'd had his pick, could've chosen anyone, but he'd fallen for her. She'd been truly lucky then, before the fire.

Sawyer probably had a lot of *fun* on a regular basis, and it was none of her business. Only this case was.

Giving herself a stern mental shake, she looked away as Sawyer replied to Tessa too low for Liz to hear and turned to Gareth. "Has anybody talked to the crowd?"

"Yeah, Sawyer's brother Holden." Gareth looked around. "He's out there somewhere."

"I'll find him."

"Hey." Gareth stopped her from walking away. "We didn't really know each other well back in the day."

She tensed, bracing herself for it. She'd run into more people from high school than she cared to remember since she'd been back. Gareth was going to be the first to bring up the fire. "We didn't hang out in the same circles. But I hear you and Ted are still best friends."

Whenever you saw one, you saw the other. Frick and Frack was what everyone called them in school.

Odd how things and people she hadn't thought of in ages were coming back to her now.

Gareth's smile was tight and didn't reach his eyes. "Ted can come across a bit abrasive." He lifted a brow. "But he's a good guy."

"If you say so."

He met her gaze squarely. "Anyway, what happened to you back then was awful. It's good to see you again, doing so well."

"Yeah." She never knew how to respond when all she wanted was to walk away. "Thanks."

"Hotshot FBI. I bought a copy of your book. Most of us at the station did. It's signed, but before you leave town, would you mind personalizing it for me?"

Inwardly, she cringed but kept her discomfort from surfacing on her face.

Sawyer left Tessa Anderson's side.

"Sure, I'll sign it if you want. Excuse me." Liz stepped away from Gareth. "Sounds like you've got a hot date tomorrow night." As soon as the words left her mouth, she regretted saying them. *Why did you go there?*

He stopped and stared at her. "Do you care?" he shot back, his gaze boring into hers.

She shouldn't, but she did. "You're free to do what you want when you're not working. Everyone needs downtime to blow off steam. You deserve it."

"That includes you, too, right?"

Nice going. "I'll go for a run. It's how I unwind. I'll be fine."

"You're fine a lot. Fine working for the FBI. Fine out in Virginia. Fine with your solitude. Fine staying at that old house in Bison Ridge alone regardless of the risks. Fine going for a run instead of getting sweaty with someone. But are you ever happy, Lizzie?"

She rocked back on her heels. Why was she suddenly under attack? And how dare he analyze her and try to dissect her life. "I shouldn't have made the comment about the hot date. It's not my business. I wasn't judging."

Sighing, he lowered his head. "I'm glad you said something. It's the only way I'd know if you cared." His gaze flickered back up to hers. "And, no, I don't have a date. Tessa claims she wants fun, but I know better. What she really wants is a husband."

"You'd make a great one. You're the settling-down type. Clearly you two have chemistry."

A muscle ticked in his jaw. "Chemistry isn't the same as compatibility. No marriage should be based on sex. Even if it is mind-blowing."

Not only did he have fun with Tessa, but it was *mind-blowing*. A detail she did not need or want to know.

"Bottom line," he continued, "I'm not the guy for her and she's not the woman for me. Not that you care though, right?"

Movement from the corner of her eye told her this conversation wasn't private.

She pivoted and faced Holden Powell.

"Sorry to intrude. I didn't realize," Holden said to Sawyer. "Hey, you." He wrapped her in a big hug, lifting her from her feet.

It was unexpected and warm and lasted way too long.

Finally, he put her down, leaving her breathless. She wasn't used to affection anymore, much less the big, cowboy kind.

"It's been ages since I've seen you," Holden said.

She pulled up her scarf that had slipped down her neck. "Yeah." She glanced at Sawyer, but he didn't meet her eyes, wouldn't even look at her. Did she want him to?

Staring at him, she no longer knew *what* she wanted besides solving this case.

"I need to go inside the shop." Sawyer turned for the department SUV, with Liz and Holden following behind him. He grabbed his boots from the trunk and sat on the tailgate.

Liz watched him slip them on, his jaw clenched, his fingers clumsy on the clamps of the boots. This type of emotional distraction, worrying about him and herself, rather than concentrating on the job, was precisely what she wanted to avoid. It was bad enough that doubt always found a way to slide in regardless of how many cases she closed. For her, there were always waves of self-confidence with an undercurrent of insecurity. She didn't need complicated emotions thrown into the mix. "This is why I wanted to keep things professional. Not make it personal. Can you let this go?"

Giving a chuckle full of ire, he grabbed his kit. "*You* brought up *me* having a hot date," he snapped. "You got personal. But sure, I can let it go. I'll store it in my locked box where I keep everything else bottled up until I have your permission to unpack it."

Holden whistled softly.

She opened her mouth to set him straight, and her mind went blank. Except for one thing. He was right. About all of it. Her focus had slipped. She'd gotten jealous when she had no right and then opened a giant can of worms by discussing it.

Liz let out a long breath.

Holden put a hand on his brother's shoulder. "Are you okay to go in there injured? You've got stitches."

"I'm medically cleared to do my job, Mom." Shoving past them, Sawyer flipped on a flashlight and stalked off into what remained of the tattoo shop, carrying his kit.

"Man, you got him riled up." Holden elbowed her. "Deep down, he's just happy to have you back in town."

"I can tell." She looked up at him. He was a little shorter than Sawyer and no longer broader. When Holden played football, he was beefy. Since then, he'd gotten leaner, which suited him. He was clean-shaven. None of the scruffy rough-and-tumble two-day stubble Sawyer had down so well, making him look edgy.

Holden stared at her with those kind eyes of his and flashed a sympathetic smile. "You've been gone too long."

"Or not long enough."

"He always swore you'd come back. And here you are. Getting a wish fulfilled after fifteen years is a lot to process when you're simultaneously investigating the toughest case of your career alongside the woman who was the love of your life."

But she didn't come back for him. A pang of guilt lanced her chest.

Get to work. She bit down on the inside of her lip and refocused on the task at hand. "What did you learn from the crowd?"

"Not too much. The hours at the shop varied. According to the owner of the store next door, Mike didn't take many walk-ins. Mostly appointments. Whoever did this might have made one to get him here when he wanted. No one saw or heard anything suspicious other than the smoke. You'll want to speak to Neil Steward. He claims he received a strange phone call. Someone threatened to hurt Mike. Hard to get more out of him right now. Might be best to speak to him tomorrow."

Gareth was giving the Stewards the news about their son. The wife wailed and Neil broke down in tears. The couple needed a chance to grieve.

"Yeah. Can you ask them to come in?" she asked.

"Sure. Is the sheriff's office okay?"

She nodded. "Could you also go through the pictures Deputy Russo is taking? See if anyone stands out for any reason?"

"We'll take care of it."

"Chief Deputy! Miss FBI!" A man pushed through the crowd and slipped under the police barricade. He was holding an open bottle of whiskey. "It's high time you put a stop to this!" He took a long swig from the bottle.

Liz couldn't put a name on the face, but she recognized him.

"Chuck." Holden approached him. "I can't have you drunk and disorderly on the streets with an open container."

"I've lost everything. The restaurant. My house that I put

up for collateral on the loans. Penny is gone, too. Packed a bag. Went to her mother's in Nebraska. And you want to give me a citation for trying to drown my troubles when you all should be putting a stop to this."

"Mr. Parrot, I'm Agent Liz Kelley."

"Everybody knows who you are. The girl who survived." He put the bottle up to his mouth and guzzled more liquor until Holden snatched it from his hands. Chuck lifted his chin, his eyes narrowed. Cold. Furious. Drunk. "When are you going to arrest Kade Carver?"

Holden put a fist on his hip. "What does he have to do with this?"

"Everything." Parrot threw his arms out wide and teetered. "He's the reason this is happening."

"Who is Kade Carver?" she asked, whispering to Holden.

"A wealthy developer."

"More like business wrecker," Parrot said, his words slurred. "He wants to buy out the entire block. Build a fancy townhouse community. Right here. In the center of it all. My restaurant. The nail salon. Now Neil's tattoo parlor. On the same damn block. Come on. Wake up and smell the conspiracy. With these fires, he'll get everything on this block dirt cheap now. I'm talking pennies on the dollar."

Liz looked at Holden. "Another name to add to the list for tomorrow." She glanced at Parrot. "We'll look into it."

"About time that you do." Parrot spun around, stumbled, swayed and lumbered away.

"Be prepared," Holden said. "Carver will lawyer up. It's going to be an exhausting day. Double shift for me since I'm in charge of the office while my brother-in-law is on vacation with his fiancée."

Liz patted his shoulder. "Congratulations on getting hitched. I'm glad you finally found someone willing to put up with you," she said, and he laughed. Then she pieced together what he'd said. "Wait a minute, your brother-in-law is the sheriff?"

He nodded. "My relationship with Grace happened fast and unexpectedly. It made things awkward at work for a while, but her brother has come around since the wedding. Now he's at the ranch all the time for family dinners. Anyway, where are you staying? B&B in town? The Shooting Star?"

"Bison Ridge."

Holden frowned at her. "After the car bomb, is it wise to stay out there alone?"

Ugh. "Not you, too. If I were a man, would you ask me that?"

He shrugged. "Maybe. I've always thought of you as a sister, and considering what nearly happened to Sawyer, I don't want any member of my family who is investigating this case staying somewhere isolated."

"I appreciate the concern, but I'll be fine." After all, she was a trained agent and armed.

Smiling, Holden shook his head. "You're just as stubborn as ever. Nice to see some things never change. You should get some rest."

If only. She'd been up since three that morning with nerves over her presentation at the symposium. "I've got to wait on Sawyer since we came together." *Joined at the hip.*

Holden raised his eyebrows. "Going to be a long ride to Bison Ridge with Mr. Grumpy Pants."

"Yeah. It is." But there were more important things to think about. "Come on. I'll help you finish canvassing the crowd."

Chapter Seven

A shotgun racking nearby made Sawyer jackknife upright from his sleeping bag. The sharp signature ratcheting sound, which couldn't be mistaken for anything else, had him wide awake. In the morning light filtering into his tent, he grabbed the pistol at his side.

"Whoever is in there," Liz said from outside, "come out slowly with your hands up, or I'll shoot first and ask questions later, provided you're still alive to answer."

Hearing her voice calmed his racing pulse. Exchanging his gun for his Stetson, he put his black cowboy hat on and climbed out of the tent, wearing nothing else but his boxer briefs and a smile. "Good morning to you, too."

Eyes flaring wide, Liz lowered the shotgun. Irritation etched across her face. She wore jeans, a tank top and an open button-down shirt that she had probably thrown on in haste. Her gaze dipped, traveling over his body, and a blush rose on her cheeks.

"When you dropped me off last night," she said, meeting his eyes, "and didn't hassle me again about staying out here alone, I thought you had dropped the issue."

His temper had simmered on the ride back, and he'd thought it best to be quiet. No point arguing. Nothing would've been achieved. She'd made up her mind to be stubborn, and he had made up his to be equally obstinate. "Guess you don't know me so well anymore. I told you, now that you're a part of the investigation, you could become a target as well. It's not safe for you to be out here by yourself."

"So you decided to pitch a tent in the thicket a couple hundred feet from my house and spy on me. I'm FBI. You didn't think I'd notice?"

He chuckled. "You say 'spy,' I say 'protect.' And you didn't notice my camouflaged tent until the sun came up and you were staring out the window while making coffee."

She narrowed her eyes. "How do you know that?"

Educated supposition. She was dressed and he could see the steam rising from a mug she'd left on the porch railing. "Guess I still know you pretty well."

Yawning, he stretched, and her gaze raked over him once more, making him smile.

She put a fist on her lean hip. "I'm tempted to knock that grin off your face."

"Feel free to indulge." Tipping his hat at her, he stepped within striking distance. All she had to do was reach out and touch him. "When it comes to physical contact, I'll take what I can get with you."

She leveled a look at him, hard ice in her eyes, her expression beyond chilling, but he still felt the heat from being near her. "You're incorrigible," she said, "and you're trespassing."

"Correction. You're trespassing. Ten feet before you reach the thicket is where your property line ends and mine begins." He pointed it out. "You're standing on Powell land."

Shaking her head, she sighed. "I forgot how much of it my parents sold. On the bright side, the parcel is probably small enough to put up a high fence to keep prowlers from spying."

No fence would keep him out where Liz was concerned. "I'd strongly encourage it. The investment would mean you intend to stick around." He would love nothing more than to have her stay.

Her gaze fell, the humor draining from her face. She spun around, heading back to the house, carrying the shotgun on her shoulder.

"Can I get a cup of coffee? And take a shower?" he called out after her.

Stopping, she looked back at him. "Are you kidding me?"

He shrugged. "It'll save me from driving all the way back to the ranch." His vehicle was parked down the road, but a ten-minute ride one way. "More efficient to get ready here."

She had always been a stickler about efficiency. He hoped he'd pushed the right button.

Liz considered it a moment before waving to him to follow her.

Bingo. Smiling, he ducked back into his tent. He put on his boots, grabbed his weapon and a small duffel bag with essentials and then hurried to catch up.

In the kitchen, she set the gun on a large wooden farmhouse-style table. The place brought back memories. Most of them fond. Laughter around the table at dinner with her parents. Some of them steamy. Sneaking upstairs and making out in her room. The last few memories had been heart-wrenching.

"Did your parents leave it here?" He gestured to the shotgun.

"No, the caretaker left it for me, along with a stocked fridge." She took a mug from the cabinet and filled it with steaming black coffee. "You still take two sugars and cream?"

"I wish." He patted his stomach. "Not anymore." He was trying to keep the love handles away. "I usually just add a little protein powder to it these days, but black is fine."

She picked up a resealable bag filled with a cream-colored powder from the side of the sink. "I carry some with me whenever I travel. Better than relying on burgers every time I need a quick meal." She set it on the table. "Whatever you're doing, it's clearly working," she said, eyeing his torso and handing him the mug.

As he took it from her, their fingers brushed, and he let the contact linger. "Why did your parents keep this place?" he asked, already knowing the answer. "They never come here."

She dropped her hand. "It's been in the family forever. They want me to move back here someday. Pass the place down to my children. I keep telling them I'm never getting married or having kids, but hope springs eternal with them."

His gaze fell to her exposed throat. The side was a shade lighter than the rest with discernible scars that disappeared beneath her shirt. He took in the rest of her, silky hair reflecting the sunlight, tempting cleavage, trim waist, long legs that had once curled around his hips, holding him close.

She reached for the scarf on the table.

Setting down his coffee with one hand, he caught her wrist in his other before she could take the neckerchief. "You don't need to hide from me."

She tensed. "Habit. I hate when people stare."

"I wasn't staring," he said, honestly. "I was admiring all of you." Also the truth.

A soft laugh of disbelief came from her as she rolled her eyes. "You don't have to say things like that."

She tried to pull away, but he tightened his grip. Nothing forceful. She could release the hold if she wanted. No doubt she could knock him on his butt, too, in the process.

"Why won't you ever get married or have kids?" He stepped toward her, erasing the space between them. "You're also the settling-down type." He kept his tone gentle. "You'd make a great wife. An amazing mother. You always wanted your own family."

She reeled back with a grimace, but not hard enough or far enough to break the contact. "Stop it. You know why I can't."

He drew closer, putting her arm against his chest and flattening her palm over his heart. "I don't."

"We agreed not to talk about this." Her voice was firm, but she trembled. "About us."

"I'm not talking about us. I'm asking about you," he said, his voice low and soft. "When was the last time you let someone hug you, hold you?"

His confidential source had told him Liz didn't date. Ever. Didn't hang out with friends after work. No bestie to turn to for comfort. Only traveled for business. Didn't visit her parents. A workaholic who chose to be alone.

She hesitated, and he saw in the startled depths of her pale green eyes that it had been far too long. Years.

His heart ached for her. He at least eased his pain, the loneliness, by seeking temporary comfort with others. A warm body here and there. A distraction, a reminder of what he truly missed. It always brought him full circle in the end. Right back to wanting the one person who no longer wanted him. Liz.

"A few hours ago," she stammered.

He chuckled when he really wanted to grit his teeth at how his brother had gotten his arms around her first. Born eleven months apart, with Holden being older, they'd competed most of their lives. His brother usually came out on top. But the win of hugging *his* Liz first irked him to the bone. "Holden doesn't count."

"I say he does." Her eyes hardened. "Don't you need to get ready so we can get going? We have work to do."

This case was important. No doubt about that. Lives were at risk. Another fire could be set, another murder committed at any moment. But now he realized that she didn't simply bury herself in work, she used it as a deflection, as the greatest excuse. She'd survived the fire, but she wasn't truly living.

Deep down, if he was honest, neither was he. Like recognized like.

"I think we both need something else first." He wrapped his arms around her, bringing her into his body for a hug.

She stilled, and he thought she might pull away, but she didn't. At first, she was so stiff he could have been hugging a statue. Slowly, her body relaxed against him. He tucked her head under his chin, where she fit perfectly. Resting her cheek on his shoulder, she kept one palm on his chest, spread her fingers wide and brought her other hand to his lower back, not quite returning the hug, but he'd take it.

The searing heat from having skin on skin, hers on his, sent sensation coursing through him, warming his heart, releasing the tension he carried in his chest. He wanted to tear down the protective wall she'd built around herself. The one that kept her isolated. Surround her with light and love and affection. All the things she denied herself and deserved.

Tightening the embrace, not wanting to ever let her go, he pressed his mouth to the top of her head. Inhaled the scent of her hair, breathing her in. She smelled like spring flowers after a storm. Heady. Sultry.

Sweet.

Her spine of steel softened, her body melting into his, triggering every cell in his brain to remember the passion and pleasure they'd known in each other's arms. As well as the peace. With his thumb, he made soothing circles on her back over her shirt, dipping lower. His other hand drifted to her waist and then slid to her hip. Tenderness turned to desire in a flash. No holding back. No hiding his arousal. He soaked in the heat from her body, the softness of her curves, the smell of her.

"Liz." Only a rasp of her name filled with the longing that was growing inside him.

She sighed against his chest.

The sound slight, hinting at the vulnerability she dared

show, only stoked the wild need firing in his blood. She was everything he remembered. Everything he never stopped wanting. No matter how hard he had tried to get her out of his head, each time he'd failed.

She lifted her chin, their gazes locking, and she shuddered against him.

"You smell good," he whispered. *Feel good, too. Oh, so good.*

They were different people. Things had changed between them. They'd attempted to move on. But there was no denying they had grown in the same direction. Fighting for justice. Sacrificing everything to see it served. Through it all, this remained—heat and longing—the memories that wouldn't let either of them go. The feel of her against him, beneath him, when he was inside her. The taste of her in his mouth. The scent of her. The thousand little things about *her* he simply couldn't forget.

"You smell like you need a shower," she replied.

Chuckling, he cupped the side of her face, his palm cradling her cheek. "It was hot in the tent." Sweltering. Between making sure Liz was safe and the warm night air, he'd barely rested.

"You've gotten soft if you missed the AC."

They had slept under the stars more than once, enjoying not only the summer heat but also what they generated together. Sweat coating their skin, dripping from their bodies as they cuddled close. He'd taken it for granted that he'd have endless moments of holding her.

If only he'd known…

He ran his thumb over her mouth. Her lips parted with a tremble, her green eyes burning with unsure desire. Gravity pulled his head to hers, and he did what he'd longed to since he'd seen her at Compassionate Hearts. He kissed her, soft and subtle. She froze, making his heart pound with fear. Then her arms were around his neck as she rose on the balls of her feet and kissed him back, her tongue seeking his. Everything quickly became insistent, far more demanding. She arched against him, moaning, and he forgot how she'd walked away, turned her back on him, abandoned their plans for the future, forsaking him to uncertainty and a new kind of devastation. The heartache that had only deepened over time. Left him hollow. Uneasy. Aching.

Until this moment.

Her hands tangled in his hair, her body rubbing against his. He gloried in the surrender of her response. Oh, he'd miss this...missed her so much. Need rocked through him. He slid his hand from her jaw, cupping the side of her neck, wanting her even closer.

She stiffened and shoved him away. "I can't."

His heart squeezed at those two words. "Liz." Desperation was a cold hard fist in the pit of his stomach. "Please. I'm—"

"I can't," she repeated in a harsh whisper, tears glistening in her eyes, but her hands were curled into fists at her sides.

She was ready to charge into battle—against him.

But he didn't have a clue how to fight whatever this was. For so long, he thought she needed time. Needed to heal. Needed to regain her confidence. Needed to remember how strong she was. All of which she'd done.

"Can't what?" he demanded. Bear to be touched? Bear to be seen? Bear to love him anymore?

Pressure swelled in his chest like a balloon inflating.

"Do *this*." Pulling her shoulders back, she wiped any emotion from her face, her expression turning guarded. "There's no room for distraction."

His stomach dropped. That's what she thought of him, of fate bringing them back together? "This here, you and me, was once everything. Never a distraction."

"That was then. We can't repeat the past. Not everything we want deep inside works out."

Her words landed on his heart like hailstones.

Proof of what she'd said stood right in front of him. Rejecting him. Using work as an excuse.

She grabbed her holstered sidearm, sheathed knife, field jacket and scarf. "I'll meet you at the sheriff's office. I don't want to be late for any interviews." She stormed outside, letting the screen door slam shut.

Once more leaving him alone, sucking all the air out of the room. He couldn't breathe.

For years, he'd pushed forward, battling his own demons by becoming a firefighter and then fire marshal. As if putting out enough fires, saving enough people, stopping enough arsonists, would make up for his failure at keeping her safe. Change the fact that he hadn't gone into the stables after her, and if he had, the beam wouldn't have fallen on her and she wouldn't have been burned. That the universe would bring her back to him.

All the while, he refused to get attached to anyone else because no other woman was Liz. *His* Liz.

He'd waited for this chance to show her how much he still cared. That the accident didn't matter. And he blew it.

Thinking it would be simple. Easy. As if a hug and a kiss would change anything. He didn't know what in the world had come over him besides pure instinct. Standing in that kitchen like they'd done many times before, unable to keep his distance from her, he hadn't thought. The need to touch her had been all-consuming.

Nothing else had mattered. Not even the consequences.

Regret pooled in his gut, making him sick. He'd pushed too hard, too far, too fast and she ran away from him. Again.

Only this time, she was more out of reach than ever, and he had no idea what to do other than get back to work.

Chapter Eight

In the car, Liz couldn't stop shaking as she drove. She'd made a deal with him, had drawn a line in the sand, and he'd crossed it. No, he'd completely erased it. Even worse, she'd let him. Sure, he weaponized his good looks, standing in her kitchen only wearing his underwear, cowboy hat and boots. Oozing charm. Flexing his muscles. The sight of him, showing all that skin, was more temptation than any woman could resist. Even a hardened agent like her.

Crossing the line with him had been impulsive and wrong, despite feeling so right. He'd stopped her from grabbing her scarf and looked at her with those baby blues, turning her stomach fluttery, the same way he used to, the tingle spreading to her thighs. One touch, one look, and he slipped past the defenses she'd painstakingly built. She was at a loss as he wrapped her in his strong arms, the warmth of him seeping beneath her skin, the smell of him—pine and sweat, all man—enveloping her senses, completely overwhelming her, the sensations stripping her bare.

In that moment, it was impossible to make herself numb. To pretend she was fine being alone. To ignore the throbbing ache in her soul, a wound of her own making when she ended things with him.

Then he kissed her, melting her like warm butter, awakening something deep inside her that had been dormant for so long. His mouth familiar, like coming home, and at the same time new—an adventure she yearned for without realizing.

She couldn't breathe, couldn't think. Everything faded besides him and the burning need to be held by him, caressed and cherished, and to forget about the scars.

No matter how far she ran, how busy she stayed, the one truth she couldn't escape in his arms was how much she still loved him. How she wanted him more than her next breath.

But when his hand slid to her neck, she remembered why she'd left Wyoming. Why she'd left him.

Sawyer was deadly handsome. He deserved a partner who was equal in every way.

He had no idea what she looked like without clothes. Touching her, he remembered the girl she'd once been. Never quite as picture-perfect as him but overall attractive. Appealing.

Now, her body looked like a patchwork quilt from the grafts. Some areas smooth, some goosefleshy, others mottled. Almost Frankensteinesque. The sight of her nude nothing less than tragic.

She could track terrorists, infiltrate an extremist group undercover, subdue a suspect twice her size. What she could not do was risk baring herself to him, seeing pity or revulsion in his eyes, feeling hesitation in his touch.

That would break her into a million pieces with no way for her to recover.

She parked at the Sheriff's Department and took time collecting herself. *Only the case matters. Treat him like a colleague. Not a former lover who you miss more than anything in the world.* She needed another minute. Or two. Closing her eyes, she fell back on her training and shut down her emotions.

After tying the scarf around her neck and buttoning up her shirt, she headed inside. She approached a deputy sitting at the front counter and flashed her badge. "Agent Kelley here to see Chief Deputy Powell."

"He's not in yet, but Deputy Russo is waiting for you in the sheriff's office. We were given instructions to let you and the fire marshal set up in there. Come on through."

With a nod, she said, "Thanks."

The deputy hit a buzzer, and she entered through a half door at the end of the counter. She made her way through the bullpen to the sheriff's office and knocked on the door.

Deputy Russo, in uniform, hopped up from behind the desk and greeted her at the threshold. "Pleasure to meet you. I'm Ashley Russo." She extended her hand.

The shake was firm. "Agent Kelley."

"We left a message for Mr. Carver late last night. He called bright and early this morning to say he would swing by on his way to a worksite with his attorney. Sometime this afternoon."

He was lawyering up, but at least he wasn't stalling. Her gut told her he'd have a solid alibi. His type always did. "What about Mr. and Mrs. Steward?"

"They said they'd come in but didn't commit to a specific time."

Completely understandable. The horror of what they'd been through was unimaginable, something no parent should have to suffer. "You were the one taking photographs of the crowd last night. Have you had a chance to look through them?" Liz asked.

"Yes, I have. I came in at seven to get started on it. I pulled them up on the computer. Also, I enlarged them, focusing on individual faces and printed those for you. I started putting names to a couple. There's still a lot to go through."

Overachiever. Liz liked that. "By any chance, would you be able to continue helping this morning?"

"As a matter of fact, I can. Those were my marching orders from Deputy Powell." She glanced at the clock. "He should be in soon." Russo went around the desk and pulled the chair out for her.

Liz sat and clicked through all the photos, getting oriented. Russo showed her the ones of individuals that had been enlarged and enhanced. Some had a strip of general-purpose masking tape on them with names written in Sharpie. She took in the various expressions, searching for any that stood out. Unemotional. Excited. Aroused. Happy.

"What are we working on?" a familiar voice asked from the doorway, stirring more than the physical in her.

She looked up to see Sawyer Powell waltz into the office sporting his cowboy hat, fire marshal T-shirt and jeans that highlighted his sculpted physique. Her blood pressure spiked at how good he looked. His holstered sidearm and badge hooked to his belt reminded her that not only was he a fire marshal but also a law enforcement officer.

His gaze met hers, and instead of fight in his eyes, she only saw sadness, a haunted and desolate expression hanging on his face that stunned her.

"Putting names to the faces in the crowd last night in front of the Cowboy Way," she said.

"Find anything interesting yet?" Holden asked, coming in behind his brother.

Liz glanced back at the photos. "Not yet. Russo and I could use help identifying people. I'd say the more, the merrier, but really, it'd only be faster."

"I can help for a bit." A cell phone buzzed. "I got a text from Logan," Holden said, glancing at his phone. "He is about to board a plane to drop off the evidence at Quantico. His boss insisted on preserving the chain of custody. Nobody wants any issues if we're able to take this to trial."

"Great." The news was the best she could've hoped for, but she couldn't muster more than a humdrum response while looking at Sawyer. "Ernie will get started on it today."

As Sawyer approached the desk, she noticed he was carrying a take-out tray with two cups and a bag from Delgado's. He set one of the to-go cups down in front of her. "This is better than the sludge they perk here."

"Hey." Holden elbowed Sawyer's good side. "It's not that bad."

"Yes, it is." Sawyer opened the bag and set two wrapped sandwiches on the desk. "Breakfast. Egg whites and cheese. One has turkey bacon. The other turkey sausage."

Why did he have to be so sweet? His charm was hard to resist.

The smell of the sandwiches made her stomach growl. Apparently, he really did watch what he ate. Even last night, he'd had a side salad with his grilled chicken, making her feel naughty by inhaling the beef sub.

"No breakfast sandwich for me?" Holden asked with a teasing grin. "I am letting you guys use the sheriff's office."

Neither she nor Sawyer smiled in response or looked away from one another.

"You always eat at home since you and Grace got married." Sawyer sipped his coffee, not taking his sad eyes off her, doing his best to make her squirm.

But it didn't work. She never let a colleague get under her skin.

Holden shrugged. "The gesture would've been nice."

"I'm not hungry. You can have mine," she said flatly, holding Sawyer's gaze, no matter how uncomfortable it made her with the air backing up in her lungs. "Thanks for the coffee."

Sawyer grabbed both sandwiches and tossed them, one at a time, sinking each into the trash bin without even looking. "You want to let your blood sugar drop. Fine. Neither of us will eat."

"Hey. Why are you wasting perfectly good food? Do

you know what Mom would say?" Holden went to the bin and fished them out. "Ashley, are you hungry?"

"Actually, since I came in so early, I skipped breakfast. I'd like one," the deputy said, and Liz regretted not offering it to her.

"Bacon or sausage?" Holden asked.

"Sausage please."

He handed it to her. "I'll have the other for a midmorning snack." His gaze bounced from Liz to his brother. "This energy is different from last night. What is going on between you two this morning?" he asked, picking up on the tension that thickened the air.

"Nothing," she said, not letting any emotion leak into her voice or show on her face.

"On that we can agree," Sawyer grumbled.

She was thankful he didn't elaborate. There was a time when the two brothers spilled their guts to each other. No topic or detail off limits. Maybe Russo's presence stopped him.

Liz couldn't get over the injured expression on Sawyer, and warning clanged in her head, reminding her that wild animals were more aggressive, more dangerous when wounded.

Not that he should be the one upset. She'd only asked to wait to hash everything out until after they finished the case. Not for a reckless one-off kiss in her kitchen that dredged up in excruciating clarity everything she'd missed the past fifteen years. Aroused by pressing against that solid wall of muscle he called a chest. Teased by tasting him. Tormented by wanting to do it again. *Thank you very much.*

"Why don't we each take a stack of photos," Holden suggested. "If you can't ID the person, set it in the middle of the desk, and someone else will take a crack at it."

Everyone grabbed a chair. Russo dug into the sandwich with gusto, and before she finished, Holden had started on his second breakfast. The yummy aroma had Liz wondering if she'd made the right choice.

Deputy Russo needed it more than me.

They worked for a couple of hours, getting most of the names, discussing any contentious history between individuals that might be relevant when she came across a picture that gave her chills. White male. Late twenties. Brown eyes. Dark hair. Grinning like it was Christmas morning. The smile on his lips was subtle, but the gleam in his big bright eyes gave her pause.

Putting her coffee cup down, she held up the picture. "Who is this?"

Holden stared at the photo. "I know this guy. His name is on the tip of my tongue." He snapped his fingers, trying to think. "Released three or four months ago."

Tapping the photo, Liz said, "I bet he's a firebug."

Russo slipped in behind the computer. "I'm on it." She clacked away, typing for a few minutes. "Found him. Isaac Quincy. Convicted arsonist. Released three months ago."

"Can I take a look at the file?" Liz asked, and Russo moved aside. She skimmed through it. "According to his record, he has been in and out of jail since he was sixteen. Every arrest was for arson. Accelerants used were gasoline, kerosene and lighter fluid." She reviewed each incident. "Hmm. The fires escalated in aggression. His last two stints in jail were for burning down his childhood home while his parents were on vacation. He had been house-sitting. In the parents' statement, they said he was a 'good boy' who simply couldn't control himself. Mom didn't want to press charges. Dad did for his son's own good. The last one was for torching a dumpster while a homeless person was inside of it. Quincy claimed he didn't know the man was asleep inside. The victim suffered second-degree burns. No fatalities."

"Do you think he could be our guy?" Sawyer asked.

"It's possible." She looked around the room at the others. "He fits the profile, but these recent fires feel—"

"Personal," Sawyer said, finishing her sentence. "He didn't just set fires. He blew up the restaurant and turned the Compassionate Hearts into an inferno."

She nodded. "Not the work of a random firebug. But his recent release from prison coinciding with serial arson can't be dismissed, either."

"Maybe he was hired," Holden suggested, "by Kade Carver. I can't see him getting his hands dirty. I spoke to a couple of owners of other shops in those two blocks. They were reluctant to sell before, but after the fires, they've decided to accept Carver's offer."

"Deputy Russo, could you dig into it?" Liz asked. "See if there's any possible connection between Quincy and Carver. Find a thread, no matter how thin, we'll pull it and see where it leads."

"Sure." Russo left the office.

"I've been thinking we should set up a hotline for any tips," Liz said.

Holden frowned, not liking the idea. "Requires manpower to sort through all the crank calls we'll get."

That was a definite con. She was more concerned with the pros. "Can you spare it?"

"Will it be worth it?" he countered.

Sawyer sat back in his chair. "Do you really think we'll get a viable lead from a hotline?"

"No, I don't. I'm not going to hold my breath waiting to hear from a witness."

Holden sighed. "Then why bother?"

"Serial arsonists enjoy manipulating authorities. They like to communicate, explain themselves."

"You're hoping he'll call," Sawyer said.

She nodded. "We should check in with the medical examiner. See if we can get a time of death for Mike Steward."

"Easier to squeeze details out of Roger Norris in person. He doesn't like to talk over the phone." Sawyer stood. "It's a ten-minute walk."

Fresh air would be good. She needed to stretch her legs. "Let's go."

Neither of them initiated conversation along the way, which was for the best. He appeared resigned and she appreciated it. Maybe he'd gotten the message and would simply focus on the job. Something in her gut, though, told her not to cling to false hope since the air of misery hanging around him troubled her.

In the medical examiner's office, Roger Norris wore narrow rectangular glasses and his white lab coat over a gray AC/DC T-shirt with orange lettering. His thin dishwater blond hair was slicked back. His attention was focused on one of his many screens while he noshed on a banana.

Her stomach rumbled, and she wished she had eaten the breakfast sandwich instead of refusing out of anger. Or principle. If she had accepted the coffee, why not the food, too?

It made no sense, but Sawyer had her spinning in circles.

Roger nodded when they came in. "Sawyer Powell walks into my joint yet again. Can't stay away from me these days, can you?"

"Unfortunately not. This is—"

"Liz Kelley. I read your flattering quotes about the fire marshal in the *Gazette* today."

It was good of Egan to print it. She hoped her comments would change public opinion about Sawyer. "What can you tell us about Mike Steward?" Liz asked.

"Oh, plenty. Found something quite interesting." He scooted on his stool over to another screen. "His last meal was a burger, fries and a Coke. Based on his fractured skull, he was knocked out before his throat was cut. I got a lockdown on the estimated time of death. It was between four thirty and five thirty."

Nice and tight. That would be helpful.

"Was that the interesting part?" Sawyer asked.

"No, not at all. I'm getting to that. Saved the best part for last." Norris brought up something on his screen. A picture of a small typed note. "Found that stuffed in the victim's mouth toward the back of the throat."

It read, *SINS OF THE FATHER.*

"Any prints?" Sawyer asked.

Norris shook his head. "The perp was careful."

"Our guy wants to talk to us," Liz said. Just like she thought. "We've got to persuade Holden to dedicate manpower for a hotline."

"Consider it done." Sawyer glanced at her. "The only question is what sins did Neil Steward commit?"

Chapter Nine

The awkward silence between Sawyer and Liz, when they weren't discussing something pertinent to the case, unsettled him. She made it look easy, shutting off her emotions, staying laser-focused on work while he was struggling.

Back in the sheriff's office, Holden agreed to the hotline without protest after learning about the note the killer had left inside Mike Steward's mouth. By the time they'd eaten lunch, not a word exchanged between them, it was up and running.

"The *Gazette* and local news station will spread the word about the hotline. Everyone will know about it. We'll weed through the garbage," Holden said. "I'll only bother you with any tips that might be legit or if the perp calls in."

"Thanks," Sawyer said to his brother while keeping his gaze on Liz. Not that it seemed to faze her at all.

"I think Carver is here." She hiked her chin toward the hall.

Two men in business suits had entered the Sheriff's department.

Holden glanced over his shoulder. "Yep. That's him and his lawyer."

She shoved back from the desk and got up. "I can do the interview alone if you'd rather not do it together," she said, her voice flat.

"This is my case." He wiped his hands and crumpled

up the wrapper from lunch, throwing it away. "You're welcome to join in the interrogation room. If you can handle it."

"I don't see why I wouldn't be able to. There's nothing personal about this for me."

Her rejection earlier was like a knife in the gut, and here she was twisting it. "You've made that clear. We can talk to them in interrogation room one."

She pulled on a phony professional smile. "I'd like to question him here in the office instead."

"Why?" Sawyer asked.

"It'll make him less defensive. He might let something slip since he'll be less guarded."

Sawyer nodded. "Fine with me."

"I'll show him in," Holden offered.

"If you don't mind, I'll do it." She headed for the door. "Believe it or not, I'm good at putting suspects at ease."

Watching Liz walk away down the hall, Sawyer wanted this *wound*, deep in his heart, to scab over, to scar and fade. Instead, it festered and hurt. Infected by the past.

Holden turned to Sawyer. "Why is Liz acting like a robot? Her voice is all monotone and her eyes are blank. And you threw away food earlier. Fess up. What happened?"

Sawyer watched her greet Carver and his lawyer with a plastic grin. "I happened. I kissed her this morning."

"Well, that's a good thing, right?"

He glanced at his brother out of the corner of his eye. "Based on what you've observed thus far, does it look like it was a good thing?"

"Sorry." Holden folded his arms across his chest. "You've waited fifteen years for this. What's the plan?"

Liz said something that made Carver grin and look down at his suit with pride before he ran a hand through his white hair.

"There is no plan. All she wants to do is give me the

Heisman or run away from me." Each time it was like being kicked in the teeth. "She doesn't want me."

What if their time together had been lightning in a bottle? Not meant to last or not meant for them to have a second chance.

Then he thought of her pressed against him. The way she'd tightened her arms around him in the hug, sighed like she wanted more. Kissed him back. No restraint. Full of desire like she *did* want him.

"Maybe it's not you she doesn't want," Holden said. "Maybe she just doesn't want to get hurt."

"But I'd never hurt her."

"She might not be so sure of that."

Sawyer glanced back down the hall. He noticed Liz tugging up her neckerchief as she had a deputy get two cups of coffee for Carver and his lawyer.

What she'd said to him in the kitchen came back to him. How she'd never get married and have kids and that he knew why.

His heart sank at the thought of her denying herself the kind of life she wanted because of the scars. The accident had never mattered to him, but it still mattered to her. Perhaps in a way he couldn't fully understand.

Holden put a hand on Sawyer's shoulder. "Remember that basketball game you finished with a broken foot sophomore year?" his brother asked.

It had hurt like hell. "Yeah, of course." He'd never forget it.

"Any other player would've stayed off that foot. Avoided putting any pressure on it. Human nature to protect yourself from what's going to hurt. But not you, because you don't quit," Holden said. "No matter how painful, no matter the consequences, you don't give up when you're going after something you want. Your Liz is back in town. You can't quit now. Stop moping like a puppy that lost its home. Remember what you are."

Liz started escorting them over.

"And what's that?"

"A coyote," Holden said, referring to their high school mascot. His brother howled low enough for only them to hear and then crossed the hall to his office and closed the door.

The pep talk lifted his spirits. Holden was good at that. In fifteen years, Sawyer hadn't given up hope. Today, he had not only held Liz, but he got to kiss her, and for a moment it was everything.

Progress.

Only a coward or a fool would quit now. Sawyer was neither.

He grabbed an extra chair and brought it around behind the desk. Liz ushered them into the office. The two older men sat across from the desk.

Sawyer took the seat near the computer.

"Once again," Liz said, sitting beside him, "we appreciate you taking the time out of your busy schedule to come down here."

"Of course. I'm happy to help." The fifty-five-year-old man took a sip of his coffee, gagged and set the mug on the desk. "I just don't know how I can."

"We understand you're interested in purchasing all the businesses between Second and Third Street from Kern Avenue to Sycamore Road," Sawyer said.

"I am. It's to build a townhome community in the town center." Carver folded his hands in his lap. "Part of a housing growth plan I've coordinated with the mayor."

"Would you say you're hands-on with your businesses?" Sawyer asked. "That you're aware of details."

With a nod, Kade Carver grinned. "Certainly. It's how I became so successful. I even know the name of every tenant. The devil is in the details."

"Have you had any holdouts who have refused to sell?" Sawyer asked.

"A few."

"Chuck Parrot recently invested a lot to renovate his restaurant." Liz's tone was soft, casual. "Was he interested in selling?"

Clearing his throat, Kade Carver narrowed his eyes. "He overextended himself with the loans he took out for the renovation. He was having trouble making the payments, so he was considering my offer."

"What about the nail salon?" Sawyer sipped his coffee that had been delivered with lunch.

Carver's mouth twitched. "We were in negotiations for a price we both felt was fair until the fire."

"Did Mr. Steward, the owner of the tattoo parlor, indicate he was interested in selling?" Liz asked.

Carver's gaze slid over her. "I'm not exactly sure where this line of questioning is leading. Are you accusing me of something?"

Smiling, Liz shook her head. "Sir, you are not being charged with a crime. Can you answer the question?"

His lawyer leaned over and whispered in his ear.

"No, the Stewards didn't want to sell," Carver said. "At first. But like any good businessman, I got to the root of their hesitation and came up with a viable solution. I assured them I would find them a suitable replacement location, which was the sticking point. Neil agreed to sell his place if he liked the alternate site. Otherwise, no deal. Seemed fair to me. I wasn't worried about it. They have a cult following and a reputation that'd ensure the business would thrive regardless of where it was moved. Or at least it did."

"The recent fires have lowered the property value of the businesses located on the two blocks you're interested in purchasing." Sawyer let that hang in the air for a moment. "Isn't that correct?"

The man shifted in his seat, looking a tad uncomfortable, but his lawyer saved him from responding. "My client hasn't had a chance to thoroughly review how the fires have affected the value."

"I hope you don't think I'm running around town torching these places," Carver said. "I may be a cutthroat businessman, but I am no killer. And why would I burn down a cabin? Or Compassionate Hearts? Huh?"

"To throw off the investigation," Sawyer said pointedly. "To keep the trail from leading to you. It's called misdirection."

Carver puffed up his chest, his cheeks growing pink. "I was at home last night. With my wife."

Liz nodded. "Of course you were. I'm certain she'll verify."

"She will indeed. And when the cabin was burned down and those hunters were murdered," Carver continued, "I wasn't even in the state. I was in Florida. With my wife."

"Mr. Carver," Liz said, holding up a gentle hand, "we don't think you doused any of these places in an accelerant and lit the match."

The man gave a smug grin. "I should hope not."

Leaning forward, Sawyer rested his forearms on the desk. "But it is entirely possible that you paid someone to do the dirty work for you," he said, and Kade's jaw dropped. "You're the only person who would financially benefit from any of these fires. Mr. Parrot swears you're behind it."

"Chuck Parrot is a drunk and a liar." Carver's tone turned vicious. "Only a fool would listen to him."

"This interview is over." The lawyer set his coffee mug down and stood, prompting Carver to do the same. "We've cooperated and graciously answered your questions. Unless you charge my client with a crime, he has nothing else to say. Good day."

"Mayor Schroeder is going to hear about this." Carver

wagged a finger at them. "Trying to pin this on an innocent businessman because you can't do your job."

The lawyer beckoned his client to hurry along. As they stalked out of the office, they ran into Neil Steward, who was coming into the department.

Mr. Steward marched up to them, shaking a fist in Carver's direction. "If you're behind this, like Chuck is saying, if you're the reason my boy is dead, I'll kill you." The deputy at the front desk jumped up and got between them. "Hear me? I'll kill you!"

"Thank you for threatening my client, not only in a room full of witnesses, Mr. Steward, but also law enforcement. Should any harm come to him, they know who to arrest." The lawyer steered Kade Carver out of the department.

"What do you think?" Sawyer asked Liz.

She glanced at him, and he could see the wheels turning in her head. "I hate it when loved ones are used as alibis because it can be hard to get to the truth, but it's a lot of people to kill just for profit."

"More have been killed over less."

She nodded. "Unfortunately, that's true. The restaurant was the first fire set. Then the nail salon. The cabin and the thrift store could be about misdirection."

Neil Steward was headed their way.

"I hate the type of conversation we're about to have with a grieving parent," she said.

"Me too." It was the hardest part of the job.

"I'd never given it much thought before, how fire marshals also have to do this." The first glimmer of emotion flickered in her green eyes.

They stood as Neil Steward walked into the office. In his midforties, he was a burly guy, full mountain man beard, tattoos covering his exposed arms.

"I'm Agent Kelley and this is Fire Marshal Powell. We're sorry for your loss. You have our deepest sympathies."

Liz shook his hand. "Please have a seat. Is your wife joining us?"

With bloodshot eyes, he dropped down into a chair. "She's too distraught to get out of the bed."

Understandable. They had just lost their only child.

"Can we get you a coffee?" she asked, and he shook his head. "We understand you received a threatening phone call right before the fire started."

"Sure did. Some weird guy. Said I deserved what was about to happen. 'Fireworks.' That was the word he used. I thought it was a buddy of mine messing around, but then he said he was going to take my boy and my shop."

Sawyer exchanged a look with Liz. "Did he say why he believed you deserved it? Have you crossed anyone that you can think of?"

Scratching his beard, Neil thought about it. "No, no, he didn't give me a reason. I just assumed the guy was a whacko. He was talking bananas. My wild days are long behind me. I don't make trouble with anybody. You can ask my wife. She'll tell you."

"May we see your phone?" Liz held out her hand. After he unlocked it and placed it in her palm, she looked through his calls. "Is this it? At ten thirty-five?"

The grieving father nodded. "Yeah. That's the one."

"From the exchange, it looks like it's from a disposable phone. A burner." Liz wrote the number down along with how long the call lasted. "Did you recognize the voice?"

Another shake of his head.

"Are you sure the guy didn't say anything else? I only ask because one minute and forty-five seconds is a long time." More had been said, Sawyer was certain of it.

Neil glanced around the room, once again thinking. "No. He, um, repeated it a few times. Yeah." He scratched his beard. "Wanted to make sure I got the message."

"Fireworks, he was going to take your son and your shop

because you deserved it, but no reason was given. That's all?" Sawyer asked, wanting to be clear, and Neil nodded. "Do the words *Sins of the father* mean anything to you?"

Neil swallowed convulsively, his Adam's apple bobbing in his thick neck as his eyes turned glassy. "No," he said in a pained whisper. "Should it?"

It was plain to see that it did. Why not share everything he knew to help them catch this killer? What was he hiding?

"When was the last time you spoke with your son?" Liz asked.

"Sometime earlier. Before dinner. It's in there." He pointed to his phone.

Mike's name came up a little after four.

That confirmed the estimated time of death the ME had given them, between 4:30 p.m. and 5:30 p.m. "What did you two discuss?"

"Not much." Neil shrugged. "Someone had called him earlier and made a same-day appointment for that night. Mike planned to be in the shop for five to six hours."

Liz made a note. "Did he say who the appointment was with?"

"A guy who requested Mike. Insisted on having privacy and didn't want a bunch of other tattoo artists gawking at him. He wanted a really intricate tattoo on his chest of Vulcan, the god of…" His voice trailed off.

"Fire." Sawyer got up and came around the desk, sitting beside him. When Neil raised his head, with tears brimming in his eyes, Sawyer put a comforting hand on his forearm.

"The sicko who killed my boy and burned the place to the ground made an appointment?" Horror filled his face.

"It's our understanding the shop's hours varied." Liz's tone softened. "The only way to ensure Mike was the tattoo artist available at a specific time was to make an appointment."

Neil dropped his head into his hands and sobbed. "Do you think the murderer made Mike give him the tattoo before he killed him? If so, that's how you could find him. Right? Look for the tattoo."

"No. I don't believe he actually got a tattoo from Mike." Liz clasped her hands on the desk. "The killer wouldn't want to linger any longer than absolutely necessary."

There were no CCTV cameras near the front of tattoo parlor to capture the person going in around the time in question. "Did you have security cameras inside the shop?" Sawyer wondered. "With a backup downloaded to an online server?"

"No need. We don't keep cash in the shop. Debit or credit card only. Nothing inside a meth head would break in to steal. We've never had a problem. Until now."

"Did Mike live with you?" she asked, and Neil shook his head, tears leaking from the corners of his eyes. "Did he usually call when he was done for the night? Maybe after he locked up?"

"No, we didn't keep tabs on him like that. He was twenty-three. Did his own thing. We spoke to him once a day. Sometimes every other day."

"Mr. Steward, did you agree to sell your tattoo parlor to Kade Carver under the right terms?" Sawyer asked.

"I was willing to consider it." Neil sniffled. "If he found a new location that I liked. The offer, the money was pretty good. Evelyn, my wife, wanted me to take it. Mike didn't care either way."

Sawyer glanced at her to see if she had any more questions.

She shook her head. "Mr. Steward, if you can think of anything else, perhaps, if more details about the phone call come back to you, please don't hesitate to contact us." She handed him her card.

"You have to catch whoever did this." Neil stood and trudged out of the office.

Watching him pass the front desk, Sawyer turned to her. "You think he's holding back about the phone call, too?"

"A hundred percent. Whatever was said might be the key to helping us find the killer, but for some reason he's not sharing."

Deputy Russo made a beeline to the office. "There's a connection between Kade Carver and Isaac Quincy. Kade owns an apartment complex. Four buildings. One hundred units in total. Quincy is one of his tenants."

"Good work." Liz flashed a genuine smile.

"Carver is into details. Claims to know the names of all his tenants. He'd also know that Quincy has a record, and it would be easy enough to find out he's got a penchant for playing with fire," Sawyer said. "It can be hard for a convicted felon to reintegrate in society. Get a job. Maybe Carver offered him money or free rent to start the fires."

"Only one way to find out." Liz stood. "You got an address?"

Russo held up a piece of paper.

"Thanks." Sawyer took it from her, and the deputy left. "Are we riding separately or together?" he asked Liz.

"I didn't realize you were going to give me a choice."

He grabbed his cowboy hat from the side table and put it on. "That's the thing, Liz. You decide for both of us. It's always been about your choices." He could've kicked himself for going there. He hadn't meant to; the words had just slipped out and there was no taking them back.

A blank expression fell over her face like a mask, and the distance between them grew without either of them moving.

After holding his gaze, without responding for so long, tempting him to speak first, she finally breezed past him and out into the hall. The clipped pace of her steps all business. No seductive sway of her hips, no grace. A formidable stride that he loved.

He hurried to catch up.

"One car," she said flatly over her shoulder, not looking at him. "It's more efficient."

She was something else, and man, did he love her.

Chapter Ten

After the quiet car ride, where they each stayed in their respective corners, Liz let Sawyer take the lead at Quincy's third-floor apartment.

He approached the front door and knocked. Hard. "Isaac Quincy. LFD and FBI. Open up."

Movement came from inside, a shuffling sound and then hurried footsteps, but not toward the door. Metal creaked. "Fire escape?"

"He's running." Sawyer drew his weapon and kicked in the door, busting the frame. Glock at the ready, he swept inside.

Pulling her sidearm, Liz followed behind him.

The window at the back of the living room was wide open. She caught a glimpse of the top of Quincy's head as he pounded down the steps.

Sawyer darted through the living room and ducked out the window. Liz was right behind him.

Lifting his head, Quincy glanced at them with a panicked look and clattered down the first flight. The fire escape led to the roof of a smaller adjacent building. Quincy leaped over the metal railing, landed on the smooth blacktop, slipped once and took off.

Liz swore under her breath. "Quincy, stop!"

Sawyer hopped the railing with the skill of a gymnast

over a pommel horse, but when his feet touched down, he clutched his injured side with a groan.

With little effort, she made it over the railing and kicked it into high gear. Sawyer chased him. Liz followed.

They ran across the rooftop. At the edge, Quincy jumped to the next building, making the six-foot leap, but dropped to his knees.

"Sawyer! Stitches!" she called out, not wanting him to aggravate or reopen his wound from absorbing the shock of the landing.

He halted at the ledge, either listening to her or using caution, and raised his weapon, taking aim. "Freeze, Quincy. Or I'll shoot."

The man dared to get up and take off running again.

Holstering her sidearm, Liz lengthened her stride, jumped to the next rooftop and landed in a tuck and roll. Then she popped up to her feet. "Stop!" she yelled.

But he didn't.

And neither did she.

Liz dashed after him and lunged, tackling Quincy, forcing him to his belly. She wrangled his arms behind his back and slipped on handcuffs. "Now we're going to chat down at the station instead of your apartment."

STARING THROUGH THE one-way glass of the observation room in the sheriff's department, Liz studied Isaac Quincy and considered how to play the interrogation.

Sawyer was standing in the back of the room, silently plotting how to throw her off guard, no doubt. She could feel his gaze on her, burning a hole in her backside.

"You were impressive back there." Sawyer came up beside her. "You jump from rooftops a lot?"

"Not every day." She glanced at him. "How is your side?"

"Sore, but I'm good." One corner of his mouth hitched up in a half smile.

Maybe it was the irresistible look he gave her or the adrenaline still pumping in her system that made her want to caress his cheek. Whatever the reason, she put it in check. "Are there any smokers out there?" She gestured to the bullpen.

"I think there are a couple. Why?"

Without answering, she headed out to the main area of the station. "Who has a lighter I can borrow?"

The deputy manning the front desk stood. He dug into his pocket, pulled out a Zippo and tossed it to her.

Catching it, she said, "Thanks." She dropped it in the pocket of her FBI jacket that she was still wearing and turned to Sawyer. "Let's go question him."

They headed down the hall. He opened the door for her.

She went in first, taking a seat at the metal table across from Quincy. The young man was pale and lean. A bit sweaty, which was to be expected after he ran. Wary brown eyes. Dark hair.

Sawyer pulled out the chair next to hers, making it scrape across the floor.

Straightening, Quincy began to fidget.

Liz met his nervous gaze. "We want to talk to you about the recent string of fires."

"I didn't start any of those fires." He spoke, using his hands in an animated way. His tone was immediately defensive. "I swear, I'm innocent."

"Of course you are." Sawyer leaned back in his chair. "That's why you were doing wind sprints across the roof, forcing us to chase you."

Perspiration beaded Quincy's forehead. He was anxious, but his eyes were angry. "I'm just tired of being harassed every time someone lights a match in this town."

"You're a convicted arsonist." Liz eyed him. "It's routine for us to question you when something like this happens."

"I did my time." Quincy put his elbows on the table, his expression turning indignant. "I got treatment inside. I'm rehabilitated. Ask my parole officer. Better yet, ask my court-appointed therapist."

"Oh yeah?" Liz wished she had a dollar for every time she heard that one. "So you don't get off on fires at all anymore?"

"That's right." He gave her a smug smile.

She reached into her pocket and slowly pulled out the Zippo. Watched Quincy's gaze drop to it. She fiddled with the metal lighter, turning it in her hand while he stayed transfixed. Flipping it open, she made him wait a few seconds before letting him see the flame.

Wrapping his arms around his stomach, he tried to look away, once, twice, and failed.

Liz snapped the lid of the lighter closed and watched the disappointment cross his face. "Want another?" She already knew the answer.

He nodded like a junkie in need of a fix.

She gave it to him. Holding the Zippo at eye level, even closer to Quincy's face, she struck the flint wheel, producing a flame. "Tell me about the Cowboy Way shop fire."

Licking his lips, Quincy smiled. "Perfection. It was a thing of flipping beauty." His eyes glazed over with that same Christmas-morning look. "In full swing by the time the fire department showed up."

Sawyer crossed his arms. "You admit to being there?"

"Well, I was at the grocery store two blocks away. Smelled the smoke. Had to follow it, and I found that glorious sight. So, yeah, I watched it. Along with half the town. No crime in that, or are you going to lock up everyone who was there?"

"Not everyone." Sawyer shook his head. "Only the fire-bug with a record."

"What did you think of the other fires?" Liz waved the flame. "Were those beautiful, too?"

Quincy shrugged with his gaze on the lighter. "I didn't see them. I was working the night the restaurant and the nail salon burned down. No reason for me to go to Bison Ridge."

"What about the inferno at Compassionate Hearts?" Warily, Sawyer studied him. "I'm sure you didn't miss that one."

"Wish I'd seen it, from what I heard on the news, but when I got off work, I went straight to bed. The fire happened sometime later while I was asleep."

Not unusual for him to keep track of the fires. "Where do you work?" She closed the lighter.

"Night shift. Road work. We're repaving Route 130." Quincy rattled off the name and number of his supervisor.

"Has Kade Carver ever asked you to work for him?" Sawyer asked. "In exchange for money or free rent?"

Confusion furrowed Quincy's brow. "Mr. Carver? No."

"What about any of Mr. Carver's employees?" Sawyer followed up.

The young man shook his head.

"Have you ever set a fire for someone else?" She put the lighter in her pocket. "For money?"

Quincy snickered. "That's not why I do it."

No, it wasn't. "Please answer."

"Never."

"Hard to believe," Sawyer said, "considering the way you looked at that lighter. Like a man willing to set a fire for any reason at all."

"You don't know me. You cops are all the same. I want a lawyer. Or I want out of here right now."

"You're free to go." Liz gestured to the door, and Sawyer gave her a side-eyed glance.

Isaac Quincy didn't waste a second scurrying out of the room.

"What are you doing?" Sawyer sighed. "We didn't even verify his alibi."

"He admitted to being at the Cowboy Way fire without him knowing we already had proof he was there. Quincy talked about it like he was admiring someone else's work. Not his own." She shifted in the chair, facing him. "It's natural for him to follow the other fires in the news, to remember when they happened. His alibi will check out."

"Don't tell me you believe he's rehabilitated."

Standing, she headed for the door. "Not at all. It's only a matter of time before he sets another fire. When he does, it won't be for someone else and certainly not for money."

They walked together down the hall.

"Some arsonists are paid," he said.

"True." She stopped in the doorway of the sheriff's office and leaned against the jamb. "But not Isaac Quincy. He's a pyromaniac."

He rested his shoulder on the other side of the door across from her, standing close. Intimately close. "That's exactly my point."

She could feel the heat radiating from his body. "I came here after giving a presentation at a symposium. During my seminar, I asked the participants—fire agency personnel, law enforcement, even a few insurance investigators—what was the definition of pyromania? Not a single one got it entirely right. Pyros deliberately set fires more than once. Showing tension or oftentimes arousal before the act. They are fascinated and attracted not only to fire but also to its paraphernalia. They feel pleasure, a sense of relief when setting them. But above all, they must also set fires for fire's sake. Not for money or revenge or attracting attention."

He hooked his thumb in his belt and leaned in. "Well, I guess I'll have to reread that chapter in your book." His minty breath brushed her face. "But if you're so sure Quincy is a pyro and not our guy, why did we haul him in for questioning?"

"I suspected earlier, but I wasn't sure until we had him in the interrogation room. Running didn't help him, either. The more I think about this, whoever is behind the fires isn't a professional arsonist providing a service or doing it for profit. This is way too personal. Especially with Mike Steward's throat being cut. Then calling Neil, luring him to the fire, making him watch."

"Revenge. For the sins of the father."

"Most adult arsonists who aren't for profit are almost always seeking revenge."

"If only we knew why Neil Steward 'deserved it,'" he said, using air quotes.

"Makes me wonder if the others 'deserved it,' too, in the mind of our perpetrator. Did Chuck Parrot say whether he got a call before the fire?"

"When I talked to him, his entire focus was on the substantial amount of money he'd just lost and the fact he was financially ruined. He didn't mention it, and I didn't know to ask at the time."

Someone came into the station, drawing her gaze. "Don't turn around."

Sawyer did exactly what she told him not to do. A string of curses flew from his lips. "Bill Schroeder."

The mayor beckoned to someone with a stiff hand, and Deputy Russo hurried over to talk to him.

Liz grabbed Sawyer's arm and tugged him into the office. "Do yourself a favor and let me do the talking."

He glanced down at where she was touching him. "You expect me to stay tight-lipped and simply accept whatever horse manure he decides to dump on me?"

She let him go. "You're angry with me, I know—"

"I'm not angry." He stepped toward her. "I'm hurt. Confused. Because you won't talk to me. Fifteen years of no returned calls or emails. Here we are standing in the same room together, and I still can't get any answers."

Something in his eyes squeezed at Liz's heart, and she had to batten down her emotions. If she could have the toughest conversation of her life while working on this case with him and not lose focus, she would, but even she had her limits. "After things settle down." She looked back at the bullpen, where Russo and Schroeder were still talking.

"We could've been killed by that car bomb yesterday," he said, drawing her attention squarely back to him. "Things never settle down. There's always something."

Looking irate, Bill Schroeder headed for the office.

"Right now, that something is the mayor." She took a deep breath, wishing he'd stop pushing, even though he made a valid point. "But there is one thing I can do for you."

"What?"

"Protect you." When this case was done, he had to live in this town. Mouthing off to the mayor would not make his life easier. "Let me."

With a reluctant nod, Sawyer went around the desk, sank into a chair and propped his boots on the corner as Bill Schroeder charged inside the office and slammed the door shut.

"Why on earth would you accuse an upstanding citizen from a good family such as Kade Carver of arson and murder?" he asked, staring at Sawyer like Liz didn't exist.

"Bill." Removing her FBI jacket, she took a tentative step toward him. "Liz Kelley. I don't know if you remember me."

He'd been ahead of them in school by a couple of years and had also been a teen camper at the Wild Horse Ranch, but his last summer had been the one prior to the fire.

Finally, he met her eyes. His scowl softened. "I remember you. I also know about your little book. You're supposed to be an expert. I shouldn't have to tell you that the guy doing this is probably some lowlife who comes from a broken, abusive home with a history of violence and couldn't possibly be Kade Carver."

"Mr. Carver wasn't accused or charged," she said. "Simply questioned as part of this investigation."

"When I was informed the FBI would be assisting with this case, I was relieved at first. But now I see why nothing is getting done," Bill said, with a sneer. "Are you here to work or to canoodle with your old boyfriend?"

Sawyer let out a withering breath, but without uttering a word, he took out his phone and lowered his head.

Clasping her hands in front of her, Liz held tightly to her composure. "I'm here in a strictly professional capacity. My colleague, who, even after an attempt was made on his life to impede this case and was injured, has been working tirelessly to see justice served."

Bill rolled his eyes. "Spare me the song and dance. Save it for the press. Apparently, Erica Egan is lapping it up. Great article in the *Gazette*, by the way. Really pulled at the heartstrings," he said sarcastically. "What I want to know is if you're both incompetent? I demanded an update from Deputy Russo. She informed me that you had a convicted arsonist in your custody as a suspect and released him."

"Because he didn't set these fires." She strained for calm. "Would you like us to arrest anyone who fits the profile regardless of innocence or guilt?"

"How about you arrest someone? That'd be nice. The longer this goes on, the worse it looks for me." Bill smoothed down the lapels of his suit. "My opponent is running a tough-on-crime campaign. I need to be tougher. Do you understand?"

She swallowed a sigh. The man only cared about himself and getting reelected. Some people never changed.

He and Sawyer were both from old money, the kind

that came with influence and power. Bill's family made it from the Schroeder Farm and Ranch Enterprises, part of the largest distribution network of major suppliers of agricultural inputs. Sawyer's family made it from the Shooting Star Ranch, one of the biggest in the Mountain West region. That's where the similarities between the two of them stopped.

"I can assure you, Bill, that what will not help us resolve this case any faster is you getting on television talking about the arsonist, giving him all the attention he craves. Less than twelve hours after your reckless appearance on a major news network, which only served to embolden the perpetrator, he burned down the Cowboy Way and killed Mike Steward."

"How dare you accuse me of making this situation worse," Bill said, fury giving his voice a razor-sharp edge. "As though exercising my first amendment right somehow encouraged him to strike again."

"If the cowboy boot fits," she said.

"I could have your badge. Do you know that?" Bill crossed the room, coming up to her. "One call to my daddy." He held up a single finger, his tone setting her teeth on edge. "He plays golf with the governor, who knows the attorney general. Your boss's boss," he said, now pointing in her face, and she was half tempted to break the digit that was an inch from her nose to teach Bill the consequences of bad manners.

Sawyer barked out a laugh. "Did you really pull the Daddy card?"

He had been doing so well being quiet. Of course, it couldn't last.

Bill's gaze snapped to Sawyer, fixing on him.

But she stepped in front of the mayor, redirecting his anger. "I suggest the only comments you have to the press about this case are 'No comment.' Let the professionals working on this speak to the media about the facts. My boss is SAC Ross Cho." She scrawled his number, including extension, on the back of one of her cards. "Give him a call, he'll tell you the same, and by all means, take your chances trying to get me fired." Her record spoke for itself. No one at the bureau was going to cave because an entitled man-child was having a tantrum.

"We'll see if you're untouchable, *Lucky Liz*," Bill said, and hearing the nickname sent a chill through her. "As for lover boy, if he doesn't solve this soon by putting someone behind bars or in a grave, I'll call a city council meeting and have his badge. You can bet your bottom dollar it won't be a game of chance then. That's a promise."

Bill waltzed out, leaving the door open and her exasperated.

"How did he get elected?" Spinning around, she waited for an answer from Sawyer.

"His daddy's money. Also, he puts on a good show at town hall meetings. Packs away his real personality and pretends to be someone pleasant."

"I forgot what he was like." She ran a finger under her scarf, longing to take it off. "How awful he could be."

Sawyer put his feet on the floor and sauntered over to her. "I didn't." He held up his phone, showing her what he'd been doing.

"You recorded the conversation?"

"Bet your bottom dollar I did," he said, imitating Bill.

She laughed, as he'd meant for her to.

"Let that schmuck call his council meeting." He smiled, his eyes glittering. "You did a great job drawing his fire away from me. Once again, impressive."

Fighting for him, having his back was nothing. She'd do anything for him. Sacrifice everything if it meant he'd be happy.

Snapshots of their teenage days together flickered through

her head. Then she remembered something Bill had said. "Have you seen the *Gazette* today?"

Sawyer walked over to the side table, picked up a copy and quickly scanned it. When she tried to look, he pulled it away from her line of sight. "You don't want to see it."

Dread slithered down her spine. "Give me the gist."

"Egan dug." He grimaced. "She brought up the past. The fire. Us. All of it."

She cringed. This town was already overflowing with busybodies who delved into everyone's business for sport. Now her painful past had been rehashed as entertainment. It wasn't news.

Sawyer put a hand on her back and rubbed. She was tempted to accept the comfort, almost did, but she noticed everyone in the bullpen watching them.

Adjusting her scarf, she moved away, turning her back to the gawking deputies.

"Let's get back to work." He tossed the paper in the trash. "Instead of focusing on garbage."

He was right. She should've said it first.

"We need a lead. We're missing something with this case." But what?

Sitting behind the desk, she brought up on the computer screen the original pictures Russo had taken, not the zoomed in versions that focused on individuals, and looked them over, one after another. A sinking sensation formed in the pit of her stomach. Staring at the photos, she should've seen it sooner.

"What is it?" he asked. "You're thinking something dark."

"There's a possibility that we have to consider," she said, reluctantly. "Investigate to rule it out if nothing else."

His brow furrowed. "I'm not going to like this, judging by your tone, am I?"

She shook her head. He was going to hate it. "Some arsonists are firefighters."

"No," he snapped.

"Hear me out. It's a persistent phenomenon and a long-standing problem. Sometimes they suffer from hero syndrome, but I don't think that's the case here. It's clear this is about revenge."

"Not in my station," he said with a definitive shake of his head. "I know those people. Trained with them. Battled fires with them. No."

"Arsonists start early. Usually in their teens. If he was never caught and convicted, he could be flying under the radar. He's skilled. Knows how much accelerant to use, where to place it, the timer, the car bomb. It would be easy for him to hide in the department," she said, and he scrubbed a hand over his face. "We'd be looking for someone with a decreased ability to self-regulate. Might drink a little too much. Unlikely to succeed in relationships. Divorced. Never married. White male. Sixteen to thirty-five."

"That's half the station. Most are divorced or unmarried. Hell, I fit that profile."

"If there's a firefighter with a vendetta, who is using arson to kill his victims—"

"You're reaching. Yesterday, you thought this string of fires and murders might be related to what happened at the summer camp."

She took a deep breath, hating the unease worming through her over having been mistaken about the link to the summer camp. "We have a time of death. Let's question them to see where they were." Since all the fires had started using a timer, they had no way to pinpoint when the devices had been planted. Mike Steward's death, as horrific and senseless as it was, might be the only way to find the killer. "Verify alibis. Investigate those who don't have one. Rule them out as suspects, if nothing else, and move on." *Hopefully.*

His frown deepened as he raked his hands through his hair, considering it.

"Do you have a better idea?" she asked.

"We talk to Chuck Parrot again to see if anyone called him before the fire."

"That will take five minutes. Questioning all the firefighters in your station as well as the volunteers will take hours. Possibly days. And that's with help from the deputies that Holden can spare. We need to get the ball rolling tonight. We can do it at the fire station to minimize the inconvenience and impact. Chuck Parrot can swing by there. What do you say?"

He groaned. "The olive branch they extended to me, consider it kindling."

Chapter Eleven

In his office at the fire department, Sawyer sat on the sofa trying to prepare himself to do this. Question his own as though they might be guilty. It left a bad taste in his mouth.

Gareth took a seat in the chair opposite him and Liz. From his expression, he wasn't too happy about this either but had agreed to let them interview everyone currently on shift and had someone calling those who were off to see if they didn't mind swinging in tonight. Otherwise, they'd be expected to come in tomorrow.

"Thank you for letting us get started with this as soon as possible," Sawyer said.

Resting an ankle on his knee, Gareth settled back in the chair. "Don't thank me until after you've spoken with Ted," he said, his lips giving a wry twist.

Sawyer wasn't looking forward to it.

Liz picked up her pen and notebook, about to get started, when the alarm in the building clanged. "Just when I thought we'd get through the day without a fire."

Gareth was up on his feet, rushing for the door. "Let me find out what it is." In less than a minute, he was back, already pulling on his gear. "Not a fire. Bad accident on I-80. A fuel truck and three cars. Interviewing the team will have to wait until tomorrow. But one off-duty person showed up. Tonight isn't a complete bust for you." Ducking out of the office, he waved at someone to go in and then was gone.

Tessa strutted inside, flashing a tentative smile. She was a slender woman with tempting curves on display in a form-fitting sundress pulled off the shoulders. The hem was only a few inches lower than her backside. She wore matching cowboy boots and makeup, lips a bold, daring shade of red. Her dark blond hair was all glossy curls, skimming her bare shoulders. And she smelled good, too.

There was no denying she was a beautiful woman or that his hormones recognized it, but his heart only beat for Liz.

"Gareth told me you had some questions for everyone," Tessa said, her gaze fixed on his, and flipped her hair over her shoulder, kicking up the scent of her sweet perfume.

Clearing her throat, Liz tensed. "We do. Please have a seat. We'll try to make it quick."

Tessa slipped into the chair and crossed her legs, flaunting a dangerous amount of skin.

"You were on duty yesterday?" Sawyer asked.

"Yep." Smiling, she swung her leg and drummed her red-painted fingernails on the arms of the chair.

He kept his gaze up above her neck. "Did you leave the station at any time while on duty?"

"Twice. To respond to the fire in the morning at Compassionate Hearts and later that night to respond to the fire at the Cowboy Way."

"You were here in the station between four thirty and five thirty, and someone can verify it?" Liz asked, staring down at her notepad, even though she wasn't taking any notes. She was clutching the pen so tight her knuckles whitened.

"I was. We had gotten up from a nap around three. Then a group of us played cards until dinner."

Liz jotted it down. "Who did you play cards with?" she asked, and Tessa provided the names. "Then I think that's all we need from you."

"When I got here," Tessa said, "I was told I'm the only

one coming in tonight," she said, and Sawyer wondered if her buddy Bridget was the one making the calls and had ensured no other off-duty personnel would show up.

He glanced at his watch and then at Liz. It was almost nine. "I guess we'll call it a night. It's late anyway." They could start fresh in the morning.

The three of them stood.

Tessa slinked up beside him and slid a hand up his arm, curling her fingers around his biceps. "Sawyer, can I speak to you privately?"

He turned to Liz, her face inscrutable, and then caught a flash of jealousy in her eyes. Or was it his imagination and he was seeing what he wanted?

"Take your time." Liz's voice was encouraging, even enthusiastic. She grabbed her things and headed for the door without looking back at him. "I'm going home. See you tomorrow," she said in a rush, disappearing out the door and shutting it behind her.

He gritted his teeth that they'd driven to the fire station separately to avoid the hassle of doubling back to pick her vehicle up later. He knew how this must appear to her and didn't want her leaving with the wrong idea. More importantly, he didn't want her at the house alone.

"Can we sit for a minute?" Tessa glanced at the sofa.

Sitting was how it would start. Then she'd climb onto his lap and lower his zipper. "I'll stay standing. What'd you need?"

"I know your heart and head is in the right place, but I don't think questioning everyone is going to go over well with the others," she said cautiously.

"There might be some tension for a few days, but once we catch this guy, it will all be worth it."

She moved closer, brushing her curves, the ones that could make a monk ache to touch her, against his body. "I know you said not tonight, but I'm free and you're free, and I could use the pleasure of your company." Running her hands up his chest, she wrapped her arms around his neck. "Let's go to my place and get dirty together." She moistened her lips. "Or we could lock the door and do it right here while everyone's out."

Many men would've loved to take what she was offering. He wasn't one of them.

Sawyer pulled her arms from around his neck and put lots of space between them. "Tessa, we won't be hooking up anymore." They hadn't for a while, not since she asked him if he ever wanted to get married and have kids and when would they start going out to dinner on a proper date? Alarm bells went off in his head, and that had been that for him. He had hoped they could've avoided the dreaded conversation. "It's not you. It's me."

"I scared you off, didn't I? I figured if I gave you a little time, a lot of space, you'd come back because you missed me."

He only thought of her when he saw her in passing and hadn't missed her, which was telling. But he didn't want to hurt her, either.

"I don't need things to get serious right now. I'm good just having fun. No strings attached," Tessa said, lying to him, possibly even lying to herself.

Putting his hands in his pockets, he edged farther back. "This isn't what I want."

"Tell me the truth. I know you've got needs, and one day you'll settle down."

"The truth is I want to get serious."

Her gaze flickered over his face as understanding dawned in her hurt eyes. "Just not with me."

He picked up his hat and put it on. "The right woman is back in my life. I can't lose her again."

"Liz."

Sawyer gave one firm nod.

"I got that feeling last night. When I pulled you to the side, you kept glancing over at her while we spoke. I had to give it one more shot."

"Did Bridget make sure no one else was coming in tonight?"

Biting her lower lip, she gave him a guilty smile.

"You're going to find the right guy," he said. "When you do, he's going to be lucky to have you."

Tessa sighed. "I got all dolled up for nothing. At least tell me I look nice."

"You look really nice."

"Thanks for being honest with me. I know plenty of guys who would've taken me up on my offer for a good time on that sofa and, once finished, would've chased after the woman he really wanted."

"I'm not that kind of guy." And Tessa deserved better.

She pressed a palm to his cheek. "Which makes this even harder. Because you're one of the good ones."

"I have to go."

"To chase after her?"

In a manner of speaking. "Yeah."

Confronting Liz about the past and getting answers he deserved was one thing. Knowing for certain whether she was still attracted to him, wanted him or cared for him was another story. The idea of her being afraid of getting hurt—by him—made something inside his chest crack open and bleed. And if that was the case, then he needed a different approach.

LIZ FINISHED BRUSHING her teeth and slipped on her cotton pajama bottoms and tank top. Turning off the light, she couldn't stop thinking about Tessa, her svelte figure or the dress she wore, which left very, very little to the imagination.

Not that Sawyer needed to imagine. He'd already enjoyed Tessa Anderson's entire package.

He was probably doing it again right now.

Good for him.

Acid burned through her veins. She needed to finish this case and get back to Virginia.

A car pulled into the drive.

Grabbing her weapon, she jumped from the bed and crept to the window. She shifted the edge of the curtain to the side and peeked out.

It was a red Fire Department SUV. Liz checked the time. She'd only been home for thirty minutes. He must have turned Tessa down. Surely, no easy feat, considering the dress, the hair, the cowboy boots.

Relief and regret battled inside her. He deserved to act like it was business, or rather fun as usual, not restricting himself simply because she was in town. Soon enough, she'd be gone.

Sawyer climbed out of the vehicle and shut the door, but instead of traipsing off toward the trees, he was making a beeline for her front door.

Her pulse spiked.

As if he sensed her watching him, he looked right up at her window, straight at her through the silver of darkness where she hid. Then he disappeared under the porch.

The doorbell rang. Her chest tightened. It rang again. And again.

What did he want? It was late, she was exhausted, the lights were out, and the house was quiet. Obvious "do not disturb" signs.

He knocked at the door.

Maybe there was another fire or murder and rather than call, he wanted to tell her in person. She put her weapon on the nightstand beside the knife she wore strapped to her ankle, grabbed her long-sleeve pajama top, buttoned it and headed downstairs. As she made it to the first floor, the knocking turned into a fist pounding.

She opened the door and yawned like he had roused her from sleep. "What is it that couldn't wait until morning?"

"I had a question." He stepped across the threshold and stalked toward her.

Liz shuffled away, but he kept coming. She backed up until she had no place left to go. He didn't say a word as he placed his palms on the wall behind her, on either side of her head. He leaned in, and his mouth crushed hard on hers, making her breath catch and her legs turn to jelly. She didn't fight. Didn't pull away. The wind had been knocked out of her by the suddenness, the urgency under it, and the scorching need that slammed into her like a force of nature.

He was kissing her with a hot, focused intensity. She couldn't stop herself from kissing him back, drinking in the taste of him, slipping her fingers into his hair, bringing him even closer. A moan slid up her throat, and the next thing she knew, her mouth was free.

He'd taken a step back and stared down at her, studying her, assessing something.

"What are you looking at?" she asked, her voice shaky, fragile. She hated the sound.

"I've got my answer." Sawyer winked, spun on his heel and headed for the door. "Good night." He slammed the door closed.

Had he asked a question?

THE NEXT MORNING, Liz rolled over in bed and hit Snooze on her beeping alarm clock for the fourth time, which was unlike her. She usually forced herself to get up, threw on her clothes and went for a run. Today, she was physically, mentally and emotionally exhausted. Between the arsonist-murderer on the loose and Sawyer wearing her down, she'd earned the extra rest.

Last night, after he kissed her, leaving her lips swollen and awareness coursing through her body, she couldn't sleep for hours. She'd ached.

Ached to be touched.

Ached to be with him.

Still did.

Looking down at her bare arm on the side that was worse, she ran her fingers over the variation in shades and texture.

As a rookie, she'd tried to get intimate with a guy, a fellow agent. They'd met during the academy, became friends, flirted. She told him about the accident. Downplayed the scars. Why go into graphic detail? After graduation, he asked her out. Back at her apartment, she'd swallowed her fear and thrown caution to the wind following a couple of shots of whiskey. Once her shirt came off, their make-out session changed, the gleam in his eyes slid from desire to distaste.

The awkwardness lasted for a moment and an eternity. She fumbled to shut off the light, as if that'd make a difference. The sun eventually had to rise—no hiding forever. He uttered an excuse about forgetting something work-related and having to get up early. That was that.

Even though she had built a life, stitched herself up with so many missing pieces, to this day, she wondered if some holes could never be filled, some wounds never healed.

Staring at her arm, she was painfully aware of the stark difference between knowing a thing and seeing it. Touching it.

The ache inside swelled. Tears gathered in the corners of her eyes. She clenched her jaw against the loneliness closing in around her.

I'm fine. I'm fine.

A buzzing pulled her from her thoughts. She glanced

at her phone and cringed. Was there another fire? Another victim?

This case was a mess of cruel death and fiery destruction.

Shaking off her self-pity, she answered the phone. "Agent Kelley."

"Hello, this is Nurse Tipton calling from Laramie Hospital. Mrs. Martinez didn't make it through the night. She's passed."

Sitting up, Liz shoved back the covers and put her bare feet on the worn wooden floor. "Thank you for letting me know." She clicked off.

The weight of another senseless death was heavy not only on her shoulders but also in her heart. They had to find this guy before he did more harm.

She rushed through a shower. Not bothering to blow-dry her hair, she brushed it thoroughly. She decided on slacks, a gray scarf with delicate blue polka dots, and light blue button-down.

In the kitchen, she made coffee as she stared out the window at the tent Sawyer had slept in again. She fired off a text to him about Aleida and got to work on whipping up a quick breakfast. She was at the stove scrambling egg whites and chopped up veggies with her back to the door when she heard him come in. The screen door snapped closed behind him.

"I'm sorry," he said. "About Aleida."

She didn't turn to look at him. Simply nodded.

He stood still a minute and then headed upstairs, and the shower started. She made a couple of breakfast burritos and, after leaving one for him on the table, took hers and coffee in a travel mug outside onto the porch.

She sat in one of the old rocking chairs and, though her appetite hadn't kicked in yet, munched on the food.

Her father had been a fourth-generation farmer. Their

property—before they'd sold most of it to the Powells—reached up from the break land plateau to Big Horn Ridge. She loved the snowcapped rolling mountains, the brown and green hills, wide open space, clean air, the lack of congestion. The view helped put things in perspective, making it hard to deny the sense of loss inside, the gnawing emptiness that hollowed her out that had nothing to do with the case.

Not once in her career had she allowed her personal business to interfere with her job. Somehow, she had convinced herself it was due to the fact she was a good agent. Every time she looked at Sawyer, she questioned that conviction. Not her being a good agent part. Maybe it had been so easy for her to separate the personal from the professional because she'd never had anything else in her life before that she cared about.

And she did care for him. Deeply.

The screen door creaked as he stepped outside, shutting the front door. "I'm ready if you are."

Getting into his vehicle was her response. Sawyer drove while he ate. With her fingers laced together, hard, she stared out the window until they pulled up to the fire station on the side of the building where his office was located.

There was a long moment of silence, the only sound the running engine and AC blowing. Sawyer reached over and covered her hands with one of his palms. She hadn't realized how cold she was until his warmth penetrated.

A knock on the driver's side window drew their attention, and he moved his hand. Erica Egan stood on the other side wearing a skintight tank top, bent over, with an enviable amount of cleavage on display. She held up a tray with three coffees and flashed a pearly white smile. "Time to chat."

As Sawyer groaned, they both got out of the car.

He slammed the door shut. "After the last article, no more quotes." He headed for the door to the building.

Wearing khaki shorts and heels that showed off her long, taut legs, she click-clacked ahead of them and threw herself in front of the door. "We had a deal."

Liz's gaze swept over Erica, her bare arms, smooth legs—her effortless sex appeal. It made Liz wonder why she hadn't ever appreciated the curve of her neck when she was younger, the smoothness of its skin. How she had even taken for granted her pale freckles.

She tugged on the neckerchief.

"You brought up painful things that should've been left in the past and out of the *Gazette*." Sawyer crossed his arms. "Things that have no bearing on this case."

"I beg to differ," Erica said. "You two have history, and I picked up on a certain vibe between you, which might affect how you handle the investigation."

"What you picked up on was that I'm not interested in letting you sidle up to me for information." He reached for the door handle.

The journalist blocked him. "I framed both of you in a positive light and used the entirety of Agent Kelley's glowing quote about you."

Erica offered Liz a coffee cup. She accepted it, though she wouldn't drink it. Paranoia prevented her from consuming food and beverages from strangers. Not that she thought the reporter was going to poison her. She simply couldn't do it, but accepting the coffee was a gesture of good will.

"I also did as you asked," Erica continued. "No vivid descriptions of the fire. I painted the perpetrator as a monster and highlighted not only the loss of two parents but also the awful impact on the entire community."

"You read the article, Sawyer." Liz glanced at him. "Did she?"

By the tightening of his jaw, Erica had. "Nothing else about the fire fifteen years ago or describing Liz as the girl who survived. Agreed?"

Grinning, Erica handed him a cup.

He took the peace offering.

"A source told me you are changing the focus of your investigation to the firefighters, as you may suspect one of them is the culprit. Can you confirm or deny?"

How did she find out so quickly? Sawyer had to call Gareth, who in turn called Ted, last night to set up the interviews for all personnel today, but word had traveled much faster than either of them had expected.

"Who told you?" Sawyer asked. "And don't give me any hogwash about confidential sources."

"I overheard a couple of firefighters griping about it at the bar last night. Beyond that I can't reveal my sources. Is it true?"

"We have to examine every possibility," Liz said. "Today we're only conducting routine interviews. We thank the fine men and women of the LFD and VFD for their cooperation and appreciate their invaluable service to the community."

"Have a good day, Ms. Egan." Sawyer grabbed the handle and opened the door, letting Liz inside first. Once the door closed on the reporter, he said, "Holden and his deputies will be here soon to help out."

"It's going to be a long day." Probably grueling. "Are you ready for this? For their skepticism. For the hostility." She'd been in this situation before—questioning firefighters—and what she'd faced was nothing short of vitriol.

"Does it matter if I'm ready? We have a job to do."

Chapter Twelve

"This is unbelievable," Ted Rapke said, sitting in a chair in Sawyer's office, his face rigid with tension. "You actually think it's one of us?"

"I don't." Sawyer's head was throbbing after going through this for hours. The same questions, similar responses, different firefighters. "But it's necessary."

Scooting to the edge of the sofa beside him, Liz rested her forearms on her thighs. "Please answer the question. Where were you between four thirty and five thirty last night?"

Ted sighed. "I left my shift early. Around three. Three-thirty. I met my fiancée, Cathy, and was with her the rest of the night."

"I'm sure she'll verify." Liz gave a tight smile. "Why did you leave early?"

"We recently got engaged. I haven't given her much input on the engagement party. Telling her whatever she wanted was fine with me apparently wasn't good enough. Her mom was coming into town this morning, and she wanted to go over things the night before. Put on a good show. You know? Gareth agreed to cover for me."

"Has your relationship been rocky?" she asked.

Ted's gaze swung to Sawyer and then back to Liz. "What has that got to do with anything?"

Sawyer gritted his teeth, hating to subject the guys to this. "She needs to form a complete profile of everyone."

"Not per se." Ted rubbed his hands up and down his thighs. "I've been married twice before. I want to make this one work."

"What time did you meet her and where?" Liz opened a bottle of water and took a sip.

Ted shrugged. "Maybe four. At her place."

"Do we have enough?" Irritation ticked through Sawyer.

Liz sat back and crossed her legs. "Sure. We'll need to contact your fiancée, but that's all for now."

"You know we've all been through a background check. We risk our lives every day to save people. It's one thing to question us, dragging us in on our day off, or asking us to lose sleep, but you shouldn't put the volunteers through the wringer." He pushed to his feet, with disgust stamped on his face. "Their numbers dwindle every year."

"One more question," Liz said. "You know everyone in the department and the volunteers very well."

Ted narrowed his eyes at her. "That's a statement, not a question, but yeah, I do."

"Do you have any rock stars? Someone who can't get enough of the job, works extra shifts, a volunteer who joined young and is at every single call, at the front of every work detail."

Ted's face hardened. "You should be ashamed of yourself, Liz. Now you want to go after someone who's dedicated and earnest. Is this a joke? What kind of investigation are you running?"

"Sadly, this is no joke." Liz stood. "At least one hundred arsonists who are also firefighters are convicted every year. In North America alone. That's only the ones who've been caught. If this arsonist is a firefighter, then 'earnest' is precisely who we are looking for, because beneath that layer of dedication is a need for self-importance. It's the type we go after when a serial arsonist is running around, and frequently enough, there's good reason."

Waving a dismissive hand at her, Ted walked out of the office.

Sawyer jumped to his feet and went after him. "Hold up," he said, and Ted stopped but didn't turn around. He hurried around to face him. "I don't like this any more than you do. The goal is to eliminate everyone in the LFD and VFD as suspects. But if this guy is hiding somewhere in our ranks, it's unacceptable. One thing we take pride in is our integrity and the trust that the community has in us. If one of our own is an arsonist and a murderer, he's everything we detest."

The words gave Ted pause, deflating the anger in his face. Slowly, he nodded. "You're right, but that's still a mighty big *if*."

A door across the hall from them opened. Holden and Joshua Burfield stepped out and shook hands.

Ted walked away, heading over to Josh. "Want to get out of here and grab a quick drink before I have to explain to my future mother-in-law why we're being questioned?"

"Sure, let's get Gareth," Josh said. "Hey, have you set a date for the engagement party?"

After this, Sawyer doubted an invitation was in the cards for him.

"Not yet." Ted gave a weary shake of his head. "Can't agree on a venue. I don't want to spend as much money on this party as we will on a wedding."

Holden followed Sawyer back into his office and closed the door.

"How's it going?" Liz asked.

"So far, most everyone we've questioned have had alibis."

"Let me guess." Liz sighed. "Thirty percent were here on duty. The rest were with loved ones."

Holden put his finger on his nose. "Bingo. Girlfriend, fiancée, brother, mother. I'll have a deputy verify them all."

"We have a list, too," Liz said. "At the top of ours is Ted Rapke. We need solid times from the fiancée."

Sawyer bristled. Ted could be aggravating and hold a grudge. That didn't make him a murderer and an arsonist.

"I've also got two we have to look into deeper," Holden said. "Alibis are weak."

"Who?" Sawyer sat down.

"Gareth McCreary. He wasn't on duty at the time in question because he was getting ready to fill in for Ted. States he went to the grocery store on Third to pick up stuff to cook dinner for the company, paid cash and can't find the receipt. Arrived at the station at five. Someone else said he didn't arrive until five thirty. We'll check the surveillance cameras at the grocery store to see when he was there."

"The store is only two blocks from the Cowboy Way." It had been a quick walk for Isaac Quincy.

"The other person?" Liz asked.

"Johnson, the probie."

Sawyer recalled seeing him at the fire. "But he was on duty."

"He was, but he left the station earlier that day to run an errand. Picked up a prescription and pastries from Divine Treats."

Not good. Wincing, Sawyer scratched the stubble on his jaw. He needed to shave. "The pastry shop is around the corner from the tattoo parlor."

Liz stretched her neck and adjusted her scarf. "What time?"

"He was gone from five to six. It'll be easy to establish exactly when he picked up the prescription. Divine Treats is a different story. There are no cameras inside or at the traffic lights on the block. We'll check with the stores across the street. I think there's even an ATM, too."

"Sounds good." Liz finished her water. "If we can't clear McCreary and the probie, let's see if they'll agree to take a polygraph test."

"All right. One more thing. Josh Burfield couldn't convince all the volunteers to come in for questioning. Two took it as an offense. One quit. I'll talk to them personally tomorrow." Holden yawned, and exhaustion was starting to set in for Sawyer, too. "It's getting late. I'm cutting my deputies loose, but I'll stick around a few more hours to help you question the next team on the way in. Best to push through what we can tonight." His cell phone buzzed. He answered it. "Chief Deputy Powell." While he listened, his gaze slid to him and then Liz. "Okay. Wait a sec. I'm going to put you on speaker." As he did so, he said to them, "We got something on the hotline Russo thinks you need to hear." He moved closer. "Go ahead and play it, Ashley."

"This came in a few hours ago, but we just now got to it because we've been inundated with worthless calls and phony tips. Here you go."

The message played. "You think I'm a monster. I'm anything but." The voice was deep and sinister. Electronically modified. "I am vengeance, making them reap what they have sown. Ask them how they built their businesses, where they got the seed money. And they will lie. Ask what they're hiding. And they will lie. I took a son for the sins of the father. Did he tell you about our chat? Did he tell you why he has been punished? Or did he lie? I have taken everything from two, leaving them their lives and their lies as their cross to bear. Fire was my weapon. My anger, my hatred, was best turned into a flammable fuel. Because it's effective and nothing burns as clean."

"That's the end of it," Russo said. "We're trying to trace where the call came from."

Sawyer swallowed around the thick knot in his throat. "I thought I'd be relieved if he left a message," he said, feeling the complete opposite. "Like we'd get a clue, or he'd tip his hand, and we'd see some way to stop him."

"Can you play it again?" Liz asked. The second time they listened to it, she took notes. "Russo, we're going to speak to Parrot today. Can you contact Neil Steward and ask where he got the money to open the tattoo parlor? The same with Aleida Martinez's husband. He might be able to fill in some blanks for us."

"I'm on it."

Holden disconnected.

"He may not have left us a clue," Liz said, "but he gave us a way to find one. It's getting Steward to tell us what he's hiding."

"Maybe Parrot will be more forthcoming," Sawyer said, hoping for the best but expecting more lies. Neil had lost his son and his shop, and still he was determined to protect his secret.

A deputy poked his head into the office. "I've got another firefighter for you to question."

"I'll take him," Holden said, moving to the door.

Sawyer glanced at his watch. It was only five, but it felt much later. "Thanks, Holden."

"No problem." His brother gave a two-finger salute. "Here to serve." He left the office.

"It almost sounded like our guy was finished." Sawyer grabbed a bottle of water. "The way he used the past tense."

"Possibly. It's been two days with no fires. No car bombs. No murders." She stared at her notes. "But part of it was also in present tense. I *am* vengeance. *Making* them reap what they have sown. He was careful with the way he worded it for a reason. His type gets a thrill out of manipulating law enforcement."

"I hope he's done and that there are no others he intends to punish. But he does want us to find out what Steward and Parrot are lying about. Perhaps that's part of his plan.

How he gets to us. If it's illegal, then we'll finish the punishment."

"That's what they do. Manipulate while reminding us that he's in charge. Even if he is finished with his vendetta, we're not going to let him get away with murder and arson." Resting her head on the back of the sofa, she pinched the bridge of her nose and closed her eyes. "We need a break in this case. What if you're right and we're wasting time conducting these interviews?" She heaved a shuddery breath. "What am I missing?"

"I never said it was a waste of time. I don't want to believe someone I know, I trust and I've worked with is capable of something like this. Have your instincts been wrong before on other cases?"

Her lashes lifted. "No, but—" she tilted her head toward him "—being back here is messing with my head."

She neglected to mention whether he was having any effect on her heart. He didn't want to be a distraction. Something to avoid. He wanted to be a safe place for her to fall when she needed it. He wanted to be there for her in every way.

Sawyer took her hand in his and the minute their skin touched sparks fired through his whole body. He rubbed the tendons along her inner wrist, a careless caress. Or maybe a careful one. He wasn't sure, but when she didn't pull away, he was starting to think that if he wore her down bit by bit, she'd eventually stop running. Talk to him.

"What's your plan tonight?" she asked.

"What do you mean?"

"Where do you intend to sleep? I hope it's at home in your bed and not in the tent again. You need a good night's rest."

Still rubbing her wrist, he stretched his torso until a twinge in his side made him stop. "I'm touched you care, even though you keep denying it."

"If you're tired, you're not going to be at your best during this investigation."

Leaning back, he angled toward her so that their thighs touched. "I see. You're only concerned about my job performance."

"That's not what I meant." Her voice softened.

Sawyer brushed hair away from her face, trailing his fingertips along her cheek to her chin and let it linger there. That was the thing about Liz. She always made him want to get closer. Always pulled him in, without even trying. "Care to clarify?"

A charged silence bloomed between them. She stared at him, her eyes pale green pools of warmth and uncertainty. All he wanted was to erase her doubt. About herself and him.

"I don't want to repeat the past," he admitted. "I know you've said you can't, but you need to know that I can't stop trying because I've never stopped loving you."

Her lips parted, her eyes going wide.

A sharp rap on the open door had them pulling apart. Chuck Parrot entered. "I guess the *Gazette* got it right about you two."

The last thing Sawyer wanted was for anyone to mention the article again.

Liz's shoulders tensed. "What do you mean?" she asked, and Sawyer was grateful she didn't know all the details in the article.

Parrot schlepped in—his thinning red hair wild and wiry as though he hadn't combed it—and plopped down in a chair like he'd been drinking or hadn't stopped in days. "Erica Egan wrote that you two had been lovers years ago until tragedy separated you and that this case has rekindled your connection."

The reporter had swapped one sensational focus for another. "Egan only cares about seeing her byline beneath the front-page headline."

"Doesn't mean she's wrong." Chuck pulled a flask from his back pocket.

"You'll have to wait," Sawyer said, "until we're done here to resume drinking."

Flattening his mouth in a thin line, Chuck sagged in his seat but kept hold of the flask, resting it on his round belly. "Well, hurry up so I can get back to drowning my sorrows." He shook the metal container.

Sawyer glanced at Liz to see how she wanted to handle it. She intensely eyed Parrot like a puzzle she wanted to piece together. So he got to the point. "Did you receive a threatening phone call shortly before your restaurant was burned down?"

The question sobered him quickly. He straightened, his eyes turning alert. "Excuse me?"

Sawyer waited for a beat, studying him. "Did someone call you minutes before the fire and threaten you?"

Chuck hesitated, and Sawyer could see the deliberation on his face. "No. No one called me. Why do you ask?"

"Because someone called Neil Steward right before the Cowboy Way was torched," Sawyer said. "Threatened to take away his son and his shop."

His gaze bounced around as Chuck lowered his head. "Did the man say why he was going to do that to Neil?"

"I never said it was a man who called Neil."

Chuck opened the flask and took a sip. "Merely assumed."

"I know you from somewhere," Liz said. "Don't I? Your face, your voice, very familiar."

"I don't think so. Maybe I have one of those faces. People seem to think they know me for some reason."

The round shape. Freckles. Pale complexion. Orange-red hair. His face was distinctive. Chuck was forty-two, ten years their senior, though he looked older, so Liz didn't know him from school.

"It'll come to me. In the meantime, may we see your cell phone?" she asked.

His brows drew together, and he moved his hand, covering his pocket that had the bulge of his phone. "No, you may not."

"Withholding information or evidence in a criminal investigation is obstruction of justice." Her tone was soft.

"I'm the victim here. You might want to remember that."

"Don't you want to help us catch this guy?" Sawyer asked.

"Yeah," Chuck spat out, nodding, "of course."

Sawyer cocked his head to the side. "Then tell us about the phone call."

"I would." Chuck stood. "But I didn't get one." He headed for the door.

"CP," Liz called out, and Parrot spun around. "That's what everyone called you on the Wild Horse Ranch."

He didn't say anything, his face turning ghostly white.

"It took me some time to recognize you. Easier here in the light of the office. You've put on weight. Your hair has thinned. Aged quite a bit. But you worked there my first year." She rose and edged toward him. "As a ranch hand, but you weren't there the next summer when the fire that killed the Durbins happened, right?"

Chuck shrugged. "Sure. So what?"

"Why did you say I didn't know you?"

Another shrug from him. "Guess I didn't make the connection. I don't recall every stinking kid that passed through there. Why? Is that a crime, too?"

He was a bad liar. Chuck Parrot had already admitted to reading the article in the *Gazette*. The Wild Horse Ranch fire had been mentioned. Even if he didn't remember Liz, he was aware of the connection.

Liz smiled in that practiced saccharine way Sawyer recognized. "Did Neil work there around the same time as you?"

Chuck turned the flask up to his mouth, taking another hit. Probably stalling. "You'll have to ask him about his previous work history."

"Where did you get the seed money to open your restaurant?" she asked.

Chuck's brow furrowed, and he rocked back on his heels like the question had been a physical blow. "Wh-what difference does it make?"

Maybe all the difference in the world.

"Where?" she pressed.

He rubbed his hand over the back of his neck. "Loan from the bank."

Ask and they'll lie.

Why?

"Which bank gave a ranch hand a five-figure loan to open a restaurant with nothing for collateral?"

Sawyer loved watching Liz work. She was sexy as she closed in, throwing razor-sharp questions to get at the truth. Not to mention seeing her chase down a suspect had been oddly thrilling.

"You don't know me or what I had to use as collateral," Chuck said defensively. "Frankly, it's none of your business. What should be is finding the sick SOB who took everything away from me. Is there anything else?"

She shook her head and followed him to the doorway, where she watched him leave. "How much do you want to bet Neil worked there, too?"

"It was a popular place. The Durbins hired many ranch hands over the years, and they were the only camp within a hundred miles that catered to older teens."

She cast a glance at Sawyer over her shoulder. "You still don't think there's something there, at the very least, something about the Wild Horse Ranch, rather than the fire, is the connection?"

"I'm not saying that." He was playing Devil's advocate. Statistically, this was more than coincidence. "We've got to look at it from all angles. Test the theory."

"I wonder if any records from the ranch still exist."

"The fire wiped out the main house and the cabins. The property was sold. Everything leveled. The Durbins didn't have any kids who we could speak with. But I do think there's something there." He came up alongside her. "Chuck knows you, but he lied about it because he didn't want us to associate him with the ranch. He also lied about not getting a threatening phone call and where he got his seed money for the restaurant. For whatever reason, Chuck and Neil are hiding the same thing. If we can figure out what it is, the connection will be solid."

"It'll have to wait." She gestured down the hall.

The next team of firefighters had arrived to be questioned.

Chapter Thirteen

He had enjoyed calling into the hotline, airing his grievance, giving his retribution a voice. Now others would wonder about the dirty deeds of those on his list. What he didn't enjoy was Liz's meddling. Yet again. He thought he'd be able to savor making her suffer, taking Sawyer away while she was forced to watch and dealing with her later in Virginia.

Turns out, she was a sharper agent than he'd assumed and should have given her more credit. She and Sawyer were asking all the right questions to all the right people, circling like sharks, getting closer than he could allow, smelling blood in the water.

Somehow, they had even corrupted the lovely Erica Egan. In the *Gazette*, she lauded Kelley and Powell for their efforts in the investigation. Baited readers to root for the star-crossed lovers on their journey to prevail as they rekindled a connection. It made him want to gag. All the while, Egan failed to describe the glory of his handiwork. Instead, she labeled those who had sold their souls to the devil as innocent victims. Called him a monster!

When he was only seeking justice.

Removing Liz Kelley and Sawyer Powell from the playing field was the safest answer to his growing problem. Then the reporter would revert to her old style—he was helping sell more papers—and he didn't need those two meddlers to ruin his game. After all, he had a spectacular finale planned. Something no one expected. Something no one could stop once it started. Something the likes of which no one in the Mountain West had ever seen. He was going to finish with a big *boom*.

More pain and suffering and fire was necessary. The greater the effort, the grander the gesture, the sweeter the reward. In the end, he'd get what he wanted, what he needed, and all the patience he'd shown, the risks he had taken, all the blood he had shed, would be worth it.

But first, he needed Liz and Sawyer out of the way. No more underestimating them.

He watched the cursed lovebirds slide into the red SUV that was parked right in view of the surveillance camera. He hadn't been able to get anywhere close to it. The inconvenience only forced him to improvise.

Regrettably, he wouldn't be able to take care of those two himself tonight. In case something went wrong, he needed an airtight alibi that was above reproach. For this one, he needed assistance. Someone he trusted.

Liz's luck was finally about to run out. She and Sawyer were completely unaware of what lay ahead and how their night would end.

SAWYER HAD TOLD her that he still loved her. Liz didn't know if that was possible. Or healthy. Or best for him.

That was all she could think about on the nerve-wracking drive back to Bison Ridge. Maybe he wouldn't bring it up tonight. Let them get some sleep and tackle it tomorrow.

She glanced at her cell. It was on ten percent power. She needed to grab her phone charger from the rental.

Sawyer pulled up behind her vehicle, which was in front of the house, and put the SUV in Park.

"I don't know about you, but I'm exhausted." She hopped out. "Good night," she said, closing the door.

He was right behind her. "Are we going to talk about it?" His voice was dark and deep and rumbly.

No. "Tomorrow. Okay?" She headed for the rental. "I'm beat."

She wasn't up to handling Sawyer. Not tonight. He'd always been able to see right through the mask she tried to wear to hide her emotions. Training had made her better, but still, he had that way about him. Like he could see her soul. The last thing she wanted was for him to glimpse her weakness.

"I told you I love you."

She faltered to a stop, her stomach tightening in a knot. "I know."

He put a hand on her shoulder and turned her around to face him. "I deserve a response," he said, gentling his tone, making it soft as cotton. Then he waited and waited. "Give me something, Lizzie," he said, the only one she ever allowed to use the nickname.

"Thank you." The two clumsy words tumbled from her mouth.

Sawyer shook his head as if he hadn't heard her correctly. "Thank you?" He reared back, pulling his hands from her shoulders. "Thank you," he snapped. "Tell me you don't love me. Tell me what you felt died a long time ago. Tell me that you don't want me the way I want you. Or tell me that you *do* love me. But don't say 'thank you.'"

Steeling herself, she looked at him, meeting his darkening stare, concealing the agony roiling inside her. "I don't want you to sleep in the tent tonight. Call Tessa. Give her a real chance. You might be more compatible than you realize."

He nudged the tip of his black cowboy hat up with his knuckle. "You're still trying to decide for both of us. As though what I want isn't a factor in this equation. You've gotten too accustomed to acting stoic, running away from anything that makes you feel something. No boyfriend. No husband. No friends. No pet. What about your family? All you've got is that badge and a gun when you deserve a hell of a lot more to fill the empty spaces in your life."

"You're one to talk. Where's your girlfriend or wife or pet?" she asked, skipping over the friends and family part since he had her there. "Who are you to judge me?"

"I noticed you neglected to address how you keep making unilateral decisions that affect both our lives. I'm done letting you kick me to the side with no explanation. You want to know why?" he asked, but he didn't wait for her to answer. "I am not a puppy, who'll slink away and lick his wounds. I'm a coyote." He started howling.

At her.

What in the world? Had he lost his mind?

COLOR ROSE IN her cheeks. The only proof he was getting to her, making her feel something.

"Please," she said, "stop howling like some wild thing."

He howled again, this time even louder, letting out his frustration and his misery.

She heaved out a breath. "You have no right to make unfounded assumptions about my life," she said, raising her voice over his howls. "I have a great job. I'm proud to be an agent. To have a purpose." She glowered at him.

There she went, bringing up work as a deflection, so he kept on howling.

"I've built a good life and I'm perfectly f…" Her voice trailed off as she caught herself, something dawning in her eyes.

"What? You're perfectly *fine*?"

He must have struck a chord. She narrowed her eyes, lips thinning, spun around and opened the door to her rental car.

"I appreciate your concern, but go home." Her tone was weary. She reached inside the car and grabbed something.

"This day has pushed us to our breaking point. You need to get some sleep. We both do."

Go home. He should do as she asked and let her be, but something inside him demanded he stay. This was where they needed to be, at their breaking point, so they could have a breakthrough.

She slammed the car door, holding a phone charger, and turned toward the house.

But he was right on her, closing the distance. He gripped her arms, making her face him. "Every good memory I have is tied up with you." His heart thudded in his chest.

Tears glistened in her eyes. "Then it's time to make good memories with someone new."

"Do you ever think about us?"

Her bottom lip trembled. "I try not to," she said, her voice breaking right along with his heart.

"I think about you every single day." Though his nights were the hardest. Yes, he'd had other lovers, but being with them only made him miss her more. When he was alone in his bed with only his memories for comfort, his regrets tortured him. "I've loved you for so long that I don't remember what it's like not to."

He'd let her run away before, but this time, things would be different. This time, he would fight for her and not give up.

A vehicle approaching, the engine a loud growl, had him pivoting toward the sound. A black motorcycle came down the road way too fast for the speed limit. Alarm pulsed through him. The person was wearing all black, a helmet covering his face. Sawyer had a split second of recognition as the motorcycle slowed, moonlight bouncing off steel. A gun.

An icy wave of fear rushed over him.

"Sawyer!"

Liz's voice barely registered as instinct kicked in. He

whirled her away from the line of fire, and then they were both on the ground with his body covering hers, pain flaring in his side as a shot cracked the air.

The window where they had been standing shattered. Glass rained down on them. Thunder from more gunshots breaking windows in the house. He pressed her flat to the ground as another shot punctured a tire. He drew his weapon. A third bullet pinged off the frame only centimeters from his head, close enough to feel biting heat. He shifted even lower.

The motorcycle sped away, gunning the engine, tires screeching, leaving the odor of burnt rubber in the air.

Sawyer lay there, his body fully covering hers, one arm curled around her head, his face buried in her hair. He waited for a fourth shot that never came. They were gone. For now. He strained to hear if the vehicle had turned around and was coming back. Or perhaps stopped down the road and the gunman was on foot.

It would have been reckless, not to mention foolish, for the person to get off the motorcycle or give them a chance to catch the license plate. Then again, their assailant shot at an FBI agent in front of her house, so how wise could he be?

Sawyer's shoulder had taken the brunt of the fall when they'd landed. Her right arm was beneath him, her Glock looking heavy in her small hand. She'd drawn her weapon as he'd pulled her down, and he'd done likewise. "Are you hit? Injured?"

"No, but you're smothering me. Does that count?" She pushed his chest and he moved.

"I'm going to go after him." Anger burned along his nerves. This had gone too far. Liz could've been hurt. Or worse killed. Before he could get up from the ground, she caught his arm.

"You were shot. You're bleeding." She touched his forehead.

It stung. "Just a scratch. The bullet grazed me." He hadn't even realized how close he'd come to getting shot in the head. "He's getting away."

Still, she held on to him, worry heavy in her eyes. "He's already gone. Made it to the fork in the road by now. We can't be sure which way he went, and the motorcycle gives him off-road options. We are not splitting up."

Was that all it took, nearly taking a bullet for her to see reason?

"We'll call it in, and I'll get you cleaned up." She holstered her weapon and found her phone.

"You're not staying here."

"This is my house. I won't be run off."

"It isn't safe. First the car bomb. Now this. We're going to the ranch." His voice brooked no argument. He would do anything to keep her safe.

She squeezed her eyes shut. "I don't think I can face your family, handle the hugs and kisses and questions—"

"I live in the apartment above the garage. No one has to know you're there, if you stay with me instead of a guestroom in the main house." There was also the B&B in town, but it was much more exposed, leaving their vehicles vulnerable. "You can have the bed and I'll take the sofa. Okay?"

He waited for more arguments and was ready with alternative solutions. No matter her response, she wasn't staying. He was going to make sure she was protected.

Reluctantly, she nodded. Her gaze flew back to the cut on his head and she threw her arms around him in a tight hug. "I'm so glad you're alive."

So was he.

Glad they were both alive.

Chapter Fourteen

Liz was still shaken by the close call. Whoever had shot at them had gotten away without a trace. They didn't catch the license plate to have something substantial to go on.

The sheriffs in Laramie and Bison Ridge as well as the police in nearby Wayward Bluffs had patrols on the lookout for one man, wearing black, riding a black supersport bike. Neither she nor Sawyer had caught the make to narrow down the field of what they were looking for.

Sawyer pulled up to the wrought iron gates emblazoned with his family ranch's shooting star brand. He punched in the code and the massive gate swung open. They pulled through, taking the long, tree-lined driveway illuminated by LED lights, and a wave of memories assailed her. All good and warm but still hard to face.

The Powell ranch was something out of a fairy tale or a movie, and she had once thought this would be her home.

"Are you sure no one will know I'm here?"

"It'll be fine," he said. "With the hours I'm working on the case, no one is going to come out to the apartment. Trust me."

She did trust him. Always had.

They passed the enormous main house that even had wings. Ten bedrooms. Twelve bathrooms. Buck and Holly Powell loved their family and wanted to keep them close. They built the main house hoping to have weddings, host holiday celebrations and throw big birthdays there. Enough space for grandkids, extended family, in-laws and friends to stay. They were a loving, close-knit family. Buck and Holly wanted part of their legacy to be keeping it that way for generations.

Liz had not only appreciated their vision but had also shared it. Believing this was what her life with Sawyer would look like. That they would have been married here. Raised their kids on this ranch alongside their cousins.

He parked at the side of the garage near the outdoor staircase that led to the apartment. No one peeking out of a window in the house would be able to see her exit the vehicle.

She grabbed her laptop bag, he took her carry-on suitcase, they got out, and they hurried up the stairs. Quickly, he opened the unlocked door and ushered her inside.

After closing it, he flipped the lock and slipped on the chain. "Mom has a spare key. It's an extra precaution. She usually gives us plenty of space when we're in the grind. And Dad, well…" He shrugged.

Buck Powell preferred to have his children come to him, call him, let him know when he was needed. He was an anti-helicopter parent to the extreme, while Holly was a mama bear who wanted her children to be happy, healthy and safe.

"I'll put your bag in the bedroom." He started toward the room at the far end with the double French doors.

The garage apartment had been an idea for Monty, not yet realized the last time she was on the Shooting Star Ranch.

On the opposite end of the spacious apartment was a kitchen equipped with the essentials, including an island large enough to eat on. White cabinets and black quartz countertops. She took in the place. Hardwood floors and large area rug defined the living room with a cognac-colored leather sofa and large television. The place was cozy and warm and tidy.

Following him through the living room, she stopped in front of the framed picture hanging on the wall—an eighteen-by-twenty-four-inch poster of her posing with a copy of her book. It was surreal.

"I'm sure all the ladies you bring here love to see this." She gestured to it like she was Vanna White on *Wheel of Fortune*.

"As a matter of fact, they tell me it's what they like best about my place."

Surely, they loved the bed with Sawyer naked in it the best. "Did you get it from the bookstore?"

"Yeah. It's the one your mom custom-made. She paid a pretty penny for shipping." He stepped closer, eyeing it before looking at her. "Seriously, I don't bring anyone here."

"Why not?"

"Too personal. The ranch is about family." He went to the bedroom and set her bag down. "To bring them here would mean I'm interested in a future with them."

Questions rushed through her mind, but to ask them would only lead to trouble. "Mind if I shower?" She followed him into the room in the back.

The king-size bed was made, complete with accent pillows. The apartment looked like something out of a magazine, only lived in. His mother must have decorated.

"You let me use yours. Feel free to use mine." He flashed a weary smile, his eyes warm and sincere.

She looked at the bandage on his forehead, thought about the stitches in his side and ached to hold him close. Pulling her gaze away, she unzipped her suitcase. "Bathroom?"

He pushed open the door to the en suite. "Right here."

She fished out her toiletry bag and hurried into the bathroom before she acted on an impulse she'd regret. "Thanks." She closed the door and turned on the light.

The tile and stonework were dark and sophisticated. Masculine. Yet, there was still an airy spa-like feel. In the daytime, the skylights must have provided plenty of natural light. The large shower had smooth stone flooring and two showerheads. She started one of them.

She didn't take long getting cleaned up and brushing her teeth. Once finished, she looked around the bathroom and realized in her haste, she'd forgotten to bring her pajamas.

No way was she going out with only a towel wrapped around her. Sawyer was sitting on that bed waiting to talk to her. She just knew it.

She grabbed his navy robe from the hook on the back of the door, pulled it on and hung up the towel. Tying the belt, she rubbed her fingers over the ultrasoft cotton, nuzzled her nose in the collar and inhaled the scent of him. The loss hit her all over again. The stark reminder of what was waiting for her in Virginia. An empty condo and a cold bed.

Beyond the door waited a man who would push with questions that she owed answers to.

You can't hide in here forever, and there's nowhere to run.

She opened the door and stepped out of the bathroom. Sitting on the bed, he lifted his head and his penetrating gaze locked on hers.

A breath shuddered out of her with a lump in her throat like a boulder. She shoved her hands in the pockets of the robe, faking casualness. "Hope you don't mind I put it on."

"Not at all." He pushed off the bed and came closer. "You look good wearing my things." He flashed a sinful grin that made her heart tumble over in her chest.

Averting her gaze, she caught sight of a copy of her book on the nightstand. She thought again about the poster hanging in the living room and something he'd said. Actually, a lot of things he'd said. "Tell me something."

He stopped less than a foot away, within arm's reach. "Anything."

"How did you know my mom spent a lot of money on shipping for the poster? How are you certain that I don't have a social life or get sweaty with someone sometimes or have a pet or anything besides work?" All true, but she hadn't shared those private, embarrassing details with him. The only thing he didn't seem to know was whether she'd been in the house the day he came to Montana. And the reason he didn't know was because her mother hadn't been home.

The grin slipped from his face. He scrubbed a hand through his hair. "Your mom and I have kept in touch."

Anger whispered through her. *My mother and Sawyer have been communicating behind my back.* "All these years? Keeping it a secret from me."

"When I was in Montana, your mom happened to be in town and saw the Missoula sheriff hauling me in to the station. She got me released, made sure no charges were pressed, took me to a diner and fed me. We talked for hours. She didn't want me to pull another stunt like that. I agreed on the condition that she'd tell me everything. Give me updates about you."

Although she didn't visit her parents and didn't encourage them to fly out to see her—far too busy with work—she confided in her mother, too much apparently, since the information was routinely shared with Sawyer. "How often?"

"We talk three or four times a week."

The frequency was staggering. More often than she talked to them. "About what? It can't just be about me." Not enough going on in her life.

"Quilting. Bridge. Hunting. My job. My parents. She knows everything going on with my brothers. Your parents even came to Holden's wedding."

Her parents were invited when she wasn't? Not that she

would've gone. Still, the sting of betrayal cut deep. "You had no right."

He sighed. "Lizzie, just because you cut me off, didn't mean I was ready to let go. You...you were my everything."

Her heart lurched. He had been her whole world, too. The first person she wanted to talk to about anything, good or bad. When they were together, everything felt possible because he was hers and she was his. Then the fire burned away the future they wanted, reducing it to ashes, but letting Sawyer go had been a different kind of devastation.

"I thought it would be easier if we didn't have any more contact." Her voice was a whisper.

"Easier for you maybe. But not for me. I loved you. With everything I am. I still wanted the future we had planned. Going to college together at SWU. Getting engaged after graduation. Married once we had settled into our careers. I didn't stop wanting a life with you because of the accident."

"We were silly kids. With preposterous plans. Your high school love isn't supposed to be your only one."

Yet he was hers. Not just her first but her only.

"Who says? Try telling that to my parents."

The ideal couple. High school sweethearts. Never had an off year to explore other romantic interests. Married for forty. Four kids. Unbearably affectionate. An impossible standard.

"I was there at your side every day as you recovered in the hospital. You lost twenty pounds in one week. I saw the pain. All your struggles. Tried to help you through recovery, but you slowly started shutting me out until you moved away and cut off all contact."

A jolt of sorrow sliced through her. "I was doing you a favor. I thought that I'd be the only one who would suffer."

He shook his head. "You took away my choice. Made a unilateral decision for both of us." His voice was rough. Ragged.

"You were supposed to move on with some pretty girl and live the life you were always meant to have. Just with someone else."

Sawyer grimaced. "How could I move on when you haven't?" he asked, his tone intimate, bare. "How could I fall for someone else when all I do is compare them to you and hate how they don't measure up?" Lowering his head, he blew out a long breath. "Were you there that day in Montana? Were you home? Did you hear me, screaming for you until I was breathless?"

Her throat closed. A fresh wave of pain flooded her, but the ache was in her heart. "I was."

"Why didn't you come out and talk to me?"

Tears welled, threatening to fall. "Because I didn't want to be without you. I would've looked into your eyes, fell into your arms and never let go."

"That was all I ever wanted." He ventured even closer. "Why didn't you?"

She shut her eyes. Hot tears rolled down her cheeks. "I was broken. I'd lost myself. Everything good and beautiful and strong was tied up in you." As though there was no Liz without Sawyer. Using him to fix what was fractured inside of her wouldn't have been right. Wouldn't have been healthy. "I had to let you go, so we could both be free. Even though it had killed me to do it." She looked up at him. "I had to heal, find a way out of the darkness and back into the light, alone. Eventually, I did, and it led me to the FBI." The bureau gave her a renewed sense of purpose.

"Then why are you still running from me?" he demanded, sounding bereft.

"You haven't seen it." A pang returned to her chest. "The scars. The skin grafts. What I look like."

Hurt flashed on his face. "Because you never gave me a chance."

"A chance? For what? To reject me?" Her back teeth

clenched. "To stay with me out of obligation? Some twisted sense of loyalty. Or worse pity?" Burdening him with the expectation to love her after the fire had left her *damaged goods*. "Why drag out the inevitable part where you eventually wanted to move on and dumped me."

"Since you thought me leaving you was inevitable, you left me first. When all this time, you should've believed that *you* and *me* being together is what's inevitable."

"The fire *ruined* me." The only way he'd understand was to show him. Loosening the belt, she turned her back to him and shrugged off the top of the robe, letting it fall to her waist. Then she pulled her hair over one shoulder. "Nobody wants to look at this, much less touch it. Especially not…" A lover.

She trembled, baring herself to him, exposing the scars and grief she carried.

Her heart throbbed so hard it hurt until he wrapped his arms around her, bringing her against him, with his warm chest to her back. She nearly pulled away, the heat of his body was scorching, but she was tired of running from the one person she wanted to cling to.

"You are not ruined." He pressed his mouth to the nape of her neck, his breath sending a tingle down her spine.

Over the years, she'd imagined what it would be like to see him again, to hold him, to be held in return.

This was real. Not a memory. Not a fantasy she'd had a thousand times.

"You're a warrior who goes into battle against the worst of the worst." Kissing her softly, he trailed a path across her back. "You're brilliant and brave and beautiful. Even more so now. Not despite the scars. Simply beautiful, scars and all. And you're still the sexiest woman I've ever known."

Curling her hands around his forearms that were banded tight around her, she closed her eyes and reveled in his touch, in the sincerity in his voice, in the way he smelled, in how he accepted all that she was.

He brushed her shoulder with his lips and slipped a hand inside the robe, palm pressed to her stomach.

His warmth penetrated past the scars and muscle, deep into her bones. With Sawyer, she was exposed. Vulnerable.

And it frightened her.

But then he did something even more terrifying.

He untied the belt, letting the robe fall to the floor and turned her around. His gaze swept over her body and there was only tenderness in his eyes. *Appreciation.*

Looking back up at her, he cupped her jaw, running his fingers into her hair. "I love you, honey. So much." He pressed the sweetest kiss to her lips. "Still. Always."

She was smiling and crying and shivering at the same time. "I love you, too."

A devastating smile broke over his face, and her thoughts scattered. He crushed his mouth to hers, his lips full of desperation and hunger. She kissed him back hard, longing sliding into every stroke of her tongue against his, concentrating on the taste of him.

He shuffled them backward, somehow caressing her as he pulled his shirt over his head. Their lips parted for a breath. Then his mouth claimed hers again, and they let out twin sighs of relief.

The years they'd been apart disappeared as if they'd always been and should always be together.

She unbuckled his belt, shoved down his pants and boxer briefs. A sigh escaped her. He was gorgeous. Everything about him sexy and strong.

"Do you want me to shower first?" He kicked off his boots, working his jeans off the rest of the way.

After fifteen years, she should be able to wait five more minutes. But she couldn't. "I need you right now. We'll shower after. Together. Put those two showerheads to good use."

"Then we can get dirty again."

She laughed as they tumbled onto the bed in a tangle. The delicious weight of him on top of her settled between her thighs, his hands exploring her body while she delighted in the feel of his skin and muscles and strength.

Her body relaxed and tensed with anticipation. "It's been a long time for me. I haven't done this since…you."

He stared down at her and smiled. "We can go slow. Start with me kissing every inch of you." He pressed his lips to the base of her throat, licked across her collarbone and nipped her shoulder, sending a shiver through her.

Although that sounded like a dream come true, she didn't want to slow down. She wanted to rush forward. With him. "Let's save slow for tomorrow morning."

He kissed her again, his mouth warm and demanding as his hand slid down between her legs. The need unleashed within her was immediate—too powerful to deny. So much emotion in his touch. Love and joy and hunger. She felt the same. Fear wouldn't hold her back any longer.

Clinging to each other, tangled together. Connected. She thought needing him made her weak. Only now she saw their love made them stronger.

That need for him all-consuming. No restraint between them. Only intensity and heat and love.

This was everything.

She'd been running all this time from where she belonged. Where she was always meant to be.

They were inevitable.

Chapter Fifteen

Missed? How had his brother missed?

He never did like guns, in part because of the uncertainty. Is someone alive? Dead? Is the wound fatal?

And guns were too loud. Crude. Say nothing of the mess they caused. Unlike fire. That was a different beast. His animal of choice. Sophisticated when done right.

His brother thought Sawyer or Liz might have been injured, but he was certain they were alive. What if she called in more agents to assist with the case?

Even if she didn't, the sheriff's department was going to throw their full weight behind solving this case. Deputies were already conducting interviews to speed things along. This drive-by shooting was only going to fuel their efforts.

Then there was Sawyer. His protective instincts would put him in overdrive. That Powell would stop at nothing now.

At least his brother had removed the license plates from the motorcycle and evaded the roadblocks authorities had set up. No danger of them figuring out who they were.

Gritting his teeth, he groaned. He was under pressure to see this through. Instead of being able to draw this out, like he wanted, he needed to accelerate his timeline.

Somehow, someway he would finish the list. No better time than now to make it happen. Starting with Neil Steward and Chuck Parrot. No protective custody had been given to them. Neither man had provided the authorities with enough to warrant it, too busy hiding their precious secret. Liars until the end.

And I was smart enough to bait Liz and Sawyer into thinking I was finished.

Far from it.

In order for this to work, before the sun rose, he needed to make sure Steward and Parrot were dead.

SAWYER WOKE WITH light streaming in the windows and Liz nestled up against him. And it was perfect.

She was perfect. For him. He only wished they hadn't wasted so much time not being together, but he finally understood why she'd needed to recover and grow on her own without him. Saw how she'd suffered. How she'd sacrificed for him.

Last night as he held her close, she'd told him about the rookie agent who had made her question if any man would find her desirable. What a weak fool that guy was not to see she was gorgeous. His loss was Sawyer's gain.

Now Liz knew that he'd had other options and still only wanted her. There would be no fear of entrapment. Of obligation. Of resentment.

No doubt.

With open hearts, they were choosing this—to be together.

Liz snuggled closer, her leg between his thighs, nuzzling her mouth against the curve of his neck. "Good morning," she whispered, her voice throaty and sexy.

He tightened his arm around her. "How are you feeling?"

"A whole lot better than fine." She gave his shoulder a playful nip. "Amazing, actually." She ran her palm across his chest. "It was like riding a bike. You?"

Like he'd been living with one lung, barely able to breathe. Now? "Everything is right in the world with you back in my life." In his arms where she belonged. Sex had never been an issue for him. Intimacy had. She was the one woman he'd been truly intimate with, sharing his deepest secrets, his real self. "There's nothing like this." He caressed her face. "Like us."

"I'll never let go again," she promised.

"You better not." He wouldn't survive if she did. "And last night." He gave a low whistle and kissed her. "I thought it was mind-blowing before, but that was next level."

"You're full of it." She leaned up on her forearm. "You said it was mind-blowing with Tessa."

"No, I didn't. I spoke in generalities that could be applied to any relationship." He brushed hair from her face and tucked it behind her ear. Caressed her cheek. Cupped the side of her neck. Felt incredible for her not to cringe. "Chemistry and compatibility aren't the same. We have both. Marriage shouldn't be based on sex, even if it's mind-blowing. That's what Dad told me after I informed him that I was going to marry you one day."

Her brows pinched together. "I don't know if I should be flattered that you were referring to us when you said 'mind-blowing' or creeped out that your dad knew so much about our sex life."

He chuckled. "Some private things had slipped out in an argument we had. I wanted to marry you right after high school. He thought we were too young and believed I was confusing great sex with love. That's when I came up with the plan to do it after college. But the takeaway is you should be flattered."

There was a loud knock on the door, and Liz tensed. His front doorknob rattled, someone trying to get in.

Good thing he'd locked it.

She yanked the sheet up, covering herself. "I thought you said no one would come here."

"Sawyer!" Holden's voice was urgent. "Open up."

"One minute," he called out and turned to Liz. "Sorry. I forgot Holden and Monty drive past the garage on their way out of the ranch." He jumped up and shoved his legs into his jeans. Leaning over the bed, he gave her a quick kiss.

After closing the French doors to the bedroom, he hustled to the front door, slipped off the chain, flipped the dead bolt and opened it, but stood holding on to the knob and frame so his brother wouldn't cross the threshold. "Hey, what's up?"

"I was heading out, about to call you and spotted your car. I thought you were camping out at Liz's. What happened? Did she run off the whipped puppy?" His brother tousled Sawyer's hair, and Holden's gaze flew to his forehead. "And what happened to your head?"

After Liz had called in the shooting, the Bison Ridge sheriff had responded, coming out to the house to take their statement. Sawyer had asked the deputies in Laramie not to notify his brother because Sawyer wanted to explain himself.

"Why were you going to call me?" Sawyer asked, redirecting him.

"Are you going to let me in?" He stepped forward, but when Sawyer didn't budge, Holden narrowed his eyes. "Is she inside?" he asked in a whisper.

Thankful his brother was discreet for once in their lives, Sawyer gave a casual nod.

Holden gave a loud howl that made Sawyer's gut tighten with embarrassment. "Way to go Coyote." He patted his brother's shoulder. "Morning, Liz!"

Sawyer groaned. He should've known better.

"Morning, Holden," she said from the back of the apartment.

"I'll give you both a minute to throw something on, and then I'm coming in. I need to speak with you two."

"Don't tell Mom she's here," Sawyer said.

"Why? She'd love to see her."

One step at a time. Sawyer let out a heavy breath. "Please. If not for me, then for Liz."

Holden gave a one-shoulder shrug, which was noncommittal at best. "Go get dressed, you filthy coyote."

Shaking his head, Sawyer closed the door and went back to the bedroom. Liz was already in the bathroom, brushing her teeth. After running a quick comb through her hair, she threw on clothes. While he waited for her, he got coffee started.

Coming into the living room, she was dressed in trousers and a button-down shirt—sans scarf. He didn't know if she'd leave the apartment without one but was happy to see she didn't feel the need to have it on when speaking with Holden.

Sawyer let his brother in, and he gave Liz a hug and a kiss on the cheek.

"We've got something to share, too." Sawyer grabbed three mugs and set them on the kitchen counter. "Who goes first?"

"Well, if your news has anything to do with that nasty cut on your head and the roadblocks that were set up last night around Bison Ridge, then you're up."

Sawyer poured the coffee and filled his brother in on what happened, as well as the necessity to keep Liz out of harm's way by bringing her to the ranch.

"Wow," Holden said with a grim look. "I'm glad you two are all right. You should've been out here at the ranch all along." He eyed Liz. "Am I supposed to keep this from Mom and Dad? The Liz secret is big enough. And don't expect me to keep it from Grace. My wife and I don't keep secrets from each other. Speaking of which, Grace is going to want to meet you, Liz. I promise you'll love her."

Liz drew in a deep breath. "I'll see everyone before I go back to Virginia." She patted his arm. "I promise."

Sawyer's chest tightened. He didn't know how things would work out yet, but he didn't intend to be separated from her, doing this long distance.

Holden glanced at him, most likely sensing what was on Sawyer's mind. "Well, I stopped by to let you know that Neil Steward and Chuck Parrot are dead."

"What?" Liz gasped. "How?"

"Car bomb with Neil. Same set up as yours, Sawyer. Parrot was different. His house burned down with him inside."

Another gruesome way to go. "Why wasn't I called?" Sawyer asked.

"It was clearly arson. Parrot must have fallen asleep drunk on his sofa. The window in his back door was broken. That's how our perp got in. He poured gasoline around the couch, and based on how severely Parrot's body was burned, we suspect he doused him, too, and then set it on fire."

"That's terrible." Horror soured his stomach. "Are they sure the accelerant was gasoline?"

Holden put a fist on his hip. "Here's the kicker, the guy left the five-gallon plastic gas can behind on the back porch steps. We dusted for fingerprints, but nothing."

Liz held her coffee cup in both hands. "Was Russo able to get anything out of Neil Steward before he was killed? Or Aleida's husband, Mr. Martinez?"

"Neil had nothing new to share. Claimed he got a business loan."

"Same as Parrot," Sawyer said.

"As for Martinez, Aleida told him it was family money that allowed her to invest in Compassionate Hearts franchise and open a store. He told Russo that Aleida was determined to give back to the community and to make a difference. Like a woman on a mission."

"Maybe one of redemption." Sawyer glanced at Liz. She

had that faraway look in her eyes. Her wheels were turning. "What are you thinking about?"

"How Holden doesn't keep secrets from his wife," she said, glancing between them. "We need to talk to Evelyn Steward." Liz sipped her coffee. "She was married to Neil for twenty-four years. She must know something, and if she does, with Neil dead, there's no longer any reason for her to protect his secret."

THEY FOUND EVELYN STEWARD coming out of the funeral director's office.

She shook the man's hand. "Thank you for the support and the guidance. For taking care of everything."

"Certainly. That's why we're here."

Liz was never comfortable at funerals. The music, the flowers, the ceremony of endless words and weeping. She recognized it was necessary for closure and to celebrate a deceased person's life. An opportunity not to grieve alone. It simply made her uneasy.

Turning, Evelyn lumbered down the hall, her clothes disheveled, her eyes red-rimmed. Liz and Sawyer approached her.

"Mrs. Steward, I'm Agent Kelley and this is Fire Marshal Powell. We're very sorry for your loss. We know this is a difficult time for you, but we need to speak with you for a moment."

Wringing her hands, the grieving woman nodded.

Sawyer showed her into an empty room where they could speak privately. "Mrs. Steward, we'd like to talk to you about Neil."

Evelyn sank down into a chair and burst into tears. Digging into her purse with a shaky hand, she pulled out a tissue. "First Mikey. Now Neil. I have to organize a double funeral." She sobbed uncontrollably.

Giving her a minute, Liz sat beside her and put a comforting hand on her shoulder. She had no idea what a mother must feel, or a wife, much less someone who had to bury a son and a husband at the same time.

Liz waited for Evelyn to regain her composure. "Did Neil tell you about the threatening phone call he received the night the Cowboy Way was burned down?"

"The night Mikey..." Dabbing at the tears in her puffy eyes, she nodded.

"What did the perpetrator say to Neil?" Sawyer asked.

"Um, the guy told him Neil deserved what was about to happen." Evelyn wiped her nose. "Fireworks. That he was going to take the shop and our son." Her voice quivered.

Liz leaned forward, putting her forearms on her thighs. "Did he tell Neil why he was being punished?" she asked, and Evelyn hesitated. "If you keep Neil's secret and don't tell us what he was hiding, we won't be able to bring the man who did this to justice."

"I told Neil the same thing." More tears swam in her eyes. "That's why he wouldn't let me go with him to the sheriff's office. He thought I might let something slip. By accident or on purpose."

She exchanged a knowing glance with Sawyer. "Let what slip?"

"Neil was being punished for what happened to Timothy." Evelyn took a shuddering breath. "That's what the man said."

"Who's Timothy?" Sawyer asked.

Evelyn shrugged. "I don't know."

Impatience flashed through Liz, but she reminded herself of what this poor woman must be going through. "You know more than you realize. Your husband must've said something about it. I'm sure you questioned him."

"Questioned him?" She shook her head. "Not at first. We were too busy trying to find Mike, and by then, it was too late. But later, yeah. We got into a horrible fight. He said he couldn't talk about it. To protect me. From legal action. In case I went to the authorities."

"What kind of legal action?" Liz wondered. "Was he worried you would be implicated in a crime and that we might arrest you?"

"No." Tears spilled from her eyes. "He was worried about us getting sued."

Liz looked at Sawyer, and he shared in her confusion.

"We don't understand," he said.

"Neil signed an NDA."

"A nondisclosure agreement?" Liz asked for clarification because it came out of left field.

"Sixteen years ago, Neil up and quit his job at the Wild Horse Ranch. Out of the blue. Something happened. Something bad. He wouldn't talk about it. Because he'd signed an NDA." Her fingers clenched in her lap. "He was worried I might tell my mother. Or my sister. Or my best friend Kim. It's true, it's hard for me to keep secrets. My husband, knowing me so well, never shared the details. But he had a stack of money. Fifty thousand dollars. I'd never seen so much cash in my life. He decided to pursue what he loved. Drawing and ink. Eventually we saved enough and opened the Cowboy Way." Tears welled in her eyes. "We never talked about where the money came from or why it was given to him. Not until he got that phone call. He said he couldn't talk about Timothy because of the NDA. That's when I realized it was tied to whatever happened back then. I pushed him and I screamed at him, demanding to know if he had hurt or killed this Timothy. Needing to understand what was happening to us and why. He swore to me that he wasn't the one who had killed him."

Killed him? "It happened during the summer, sixteen years ago when Neil quit and came home with the money," Liz said.

"Yeah." Evelyn nodded. "Right around the Fourth of

July. I remember sitting outside with him, drinking a beer, fanning myself with some of that money while we watched the fireworks."

Fireworks.

Liz combed through her memories, trying to remember any Timothy from the Durbin's. A camper or ranch hand.

Then it came to her. "Thank you, Mrs. Steward. You've been very helpful." She rose and started to move away when Evelyn caught her arm hard and it was all Liz could do not to flinch. She didn't, shaken when the woman's eyes filled with tears.

"Please find the wretched person who did this," Evelyn whispered, then let her go.

Liz straightened, her arm stinging like a live wire had zipped through it. "We will." She handed her one of her cards. "If you need me, call."

"Can you get their bodies released as fast as you can so I can—" her voice broke "—so I can bury them?"

"We'll do everything we can." Liz stalked out of the room with Sawyer beside her and they headed for the parking lot.

"I saw it in your eyes," Sawyer said. "What is it?"

"I remember a camper from that summer. New kid like me. Timothy. But he didn't die."

Chapter Sixteen

"I checked the records, sixteen years ago, around the Fourth of July," Holden said, setting down a folder on the desk. "There is an incident report. No 911 call, but Sheriff Jim Ames was called out. A kid died. Timothy Smith."

Shock washed over Liz's face.

Sawyer opened the folder, setting it where she could look along and read through it.

"I don't understand," Liz said. "A group of us were going out riding. Before we got too far out, I realized my horse had lost a shoe. One of the ranch hands, CP, told me to head back to get it fixed. When the others got back, the group was quiet, uneasy. Someone told me that Timothy had fallen. Broken his leg. But I remember the sheriff showed up and, a while later, an ambulance."

"Right here." Sawyer directed her where to look. "A fatal injury sustained from fireworks. The death was ruled accidental."

"If he died, wouldn't it have been in the news?" she asked.

Holden sighed. "I checked that, too. There was nothing in the paper."

"Whatever happened, they covered it up." Liz pressed a palm to her forehead. "The Durbins paid for silence."

Sawyer glanced at the list of kids and ranch hands who had been interviewed. Albert Goldberg, Chuck Parrot,

Courtney O'Hare, Ermenegilda Martinez, Flynn Hartley, Neil Steward, Randy Tillman, Scott Unger. He got to the last name and clenched his jaw. "I don't think it was the Durbins who paid."

He pointed to the name William Schroeder. "I think Bill's daddy did."

"What I don't get is the sheriff came to the ranch." Liz pushed hair back behind her ear. "How was there a cover up, with people signing NDAs and getting paid off?"

A deep line creased Holden's brow. "You've missed a lot. Sheriff Ames ended up being dirty. You remember Dean and Lucas Delgado from school?"

She nodded. "Yeah, of course. It was because of Dean that Delgado's became the hangout spot."

"They killed Ames." At her surprised look, he continued. "Long story, but they're CIA now."

"Guess I have missed a lot."

"In the fallout of the scandal surrounding Ames, Holden went through a rough patch," Sawyer confided.

Holden shook his head. "Don't bring that up."

"Why was it rough?" she asked.

Holden sighed. "I'll tell her. I was deputy when everyone found out about the sheriff being dirty, and I didn't see the corruption right under my nose. Everybody thought I was either dirty, too, or an incompetent fool. That pretty much sums it up."

Liz reached out, took his hand, and gave it a squeeze. "I'm sorry."

"I got through it."

"My guess is that back then," Sawyer said, "with the Durbins and Schroeders being tight, Dave called Bill's dad and asked him how he wanted to handle the situation. From there, one of them contacted the sheriff, knowing he would go along with a cover-up for the right price."

Her shoulders stiffened. "If Bill's father orchestrated the payouts and the NDAs, then Bill must be responsible for

Timothy's death. That would not only make him a target but the biggest one. Maybe our guy blames him the most and is saving him for last."

Holden headed for the door. "I'll get a deputy over to city hall to protect our esteemed mayor."

Picking up the file, Liz sat back in her chair as she looked it over. "Do you know if Roger Norris was the medical examiner at that time?" she asked Sawyer.

"I've been fire marshal longer than he's been ME. You want me to check with him, pull the case and give us his assessment of whether the death was accidental or not?"

"Exactly." She leaned over and gave him a quick kiss before turning her attention back to the file.

Although she had chosen to wear the scarf around her neck, she was lighter, looser, but not any less focused or dedicated. He liked it. A lot.

Sawyer made the call to Roger. Voicemail. Stifling a groan, he left a message and marked it Priority.

"Hey, I noticed something reading the sheriff's report. He wrote that he'd taken ten statements. But there are only nine. They're pretty much all verbatim. Like reading a script."

"Ames could've made a mistake." He got up and stretched his legs. "Or maybe he did take ten statements, but one person wasn't willing to accept the hush money, so they found a different way to silence them."

"Sloppy not to go over the report with a fine-toothed comb to ensure no errors in your counting," she said.

"Well, he was the sheriff, with powerful friends. His arrogance probably made him careless." He touched the cut on his forehead but didn't let Liz see him wince.

"If our guy is doing all of this because of something that happened sixteen years ago, why now?" she asked. "Why not last year? Why not eleven years ago?"

Unease trickled down his spine as a thought occurred to him. "What if he did try before? Fifteen years ago."

She stiffened. "The fire at the camp that killed the Durbins. It would've been around the anniversary of Timothy's death." Her hand went to her throat. "It would make sense. They never found out who did it. No suspects. But why wait fifteen years to go after everyone else?"

At a loss, Sawyer shrugged. "They all have more to lose now than they did then."

Considering it, she nodded slowly. "We should talk to Timothy's mother. Louise Smith. The father died twenty years ago."

"Then let's."

She sighed. "I prefer to do it face-to-face, but Mrs. Smith lives in Big Piney."

That was a four-hour drive. He picked up the phone. "What's the cell number?" She read it off and he dialed. Once it started ringing, he put it on speaker.

"Hello," an older woman said.

"Hi, is this Mrs. Louise Smith?" he asked.

"Yes, yes, it is."

"My name is Sawyer Powell. I'm a fire marshal with the Laramie Fire Department and I'm here with Special Agent Liz Kelley."

"Are you calling about the recent fires? If so, I don't have any information that could help."

His gaze slid to Liz, and she sat forward with a shrug.

"Mrs. Smith, why would you think we're calling about the recent fires in Laramie?" Liz asked.

"Because that's all anyone in town can talk about."

Sawyer scratched his chin. "In Big Piney?"

Mrs. Smith chuckled. "Why heavens, no. Here in Laramie. I'm in town staying at my mother's place. Well, actually, it's my daughter's now. She got it in the will."

"May we stop by and talk to you in person?" Liz scooted to the edge of her seat. "We had some questions about your son, Timothy. About his death."

"Oh, um, well, I don't see why not." Louise gave them the address.

"Thank you. We're headed over now. See you shortly." Sawyer disconnected and grabbed his hat.

LIZ TOOK THE glass of lemonade Mrs. Smith handed her from the tray. "Thank you."

"Certainly." A petite graying woman in her late fifties, Louise Smith handed one to Sawyer. "I whipped up some sandwiches for you. I didn't have time for anything else. They're made with Wyomatoes."

They looked lovely—little tea sandwiches with the crusts cut off. Liz salivated, thinking about eating one. She loved Wyomatoes. Another thing she missed living in Virginia. The organic tomatoes grown at a high elevation in Big Piney at the Wyomatoes Farm. They had a specific sweetness and juiciness to them unlike any others. But she found it difficult to stomach food when discussing death, and her paranoia didn't allow her to eat anything prepared by a stranger unless it was in a restaurant.

"Thank you." Sawyer grabbed one and took a bite without hesitation. He moaned with delight. "This is delicious."

"Dill is my secret ingredient."

Clearing her throat, Liz set the lemonade down without tasting it and opened her notepad. "As we said on the phone, we wanted to talk to you about Timothy's death. What were you told?"

Louise crossed her legs at the ankle. "The sheriff came by. Told us, me and my daughter Birdie, that there was an accident at the camp. Some kids were horsing around with fireworks. Timothy didn't know what he was doing and hurt himself. Didn't survive the injury."

"Did you have any reason not to believe the story?" Liz asked.

"Kids mess around. Sometimes they do silly, dangerous things. But Birdie didn't buy it for a second. She swore

Timothy was being harassed at that camp and that he was killed."

"Did Birdie go to the camp with him?" Liz glanced at Sawyer, who had finished his lemonade and was taking a second sandwich.

Louise shook her head. "I'm afraid not. Wish she had. We were all living in Big Piney at the time. Every summer, the kids would stay here with my mother. One year, my mom thought it best to send him to the camp at the dude ranch. Timothy was a frail boy, sickly, the brainy kind who got along better with animals, horses you know, rather than people. Though, my mom said they had a couple of close friends in town that they met at the local rec center." Louise refilled Sawyer's glass from the pitcher on the table. "Birdie didn't want to go to camp, decided to hang out with her friends instead. My mom cajoled Timothy into going. Birdie said he called her almost every night complaining about the bullying. Mom thought he needed to toughen up. Stick it out. I was torn, thinking it was a good idea for him to be around some men, with his father gone." She sighed. "To this day, Birdie believes he was killed. She's never gotten over it. Blaming herself for not going with him."

Sawyer wiped his mouth with a napkin. "We'd like to speak with her. Is she here?"

"If she isn't working, she's working out. Today is her day off. I expect she's cycling, running, swimming." Louise laughed. "Anything to lose ten pounds before she gets married. I keep telling her that she's thin enough. It's the curves that she has that got her the man."

Liz gave a polite smile. "What does she do?"

"Health inspector. Good head on her shoulders. Actually uses her biology degree."

"I think that's all for now. Thank you for your time." Liz rose and shook her hand.

Sawyer did likewise before taking another sandwich to go.

"I'll see you to the door," Louise said, rising from her seat.

As they walked through the house, Liz wrote Sawyer's name and number on the back of her card and handed it to Louise. "When your daughter gets home, let her know that we'd like to speak with her. Preferably in person." She noticed Sawyer had stopped and was looking at a picture on the wall. "We're working from the sheriff's office. She can find us there or give us a call."

"Oh, I thought you would be over at the LFD. Aren't you questioning all the firefighters as suspects?"

For someone who lived out of town, Louise Smith was well informed on everything happening in town.

"Mrs. Smith, is this your daughter?" Sawyer pointed to the picture of a woman wearing a cap and gown. Something in his voice raised the hairs on the back of Liz's neck.

"Yes, it is. That's the day Catherine graduated from SWU. Proud day. Happy day."

"Ma'am, if you don't mind me asking, why do you call her Birdie?" Sawyer asked.

"I'm a bird-watcher. When the kids were little, my husband and I would take them all over to the best birding spots. Yellowstone, the Red Desert, Hutton, Seedskadee, Grand Teton, you name it. Back then, Catherine was this delicate, beautiful—she's still beautiful—perfect creature. Like a bird. Been calling her Birdie since she was three. Everyone does. Or used to. When she started college, she preferred it if folks called her Cathy, but I'm her mama, birthed her. I'll call her what I want."

"Please pass our message to your daughter," Sawyer said, his face set in stone. "We have to be going." He took Liz by the elbow and hurried her along to the car.

"What is it? You look like you've seen a ghost."

He rounded the car over to the driver's side and opened the door. "Birdie. Catherine Smith. Is Ted Rapke's fiancée."

Chapter Seventeen

As much as Sawyer disliked it, they had to question Ted in the interrogation room at the sheriff's office. His association with Catherine Smith was too damning.

"He brought a lawyer," Liz said, as though it were an admission of guilt.

Standing beside her in the observation room, he glanced at her. "Only a fool wouldn't have. Our second time speaking with him, he gets summoned to the sheriff's office on the heels of a string of fires and murders. He knows it's not a routine 'let's rule everyone out' chat this time."

She raised a brow. "Why are you so quick to defend him?"

"I'm just not ready to condemn him. He's only known her a short while. Ted didn't start that fire fifteen years ago."

Liz sighed. "Catherine has had friends here for years. It's possible she knew him back then and they've reconnected. The town is small. Catherine spent summers here. It's also possible that the same person who burned down the Wild Horse Ranch isn't the same person exacting revenge now. Catherine could be some siren luring men to do her bidding. All the possibilities need to be examined," she said, and Sawyer heaved out a frustrated breath. She put her hand on his chest. "We need to get to the truth, and you need to be prepared that you may not like it."

He nodded. Unclenched his fingers. "Only the truth and seeing justice served matters." Didn't mean he had to like it.

The door opened and Holden came in. They'd been waiting for him to start the interview since he wanted to observe.

"We can't find Mayor Schroeder," his brother said. "His staff haven't seen him since this morning when he left for a meeting. He was supposed to check out a potential site for an entertainment complex between here and Cheyenne with Kade Carver. They've tried to reach him on his cell." He shook his head. "I've had deputies looking everywhere. They found his vehicle about ten miles outside of town. His phone was in the floorboard of the driver's side."

This horrific nightmare kept escalating. The stakes mounting. What was next? When was it going to end?

Liz eyed Sawyer with a frown. "He was last seen at what time?" she asked Holden.

"Ten a.m. at city hall. He was supposed to meet Carver at ten thirty."

She put a hand on his arm. "Ready?"

With a nod, he said, "Yeah." He'd never had an investigation hit this close to home, pushing so many personal buttons. Something about this case had slithered under his skin, prickling him from the inside out. The sooner they found the perpetrator, regardless of who it was, the better.

They entered the interrogation room and sat across from Ted and his lawyer.

"Why am I here?" Ted asked. He was wearing jeans and a green T-shirt. His black hair looked shorter, as if he'd gotten it cut since they last spoke. "Was there another fire I haven't heard about?"

"Can you tell us where you were this morning between ten and ten-thirty?" Liz started.

"On a run," Ted readily answered, but then he swore. "Alone. I don't have anyone who can verify it. I slept in at my place, decided to go for a long run on one of the trails through the foothills of Elk Horn range."

"How long were you out there?" Liz asked.

Ted shrugged. "I did a six-miler. Maybe from nine thirtyish to ten thirty."

With no one to corroborate where he was this morning and his fiancée as his sole alibi for Mike Steward's murder, they needed to explore motive. "When did you meet Catherine Smith?"

His eyes narrowed, his brow creasing. "This again? Why do you keep circling around my relationship? How is it relevant to this case?"

Liz folded her hands on the table. "Please answer the question."

After his lawyer nodded, Ted said, "A year ago at Delgado's. She was inspecting the place and struck up a conversation, started flirting. One thing led to another."

"That's when you started dating," Liz clarified, "but was that your first time ever meeting her?"

Ted straightened. "Um, no, it wasn't. I'd seen her around over the years. During the summers at the rec center. We'd go there to shoot hoops. Play football on the field. Go swimming. Goof off. We knew each other in passing. Why?"

Liz slid a glance at Sawyer before turning her focus back to Ted. "The fires, the murders, are all about getting revenge. For the death of Timothy Smith. Catherine's brother."

His eyes flared wide. Ted looked between Liz and Sawyer in disbelief, which appeared genuine. "Are you sure? I mean, do you have concrete proof that's what all this killing has been about?"

Sawyer nodded. "We do."

"And you think it's me?" Ted asked, pointing a finger at his chest.

Liz leaned forward. "You're a person of interest."

"What did Catherine tell you about her brother?" Sawyer asked.

"Only that he died years ago. That he was killed and his murderer was never punished. I could tell the subject was painful for her, so I never pushed about details."

"Did she seem angry about it?" Sawyer wondered.

"No," Ted said flatly. "It happened a long time ago. Still upsetting, but not enough to turn her into a cold-blooded killer."

"When did you get engaged?" Liz asked.

"About three weeks ago."

"Right after you got engaged to Catherine Smith, the fires and murders started." The statement from Liz hung in the air like a bad smell when she didn't follow it up with a question, only staring at Ted.

The fire chief pulled back his shoulders. "What are you implying? That I burned down businesses and killed people as—what?—some kind of sick, twisted gift to my bride-to-be?" He made a sound of outrage. "I'm no killer, and I certainly wouldn't do it for a woman. I love Cathy. I'd do almost anything for her. *Almost.* I come up short in that area a lot. Ask my ex-wives. That's why I'm about to get married for a third time."

"Stick to answering the questions only," his lawyer said to him. "Don't elaborate. Don't offer anything additional. Understand?"

Ted nodded.

"Let's say it's not you." Sawyer sat back in his chair. "Then it's somebody you know. Someone Catherine knows. Someone who knew her sixteen years ago. Someone who shares her pain and anger. Someone who knows fire. Compassionate Hearts was deliberately turned into an inferno. The restaurant was blown to smithereens. But the cabin was more controlled. Like the one at the Cowboy Way.

Help us clear you so we can focus on the real bad guy. The real killer."

As Ted thought about it, his face became stark with tension, and he looked away, causing Sawyer to groan. There was something.

"Ted," Liz softened her voice, "share what you know."

His gaze flashed up at them, his mouth thinning. "I didn't hear a question."

"You thought of someone," Sawyer said, calm and low, hoping to get through to him. "Who?"

"You want me to give you a name and put someone in the seat I'm sitting in right now based on—what?—conjecture," Ted said through gritted teeth. "I won't do that."

Liz's cell phone buzzed. She glanced at the screen. "Would you be willing to let us fingerprint you and administer a polygraph?"

The lawyer whispered in his ear, undoubtedly explaining his options and consequences of each.

Ted nodded. "Sure, fingerprints, DNA, polygraph," he said easily, like a man who wasn't guilty. "I'm willing to do it."

Liz gestured to the hall. Sawyer stepped out with her, and Holden joined them.

She accepted the call. "Kelley." She listened for a moment. "Let me call you right back, Ernie." Liz clicked off. "Forensics are in."

In the office, Liz dialed Ernie and put him on speaker. "You've got me, Fire Marshal Sawyer Powell and Chief Deputy Holden Powell."

"Must be nice to be a Powell in Laramie," Ernie said lightly. "Let's get into the meat, starting with the car bomb. Ammonium nitrate was used. A rudimentary, fairly simple timer with a remote detonator. Small, quite compact. That's where the skill factor comes in. The cap from the gas tank was removed, and the device was inserted there. Moving on to the fires. The marshal's guess was correct. The accelerant used was indeed gasoline. The device consisted of a plastic container, housing the gas with a similar timer but modified to trigger the tool that started the fire. This is where it got intriguing for me and explains why your fires burned so hot. A flare was used each time."

Happy to have his assessment confirmed, Sawyer nodded. "Like I suspected."

"Was it a road flare?" Liz asked.

"Nope," Ernie said. "It was a short fusee that burns at nineteen hundred degrees Fahrenheit. The kind they use in the forestry division."

Liz turned to him in confusion. "They use flares to suppress wildfires?"

"As counterintuitive as it seems, yeah," Sawyer said. "The folks fighting the wildfires are also purposively setting them. Prescribed burns and backfires to starve the fire of natural fuel before it has a chance to break through a certain line. The best defense is a good offense."

"That's all I have for you," Ernie said.

"Thanks. We really appreciate it. Lunch is on me when I get back."

"Lunch for a week."

Liz smiled. "You got it." She disconnected. "We need to speak to Ted again."

Sawyer led the way to the interrogation room. Neither he nor Liz bothered sitting.

He pressed his palms on the table and bent over, staring Ted straight in the eyes. "Forensics came back. Fusees were used to start the fire. It is a firefighter. One who works for the forestry division."

Clenching his jaw, Ted looked sick.

"Give us a name," Liz demanded. "Time is running out. The mayor is missing. This guy blames Bill Schroeder for Timothy's death."

Ted squeezed his eyes shut. Lowered his head as though the truth was unbearable. "I didn't know it was him. I swear it. Right under my nose the whole time." He cursed and pounded a fist on the table. "It's Cathy's best friend. Joshua Burfield. Sometimes I'd wonder if there was something going on between them, maybe they'd dated before, but she swore they hadn't. That they were just friends. But they have a weird bond." He sighed. "Honestly, I think he's in love with her," Ted said, and Sawyer understood why the chief had kept Burfield so close. "Josh has been a wildland firefighter with the forestry division since he was eighteen. A volunteer firefighter at twenty. One of the best—intense, yeah, but dedicated. I didn't know. I swear, I had no idea he was capable of this." Ted looked up at them, eyes filled with anger and disbelief.

"You did the right thing in telling us." Sawyer patted his shoulder and then hurried behind Liz out into the hall. "What was Burfield's alibi for the night of Mike Steward's murder?" he asked Holden.

"His brother, Caleb, confirmed they were together."

Liz shook her head. "This is exactly why I don't trust it when an alibi is a loved one. We need to find him and the brother and bring them both in."

Holden was already moving down the hall. "I'll put out an APB on them," he said over his shoulder.

"We also need search warrants for both their houses," Liz said. "Fast."

Holden gave a dark chuckle. "We'll only need one search warrant. Burfield and his brother live together. Don't worry about fast. The mayor is missing. The judge will hop to it."

Chapter Eighteen

From his usual discreet spot, he spied on Birdie as she finished her laps in the swimming pool at the rec center. The way she glided through the water was beautiful. Such long, clean strokes. Such stamina. He loved watching her do anything. Run. Eat. Sleep.

She was his favorite thing in the whole wide world.

And today, he was finally going to win her heart, take back what was his from Ted Rapke.

She climbed out of the pool, graceful as a swan, water glistening on her skin. Wrapping the towel around her lithe body, she slipped into flip-flops and went to the locker room.

He walked outside to wait for her. Wearing his sunglasses and Stetson, he leaned against his truck. His last gift for her was tucked securely away in the flatbed with the aluminum cover, keeping it a surprise. He imagined what it would be like once she found out how hard he'd worked—the effort, the planning, the sacrifice—to make her happy.

The love nest where he was taking her was prepared. Champagne on ice. After lighting some candles, he'd confess everything. She'd be so grateful, so overwhelmed with emotion that she'd realize how much she loved him. More than anyone else. More than Ted. Because only he would go to such lengths for her.

You're so cool. That's what she'd say to him. *No one loves me like you do.*

Then they'd make love. It'd be like the first time. The only time. After he burned down the Wild Horse Ranch.

This was going to be a *true romance.* One for the storybooks. They'd tell their children about it, omitting a few incriminating details.

The door to the rec center opened and Birdie breezed outside. He smiled, excitement buzzing and crackling like electricity in his veins. He waved and she caught sight of him.

Surprise flittered across her face followed by a bright grin. "Hey, Josh, what are you doing here?" she asked, coming over. "Going for a swim?"

Her inky black hair was wet, her milky white skin damp, and she smelled of chlorine and vanilla.

"I came to get you."

"Me?" She cocked her head to the side. "How did you know I was here?"

"I knew you were off today." He brushed damp strands from her brow, and she pulled away. She did that a lot lately. "Guessed you might be here."

"It's like we have a psychic connection."

No telepathy involved. He always knew where she was, what she was doing, who she was with thanks to the spyware he'd downloaded on her phone.

She was his hobby. His addiction. His love. His world.

"Yep. Psychic connection." He opened the passenger's side door of his truck. "Get in." He offered her his hand to help her up. "I've got a surprise for you."

She glanced around, as if looking for someone or something. "What kind of surprise?"

"The best kind. Trust me, you're going to love it."

"What about my car?" she hiked her thumb over her shoulder at her Jeep.

"We'll come back for it later."

Birdie hesitated, thinking about it, a flicker of something she hated flashed in her eyes. But she took his hand, stepped on the running board and slid inside. He shut the door. Grinning, he ran around, tapped the flatbed, hopped in and pulled off.

She took out her cell phone.

"Who are you calling?" he asked.

"My mom. I don't want her to worry."

No need for nosy Louise to know. He snatched the phone from her fingers and tossed it under his seat.

"Josh. What are you doing? We've talked about this. Boundaries are important."

Boundaries were for the Teds of the world. Not for him. "After the surprise, you can have it back. Come on, you love our games."

They'd played all sorts. The flirting game. The teasing game. The jealousy game, like the one they were playing with Ted, though the fire chief had lasted the longest, made it the furthest. And her favorite—the denial game, where Birdie made a wish for something bad to happen, he'd make it come true, she'd ask if he did it, and he'd deny.

Deep down, she must've known it was him. The denial gave her the luxury to enjoy it without any nasty guilt.

When Birdie didn't respond, he asked. "Trust me?"

Doubt flickered in her eyes again, but she still trusted him. If she didn't, she wouldn't have gotten in the truck. The bond they had was strong.

Unbreakable.

Sixteen years ago, she'd told him her brother, Josh's friend, was being bullied. He'd talked to his manager at the feed store and arranged to make the deliveries at the Wild Horse so he could check on Tim. Witnessed the harassment and how evil and cruel Bill could be. Even spoke to Dave Durbin about it. The day of Timothy's murder, Josh had been there. He saw the group of them riding off. Timothy, Parrot, Unger, O'Hare, Flores, Goldberg, Tillman, Hartley, Schroeder, Steward and Kelley.

It wasn't until later, after he'd given a statement to the sheriff that had been ignored, after he'd overheard a drunk Parrot and Steward talking about the truth and the payments, that he knew what needed to be done.

He and Birdie had bonded in grief over Tim. Bonded in relishing the horrible deaths of the Durbins and the end of the Wild Horse Ranch. He'd promised Birdie he'd always take care of her, and he had.

"Yeah, I trust you," she finally said. "Where are we going?"

To the love nest. A little cabin he rented outside of town, where she'd be safe. Also, remote, just in case. "Someplace special."

"I hope this isn't anything romantic." The enticing twinkle in her eyes said otherwise. "We've talked about this."

Oh, yes. They'd talked while she flirted and teased—how she enjoyed their games. He was the only friend in the world who understood her pain. The one who made her feel safe. The one she could turn to no matter what. The one who would hold her. But not the one she wanted to have sex with. Not the one she wanted to marry.

Tonight, that would change with a new game. *The love game.* He'd show her she could only count on him, that he was the best man for her—with the greatest, grandest romantic gesture.

He put on a playlist, her current favorites. Once he got her singing, she started to relax. Twenty minutes in, her bare feet rested on the dashboard, and her sundress had slid to her hips, taunting him with the sight of her creamy pale thighs.

The cabin was right down the road, only a minute away

when his cell phone rang. He took it out. His brother Caleb. "What's up? I'm almost there."

"No fair you get to use your phone," Birdie snapped, "and I don't."

"What am I supposed to do?" Caleb asked with urgency, which meant something was wrong. "The sheriff is here with two deputy cars. FBI. Fire marshal. They just pulled up. They're getting out of their vehicles. Shoot. Kelley and Powell are eyeing my motorcycle."

No, no, no.

Alarm was a gaping pit in his stomach, but he couldn't panic. Not now. "Grab the lighter fluid from under the sink. Go to my office and burn everything." He didn't want them to know about his big finale. "Then take the spare bike. Try to get here. We'll do plan B."

Caleb disconnected.

Don't lose it. Don't lose your cool in front of Birdie.

"What's happening?" Straightening, she stiffened in her seat. "What's wrong?"

He parked in front of the cabin. "Nothing. A project Caleb is helping me with."

Boom. Boom. Boom. Thudding came from the rear of the truck.

Her brown eyes flaring wide, Birdie spun around in her seat. "Is someone in the flatbed?"

This was not how he wanted things to go. How he wanted to show her proof of his love. He had it all planned out in his head: the champagne, the candles, slowly revealing what he had done. Putting an end to the denial game, because it hadn't served him winning her heart.

Boom. Boom.

Ugh!

"Who is in the flatbed?" Birdie demanded.

Rolling his eyes, he pressed the button on the remote,

retracting the aluminum cover over the flatbed. "Go see for yourself."

She got out and ran to the back while he reached over, popping the lid of the glove compartment. Quickly, he opened a bottle and saturated a cloth with chloroform.

The door to the flatbed lowered with a clunk. "Josh!" Birdie screamed.

Holding the cloth behind his back, he hopped out and went to the rear of the vehicle.

"It's the mayor! Why is Bill Schroeder tied up and gagged in your truck?"

Wrists zip-tied behind his back, ankles bound, Bill tried to plead for help around the rancid gag Josh had shoved in his mouth. A big red shiny bow had been tied around his neck.

This was not the ta-da moment he had imagined. "I brought him for you," Josh said. "The one who killed Tim. I made the others pay, too, just like you wanted."

"What are you talking about? I never wanted this!"

"You inspected Chuck Parrot's restaurant, getting him on every violation possible. The rating was so bad he had to close and renovate. You told me you wished you could blow his place sky high. Get back at all the liars. All those who sold their soul to the devil named Schroeder."

"Oh my god! That was you?" The horror and fear in her eyes was real, only making his anger burn hotter. Before Ted came along, she would've been grateful. "Josh, you killed all those people?"

Of course he did. He narrowed his eyes. "Who else?"

Birdie's frantic gaze volleyed between him and Bill. "You burned down the Wild Horse, too, didn't you? I thought you had, loved you for it, even though it was wrong. But you kept denying it."

That was the game.

She wished to see the Durbins dead and the Wild Horse Ranch in ashes. He made it happen. No guilt for Birdie.

She wished for hell to rain down on the others. He made that happen, too. Once again, no guilt for Birdie.

But also no acknowledgment, no appreciation for him.

Did she think she had a fairy godmother of doom waving a magic wand on her behalf?

"I did it because I love you." *I want you. I need you. More than anything.* "You can't marry Ted. He'd never sacrifice for you. He's selfish. There's no way he'd do anything for you the way that I have. This is proof." He gestured with his left hand at the high-and-mighty mayor, keeping his right hand behind his back.

"I love you, but not in that way. I've told you that. You're like a brother to me." She backed away. "Ted was right about you. He said you were obsessed with me."

"That twice-divorced loser wouldn't know what real love looked like if it punched him in the face. I won't let you marry him. He doesn't deserve you. I do. I've put in the work. I've lit the fires. I've shed blood for you. You're mine!"

Birdie whirled, trying to run, but he grabbed her by the hair and shoved the cloth over her mouth and nose. She fought to break free. The struggle didn't last long.

"We'll work this out in Canada," he whispered in her ear, even though she couldn't hear him. "You, me and Caleb." Only a ten-hour drive.

There I'll make her feel right about all this. About me.

He kissed her forehead. Then he picked her up in his arms and carried her inside the cabin. Fishing in his bag, he got the zip tie and bound her wrists. He also grabbed his just-in-case rope. No gag. Nobody would hear her scream out here. He put a blanket on the floor in the bathroom, laid her down gently and, using the rope, tied her bound wrists to the pedestal of the sink. She had enough room to reach the toilet. If she got thirsty, she could get water from the sink. He'd already removed the mirror as a precaution. *Just in case.*

Wiping his brow with the back of his hand, he locked the bathroom door. He'd get rid of Bill in the big finale. Hopefully Ted as well. Every firefighter between Laramie and Bison Ridge would have to respond to the crisis, including the chief, whether on or off duty. Many would die.

With any luck, Ted would be one of them.

Chapter Nineteen

Two deputies shoved a handcuffed Caleb Burfield into the back of a sheriff's cruiser. Liz waited outside while Sawyer finished putting out the fire in the office in the house and started airing it out enough for her to come in soon and take a look. In the meantime, she glanced at the motorcycle that either Josh or Caleb had used in the drive-by when they tried to gun them down.

The radio clipped to Holden's shoulder squawked.

"Chief, you there?" dispatch said, and Liz moved closer to him out on the lawn to hear.

"Go ahead, over."

"The ME got back to us. Norris claims the old report is hogwash. He used harsher language, but you get the gist. Based on the wound, someone else hit Timothy Smith in the chest with a large powerful firecracker. Impossible that it was self-inflicted. Also, a traffic cam on US 30 picked up Joshua Burfield's car traveling north. We enhanced the photo. Burfield was driving. Catherine Smith was sitting in the passenger's seat."

Holden mouthed to Liz, *Are they in it together?*

She shrugged. Entirely possible, but Smith's involvement with Ted Rapke gave her serious doubts. The engagement seemed to be the trigger for Burfield, answering Liz's question about what prompted the murderer to act now. His jealousy and anger were the only things that explained why the fires and murders would coincide with the proposal.

Burfield was afraid of losing her. Must want Catherine for himself.

Was this some grisly romantic gesture? The thought gave Liz goose bumps.

"Does she appear to be under duress?" Holden asked.

"Uh, no. It sort of looks like she's…singing."

"They're close friends," Liz said to Holden. "Best friends. Maybe to her, this is any other day. Business as usual. But we should consider her a suspect as well until we talk to her."

"Roger that," Holden said into the radio. "Deputy Russo and I are going to head up on US 30. Have Deputy Livingston notify the state troopers of the last mile marker where he was spotted. I also want him to track the vehicle as far as he can and check Burfield's recent financial transactions."

"Let the FBI track the financials," Liz said. "We're faster and can go deeper."

"Sounds good. Got that?" Holden asked dispatch.

"Got it."

Holden headed for his sheriff's SUV. "Let Sawyer know," he said, and she nodded. He and Russo climbed in and sped off.

Liz took out her cell, dialed her boss and filled him in. "The suspect is Joshua Burfield. A wildland firefighter with the forestry division and part of the volunteer fire department." She relayed his address and last known whereabouts. "In case Catherine Smith is an accomplice, we should check her financials, too."

"We'll get right on this. Good work. How is everything else going for you?" SAC Cho asked.

"Close call with a car bomb and drive-by shooting, but I'm still standing."

He sighed. "One thing you won't have to worry about

is the mayor. I spoke with Schroeder. He got the message you're insulated."

"Speaking of the mayor, he's missing. We believe he's Burfield's next target."

"You've got your hands full out there. If you need any other assistance, don't hesitate to reach out. We're here for you. And Liz, stay safe."

"I'll do my best, sir."

Sawyer came to the doorway of the house and waved her inside. "It's okay for you to come in."

Crossing the threshold, she passed him. "Hope you didn't take in too much smoke."

"I'm good. No worries." He led the way to the office. "You're not going to believe what's in there." He let her step inside first.

On the large wall facing the desk a myriad of photos and notecards had been pinned up. String had been tied to certain pushpins, linking them to others. Caleb had sprayed lighter fluid in a rush, struck a match, and ran. He made it to another motorcycle and had gotten it started, but a deputy tackled him before he took off. The haphazard arcs of fire had burned through entire notes and pictures, leaving others partially intact, a few in their entirety.

Burfield had created a detailed problem-solving flow-chart.

Liz went up to a partially burned card that had YER POWELL on it, along with notes beneath Sawyer's name. Then she followed the threads to other cards. "Look at this. He anticipated you being a problem. Saw the Shooting Star Ranch as an impediment to neutralize you. That's why he went with the car bomb. And here." She directed his gaze to what Burfield had considered a subset issue. "He saw Holden as a secondary problem until you were eliminated."

"One problem he didn't anticipate was you." He put a hand on her lower back.

It was warm and comforting. Together they had gotten this far. They had to keep pushing. They were close to getting him.

She stepped back, taking in the full picture, piecing it together. The various problems with multiple solutions, or rather multiple ways, to enact his retribution.

This wasn't a flowchart at all.

"He visually brainstormed murder using a *mind map*," she said, half to Sawyer and half to herself. Fascinating and creepy, but fascinating, nonetheless. "He's a nonlinear thinker. This type of tool works best for them."

"What if he were linear?"

"For someone who thinks in terms of step-by-step progression, a flowchart works better. Partially destroyed, that's what I thought it was at first."

"What's the difference?"

"With a flowchart, the steps you take to solve a problem are easy and straightforward until you find a logical solution."

"Seeing as how a killing spree isn't logical, I can understand why he'd bypass that one."

She gave him a grim smile. "Now, with the mind map, the center is where he'd start, his main focus and branch out from there." Right in the middle was a card with the remaining letters LL SCHR. "This has always been, ultimately, about getting Bill Schroeder. Everyone else was a lesser piece on the game board to him. Bill's the one he holds responsible for Timothy's death."

"Then his punishment will be worse," Sawyer said. "Look at what's left around Bill's card. One for Ted. And a device."

"He only plans to use one, a single timer, but more complex. Sophisticated. This is different than the others he's used." A tremor of fear raced through her. "To be used where? How?"

"Car bomb isn't good enough for Schroeder. Right? Burfield has taken the more complicated route. It needs to be big for the last one."

"More painful. He didn't just want to kill the others, he wanted to make them suffer. Took away what was important to them. The charity store for Aleida. The restaurant and financial ruin for Parrot. Steward lost his son and shop."

"Schroeder is the mayor, but if he wanted to take out city hall, he wouldn't have kidnapped him. He could've shown up one night while he was working late."

"Bill's reputation and money are everything to him," she said, thinking aloud. "But how could Joshua Burfield take that away from him? And how would it solve his Ted problem?"

Turning, Sawyer looked around the office. "The brother didn't just burn the wall. He tried to burn the desk also. But he was in too much of a rush. Didn't have time to do it right." He went around the desk. Pulling on latex gloves he took from his pocket, he sat down. A cabinet drawer squeaked open. He thumbed through files. "This guy is macabre. He has a folder labeled *Finale*."

Liz came around the desk beside Sawyer as he opened the folder. They riffled through the contents. Page after page of information about the Schroeder Farm and Ranch Enterprises.

"Bill's family holdings are more than one company," she said. "It's way too big and diversified to take out with one device. They have various offshoots in different locations. Seeds, seed treatments, crop protection, financial services for the smaller farmers, precision agriculture services—"

Sawyer swore. "There might be a way. A horrible way." He fingered through pages quickly, stopping when he found what he wanted. "The fertilizer plant." He pulled out a collage of photos that had been taken of the plant the Schroeders owned.

Liz took a page and scrutinized the angles, what he had zoomed in on. "Burfield took pictures of all the weaknesses. No fenced perimeter. No guardhouse. It doesn't even look like there are cameras on the buildings. How is this possible?"

"Unfortunately, it's more common than you'd realize. This is where he stole the ammonium nitrate that he used for the car bombs."

"How bad are we talking if he sets a fire there?"

"The most recent incident at a fertilizer plant that I can think of was in North Carolina."

"Yeah, I heard about that. The entire town had to be evacuated."

"They had five hundred tons of combustible ammonium nitrate housed at that plant. That's almost more than double was present at the deadly blast in Texas, which killed many, injured hundreds, damaged homes and left a hundred-foot-wide crater. Doesn't he realize or care that most of the people who died there were first responders?"

"I think he's interested in one particular first responder dying—Ted Rapke." All this to get rid of one man and to have one woman? Sickening. "Doesn't OSHA regulate these facilities?" she asked, referring to the Occupational Safety and Health Administration.

"It's complicated." Sawyer homed in on a different page. After poring over it, he handed it to her. "Looks like OSHA didn't put the Schroeder Fertilizer plant on their national emphasis plan that has strict guidelines because it's exempt as a retail facility." He slid another page over to her. "This isn't good. Burfield pulled a copy of the Schroeder's last filing with the EPA."

She picked up the document. "This is public data?"

"Sure is. Do you see it?"

"What exactly am I looking for?"

"Any facility that has more than one ton or four hundred pounds of ammonium nitrate on hand is supposed to report it under federal law. Based on these pictures of the facility that Burfield took, there's close to a thousand tons at the Schroeder plant, but they haven't been reporting it."

"Why wouldn't they report it?"

"Tighter federal scrutiny, additional regulations. To save on expenses."

"At the cost of jeopardizing lives," she said, disgusted.

"If Burfield sets a fire and the plant explodes, it not only destroys the Schroeder reputation and could ruin them financially, but it'll be catastrophic."

"THEY'RE GOING TO do it." Liz disconnected from the Laramie Police Department, looking somewhat relieved.

Driving to the Schroeder Fertilizer Plant, Sawyer nodded and swerved around a vehicle, then hit the accelerator. They were on their way to make sure Burfield wasn't at the fertilizer plant and, if he arrived, wouldn't be able to go through with his diabolical plan.

Calling the LPD had been their best option since his brother Holden and the sheriff's office were busy tracking Joshua Burfield, questioning his brother, Caleb, and searching for the mayor.

"They're going to start evacuating the northwest part of town that would be most impacted in a worst-case scenario," Liz said, "but they think they'll have difficulty getting the residents of the Silver Springs Senior Living and Memory Care Center out. Took longer than I expected to coordinate because the chief of police is on vacation."

"With the sheriff. They're together. Didn't think to mention it."

"Holden's brother-in-law, the sheriff, is engaged to the chief of police?"

"Yeah."

"I take it my mother is aware of that also?"

"She met them both at the wedding."

Liz stiffened.

He put a hand on hers. "She wasn't being disloyal to you. We both love you."

"I guess I'm mostly mad at myself, if I'm being honest. I was in the dark because I wanted it that way." She let out a heavy breath, but her shoulders remained stiff. "Did you have any luck reaching someone at the plant?"

"They closed an hour ago. No one answered. No emergency number was left on the outgoing voicemail."

Pulling up to the Schroeder Fertilizer Plant, Liz pointed out the three-story building with a heavily slanted roof that had been the primary focus of Burfield's surveillance. "It's that one."

They entered the premises, passing several buildings. Sawyer drove across a large dirt lot where big delivery trucks were parked, heading toward the large gray building in the back of the property. Coming around the row of trucks to the front of it, he came to a halt.

A silver truck was parked near the entrance. Same license plate that authorities were looking for. "Burfield is here."

"I'll call it in." Liz whipped out her phone again and notified the LPD. "Get SWAT out here. We have to assume he has Mayor Schroeder and Catherine Smith inside." Irritation crossed her face as she listened. "Fine. But don't send any uniformed officers here. In case this goes wrong, I don't want them getting killed in the blast. Focus on evacuation." She disconnected. "The captain told me it would take SWAT a couple of hours to get here. Why on earth would it take that long?"

"They're coming from Cheyenne. Laramie doesn't have the funding for our own special weapons and tactics team. Not that our community usually has much need for SWAT."

"This is the first time I miss Virginia."

"I'll go in through the front," Sawyer said. "You go around back."

Liz grabbed his arm, stopping him. "Move the vehicle to the side of the building where there are no windows and Burfield can't see it. Then I'll go in through the front. You through the back."

"Why?"

"Who do you think Burfield will see as the bigger threat? You or me? Of course you and Burfield would be wrong," she said, and he tried not to take offense. "Which one of us would be better at getting inside his head?"

He stifled the growl climbing up his throat.

"I'll convince him I'm here alone," she said. "You go in through the back or some other way."

"I can't put you in his crosshairs."

"Half the town is already in his crosshairs. We have to stop him. If you get a shot at him, take it. No matter what."

He didn't wait fifteen years to get her back only to lose again now. "I won't do it if you're in the line of fire."

"This is the job I signed up for. One of us might have to make a tough call in there. Trying to save me won't save the town or ultimately me. If he detonates, we're all dead anyway," she said matter-of-factly.

She was amazing, more incredible than he'd realized, and her logic irrefutable. Nonetheless, his heart protested.

He drove to the side of the building, parked and shut the engine.

Liz turned to get out, but he put a hand on her shoulder, stopping her.

He cupped her face and kissed her on the lips. Quick and hot and sure. "Marry me?" He'd never gotten to ask her, and he wasn't going to let another chance slip by.

She blinked in surprise, her lips parting before her expression turned stony. "I don't want a doomsday proposal.

We get through this and you still want marry me, ask again." She jumped out of the vehicle.

Man, he loved her. He jumped out as well. They left the doors open, drew their weapons and went in opposite directions.

In the back, he darted past the large rolling bay doors where trucks would enter to be loaded up and caught sight of exterior stairs that led to the top. On one side of the staircase was a long chute that ran from the third floor to the ground. Another way to load trucks with materials. He scanned the top. A conveyor belt system ran from the chute inside the building. That was his way in.

LIZ WAS ALMOST at the front door when her cell vibrated. She looked at the text message from her boss.

Burfield rented a cabin in Wayward Bluffs. Sheriff's dept found C. Smith tied up inside.
No sign of the mayor.

She slipped the phone back in her pocket.

Taking a deep breath, Liz slowly opened the front door. A slight creak in the hinges announced her presence. Tension twisted in every muscle in her body. She wished Sawyer better luck.

She eased inside, her gun in a two-handed hold. Passing equipment and stacks of empty sacks labeled with the Schroeder name, she inched deeper into the building. She eyed seven massive bins lined up in a row against the back wall and edged around a couple of front-end tractor loaders.

There was an aluminum wall instead of a four-foot thick concrete one per OSHA regulations, with an opening large enough for two tractors to get through simultaneously. Beyond the wall, a large mound of ammonium nitrate sat in the middle of the building.

She crept forward. Her skin crawled. Wherever Burfield was, he knew she was there, and he was watching.

Her heart hammered in her chest as she glanced around. A conveyor belt ran from the top of the building near the ceiling, across its length, down to the heap of chemicals. She eased around the pile of whitish-gray granules. Braced for anything.

Then Bill Schroeder shuffled into view, ankles bound, a red bow around his neck as Burfield hauled him forward, hiding behind the mayor. Lean, with an athletic build, Josh was taller by a couple of inches and had to hunch. Schroeder's terrified eyes met hers, sweat beading his forehead, his skin sickly pale.

Liz raised her weapon, taking aim.

"I wouldn't if I were you." Burfield held up the detonator in his other hand and gestured with his head at the device he'd planted next to the ammonium nitrate. "I'll blow us all to kingdom come right now. Where's Sawyer?"

"Not here."

Burfield laughed. "You expect me to believe that he left you all alone."

This monster saw her as a helpless damsel incapable of holding her own. "We split up. Your truck was captured on cameras on US 30. He's trying to track you down," she said, not wanting him to know they'd found the cabin and Catherine. It might set him off.

His angular face tightened with worry. For a second his concentration slipped, and he let his head edge to the side enough for her to take a shot, but his focus snapped back, and he put his head behind Bill's again.

"Sawyer wanted to keep me safe, thinking you're headed north," she said, "and I didn't want to be a distraction to him. I agreed to make sure the fertilizer plant was secure and that there were no devices hidden while he went to arrest you."

The wariness in his eyes dissipated, but it didn't vanish. "Not sure I believe you, Liz. Maybe Holden is on US 30. And Sawyer is lurking around here."

"Holden is pursuing your brother. Caleb got away on a red motorcycle out back. The entire sheriff's department is after him. The tip on you, on US 30, came in later," she said, studying him. He looked like he might be swallowing her story, but she needed something stronger. "One thing my training did for me was remove the fear of dying. I can come into this facility knowing a twisted man such as yourself, might be inside, prepared to blow the place up with me along with it. Yet here I stand. But what I *am* afraid of more than anything else is something happening to Sawyer. If I know you're here with hundreds of pounds of explosive material, I'm not letting him anywhere near it."

Triumph gleamed in his eyes and a smile tugged at his lips. That did it. He believed her. Now she prayed Sawyer didn't make any noise.

"Glad to get you all to myself. Drop your weapon."

She held her hands up, gun flat against her palm and then set her Glock on the ground.

"Come closer." Doing as he said, she got within two feet of Bill. "Stop," he ordered, and she did. "Any other weapons? Knives?"

She removed the knife from around her ankle, taking it from the sheath, and dropped it on the ground. She dangled cuffs from her finger and let them fall.

"I'm sure you've got more. What else?" he asked.

"Nothing. That's it."

"Am I supposed to take your word for it? Take off your clothes. I need to be certain." His voice was arrogant, almost amused as though this were a game.

She didn't move.

"I don't have all the time in the world and neither do

you. As soon as you saw my truck, you called the cops. They're on the way."

"They're all evacuating the town. You've proven how serious you are about vengeance."

"Big, bad FBI agent. You don't need backup?"

Everyone needed backup and she had more than enough. "I don't want innocent cops to die."

"Do it. Take off your clothes. Remember, I'm holding all the cards."

In a way, with the detonator in his hand, he was.

"Now," Burfield ordered.

Liz shrugged off her field jacket and it dropped to the ground. Next, she lost the scarf. She'd done this before when the bomb maker for the extremist group wanted to be sure she wasn't wearing a wire. For some reason, baring her scars to monsters in service of a mission didn't bother her. Slowly, she began to unbutton her shirt.

Sawyer was close. She knew it but didn't dare glance around. Her only concern was him taking a shot if he got an opening.

She tossed her shirt on the ground, leaving only her bra, feeling more naked without her weapon than her top.

"Turn around," he ordered.

Holding her hands up, she did. As she came almost three hundred degrees, she spotted Sawyer inching along in the conveyor belt at the top of the building. But he wasn't at the right angle yet for a good shot. He needed to worm his way another ten feet. Even then, with the height and the awkward position from the conveyor belt, he still might miss.

"You're the only person I've seen up close and personal who's danced with the fire." His gaze raked over her and darkened with intense energy.

"A fire you set." She needed to buy Sawyer time.

"You deserved what you got. I saw you go out riding with this scumbag." He shoved Schroeder to the ground, the man landing with a muffled grunt, and Burfield stepped closer. "You witnessed what happened to Timothy and stayed silent. Did they pay you, too? Not that it matters. Either way, not coming forward makes you culpable."

She shook her head. "I went out riding with them. My horse lost a shoe. Chuck made me turn around and go back to the ranch. I never saw what happened to Tim. They told the rest of us who didn't go out that Tim broke his leg."

"Liar!" His finger slipped off the button on the detonator.

"I would never cover up a murder, much less take hush money. That's not me. I saw how Bill bullied Tim. I confronted him myself, spoke to CP and the Durbins about it." Though it had done little good. "I want to bring Bill to justice."

A wicked laugh rolled from his lips. "Yeah, right."

"I've never liked this man. He's despicable. His family's money can't influence me. We reviewed the coroner's report on Tim. The current ME says it shows the wound that killed him couldn't have been self-inflicted. He was murdered. The old coroner and sheriff were corrupt."

"He'll claim it was an accident. Same story he tried to tell me. That they were messing around with fireworks. He only wanted to scare Timothy. Didn't mean to kill him. Bill Schroeder will get off."

"Even if Bill claimed it was an accident, he could be charged with manslaughter." She doubted it would stick since Joshua Burfield had killed all the witnesses to the crime. They had no evidence that Schroeder was the one who launched the fireworks, but she needed to talk Josh down. "Evelyn Steward can testify that Neil was paid hush money. And I found the EPA filing for the fertilizer plant. The Schroeders are breaking a federal law by not reporting how much ammonium nitrate they have here. They will see the inside of a jail cell." That was true. "I promise you."

He considered it. For a heartbeat. Maybe two. "No, no."

He shook his head. "Men like Bill and his father always find a way to wriggle out of trouble. This," he said, holding up the detonator, "is the only kind of justice I can count on."

A gunshot fired, hitting Burfield in the forearm, and the detonator dropped. Another shot and he staggered backward. Too far back. The pile of ammonium nitrate would block Sawyer's view.

The bullet had struck his shoulder near the collarbone. If the shot didn't put him down, it would make his adrenaline kick in. He glanced at the floor and he went for the detonator.

Liz scooped up her knife from the ground. Adrenaline pumping through her, she raised the blade, driving it up into his chest.

Burfield raised his shocked gaze to her and then fury exploded across his face. "Go to hell."

She backed away from him, Burfield's blood on her hands. "You first."

With a fierce growl, Burfield lunged for her.

Pop! Pop! Sawyer fired a third and fourth shot.

Burfield dropped to his knees, his eyes still with the flatness of death, and fell to the ground.

Liz raced forward and secured the detonator. Kneeling beside Burfield, she checked his pulse to be certain the monster was dead.

She climbed to her feet, put her weapon in the holster and slipped on her shirt. As she went over to Bill Schroeder, she smelled how he had soiled himself. Thinking about what an awful person he was, her dislike for him intensified. She tugged the gag down from his mouth. "Can you breathe?"

"Untie me. I can't believe he was going to kill me. I've got to get out of here."

She stared down at him and considered it. "Zip ties can be tough. Let me go find something to cut through it."

He wiggled around on the ground. "Pull the knife out of that SOB's chest and cut it with that."

"Can't." She shook her head. "It's evidence."

Liz stood and headed for the exit. Bill Schroeder yelled and cursed behind her.

Outside, the sun shone brighter now that Burfield was dead and this ordeal was over.

Sawyer ran up to her, and she fell into his arms. He held her tight, and she squeezed him right back.

"Good shooting in there," she said after a couple minutes.

"Anything for you." He pulled back a little and looked at her. "Where's Bill?"

"On the floor, writhing like the snake that he is. We'll cut him loose soon."

Chuckling, he grasped her chin and tilted her face up to his. "Those were some gutsy moves you made. Risky ones, too."

"Are you going to give me a hard time?"

"Maybe." He kissed her gently. "Definitely. You better get used to it."

"Oh, really. Why is that?"

"Because we're getting married."

She laughed. "First, you have to ask me again. Then I have to say yes."

"Nope." He roped his arms around her waist. "This time I get to make a unilateral decision for both of us."

She laughed harder. Even though they'd had another close call with death, they had survived, and it was time for her to start living.

"Liz Kelley, I have loved you more than half my life. There's no one else in the world who I want to be with. Marry me."

She took a shuddery breath. This was really happening.

"My life is in Virginia. Yours is here. And what about your family? You're all so—"

He kissed her, and the reasons why they shouldn't simply evaporated.

"I can be a fire marshal anywhere. Ted and Gareth would be thrilled to get rid of me," he said, and she chuckled. "We can get married at the ranch if you want."

"I'd like that."

"We could take the kids there every summer. We'll have Thanksgiving there with your parents. Maybe Christmases, too. Our folks will spoil them rotten," he said, painting a picture of exactly the life she wanted but had been too afraid to hope for.

"Kids, huh?" she asked, playfully.

"Only if you're still interested in having them."

She'd always wanted to have Sawyer's children. "I definitely want to have a family with you. Someday."

He brushed his lips across hers and kissed her softly. "Where you go, I go from now on. Please marry me so I don't look like a stalker."

She laughed until tears of joy filled her eyes. Her heart glowed in her chest like a bulb, getting brighter and hotter with each breath. "Yes, Sawyer Powell. I'll marry you."

* * * * *

A Q&A with Juno Rushdan

What is your daily writing routine?
I wake up at 5:30 a.m., have a gigantic cup of coffee and work out. Then I get my kids ready for school. Once they're off, I feed and walk the dogs before settling into my office. I crank up my current playlist and write until it's time to pick up my children and take them to their after-school activities. If I'm close to a deadline, I'll continue writing after dinner for a few more hours.

Where do your story ideas come from?
Most of my ideas come from my dreams, something in the news or simply pop into my head while I'm on vacation. I find fun, new environments inspirational for me.

Do you have a favorite travel destination?
I've visited more than twenty different countries, but my favorite destination is the Amalfi Coast, Italy. With the heavenly food, sumptuous wine, and stunning turquoise water of the Mediterranean, it is like paradise.

What is your favorite movie?
As a huge movie buff, I have too many favorites to pick one.

When did you read your first Harlequin romance? Do you remember its title?
I was around twelve when I "borrowed" one of my grandmother's Harlequin romances from her library. I devoured it over the weekend and was hooked.

How did you meet your current love?
We're both from New York but met in Germany while I was stationed there as an intelligence officer. We were put on the same team, deployed for three months, and fought all the time. When we returned, we crazily decided to date, knowing we either had the makings of something special or we'd kill each other. We've been together for twenty years, married for eighteen.

What characteristic do you most value in your friends?
Compassion.

How did you celebrate or treat yourself when you got your first book deal?
I would've been content toasting with champagne, but my husband, who is my biggest supporter, surprised me with a weekend at a romantic resort. He picked the place because it was pure luxury and less than a two-hour drive from home, which he instinctively knew I needed for my sanity since it was my first time away from our babies.

Will you share your favorite reader response?
"You were a new author for me. I just finished your Topaz series and loved it! Reading each book was like watching a movie. You're now one of my favorites!"

Other than author, what job would you like to have?
Without a doubt, movie critic. Maybe in my next life.